KU-166-240

THE COMING DARKNESS

GREG MOSSE

Published by Moonflower Publishing Ltd.
www.MoonflowerBooks.co.uk

ISBN: 978-1919618753

Cover design by Jasmine Aurora

Printed and bound by Jellyfish Ltd., Curdridge, Hampshire

Moonflower Publishing Registered Office: 303 The Pillbox, 115 Coventry Road, London E2 6GG, United Kingdom

MOONFLOWER

For Moose, Martha and Felix

1

It began very early one Sunday, a hot summer night in 2037, a little before one o'clock. Marseille was under curfew, a brown-out only a few minutes away. Inside Bunker Martha, the dark shift were on duty.

Alexandre Lamarque, a tall man with dark hair and kind eyes, carried a descendant of the Heckler & Koch .45-calibre pistol he'd been issued on his first day of training twelve years before, plus a sonic immobiliser, retrieved from the armoury at the local gendarmerie earlier that day.

'Guaranteed non-lethal,' the quartermaster told him. 'If that's what you're looking for.'

He stood in deep shadow in an alleyway about fifty metres from the rear of the converted U-boat base, a vast structure still known by its World War II codename. Today, it was an international data centre, housing a vast array of servers, computers, switches and routers.

The sky was almost clear, the moon and stars visible beyond the wisps of high cirrus clouds. Between Alex and Bunker Martha, a two-metre fence surrounded a pumping station. Back in the early 2000s, a pragmatic computer engineer whose grandfather had worked the mines above Marseille invented the idea of channelling groundwater from drainage tunnels in the hills, absorbing the waste heat, and then releasing it out into the blue waters of the Mediterranean.

An excellent plan, thought Alex, but also an obvious weakness.

Somewhere a siren sounded, abrupt but distant. Seconds later, the planned brown-out killed the streetlamps and plunged the docks, the pleasure-port and the entire industrial zone into darkness. Seconds later, Alex felt the backup generators rumble into life through the soles of his shoes.

He stayed relaxed, scanning the terrain – the car park with spreading lime trees, the security perimeter and, beyond that, the maritime repair yard with its four-storey boat garage.

Nothing out of place.

He heard the distinctive churring trill of a male nightjar marking its territory, followed by the faint percussive sound of its wing-clapping. It was perched atop one of the heavy gateposts near the locked entrance to the pumping station.

Suddenly, the bird shot up into the air and flapped away, disturbed by a sound.

Alex swept his gaze methodically between the lime trees, looking for what might have disturbed it.

There it was, a mid-size, light-coloured vehicle; two dark figures clambering out of the boot, stretching stiffened limbs. Then whispering, two voices, taking care but not enough care. Trusting in the curfew and the emptiness of the night.

Alex knew who they were – international students from Marseille University, charity placements supposed to foster understanding between peoples. Amaury Barra, the colleague who'd given him the tip-off about the planned attack, had said the suspects were 'little more than children'. That they were almost certainly being manipulated.

'But they're still dangerous?' Alex had asked.

'Oh, yes,' Amaury had said.

Alex had decided to confront them alone, without backup, to give them a chance to pull back. To walk away. To resume a normal life, whatever that might mean, whatever that might be worth.

A stupid decision, he suspected, but also the right one.

They were hard to make out as they bent over, busy with some kind of equipment. Presumably a bomb. Alex wondered how effective it might be. With improvised explosive devices, the death of the bomb-setter was almost as likely as the destruction of the target.

Without warning, the two students ducked out of sight.

Alex stared into the darkness. What had happened? Was somebody coming?

A few feet away, a rat disturbed a pebble as it emerged from a tangle of pipes. As he watched, it squeezed beneath the bottom rail of the gate, like a piece of paper slipping through the crack under a door.

Alex allowed all the breath to leave his body, releasing his pent-up energy, feeling the future close in, the circumstances narrow, reducing his margin for manoeuvre.

Then the two dark shapes were back, moving almost directly towards him. One carried something heavy, glowing with a small square of pale green light.

Amateurs, thought Alex. They should have waited for the screen to go dark.

Without conscious thought, he calculated the angles and distances. The gate was three seconds away, a little less than twenty-five metres. He wondered briefly how they intended to break into the caged pumping station, but the gate swung open the moment one of them touched it and he realised they knew the alphanumeric code that controlled the locks.

Not *that* amateur, then.

He waited as the shadows moved away, zigzagging between the pipes and valves, their feet crunching on the shingle, closer and closer to the rear wall of the data centre.

Alex stepped out of the alleyway, his steps silent against the tarmac. The two figures crouched down. A woman and a man. He heard their feet twist in the pebbles, saw the tiny green screen flicker as they placed it against the wall. It was now or never.

He took three long strides.

'*Police, ne bougez plus*,' he shouted. 'Don't move!'

The man lunged at him, and Alex fired. The son-imm struck him in the chest. He twitched once and fell to the ground, his muscles slack.

Alex adjusted his aim, but the woman dodged behind a thick vertical pipe.

He eased left and caught a glimpse of her face – dark skin, bright eyes – then she moved back out of sight. The figure on the ground was moving. Alex didn't want to hit him again.

'There's no need to do this,' he shouted. 'Trust me. This is a stupid idea. You can walk away.'

The woman shouted back at him, five short words in a language he didn't understand. In that moment, Alex saw the future as clearly as he could see the moon above their heads. When it happened, it was like playing a video for a second time.

The woman leaned out and fired two rapid shots into her stunned companion. Despite the darkness, Alex could make out the mess it made of the man's head – brain matter, scalp and hair smeared across the pale shingle. Then she made a break for it, firing five shots across the pipework towards where Alex crouched under cover.

Not amateurs at all, he thought, surprised. At least, not this one.

The woman sprinted from the pumping station, thumping across the smooth tarmac. An alarm shrieked.

Alex moved quickly to disengage the receiver-detonator from the IED. Then he paused to listen.

The woman's footsteps had stopped. She must still be close.

The slow-moving lights of an electric buggy appeared from the darkness four hundred metres away. A civilian security team. Probably unarmed. Definitely ill-trained to deal with a terrorist who hadn't hesitated to shoot her own accomplice in order to prevent him being captured and questioned.

None of this was what Alex wanted. He put away the son-imm and released the .45 from its holster. Crouching, he made his way to the cover of the gatepost just in time to see the woman stand up, stepping out from behind one of the parked cars. She was looking towards him, but hadn't raised her weapon.

'*Vous ne pourrez pas vous échapper,*' he called to her.

You can't escape.

She shouted back at him – the same five words, he was sure, like a slogan or a prayer. Or perhaps she simply shouted at the night. Then she raised the muzzle of her gun beneath her chin and fired a bullet into her own brain.

2

Alex's mother lived on the fourth floor of a noble townhouse on Boulevard Henri IV, near the Bastille in central Paris. Gloria Lamarque shared his high forehead and firm jawline, as well as his intelligence and determination. She questioned him closely as he told her what had happened in Marseille.

'How did they get the code to enter the pumping station, Alexandre?'

Alex, who had barely slept in the two days since he left Marseille with its smell of blood and failure, shrugged. 'I don't know.'

'And the car. You haven't been able to trace it?'

'I had to leave. I shouldn't have been there at all. I cut a hole in the fence at the far end of the alley to get in. I left the same way.'

'So no official follow-up. What do you think were they trying to do?'

'Destroying the cooling system would have taken the data centre offline, but only for a short time. So… I don't know.'

The mission had been a failure. Two dead young people and no answers at all.

'You had a hunch,' said Gloria. 'You felt the need to be there. They must have had an accomplice of some kind. The employee whose car it was, who gave them the gate code.'

'Or they might have concealed themselves in the car without the employee knowing. In any case, they're both dead.'

'Suicide,' said his mother, shaking her head.

'Technically, one murder and one suicide.'

'Not your fault,' she insisted. 'Professionals?'

Alex thought of the woman. The way she'd fired two bullets into her partner's head.

'One of them was, at least.'

'*Oui, bien sûr.*'

'I misinterpreted the intelligence,' said Alex. 'I feel…'

He didn't know exactly what he felt. There was a great shadow over everything – his thoughts, his emotions, his work, his purpose in life. It had been there since Marseille. Since the woman shot her partner without hesitation.

'I counted them,' he said suddenly. 'All the people who've died. The people I've killed.'

His mother gave him a steady look. 'People die all the time. It's a fact of history. People succumb pointlessly, without reason, without meaning. Accidents, old age, illness—'

'That's not what I'm talking about.' Alex cut her off. 'These people, the people in my memories, they died because of me. Because of my presence. Because of the ideas that…'

He stopped. That was the trouble with loss of faith. It wasn't worth explaining – it simply *was*.

'I tried to persuade you to join Professor Fayard's service,' Gloria reminded him. 'You're much more suited to strategy and intelligence. Do you know where he is now?'

'Of course I do.'

'I've a good mind to call him.'

'Don't be absurd.'

'Tout n'est pas noir, Alexandre.'

Not everything is black.

There was a long silence, and then he said, 'That may not be true.'

The air in the apartment seemed to become still. She narrowed her eyes.

'Alexandre, what can you see coming?'

'Nothing,' he said. 'No, I don't mean that I have no sense of the future. I mean I see "a nothing". An absence. A vast loss. What happened in Marseille has something to do with that.'

His mother studied his face. 'Are you sure?'

'I am.'

'When?'

'Soon.'

'And how?'

'I don't know that either.'

Alex stood up and walked to the two tall windows that overlooked the boulevard. Both were open, and he could smell the sun-warmed fruit on the apple trees that grew in the central reservation. The quiet was broken by the raucous crescendo of a rare petrol-driven truck carrying waste masonry from a building site, the fumes of its exhaust billowing. The throb of its coarse, polluting engine bounced and faded between the stately six-storey houses.

'Come and look at something,' said his mother. She stood by her desk, gesturing at a stack of papers. 'This is a history I've been writing – of exploitation, careless risk, indifference to suffering, irresponsible power.'

He glanced at the title page. 'A history of weapons testing sites in twentieth-century colonial territories, into the 2030s.'

'Okay,' he said, confused. His mother was a renowned historian, always working on something, but she rarely drew his attention to her writing. 'Do you want me to read it?'

She picked up the top page. 'You've done your best within the limits of what was possible; the limits of your life and times. Others have done much worse – and lacked your motivation to do good.'

He frowned. 'You want me to take it all in my stride and move on. But what's the point of trying to do good if it achieves nothing?'

Instead of answering, she said, 'Have you spoken to Amaury?'

Alex didn't want to tell her that it was Amaury Barra who had given him the incomplete intelligence, the person who'd put him in such a difficult position to start with.

'Why do you ask?'

'You graduated together.' She said it as if that explained everything.

'And?'

'He must confront the same feelings. He's gone through everything you're going through. You have the gift of seeing clearly, Alexandre. Use it.'

Yes, thought Alex, unhappily. That's the problem.

While Alex and his mother were speaking, in the west of the city, just outside the orbital motorway, two men in dark suits were making a delivery of sixteen heavy boxes. They were marked for the attention of in-house catering as '*comestibles*'. They looked like boxes of foodstuffs.

But they weren't.

In Calais, a man with a sequence of five letters tattooed on the back of his hand left the international travel terminal in a small electric minibus. He got out close to the maritime port and made his way to a semi-official refugee encampment, where he met an Englishman whose eyes were wild, clouded with drugs.

From a distance, the man from the terminal looked like he was being kind.

But he wasn't.

3

Alex hadn't slept for twenty-seven hours. That would normally be close to his useful limit, but in July in the Arctic Circle the sun refused to set and his body just kept going.

Should he be worried, he wondered, that his mind might give up before his physical energy was exhausted?

'Well,' he said aloud. 'There's only one way to find out.'

The hire car was capable of driving itself, but he preferred manual control on roads he didn't know. The Norwegian landscape was breath-taking – granite mountains, bare peaks, snow and spruce forests. It was a panorama in charcoal grey, green and white against a deep blue sky. The road wound left and right as the low sun jagged through the tree trunks, alternately dazzling him and leaving him in shadow. The podcast he had downloaded to keep him company droned on.

In 2005, when Alex was born, there had been 400,000 people living beyond the Arctic Circle in Norway. A generation later, in 2037, that number was almost double.

All the same, there were still thousands of square kilometres of empty space in which to hide things away. Some of them quite big things.

He emerged from the woods at the edge of a fjord, and drove onto an exceptionally beautiful bridge that seemed to skim the surface of the salt water. On the far side he stopped at a fortified metal gate, showing his false credentials to a camera lens mounted on a post.

The gate slid open silently and he drove on until he reached a silvery blue lake with a hydropower station tucked into a fold in the rocks. He rolled down the window, letting in a blast of cold, clean air. The landscape thrummed with the roar of meltwater churning through unseen turbines.

Further along the smooth, winding road, the Genetics Research and Development laboratory was in deep shadow. Alex parked and put on his coat for the short walk to reception. He passed through a hygiene station and was searched, then taken to the director's office.

As soon as he walked in, a man with deep worry lines and a pointed goatee bounced out of his leather chair. He, too, was wearing a coat. The room was uncomfortably cold. The only light came through the window.

'Monsieur Albin.' He sounded relieved. 'Welcome to Genetisk Forskning og Utvikling.'

'Thank you, Director Genmis. And I'm sorry about the circumstances. I have the basics, but can you tell me what steps you have taken so far?'

The director wrung his hands. 'None.' His voice was plaintive. 'We have done nothing. We shut everything down. That is all.'

Alex wasn't surprised. It was the right thing to do. 'Tell me when you first knew?'

'My security director called me at four in the morning. By then it had already locked every networked server, desktop, laptop, hand-held, tablet and phone.'

'Every device connected to your hard-wired network or your Wi-Fi?' Alex guessed.

'Exactly.'

'How many files?'

The man spread his hands. 'Hundreds of thousands. Several vast databases. Have you run the remote diagnostic to find out how it got in?'

'Without connectivity there are no remote diagnostics. Could you show me the ransom message?'

The director picked up a tablet and handed it over.

Alex glanced at him. 'This device is disconnected from your servers?'

'Absolutely.'

The photograph on the tablet showed a computer screen entirely taken up by a facsimile of a hand-written message, like ink on parchment:

Greetings, FRIENDS! We are here to HELP! Let's work together to SOLVE this CRISIS. Things could be WORSE. You might have gone about your business, NEVER KNOWING about the GAPING security flaw in your systems. We can help put that right and release your files from their TEMPORARY PRISON where we've encoded them with the strongest known algorithms. If you try to reset or restart your systems, they will DELETE. If you employ any decryption software except ours, they will DELETE. Let us reinstate and clean up your servers. You know it makes SENSE.

Alex handed the device back. 'I take it you were given instructions for paying ransom in cryptocurrency?'

'Yes.' Genmis's lips twisted.

'Which currency?'

'There were several. I… I don't remember.' Director Genmis rubbed his eyes. 'Forgive me, Monsieur Albin. I haven't slept. The price has risen with each hour that passes. It's a nightmare.'

'Rule one: no ransom,' Alex told him, his voice firm. 'Rule two: speak to support – that's me. Rule three: tell the world and share what you learn.'

The director looked frustrated. 'How do I tell the world? I had to go to the hydro plant just to call you.'

'Don't you have backup power?' asked Alex.

'Yes, but we don't dare use it. We were afraid the electrical wiring could be used to further the attack.'

'You did the right thing,' Alex assured him. 'But I'm going to need you to activate your backup generator now. While you're doing that, I'll need to bring in some equipment.'

'You won't be offended if I ask my security team to check it?'

'You shouldn't be comfortable with anyone you don't know having access to your research. Even me. Once my work is complete, you should wipe all my drives.'

'Thank you.' The director looked at him mournfully. 'I can't tell you how terrible it's been. Everyone is freezing cold and depressed.'

When Alex returned with his equipment, Director Genmis watched him show the security personnel the contents of his black equipment case – numerous devices held in perfectly shaped indentations in protective foam. He encouraged the guards to scan each one, making a complete log of every file and executable program. He reiterated that they could wipe all the data before he left. He noticed them becoming irritated with how careful he was making them be.

Good, he thought.

'How long will it take?' asked the director, hopefully.

'To quarantine and restart all the network modules, isolating each one physically, and purging it of the trojan?' Alex paused to consider. 'Thirty-six hours.'

'That long?' The director sounded appalled.

Alex gave him a reassuring look. 'Slow and steady wins the race.'

News of Alex's arrival had got around. When the director took him to the main laboratory, the core scientific staff gathered around as he explained his plan.

'I'll isolate each device from all other equipment. As soon as I've made them "dumb", I can analyse and restart them.'

Many stayed to watch as he got down to work. With their computers down, they had nothing better to do. But the work took several hours, all of it conducted in half-light through the windows. In the unnatural quiet the whirr of the first device turning on seemed loud.

'Okay,' Alex announced. 'Step one complete.'

One by one, the computers around the room came to life. As each set of tell-tale lights began blinking in the gloom, cheers went up.

Alex held up a cautioning hand. 'By all means check the functionality of your equipment, but don't make any changes. This is only the start.'

As the scientists scattered to check their newly dumb equipment, Alex went to work on the central-heating controls, ring-fencing them and turning off the smart controls that automatically regulated temperature, humidity, allergen control and so on. There was another cheer as the heat came on, and warmth spread through the room.

By then, it was getting late. Everyone looked exhausted. Genmis couldn't speak without yawning. Alex calculated he himself had reached thirty-two hours without sleep.

'I'm going to take a break,' he said, stretching. 'You should all get some rest, too.'

'But the ransom is going up all the time,' the director objected.

Alex shook his head. 'We're not paying the ransom, remember?'

'No, yes, of course. Good point.' The director laughed and the laugh turned into another yawn.

'You should rest, too.' Alex told him. 'Could you show me…?'

'This way.' The director motioned for him to follow him into a long corridor. 'Your room is ready.'

Alex barely noticed the functional quarters. He set an alarm, undressed and was asleep within minutes.

Alex woke four hours later. Automatically, he calculated the hours remaining. His deadline was one o'clock. He still had plenty of time.

He glanced out of a triple-glazed window, not much more than a porthole. There was no discernible change in the quality of the light on the granite slopes, on the dark trunks of the spruce trees. In the distance there was a layer of cloud, but it hadn't yet obscured the sun.

When he returned to the operation room, a few scientists were waiting impatiently. He explained that his plan was to concentrate on catering and other logistics, then move on to the security systems. An hour later, he told the director that the kitchens could be put back into service.

Genmis beamed. 'Excellent news.'

'But I need to keep the security circuits offline until the end.' Alex's tone was nonchalant, but the director gave him a steady look.

'Why is that?'

'They are, counterintuitively, a potential problem,' he explained. 'The security network is interlinked with motion sensors, follow-cameras, direction-seeking, face recognition – a panoply of insecurities. I've isolated the system but, like the rest, I have to purge it device by device. Do you know how many elements the security system includes?'

'I have no idea,' Genmis conceded.

'Neither do I.' Alex became grave. 'It can never be entirely secure, you know that, right? That's why we encourage keeping a complete backup on our servers.'

'But that isn't possible.'

'Commercial secrecy,' Alex said. 'I understand.'

Despite the director's concerns, the atmosphere in the facility had changed. The staff seemed reassured by the industrious presence of Thierry Albin of Breach Detection & Recovery SA. With each step, each restarted system and device, the mood improved.

When Alex took a short break to eat herring and boiled potatoes in the cafeteria, the staff chatted with him animatedly about his work. When he asked for the best walks to take around the extensive wooded grounds, they gave him several routes to try.

Just as he had planned it, Alex was becoming a part of the team.

4

Early that afternoon, rain began falling from the grey sky. The air turned unseasonably cold. There was a suggestion of sleet in the drops that pelted against the thick window panes.

Good timing, thought Alex.

He went looking for Genmis and found him trying to process reams of data without the assistance of computers.

'I'm sorry to interrupt,' said Alex.

The director jumped to his feet, hope in his eyes. 'Are we ready? Have you finished?'

'Not quite. I'm running dual programs that will cross-analyse the security system first. Those are going well but they will take a little while.' Alex glanced out of the window. 'In the meantime, I thought I might get some fresh air.'

The director looked uncertainly out at the gloom. 'Are you sure?'

'Oh, I don't mind the weather. I won't go far. I'll stay within the perimeter. Would you like someone to accompany me?'

'Monsieur Albin, when you spend your whole life in the frozen north, you only go out on the good days,' Genmis said. 'This is not one of the good days.'

On his way out, Alex insisted on the standard security controls. As expected, neither the full-body screening device nor the security officers' wands detected the devices concealed in the heels of his heavy boots. Nor could they distinguish the equipment hidden by the shadow of his coat's thick metal zip.

He took a marked trail into the woods, emerging onto an exposed ridge. Up there, the north-east wind was biting.

Alex stood very still. Anyone watching would think he was taking in the view. In fact, all of his concentration was focused on listening, making sure he had not been followed, that there was no one else out there with him. But he could hear nothing except the wind and distant the muffled roar of water through the hydro turbines.

The land dipped to the west before climbing again to a small hill with just a few younger trees battling for survival in poor soil. It took him another twenty minutes to reach the place. By then, his time was nearly up.

Crouching down, he rotated the heel of his left boot and removed the tiny data drive on which he had copied the lab's entire database. Returning that boot to normal, he rotated his other heel and removed a beacon whose signal would transmit up to nearly two kilometres of altitude. He connected them securely together and checked the time.

Six minutes left.

Working faster now, he carefully pulled apart the seam of his winter coat, just behind the main metal zip. From the hidden compartment he drew out a deflated weather balloon and a tiny helium canister.

He stood quietly for half a minute, listening once more. If anyone was around, he would have to abort and miss the planned fly-past. There was a second potential pickup scheduled for six hours later but he didn't want to have to make excuses for wandering the hills again. These people were not idiots.

When he was sure he was alone, he attached the drive and beacon to the flaccid balloon and inflated it. When the canister was empty, the balloon was about one and a half metres in diameter. It would grow to eight or ten metres in diameter as it rose. Big enough that, even if the beacon failed to activate, it was possible the fly-past could locate it visually.

He checked the time again – one o'clock on the dot.

He raised the balloon above his head, and let it go.

The winds were brisk. It climbed swiftly into the low clouds and disappeared.

Too quick, too fleeting to register as a threat.

Alex trekked back to the lab to find the director waiting for him in reception. A surge of adrenaline rushed through him.

'I was just beginning to worry that you might have become lost, Thierry,' said Genmis.

'All good,' said Alex. 'I got a little turned around but I found my way back. I'll just go through security and get back to work.'

'Surely there's no need for security coming back from a hike,' Genmis said.

But Alex insisted. When the thorough sweep was finished, he told the director, 'I'll put my outdoor clothes in the drying room and meet you in the main lab.'

Ten minutes later, he was back at a terminal, the director leaning over his shoulder, watching the progress dials on his twin security programs. They both indicated ninety-five per cent.

'When this is done, we'll be able to reboot your whole network and reconnect your facility to the outside world,' Alex told him.

Genmis stared eagerly at the screen. 'Have you decided how the virus got in?'

'Incorporated in some other software – perhaps a smart device like a heater or a fridge, somebody's comm-watch, somebody's smart glasses.' Alex made a vague gesture. 'It could be anything.'

'But you've found it all, and it's gone?'

'Yes.'

'It can't self-replicate?' Genmis pressed.

'Not if the security check comes up clean.'

The progress dials clicked up to ninety-six per cent.

The director lingered, watching the dials. 'How much of our data was released into the wild? Do we have any secrets left?'

Alex soothed him with a lie. 'Your data was encrypted with software provided by Breach Detection & Recovery. The encryption relies on prime number codes only you have access to. The attack prevented you from accessing your data, but no one could ever see your work.'

Ninety-eight per cent.

'Hackers aren't interested in genetic research,' Alex continued. 'They're only interested in money.'

Ninety-nine per cent.

'The attack was designed to pressure you into parting with cash, not scientific innovations. Now, I've removed the hackers' encryption layer and restored everything to how you left it.'

The counter turned green. One hundred per cent. Job complete.

'There you are,' Alex said, with a smile.

Genmis's face lit up. 'Monsieur Thierry Albin, I could kiss you.'

'But that would be a breach of hygiene protocol,' said Alex, laughing.

'So, I won't,' said the director. 'Of course not. All the same… Thank you.'

His earnest gratitude made Alex feel bad. He was no better than a thief.

It was too late to catch a flight to Oslo so Alex stayed one more night. Earlier, exhaustion had obliged him to rest. Now, though, the stress of the mission prevented him from dropping off. He made an effort to slow his breathing. In his memory he replayed his last conversation with Mariam, lying on the roof of his boat, looking up at the stars, waiting for the morning siren and the end of overnight curfew, telling her about the botched attack on the data centre in Marseille, reliving the moment.

'You tried to do the right thing, the generous thing,' Mariam whispered. She touched the back of his hand with her fingertips. 'Poor Alex.'

'I need to tell you something,' he said.

'Talk,' she said, and he heard the smile in her voice. 'I'm not stopping you.'

But, for some time, she did stop him. Afterwards they lay quietly beneath the stars. Finally, she spoke again.

'Something is bothering you. I can see it in your face.'

He sat up to look at her. 'I've set a trojan loose on an honest scientific research establishment – a good set of people doing good work on transgenic infections. The virus has just become active. It will seriously mess them up.'

'You've infected their data so that they will call you in to fix a problem that you created?'

'Yes.'

'And you don't like this because…?'

'Because the more I look at them, the more I think they're the good guys in this scenario. Which means…'

There was a pause.

'You seem different,' she said after a long moment. 'It's not like you to worry so much about your missions. Or to feel guilty about them.'

He thought about what to say. How much truth to tell. There didn't seem to be much truth in his life these days.

'Something is coming,' he told her, his voice very low.

She searched his face. 'Something?'

'An absence. A darkness.'

Marian rose up on one elbow, her brow creasing. 'What does that mean?'

'*Je n'en ai aucune idée,*' said Alex.

He had absolutely no idea.

The next morning, in the sparse visitor accommodation at the GFU lab, Alex was packing his clothes. It was seven o'clock. Outside, the midsummer light was the same drab grey it had been since he'd arrived. He drank a cup of coffee in his room, then fetched the outdoor layers he had left in the drying room.

Down in reception, he once again insisted the security guards went through the rigmarole of checking all his equipment, passing his devices through an electromagnet, then connecting each one to a piece of hardware designed to detect optical drives and scrape them clean. As each element of his kit was declared innocent, Alex replaced it in the appropriate foam bed in his equipment case. Director Genmis arrived, smelling of toothpaste, his hair still wet from the shower, effusive with gratitude.

Alex finally got away just before eight, driving south to the closest regional airport through the breath-takingly beautiful countryside on exceptionally smooth roads. He took an internal flight to Oslo. While waiting for his connection to Paris, he checked his messages. The one that mattered came from a fake uncle, telling him that his imaginary aunt was home from her trip and quite recovered.

That's that, thought Alex. The balloon had been intercepted as planned.

So why did he feel so guilty?

At the same time in a nondescript suburb of northern Paris, the two men who had delivered the fake boxes of '*comestibles*' were planning a trip to Marseille with instructions to visit a morgue. Meanwhile, the man from the Calais travel terminal was studying detailed plans of the water treatment and supply network for the ten million registered citizens and undocumented Blanks of north-eastern France.

Simultaneously, in the eastern Mediterranean, on the island of Cyprus, a severe-looking woman who ran a data centre similar to Bunker Martha was contemplating a message on her holoscreen. It was a request for access from a French commercial operation interested in investing in the network.

Time was running short. She didn't want the distraction.

All the same, after a moment's hesitation, she dictated a positive reply.

It doesn't matter, she thought.

Soon it will all burn.

Back in Paris, Alex's journey into the city centre was uneventful. He left the Métro at Bastille and walked a short distance through the sticky summer heat to the canal basin, descending the eighteen worn stone steps to the water. His boat's on-board security system recognised the presence of his comm-watch and disabled the electric current to the rail.

'*Bonsoir, Alexandre,*' said the synthetic voice.

Alex frowned. He hated it when the boat's AI spoke to him. He thought he'd already disabled it. Perhaps it had automatically rebooted.

The hatch opened and he stepped down three steps into the dark interior, activating discreet low-energy lighting. The air conditioning was extremely effective, using the relative cool of the canal water, but it had been off for several days and the interior felt almost damp. He spoke a command to adjust it then checked his hand-held, hoping for a message from Mariam, but there was nothing.

He looked out of one of the small windows. About fifteen metres from the moorings, out in the sludge-green water, two officers on a police boat were grappling with long hooks at a heavy, waterlogged body, struggling to pull it alongside. At the same moment, the streetlamps were extinguished as the power grid shut down for load shedding.

Nice, he thought, bitterly. Welcome home.

5

A week later, Alex's colleague Amaury Barra was also using a false identity. The biometric passport on his comm-watch said he was Firmin Couchant, an expert delegated by the French Ministry for Foreign Affairs from its Aid & Development programme. He had been in North Africa for a month, based in an industrial facility on the coast – a desalination plant, powered by energy from the Great Solar Array in southern Cyrenia. He was having a final meeting before heading back to Paris.

'The classic method for removing salt from seawater,' he told his visitor, 'is to boil it and condense the vapour. Heating water to a hundred degrees Celsius requires huge energy inputs. Instead, we use refrigeration. It's six times more efficient.'

Amaury's visitor looked intrigued. He was the mayor of Benghazi, sent by the Cyrenian prime minster on a fact-finding mission.

'Does freezing have the same impact as distillation?'

'Yes,' Amaury told him. 'As the ice forms, it leaves behind the salt. We separate it and, once it's liquid again, we push it through filters to remove impurities. At that point, it enters the public drinking supply.' He gestured at the huge metal tanks around them. 'This facility is state of the art.'

'But you are leaving, Monsieur Couchant.' The mayor looked round. 'Are our local staff adequately trained?'

'More than adequately,' Amaury reassured him. He felt a vibration from his comm-watch. 'Will you excuse me?'

Leaving the mayor with his deputy, Amaury stepped out of the main tank hall, removing his PPE in the pristine hygiene station. Back at his desk, he woke his French-made holoscreen with a voice command, and plugged in an encrypted USB stick. It responded to a biometric security protocol activated by his thumbprint and opened his new message.

It was, on the surface, an urgent request to be in touch with home regarding the illness of a family member. A journey to Cyrene City was suggested. 'Plan to be away for a few weeks.'

Concealed within the 'family' message were the details of a clandestine meeting.

Amaury memorised the details, replied in the same code, shut down the screen and removed the USB stick from the socket. His deputy tapped politely on his doorframe and stepped inside.

'Problems?' she asked, straightening her headscarf.

'Family business.' Amaury smiled as he sold her the lie. 'I have to take a trip to the capital before I return to Paris.'

The woman's cheerful face shadowed. 'Nothing serious, I hope?'

Of course it was serious, but that wasn't information Amaury could share. 'We'll see,' he said.

'You will be missed,' his deputy told him. 'Everything has run very smoothly while you've been here.'

'That's very good of you, but it's teamwork that counts. I couldn't have done it without your work.'

'I am personally very grateful. One day, I hope, Cyrenia will no longer need France's help.' The deputy smiled again. 'Come back and visit.'

'I will,' said Amaury, knowing how unlikely that was.

It didn't take him long to collect his few personal effects – a change of clothes, a few toiletries from the shelf above the bathroom sink, his hand-held, a dumb phone. At the gates of the plant, he hopped on a company shuttle for the journey into the centre of Benghazi, along a tarmac road almost invisible beneath a layer of dust and sand.

In Benghazi, he would look for a cheap hotel and change his appearance. Then he'd travel by another coach to Cyrene City, where he would join up with a revolutionary cell and help them infiltrate the parliamentary compound.

There, two revolutionary zealots would attempt to assassinate the Cyrenian leader, Prime Minister Souad Mourad, and he would try to stop them.

Later that day, several hundred kilometres to the southeast, an insignificant immigrant labourer trudged wearily between rows of solar panels. Her name was Zeina Yaseen. Unfortunately for her, she would not remain insignificant for long.

The Great Solar Array was made up of more than three million square metres of photovoltaics, mounted on motorised stands, tracking the sun in its passage across the dome of the sky. The hum of their motors accompanied Zeina in every moment of her day. Each panel was programmed to move independently for optimum energy capture.

Zeina worked at the southern tip of the array. At the start of each shift, she would look out at the vast sands, the dunes that flowed away from her like arid waves. Then, she would unfold her stepladder, climb up to the penultimate step and begin to clear dust and sand from the face of the first photovoltaic panel with a battery-powered vacuum-cleaner. Then she would climb down, fold her ladder, move it along and repeat the operation at the next metal pillar – twenty panels per hour, one hundred and forty panels per day, seven hundred per week, nearly seven thousand since she had been delegated to the site.

From the position of the sun in the sky, Zeina estimated the time was five o'clock. The panels were all tipped towards the light.

I am a servant of these machines, she thought. I am almost a machine myself.

Zeina was an intelligent woman. She knew her labour was important. Robots had been tried but they couldn't cope with the harsh environment as well as the refugee labourers could. But it was soul-destroying work and, on this particular afternoon, she had depressed herself by thinking about her family farm, back on the Nile delta in Egypt.

Growing up in the 2020s, she had been sent to work as soon as she was strong enough – pruning and harvesting, weeding and tying back. She could have gone to university, even studied for a profession, despite the collapse of the Egyptian education system. But she had preferred working with her hands alongside her parents, bringing in produce for her grandmother to cook.

She shook her head, making an effort to pull herself together, to be more positive. After all, the energy provided by the array was used to fuel desalination plants – one at Benghazi, one at Tobruk and one outside the capital, Cyrene City. She knew that, without the power she helped provide, her adopted nation could not survive. She half-believed what she had been told – that she was serving a great ideal, a new nation determined to provide a safe haven in a continent worn down by environmental degradation, desertification, war, isolationism and disease.

Zeina finished cleaning another panel, climbed down, and re-erected her ladder at the next. Balanced a little precariously, she could see the huge warehouses that accommodated the battery arrays, vast facilities packed with racks of lithium-ion storage. Beyond, there was the airbase and launch facility.

She put a hand on the panel. Her ears barely registered the hum of the motors but she could feel the vibrations as the servos murmured into life, changing its orientation by a degree.

Zeina moved on, still feeling nostalgic for the family farm, the fields of sorghum, cassava, sweet potato and yams – and the pleasant house, designed like a Roman dwelling, a square of rooms surrounding a central courtyard lined with shaded verandas. Whatever the time of day, whatever the season, there was somewhere to sit that was either warmed by the sun or cooled by the shade.

But rising sea levels had leached into the arable soil, making it less productive year-on-year. She remembered the first summer that they had worked the fields mostly at night, relying on the moon and touch, as the days became unliveable due to the heat. Then, incredibly, the waters of the mighty Nile began to fail – obstructed, withheld and harvested by nations upstream of Egypt. Finally, after her grandmother died, she had left, drawn by the promise of new beginnings.

Now she lived in an anonymous prefabricated unit on an energy campus at the edge of a desert.

Zeina began to move more quickly. She wanted to be at the end of the row by half past five. From there she would have an unobstructed view of a trial rocket launch, a dry-run for a more important lift-off with a payload of satellite technology destined for the crowded skies. As she emerged from the mechanical forest, she saw two friends from the cleaning team, one either side, five rows away. She waved and they waved back. They too had timed their labours to be able to watch.

The launch pad was about fifteen hundred metres away. Zeina and her colleagues perched on top of their folding ladders. She could see the nose cone of the rocket against the rich blue of the sky, protruding above one of the airbase buildings.

Suddenly, clouds of dust and sand began to swirl, roiling in yellow-brown clouds. Moments later, the sound reached the solar field, a deep and throaty roar of ignition. Then the rocket was rising, its fierce tongue of flame lapping at the azure sky as it shot away, diminishing in size, diminishing in its importance to her life, becoming just a memory that broke, for a minute or so, the monotony of her labour.

She heard the others cheer.

Zeina climbed down and sat for a few moments in a patch of shade. She took a bottle of water from her rucksack and drank. She ate a protein-and-carb bar and changed the battery in her vacuum.

Just four hundred more panels until she could return to the prefab cabin where she was relatively happy, given everything, given all she had lost, given how close she had come to death in the refugee corridor from Egypt, given the appalling hygiene standards at the reception camp outside Tobruk.

But she hadn't died. She had survived and now she had a life, all the same.

Zeina emptied the dirtbag onto the ground. The dust and sand rejoined the vast reservoir of the Sahara, ready to be whisked up by the wind, hover on the air, then descend gently back down onto the photovoltaic cells for her to clean away once more in an endless cycle – endless until, she supposed, she was dead.

She shrugged the rucksack onto her back, splayed the feet of her stepladder at the first panel of the next row in her zone, and went back to work.

6

Two days later, in Paris, Mariam Jordane parked Professor Fayard's official car in the basement of the headquarters of the Directorate-General for Internal Security. Glancing in her rear-view mirror, she noticed that Fayard seemed tired, his breathing shallow. When they got out, she handed him his walking stick and gave him an arm to the elevator. On the sixth floor, they crossed the lobby and shuffled the width of the vast conference room, opening the door in the bookshelves that led into his private quarters.

Fayard sat down heavily in a leather armchair, raising a hand to indicate she should wait. Mariam heard the soft beeping of the medical alert on his comm-watch and hurried to the dispenser to fetch a glass of water as he searched an inside pocket for a small silver box, but fumbled trying to release the catch.

'I am becoming useless,' he muttered.

Mariam stretched out a hand. 'Can I—'

'No, my dear.' He managed to open the box and took two capsules, then sat back with his eyes closed.

Mariam glanced around the room that had been a part of her working life for nearly seven years. She was grateful to Fayard for creating a job especially for her – one that kept her in the capital, able to care for her sisters.

During that time, she had never spoken about it to anyone. Even Alex. He knew she was a combination of bodyguard and driver, that occasionally she would undertake small missions of short duration. But nothing more. He didn't know precisely where she worked or who with. She knew about *his* work – he had trusted her with that. But she shared little. Every aspect of her life was compartmentalised, without overlap.

Why did she maintain a barrier of secrecy between them? Was it simply the nature of their jobs, the all-pervading ambience of secrecy, of constructed identities, of deceit?

Yes, but there was also her desire for their relationship to exist in its own bubble, out of the flow of mundane reality.

Fayard opened his eyes.

'What's happened, Professor?' Mariam asked. 'You seem much worse. Will you have to isolate?'

'I am worse but the prophylactic treatment means I can continue working,' he replied. 'Never mind. Come with me. I would like your opinion.'

He moved slowly to the far corner of the room, to a desk with three holoscreens. He stood, leaning on his silver-topped walking stick, insisting that Mariam should take his chair.

'I want you to watch this. The footage was discovered three days ago by a trainee. Will you give me a spontaneous reaction?'

'Of course.'

'Wake,' said Fayard. 'Play.'

He moved away as the middle screen came to life. Mariam leaned in.

The video showed a partial view of a church, the tops of a few wooden chairs and a pulpit. In the pulpit was a woman wearing dark glasses, thick foundation and generous red lipstick, her hair cut in a tidy blond bob, possibly a wig. The footage was low-light and grainy.

A figure passed in front of the lens, a shadow blotting out the screen. Mariam heard a voice, a peremptory command. Then the camera angle changed slightly, framing the woman more centrally as she touched a clenched fist to her heart and began to speak. The audio resonated eerily with the acoustics of the stone building.

'We have a right to breathe clean air, but clean air is denied us. We have a right to clean water, but our rivers run with filth. We have a right to live in security, but lawlessness prevails. We have a right to secure borders, but our borders are porous. We have a right to safe food, but our food is tainted.

'The crisis of our times is not a humanitarian crisis. It is an existential crisis. See, on the news, the tides of refugees, this way and that, flowing from old dangers into new dangers, bringing with them need and disease. See the shanties built on the outskirts and even in the heart of our greatest cities. See the countryside despoiled, the labour of millions replaced by huge machines, depleting the soil, ripping out the hedgerows, channelling the rivers and streams like spoilt children that need to be taught how to behave.

‘Hear the scientists who always say they have solutions, new solutions, always technological solutions, when the problem is not technological, has never been technological. When will they see that the problem is so much more than that, out of their control – a question of cycles and inevitable conflicts? Never. They will never see it. Their pride blinds them.

‘And our elites, the elites that control us, do not care. They run, for their own benefit, the first-world nations. They run the second-world nations by proxy. The third-world nations, the victim nations, they exploit through finance and repression.

‘That is all there is – power and the wielding of power. A tiny elite grown swollen, a rentier class, living on capital, living on the exploitation of entrenched positions of inherited wealth, dynastic authority, while the masses endure servitude, impotence, imbecile entertainments and subsistence labour, except for the lucky few allowed to climb, at such cost, with such difficulty, with so much effort, such pain, rung by rung, each day, each week, each month, each year just a little higher, just as a way of offering the rest an example. “See,” they say, “it is possible. You, too, might be a part of the elite if you work hard enough, if you sacrifice enough.”

‘Lies. All lies.

‘The machine is seized. The gears no longer turn. They were never meant to turn. The mechanism was only ever for show.

‘The forces ranged against us are vast. They move in measure and bind together, impossible to shift unless something enormous, something catastrophic, comes to shake the bars of the cages that imprison us.

‘The only response must be inhumanity. Nothing less will break the bars.

‘Tabula Rasa. We must start again. Tabula Rasa. Tabula Rasa.’

The video ended, the final frame held on the screen.

Mariam pinched out the image to look at the woman more closely. Around the dark glasses, she was so heavily made up she resembled a shop mannequin.

'Do we know who she is?'

Fayard made a vague gesture. 'Administrator Sabie is running voice recognition software. He tells me the resonance of the church makes this difficult.'

Mariam nodded. 'When was it recorded?'

'Camera data can be falsified but, it seems, last Sunday.'

She thought about what the woman had said at the end of her polemic. She'd heard of Tabula Rasa, but it had never come up as a serious threat.

'Tabula Rasa isn't a proscribed organisation, is it?' she asked.

Fayard shook his head. 'It is barely an organisation. More a set of ideas.'

'Is there a wider briefing note? Will Administrator Sabie send it to me?'

Fayard hesitated. She got the feeling he was weighing something up, something he hadn't yet decided to tell her. When he spoke, all he said was: 'I'll make sure you get the information.'

'Thank you.'

After a moment, as if to himself, he murmured, 'There will be time enough.'

Fayard's Sunday bodyguard – a huge man with punctilious manners and long black hair called Sébastien Ménard – was running late, otherwise Mariam wouldn't have been there. As soon as Sébastien arrived, Fayard told her she could go. Then he told Sébastien, 'I don't need you for the time being.'

Without a word, the big man turned and walked out, his broad shoulders almost touching the door frame.

Alone in his private quarters, Fayard walked slowly to his desk and reactivated a holoscreen with a voice command. His hand-held computer and comm-watch lay alongside but, for reasons of security, his rooms were impervious to wireless communication.

The system had gone into sleep mode and took a few moments to come alive. Fayard sat down carefully, his shoulders hunched to ease the pressure on his lungs, his breathing audible in the quiet room. The screen resolved. He confirmed his identity with a thumbprint and then told the Camera Control system to find Mariam Jordane.

It was nearly midday and the streets were fairly quiet. The system found her crossing the wide-open space in front of the mighty dome of the Panthéon. He watched as she entered a pâtisserie on Boulevard Saint-Michel, re-emerging a minute or so later with a box tied with a ribbon, and then heading south, past the Luxembourg Gardens where the general public were no longer admitted, and uphill towards the Observatory.

As she moved, the grainy image flicked from camera to camera. The old man recognised a residential neighbourhood, a hospital, a magnificent row of fine seven-storey dwellings. As Mariam arrived at her destination, the pictures improved in quality. He saw quite clearly the impressive, glazed lobby, the airlock that controlled access. He watched her step through, and she was gone.

Fayard closed the connection. He didn't feel better. It hadn't helped.

A notification popped up – a message from Administrator Sabie concerning the video of the woman in the blond wig.

Fayard opened the digital file and skimmed the text. It was from the chatroom of a group that believed in an apocalyptic interpretation of the Christian Bible and the 'end-times'. There was threatening talk of the 'Admonition', a symbolic period of a thousand years, followed by another symbolic millennium, the 'Tribulation', when 'those in possession of the gospel of the kingdom cannot be hurt by the dragon's deception'. Finally, in the 'Resolution' the 'work of the dragon' would be 'brought to an end' and the 'second spiritual resurrection' would begin.

As he read the notes, Fayard pursed his lips. Sabie wanted to know if the chat should be shut down.

'Of course not,' Fayard replied.

Sabie was an unimaginative man. In the crazed chatter of 'end-times' and apocalyptic visions, Fayard thought, he was lost. Alexandre Lamarque, on the other hand…

'Le passé,' he said aloud, to himself, *'ne nous guide plus.'*

The past is no longer any guide.

Fayard's watch beeped, a warning that he had been motionless for too long. He got up slowly, wondering if his body was still capable of recovery. His muscles ached and he felt weak. Was it the same illness, suddenly worse, or a new opportunistic infection? What he needed was new science, a medical breakthrough.

He paced the length of his room, trying not to lean too heavily on his stick.

He believed himself to be a good judge of character – cajoling, persuading, encouraging and prompting, always for the greater good, guided by what was best for France, for its people, and by a moral purpose. The decisions he'd made were the best he was capable of in the face of intractable circumstances. And circumstances were always intractable. There were always other factors, powerful destructive factors, outside of his control.

He had few regrets. He recognised there were limits to what he could expect to achieve. He had accumulated power and influence. In doing so, he had taken power away from others. He had managed to shape the organisation he headed, the Directorate-General for Internal Security, to his own vision of what was necessary and right. And he had staffed Internal Security with women and men like Administrator Sabie whose actions would always be guided by logic and science, by experience and history.

The missing piece was intuition. The ability to find the pattern concealed by apparent chaos. That was something he believed Alexandre Lamarque could provide. Gloria Lamarque's son had a deserved reputation for intuitive understanding.

But Lamarque worked for the parallel External Security service and had already rejected him once.

Still, Fayard told himself, circumstances change. Perhaps an appropriate pressure could be brought to bear.

His steady pacing of the room took him back to his desk. With the tip of his left forefinger, he touched the screen. It woke on the final still image of Mariam, disappearing into the luxurious lobby of the fine seven-storey dwelling.

7

That same Sunday, in a café in a working-class neighbourhood close to the docks in Cyrene City, about eighteen degrees of longitude east of Paris, Amaury Barra glanced at the old-fashioned LED flatscreen, high up in a corner. A news channel was broadcasting footage from the emergency ward in the main hospital.

Another novel pathogen. Bad news, again.

On the table in front of him was a map of the city, folded over to show the parliamentary compound. It was the signal. No one would ask for his name. He would simply be accepted as the shooter and that would be that. It was arranged.

Outside, he noticed two men hesitating by the café's door. One of them had a mass of black hair and a beard. The man brought his face close to the glass and pointed. The other – Amaury suspected the one in charge – had narrow features like an angry weasel. He pushed the door open, ordered and paid for two sweet coffees at the counter, then the two of them came and sat opposite Amaury.

'How long have you been here?' asked Weasel, pitching his voice very low.

'Not long,' said Amaury.

'Not long enough to attract attention?'

'No.'

Amaury weighed them up – the bearded one over-excited, the narrow-faced one worried.

'All right,' said Weasel, glancing at his bearded partner. 'Drink up.'

They drained their cups and left. Amaury walked between the two men. They passed a cheap hostel, the offices of a trading company, a charitable medical clinic with a long queue. The late-afternoon sun burned like a searchlight in the gaps between the buildings. Finally, they reached a narrow patch of scrubland and stepped into the shadow of a tall warehouse.

'Stop here,' Weasel ordered. 'Put your hands against the wall.'

Amaury did as he was told.

'We're good,' he assured them. 'No one knows who I am or where I'm from.'

'Shut up.'

The second man searched him thoroughly – his pockets, the seams of his clothes, every inch of his body.

'He's clean,' he said.

Amaury waited, his hands still on the wall. He heard the sound of an old-school mobile phone keypad, the numbers beeping as it dialled. Weasel was calling someone higher up for authority to proceed.

Or authority to abort.

Amaury wasn't worried. His cover was sound.

There was a brief murmured conversation then Weasel said, 'Turn round.'

Amaury did so. Weasel watched him steadily. The second man was fidgeting, pushing his hands through his thick dark hair, shifting his weight.

'We must be ready,' he said. 'My cousin is coming.'

'Stop talking,' ordered Weasel.

But the second man didn't listen. 'We can't miss this chance.' He turned to Amaury. 'I'm Tariq.'

'No names.' Weasel cut him off brusquely. 'We are nobody. We are only what we must do.'

'You're very wise,' Amaury told him. 'The only question I have is, how will we get into the compound?'

'My cousin—' began Tariq.

'Be quiet,' snapped Weasel. 'We wait.'

They sat down, each with their backs to the high warehouse wall, two Cyrenian revolutionaries and their 'shooter' – no longer Firmin Couchant, the well-liked manager from the desalination plant, nor Amaury Barra of the French Directorate-General for External Security.

He was a nameless mole, alone among enemies, hoping that Paris would not forget he was here.

At the same time, on the island of Cyprus, the data centre director was using a massively encrypted messaging service to exchange apparently bland messages with a few like-minded people on two of the world's most connected hubs – Long Island and Tahiti. She wished there were more.

In the background to each message, like a watermark, was the image of a distant sunrise over devastation.

Back in Cyrene City, with the passing of time, conversation became inevitable and Amaury began to understand his new colleagues. Tariq's job was to obey orders while Weasel had access to someone higher up in the insurrection, via his old-school mobile phone. The two men seemed motivated by personal grievance, a sense that life had done them down, had stolen their rightful prizes.

The sun set and, at last, Tariq's cousin arrived, a farmer in a small tractor pulling a flat-bed trailer piled high with mulch for the celebrated rose gardens inside the parliamentary compound.

'Like pigs,' said Weasel, angrily. 'We must go in like pigs?'

'It's a good plan,' argued Tariq. 'They search everything.'

'The waste is well-rotted,' interrupted the cousin. 'It's not harmful.'

'It will be easy,' said Tariq. 'They will not search through the heap. And, to breathe, we will use these.'

He showed Weasel three snorkels. Amaury tried not to find the scene funny.

'We will be found,' said Weasel, holding a snorkel with distaste.

But Tariq was confident. 'We'll be underneath. There are holes in the bed of the trailer. The snorkels will stick out underneath.'

Weasel addressed the driver of the tractor. 'This is not pig manure, at least?'

The cousin shrugged. 'It's what we have.'

Amaury watched with interest as Weasel took out his phone. The conversation was brief. Clearly, the handler left Weasel no alternative but to accept Tariq's plan. He turned to Amaury.

'You are the shooter. You are willing?'

It seemed it was up to Amaury to decide. If he said yes, all three of them would pass a point of no return. For Amaury, there would no longer be times in the day when he was alone, when he could let drop his guard.

He nodded. 'I am willing, comrade,' he said.

Across the city, Weasel's handler frowned. Knowing time was short, she had taken the call in the public lobby, then almost given herself away as a member of the Cyrenian parliament interrupted her, wanting to know Prime Minister Mourad's whereabouts.

'Is she in her safe room?'

'She cannot be disturbed,' said Weasel's handler, 'but I will pass on the honourable member's request.'

He left her, looking worried. For the future of the nation or for his own skin?

Both probably.

Weasel's handler climbed the stairs to the viewing gallery above the debating chamber, high in the atrium roof, and contemplated her dumb phone.

Was it a good idea, after all? Would the presence of these clowns inside the parliamentary compound be a distraction?

Now she knew of their plan to be smuggled in with the manure, she could easily give them away. And circumstances were already moving in her general's favour. Disturbances on the streets of Cyrene City were now to be expected, not just hoped for. The new pathogen was a help. A single pebble might start an avalanche.

She looked out through the atrium roof, towards the cranes at the docks a few kilometres away.

'Soon,' she murmured to herself, visualising Weasel's foolish face, 'all of that will burn. Let the fools come.'

8

On Tuesday morning, Alex found himself in the office of an extremely senior civil servant at the Ministry for Foreign Affairs.

The Foreign Ministry owned several buildings in central Paris, the most important an imposing mid-nineteenth-century building on the left bank of the Seine, between the Chamber of Deputies and the grassy esplanade of the Invalides. The office was furnished in chrome and leather and glass, but the ceiling mouldings, the wood panelling, the doors and the windows were all perfectly preserved examples of Second Empire design. The combination was a strange mixture of luxury and austerity. Alex wasn't sure he liked it.

Soon after dawn he had sent a formal email, stating his intention to resign. It had taken only four hours to filter up to Claudine Poiret, a woman with direct authority over External Security within French government. Poiret had immediately sent an official car to pick him up. For almost an hour they'd been talking in circles.

'I haven't taken the decision lightly,' he repeated.

Poiret leaned back in her chair, a calculating look in her eyes. 'You have two months left in your current tour of duty?'

'Yes.'

'What will you do then?'

Alex declined to be drawn. 'With respect, that's my business.'

Poiret picked up a screen-stylus and tapped it on the smoked-glass desk. 'You say you no longer believe your work is helping people. But surely you understand that what a government says for domestic consumption does not correspond to policy? Events move quickly. Actions are determined by the national interest.'

'By "actions", you mean robberies?' His tone was acid. 'Extrajudicial killings?'

'Actions that usually turn out to be justified.'

'Is that the only policy?' Alex asked. 'The "national interest"?'

'It isn't a bad policy.'

'When Iran bombed Haifa in 2024, was that in the national interest?'

Poiret looked confused. 'That had little to do with French intelligence.'

'France publicly condemned Israel to gain political advantage,' he reminded her. 'The consequences might have been nuclear conflict.'

'There was no certainty that Iran was capable of detonating a nuclear device.'

'You're deliberately missing the point,' said Alex, angrily. 'In any case, I'm not asking you to dismantle the DGSE. I am simply resigning.'

She left a beat before asking, 'How old are you, remind me?'

'I am thirty-two.'

'You were nineteen years old in 2024. Why did Haifa come into your mind?'

He made an impatient gesture. 'When I joined the service, I wrote a study of the events that led to the Israel–Iran War.'

She nodded. 'For Professor Fayard, I know. I've read your file. On the strength of it, he asked you to join the diplomatic service. Yet you refused. Why?'

Alex paused. It was a good question. His academic achievements had equipped him perfectly for a life of strategy and theoretical decision-making.

'I used to believe in the power of action,' he said.

'And now you are experiencing a loss of faith.'

He considered this assessment – looking for the truth in it. 'I lost faith when I was a child. This is different. The future is…'

He stopped.

Poiret looked genuinely interested. 'Is what?'

He met her gaze. 'On our current path? Dark.'

Silence fell and lasted so long he could hear a blackbird singing in the lime tree outside the windows.

Was she right? Should he stay and fight? Try and create better policies from within?

'You know, this is what the psychologists call an *abcès de fixation*,' she told him suddenly. 'You are choosing resignation as if it can mend all of your regrets and resentments. But this would mean abandoning everything you've worked for…' She stopped, as if another thought had occurred to her. 'I wonder, is it an aspect of your special skill?'

'I have no special skills,' Alex said.

'Don't you?' Poiret activated a holoscreen. Several documents appeared. 'Your career is studded with commendations for your "extraordinary intuitive understanding", your "exceptional ability to foresee outcomes". Wouldn't you say that was a special skill?'

Alex watched her cautiously before replying. 'They overestimate me.'

'I doubt that.' Poiret shut down the holo. 'On reflection, I think redeployment would be a better option.'

Alex frowned. 'And why would I agree to that?'

Poiret smiled. 'Oh, you must allow me some secrets, Monsieur Lamarque.'

9

The call came at six o'clock the following morning, rousing Alex from sleep in the cocoon-like cabin of his boat.

'I'm sorry to wake you, Alexandre. I need…'

There was something unexpected in his mother's voice – something almost like fear.

'What's happened?' he asked, sitting up.

'There's nothing to worry about,' she insisted, but Alex was experienced enough to recognise the lie.

He washed and dressed, put his hand-held in his jacket pocket and opened the hatch. For the time being, the air was pleasantly cool. Mist rose gently from the dark green water. Low clouds obscured the sky.

Alex crossed the gangplank and climbed the steps from the canal basin to the boulevard. A pair of bright white gulls stood immobile at the top, as if keeping watch. When he neared, they took off, noisily flapping their wings.

He crossed the boulevard and cut through a side-street where a rundown shopfront served as headquarters for Tabula Rasa, a political organisation opposed to hyper-connectivity, invasive security and a bunch of other things that, until now, it had been Alex's duty to protect. He barely glanced at it. They were strange, but they weren't a threat.

He emerged onto Boulevard Henri IV, a wide-open thoroughfare built for multiple lanes of traffic. Since the city had been remodelled for a smaller population and much lighter electric and hydro-cell cars, there was just one lane in each direction. The centre of the boulevard had been planted with an orchard of apple trees that looked scorched, even this early in the morning. He passed a comms store where a woman in pale blue overalls was rolling up her metal shutters. It was not long after dawn, but there was always demand in her line of business.

When he reached the nineteenth-century townhouse where Gloria Lamarque lived, he put on his mask and a pair of latex gloves before inputting the code on the keypad by the front door. He heard the lock disengage and let himself in, climbing the stone stairs to the fourth floor, spiralling around the elevator column.

He was doing something millions of people had done before him – responding to a call from a loved one, hoping it wasn't serious, knowing it probably was.

He uncovered his thumb to press it against the lock pad and went inside.

His mother's apartment was very dark. All the curtains were drawn and there was a smell of stale incense.

'*C'est toi, Alexandre?*' came a small voice from the sitting room.

'*Oui, c'est moi.*'

'What will you think of me? Burning incense because I haven't had time to clean.'

He found his mother in the spacious front room in her usual chair, looking tiny and neat, wrapped in a dark dressing gown. It was too gloomy to see her expression, but she spoke with a smile in her voice.

'I'm sure I'm fine,' she said. 'This is just foolishness. But they do say to act at the first symptoms.'

'They do.' Alex looked round at the heavy curtains. 'Are you sensitive to light?'

She made a vague gesture. 'A little.'

'Since when?'

'Oh, you know…' She tried to rise. 'Shall we have tea? Or coffee? No, you would prefer one of those awful green decoctions…'

Alex touched the curtain. 'Can I open this just a little?'

She waved an impatient hand. 'Go ahead.'

He pulled the drapes aside. The light that entered the apartment was flat and grey. All the same, she winced.

'Oh, dear.' She reached a hand up to shield her eyes.

'Let me look at you.'

Leaning over her small frame, Alex rested his gloved hands on either side of her face. Her eyes were bloodshot, her pupils contracted. Her skin looked clammy. For a moment she held his gaze, before looking away.

'Would you hand me my dark glasses?'

He found them on her desk in the general mess of books, notebooks, printouts and scraps of ideas. She put them on, her face relaxing.

'This is more than a little sensitivity to light,' he told her gently. 'How long have you been unwell?'

'I'm not unwell,' she insisted stubbornly.

'Unwell enough to call me at six in the morning and ask me to come over. Has it been hours, days, weeks?'

'Weeks? Good heavens no. Days. One or two days.'

Surveying the dishevelled apartment, Alex doubted it.

'How long since you've been outside?'

Her brow creased. 'That's a good question…'

Her voice faded as she seemed to forget what he'd asked. Was that another symptom? Losing her train of thought might mean she was dehydrated. Alex's chest tightened, but he kept his voice even.

'Where's your home-diag? When did you last drink something?'

'I'm not sure. In the kitchen perhaps…'

'Does your throat hurt?'

'A little.' She made to stand. 'Why don't I make us some coffee.'

Alex rested a hand on her shoulder, pressing her back down. 'You sit still. All illness is serious.'

'Alexandre, I am fifty-nine years old. I'm not an old lady. You sound like the public information messages.'

'Stay here. I'll be back in a minute.'

The kitchen was untidy, the remains of a small, unfinished meal adhering to a solitary plate – some kind of white fish in a congealed yellow sauce. There was a scar on the wooden draining board where a hot saucepan had been set down. Crumbs littered the floor. There were mouse droppings along the skirting board.

'I haven't cleared up from last night,' Gloria called from the sitting room. 'What you must think…'

'Is anyone else in the building unwell?' he called back.

'I don't think so, but…' Again, she didn't finish. A full sentence seemed beyond her.

He put water in the kettle and found fresh milk in the fridge.

So, she had gone out. That was foolish.

The kitchen window had no curtains and faced south, overlooking the building's courtyard. The room was bright, despite the dull day. He poured boiling water on the coffee grounds and, while it brewed, closed the slatted shutters, catching the latex on his right-hand glove and tearing it. He found a new one in a box on the breakfast counter and put it on.

The home-diag was in one of the eye-level cupboards. He put it on a tray along with the coffee and carried it through to the sitting room.

By the time Gloria had finished her second cup of coffee, she looked much more alert.

'Of course, I've been out now and then, but not every day, Alexandre. And I have taken precautions.'

Had she, though?

'You haven't met anyone, spoken to anyone, been in anyone else's home?'

'Just the shops.'

'There's no one in the building that we should warn? No one who might have spoken to you?'

'You know what it's like,' she interrupted. 'There's only Nelinha, and Monsieur Labidie on the first floor. I don't really know anyone else.'

'That isn't true. There are five apartments.'

'There's a couple with a small child on the top floor. But they take the lift.'

'And the other units are empty?' he asked.

'The people on the floor below me are sometimes here.' She took another sip of coffee. 'I heard them perhaps a week ago? But they have a country home.'

Alex nodded. It was one of the paradoxes of the city – homelessness alongside population decline and empty apartments, a toxic cocktail of inequality, illness and fear.

'You've had no visitors, seen no one? You're sure?'

'I know the law, Alexandre.'

He picked up the home-diag and pulled his chair closer, taking off her sunglasses. She shut her eyes. 'Sit still.'

'This feels like an interrogation,' she told him. 'Can you always tell when someone isn't telling the truth? I imagine you've become very skilled.'

Alex pressed the power button and waited as the software booted up. 'Experience helps. There are so many ways for a lie to resemble a lie.'

'You express yourself beautifully. You always have,' she said. 'Are you still worried by the future, the darkness?'

'Who isn't?'

'Tell me,' she said. 'What is it you see coming?'

He leaned in. 'Open your eyes. Look straight ahead.'

Her eyes blinked open. The device flashed a bright light. She cried out and turned her head away.

'I'm sorry,' he said gently. 'Turn back towards me and sit still for thirty seconds. You don't have to open your eyes again.'

The sensors in the device analysed the complexion of her skin, the thread-like blood vessels just beneath it, the rate and composition of her exhalations, her body temperature. The highly sensitive microphones listened to her heart and her lungs. Then the device gave a beep and he placed it against the side of her neck, checking blood pressure and flow.

'No,' she sighed, 'I really don't know them.'

It took Alex a moment to realise she had flashed back to an earlier part of the conversation.

'The other residents?'

'At least, I don't know them as people to discuss one's ailments with,' she said.

'So, you do have ailments?'

'Not ailments. Symptoms.'

'So, you do have symptoms?' he countered.

She glared at him. 'You are my most infuriating son.'

'Your only son.' He smiled.

The device beeped again. The tests were complete. Alex flipped open a screen.

'Symptom one,' he read, 'sensitivity to light. Symptom two, fever. Symptom three, raised blood pressure. Symptom four, ophthalmic evidence of infection. Symptom five, impeded breath sounds.'

She sighed and put her dark glasses back on. 'Please stop.'

'The diag will upload to the medical centre.' He rubbed his forehead with his fingertips. 'I have to take another trip later today, so I can't stay. I'll ask Nelinha to help you while I'm gone.'

His mother gave him a surprised look. 'I thought you resigned?'

'I have two months left on my tour.'

'I don't really enjoy Nelinha's company these days.' Gloria sounded troubled. 'Her parents are worried about her, you know.'

Alex didn't know where this was coming from. Nelinha was almost part of the family. She wasn't making sense. Maybe it was the illness.

'I'll talk to her before I leave.'

'Would you read my new paper?' Gloria asked, unexpectedly. 'The one I told you about last time you were here.'

'Is it important?' Alex asked.

'You aren't the only one with intuition, you know,' she said. 'It's in my shared drive. Search for "Gerboise Bleue". And when you're back, come for dinner. Bring Mariam, I want to meet her again. And Amaury Barra. You used to be close.'

She tried to stand again. Alex repeated his own gesture of putting a hand on her shoulder.

'Please, *maman*, you must take care of yourself.'

'Then let me rest,' she told him impatiently, 'while I prepare for the invasion of your unnecessary doctors.'

Leaving her with a glass of water and a slice of toast, Alex took the stairs down. He was much more worried than he had let Gloria know. She had waited too long before asking for help. The viruses that had swirled through the population for years now could be devastating. He'd never thought for a second his careful mother would catch one.

On the ground floor, crossing the tiled entrance hall with its scuffed oak panelling, he found his imagination disappearing into memories of his earliest childhood – playing with wooden spoons and saucepan lids with the concierge's daughter, Nelinha, while his mother was studying upstairs. How old would he have been – three, four? Or perhaps it wasn't a memory. Perhaps it was something he'd been told.

He knocked at the door of the concierge's flat. It swung open at his touch. He walked through the small but spotless living room to the kitchen. Nelinha was sitting on the back step, wearing headphones, facing out onto the courtyard, a large-format doc-reader balanced on her knees, dictating in Portuguese to her comm-watch. She had always been an early riser. Her dark wavy hair was brushed back from her forehead.

Not wanting to interrupt, Alex squeezed past her into the shady courtyard and sat quietly on a cast-iron chair.

Nelinha was two years older but Alex had been precocious, with an ear for her parents' mother tongue. In between homework in maths and history and comms, she'd made it her duty to polish his kitchen-Portuguese to an impressive fluency.

She stopped dictating, tapped her watch and the doc-reader went dark.

'*Bom dia*,' said Alex. 'How are *mamãe e papai*, Nelinha?'

'Happy to be in the country of their birth.' She gave a rueful smile. 'Perhaps, if they'd known the travel corridor would close, they might have thought twice before leaving, but they are content.'

'They don't miss Paris? I was surprised to hear they'd gone.'

'They're staying in a guest house on a promontory. They watch the Atlantic Ocean pounding the rocky coastline.'

She'd dodged the question, but he let it pass.

'It must be very beautiful there.'

Nelinha glanced up at the fourth-floor windows. 'You closed her shutters.'

'The light was hurting her eyes.'

'That doesn't sound good.' She gave him an assessing look. 'And here you are at the crack of dawn.'

'She's not feeling well. I've already notified the med-centre. She may be quarantined.'

Her eyes widened. 'It's that bad? I'm so sorry.'

'She says she hasn't seen anyone,' said Alex. 'Have you noticed her going in and out?'

'I hear the lift, but I don't always look to see who it is. You know she can get so absorbed in her work that she doesn't leave her apartment for days at a time. Sometimes she asks me to get her some shopping, but not in the last fortnight.' Nelinha looked apologetic. 'I should have noticed and checked.'

'It's not your fault. You're very good to her,' said Alex. 'To both of us.'

'She hates asking for help.'

'Can I ask you to watch her more closely for forty-eight hours? I have to go away for work.' He gave her his cover story. 'I'm assessing an investment opportunity in Cyprus.'

'What a big shot you are these days,' she smiled, but it didn't reach her eyes.

'Her diag automatically uploaded to the medical centre. Does the door mechanism to mother's apartment recognise your thumbprint?'

'Since about 2015.'

'Of course,' said Alex, smiling. 'I remember the day you got access. I was so jealous.'

Nelinha looked amused. 'What were you, nine years old?'

'And you were a grown-up eleven, but it was my apartment and you could open the lock and I couldn't. I was outraged.'

There was a pause, then Nelinha spoke. 'I'll look after her. You don't have to ask.'

'Thank you,' he said, and stood up. 'I should go. You've got work to do.'

'Alex,' she said, 'remember: *O que será*. Whatever will be. The world is out of control and there is nothing left that an individual can do to change things.'

This was so close to his own thoughts that Alex didn't know what to say.

'You go,' she told him. 'I'll speak to the med-centre. If it's quarantine, I'll let you know.'

'Thank you.' He paused, remembering what Gloria had said about her. 'How about you? Are you okay?'

She stood up, pushing her fingers through her dark wavy hair.

'Oh, you know. People live, people die,' she told him. 'The darkness is always on the horizon, *amigo do minho*. However much money you make, nothing can change that.'

10

Alex left his mother's building and went back to the boat to pack before spending several hours reading through the files one of Poiret's team had sent him on the international data and energy industries. It was early evening when he finally touched down in Cyprus, in the eastern Mediterranean. He was travelling under an identity he had used before, a venture-capital analyst called Maurice Panhard, researching potential infrastructure investments.

After a restless night in a mediocre isolation hotel, he was driven to an international energy-and-data relay station – a huge facility that dwarfed the nearby village of Kofinou.

'I want your impressions,' Poiret had told him. 'Energy and data are both of immense strategic importance.'

'And?' he had asked.

'Kofinou is an obvious target for terrorists. Use your skills. Come back and tell me where an attack might come from, how it might be organised.'

The morning after he arrived, Alex had been given a lengthy and detailed tour by an enthusiastic manager, Tani Sakelliou. Now, he sat at a desk in the control room of the electricity relay station, watching a holoscreen. Its animated graphic showed the recent expansion of the global network of undersea power and data cables, colour-coded by function, flow-direction and capacity. The lines grew, extended and multiplied, creating an expanding web across the world's seas and oceans.

When the timeline reached the present day, the graphic became still, with dotted lines showing cables still under construction. One of these ran south-east from Bunker Martha in Marseille to a repeater station on Corsica, then on for an uninterrupted 1,500 kilometres to Cyrenia on the North African coast. Another dotted line linked Cyrenia with Kofinou.

Not everywhere that served as a landing place for underwater cables was as visible as Kofinou, but it turned out good landing points were surprisingly hard to find. The first requirements were natural – sand or silt in which to bury the cables, each about the thickness of a telegraph pole. They should be places without significant marine traffic, trawling or dredging, no strong currents or moorings where heavy anchors might be dropped. In some locations, the power and data cables simply lay out in the open, visible between the tides. Some were encased in heavy steel tubing, encrusted with shellfish. Others were brought ashore beneath long concrete ramps, giving the appearance of slipways. In a few rare cases, the cables might stretch several kilometres inland before reaching a relay hub. The world's most important repeater stations were protected by multiple layers of reinforced concrete and steel, as impregnable as… Well, Bunker Martha.

That was where his vague forebodings had first crystallised. And they were connected to Amaury Barra, the colleague who'd warned him about the potential threat, but who had seriously underestimated the terrorists involved.

All this brought his thoughts back to Gloria. He wanted to be home, rather than chasing some nebulous threat Poiret had pretended to believe in. And he was worried about the heatwave in Paris. If there was a brown-out in her neighbourhood, she would lose her air con, which was the last thing she needed while running a fever. He'd called her on a satlink from the plane and suggested she should move to his boat. The backup batteries recharged from solar panels and carried sufficient power for several days. She'd refused, not wanting to be away from her furniture and her books.

It would, in any case, have made it more difficult for Nelinha to watch over her.

He refocused on his task, sliding the map with an impatient gesture, scrolling down the west coast of Africa all the way to the Cape, then east across the Indian Ocean, looking for danger. He zoomed in on the complicated nexus of cables around Singapore, then further east into the South Pacific as far as French Polynesia where, in the vast data desert of salt water, the island nation of Tahiti was the spider at the centre of its own web of cables.

The truth was, there were weaknesses everywhere. The map he was using was in the public domain. There was more than enough information out there to make it possible for a terrorist to locate innumerable targets, even on the vast ocean floor.

Alex activated speech recognition on his watch and began quietly dictating the first draft of his report. The control room receded as he became absorbed in his own thoughts, until a voice disturbed his concentration.

'I'm so sorry to have kept you waiting,' said Tani Sakelliou. 'I lost track of time. I'm afraid I often do here, at the heart of all this magic.' She waved a hand at the huge wall of lights, representing current flows between three continents. 'Amazing really, Monsieur Panhard. When you think how it used to be.'

'Energy production?'

'Exactly – those filthy, destructive intermediate technologies. It wouldn't be so bad if humanity had had some kind of noble project, a grand reason for the destruction of the natural world. But no, it's just so we could all live longer, fatter, lazier lives and end up just as dead.' Sakelliou laughed. 'As Director Philippou says, for each of us, one day will be shorter than all the rest.'

Alex raised an eyebrow. 'What's that?'

'It's an old medieval proverb,' she told him.

He nodded. 'Interesting.'

Sakelliou swept on. 'There was no reason, I mean, there was no real reason, once the networks began to expand. There were always enough renewables. It was just a question of connecting them up – Icelandic geothermal, North Sea aeolian, pumped-storage hydro from Israel, Saharan solar. It's always windy somewhere, sunny somewhere, the tides are always running somewhere. You know what I mean? And then massive battery arrays for storage. Can you believe Norway persists in burning oil?'

Still feeling guilty about how he had deceived Genmis, Alex found himself defending the scientist's country. 'Norwegian power stations are much cleaner than anyone else's.'

'Not as clean as the energy flowing through this room,' Sakelliou said. 'Well, nothing is completely clean. There's always a cost of some kind.' She paused. 'I'm sorry. You didn't come here to talk to me. Let me tell Director Philippou you're ready to speak to her.'

'You've been very kind, very generous with your time,' Alex said. 'My investors will be delighted.'

'Are you here about the new Cyrenia connection?' she asked. 'They have amazing solar plans – with French finance, I believe?'

Alex smiled a wholesome smile. 'I can't say.'

It was easy to lie convincingly when there was no truth to conceal.

While Sakelliou went to discover if Director Philippou was available, Alex sent Nelinha a message, hoping for good news, expecting bad. Then he texted Mariam to let her know Gloria's circumstances.

Just then, Sakelliou returned with the unwelcome news that Director Philippou had been called away at short notice. Sakelliou was extremely apologetic, and explained that she had rearranged their meeting for the following morning, though not until eleven o'clock.

Alex had no choice but to agree, deeply frustrated by the prospect of another night and day chasing Poiret's imaginary threats.

11

In Paris, Mariam had taken time off for a regular consultation with medical specialists at her sisters' comfortable facility near the Observatory where the two lay bed-ridden, due to damage inflicted at their mismanaged birth.

It was early afternoon. As always, she bought pastries they couldn't eat to share with their nurses. She stayed for two hours, holding first one twin's hand, then the other. Ablah was the younger by twenty short minutes and had always been the weaker of the two. Janaan at least seemed aware of Mariam's presence.

While she was there, Alex messaged to tell her about his mother's illness – that Gloria was in home isolation. She replied straight away.

Oh, no. Can I visit her?

Not before the med-centre have been. Nelinha is looking out for her.

She felt briefly cross that he hadn't asked her for help. Eight years they'd known one another, yet there remained – she wasn't sure why – a distance between them.

Afterwards, she walked on the shady side of fifty quiet streets, settling her thoughts. Thankfully, humidity was low and the air felt crisp – a welcome relief. When she reached the pedestrian walkway on the embankment of the Seine, she sat down, watching the water.

She was deep in thought when her comm-watch vibrated with a message from Camera Control about the apocalyptic speaker in the video Fayard had shown her. They had pinpointed the building, a church dedicated to Saint Genevieve in northern Paris. But they had no definitive match for the woman's voice. Her identity was unknown.

Fair enough. Camera Control was not completely reliable. Face-matching relied on good-quality images and the camera network was mostly low-res outside the heart of the city. Something as simple as a wig or a hat could deceive the algorithms.

The reliance on AI was a financial imperative, a false economy born out of a belief in the superiority of computer learning over human experience and intuition. All the same, thought Mariam, the response hadn't been exactly rapid. She sent a message to Sabie's office.

Why has this taken so long?

To her surprise, he replied in person.

I will attempt to ascertain.

Mariam felt her focus sharpen. This was meant to be her day off but she requested access to the archive of all the cameras around the church in the 18th arrondissement. By trawling the images herself, perhaps she could find something the algorithms had missed.

In north-west Marseille, a long black hearse was pulling up at an ugly, low-slung building. Two men climbed out – a mismatched pair, the younger one tall and fat, the older one short, thin and tired. They put on their masks and went inside.

Fifteen minutes later they emerged with two plain coffins, each on a wheeled trolley. They loaded them into the rear of their vehicle, and the younger, taller man got in on the driver's side. The older, shorter man hesitated as an attendant came running out after them with a tablet computer and a worried expression.

After a brief discussion, the older man signed the screen with his forefinger. Then he politely thanked the assistant for his help and climbed into the hearse.

'What was it?' asked the younger man, as he pulled away.

'Just a signature he forgot to ask for.'

'What name did you sign?'

'Charles de Gaulle.'

'Hilarious,' said his colleague, but neither of them was laughing.

The two men took the two bodies to a crematorium where they had an appointment at the very end of the day. They parked under a tree and stayed in the vehicle, watching dispassionately as a succession of family groups composed themselves for their last goodbyes. At around five o'clock the last legitimate mourners drifted away.

The fake undertakers reversed their vehicle to the service entrance and unloaded the two anonymous coffins. A weary official checked their digital paperwork. Seeing that it had apparently been provided by the police, he asked them if these were the two foreigners he had read about in the paper, the ones who attacked Bunker Martha. The fake undertakers pretended not to know.

Finally, the coffins were committed to the flames and, afterwards, the fake undertakers pulled away from the crematorium, nosing out into a bland residential suburb, weaving a complicated route through the lives of normal people, searching for the main road and the motorway north.

Back in Paris, Mariam was frustrated. It was hard work reviewing the neighbourhood footage via the pop-up holo from her comm-watch. She decided to visit the church in person and see what she could find.

She picked up an electric mobike at the bottom of Boulevard Saint-Michel and arrived in the northern neighbourhood a little after eight o'clock, with maybe an hour and a half of summer daylight left in the sky. She parked, immobilising the mobike with a thumbprint.

The church was bigger than she had expected, a warehouse of religion built of ugly rust-coloured burrstone. A set of low steps ran up to a narrow entrance beneath a rounded Norman arch. The door was propped open, so she pushed aside a heavy burgundy curtain and slipped in.

A late service was underway, with a congregation of several dozen worshippers. The nave was surprisingly airy, with two rows of wide Norman arches on either side. She tried to deduce the position of the camera in the video and decided it must have been about six rows back on the right-hand side, a position impossible to reach during the service, so she took a seat at the back and waited. She could smell cooking from another room and assumed a charitable meal would be offered after the service. That was unfortunate, but there was nothing to be done.

The hymn ended and the priest came forward to give a blessing in three languages – Latin, then French, then Portuguese. Mariam remembered that the 18th arrondissement neighbourhood was known for its immigrant population.

The blessing complete, a few worshippers stood and filed out past the burgundy curtain to the street. Others followed the priest through a side door. Within minutes of the service ending, Mariam was alone.

Time passed. She could hear conversation from the adjoining room, now and then the clank of crockery. Finally, even that became quiet, and someone turned off the lights.

The church was abruptly transformed. Without artificial illumination it became beautiful, with the low evening sun glowing through high windows. Alone and unseen, Mariam felt an unexpected sense of peace.

With some reluctance, she walked up the aisle and crouched down to examine the flagstones, methodically checking beneath each chair around where she thought the camera might have been. At the end of the row, she glanced up at the pulpit. Yes, this was the place.

She searched around the base of a pillar where the tiles didn't quite meet the dressed stone. The cracks were full of dust and grime.

And there it was, standing on its edge, invisible to a casual glance – a black plastic lens cap. Even in the fading light she could see fingerprints on the glossy surface and a human hair caught in the spring.

She thought back to the video – the dark blur that passed in front of the camera, the peremptory command. She could imagine the camera operator searching for the lens cap, failing to find it in the shadows, then giving up.

Now, she thought to herself, collecting the lens cap in a small evidence bag, I'll find out exactly who you are.

12

The next morning, Alex met Tani Sakelliou at the main gate. They crossed the huge industrial site on a converted golf cart, weaving beneath a web of high-voltage cables, supported by an immense steel forest of pylons.

Dust, midges, achingly bright sun.

They parked outside a hygiene station that controlled access into a bland concrete building the size of four tennis courts. Inside, he found himself in a medical room. While Sakelliou went to prepare him a visitor badge and the air conditioning cooled his skin, he introduced himself to an orderly in grey scrubs who found his name on his screen, and said, 'Take a seat, please.'

Alex sat down in a black reclining chair, like those used by dentists. The orderly took a tiny blood sample from the shallow flesh just below his left thumbnail and transferred it to a testing machine for analysis.

'Ninety seconds,' he said.

Alex took advantage of the delay to relax, counting his breaths, stilling his heartbeat. Finally, there was a beep.

'Clear,' announced the orderly, without looking up.

Alex pushed open the inner door. It led to a windowless waiting room with low soft chairs and a carpet that showed the marks of many dusty shoes. He had a moment of doubt, feeling he'd missed something – something someone had said, something important – but he didn't know what it was.

Before he could trace the thought, his comm-watch vibrated. It was a message from Nelinha.

When can we speak?

He selected an autoreply.

Later.

He checked the time. If all went well, he would be able to leave today and see Gloria first thing tomorrow. There was a military flight just before midnight, arriving at the airbase outside Paris early in the morning.

Sakelliou emerged from the side-office with a visitor identity card.

'Before we move on,' said Alex, 'can you clear something up for me?'

'I will try.'

'My consortium is interested in the rationalisation of the data network,' he lied. 'In some areas there's redundancy, in others inadequate capacity.'

The woman laughed. 'In all systems developed by atomised decision-making, there's a tendency to organised chaos.'

'Could I ask you about islands? Why are they so often—?'

'Geography, Monsieur Panhard. Fibre-optic cables can span great distances – from England to the USA across the North Atlantic, for example. Or Portugal to Brazil, following old colonial ties. Or Los Angeles to Chikura, outside Tokyo. But networks are more secure when they have multiple flows, shorter routes that can back one another up. Islands shorten the spans across the oceans. More than half the world's connectors come ashore on islands.'

'I was looking at a map earlier, with Tahiti the focal point of radiating connectors in the Pacific,' Alex said.

She nodded. 'In Tahiti, though there's a smallish population, there's vast network capacity because, well, when you lay a cable across thousands of kilometres of ocean floor, it makes sense to future-proof it with massive capacity.'

Alex thought of the lines of cables he'd been looking at earlier, stretching across the globe. 'And whoever controls the islands controls the flow of data?'

'The islands of Hong Kong and Taipei have more landing points than the whole of mainland China.'

Sakelliou delivered Alex to the director's office. Philippou turned out to be an austere-looking woman in a smart off-white business suit.

'That will be all, Tani. Monsieur Panhard, I'm sorry I could not see you yesterday. I'm afraid I can only give you a little time this morning.'

The director held out a hand. Alex assumed the hygiene in the facility was so secure that habitual restrictions on physical contact were not observed.

'Thank you for taking the time to see me,' he said.

Her fingers were cold.

Philippou's office was a pleasant modern room with internal windows that opened onto the data control area – two dozen workstations staffed by earnest-looking operatives. He caught a glimpse of Tani Sakelliou heading to her desk.

'How can I help you?' the director asked.

'The issue I would like to discuss is a delicate one.'

'I will do my best to help.'

'My investors are concerned that the data network might present a target.'

Her brow furrowed. 'A criminal target?'

'Terrorist,' he told her. 'Would you talk me through the potential vulnerabilities?'

Philippou considered this. 'Do you mean what one might call "purposeful" terrorism? Or random acts of nihilistic violence?'

Good question, thought Alex. He made a mental note to revisit it when he was alone. There was something about the way she phrased the enquiry that resonated.

'My investors would be equally concerned with both.' He hesitated. He had to take care not to appear to know too much. 'The data doesn't just flow like water down a pipe, I assume?'

She seemed to relax a little. 'The connectors require electricity to push the data. Three or four thousand volts for longer distances like the North Atlantic.'

'And the Mediterranean connectors?' For a split second, Alex pictured blood and brain matter on the shingle outside Bunker Martha, and he forced the memory away. 'The new cable from France to Cyrenia?'

'From Marseille?' Philippou frowned. 'I could check. Perhaps fifteen hundred volts.'

'And these high voltages, do they make the cables unstable?'

'Not at all. They are rated for the loads they carry.'

'I see. In your opinion, where are the weakest points in the system?'

'It is genuinely hard to say.'

That was a surprise. Shouldn't she have an opinion?

'Because?' he pressed.

Before she answered, the director tidied a notepad and an oversized doc-reader, lining them up with the edge of her desk. Was she prevaricating?

'The whole network is fragile,' she admitted. 'The repeater stations where the cables come ashore. The cables on the sea floor. It is possible to imagine them being attacked, especially now there are so many. But the issue would be short-lived. The complexity of the network allows for workarounds. One failure can no longer cut off a country, or even a continent, as it might have done thirty years ago.'

'How hard would it be to cut a cable?'

Philippou hesitated again, then swiped at a screen embedded in the surface of her desk. When she found what she wanted, she cast the image to a large screen on the wall – a super-saturated photograph of a yellow industrial machine that looked somewhere between a lunar rover and a tractor. It was being winched over the side of a service ship into a bright stretch of open water.

'This is a cable-burying machine, a CBM. If a CBM can lay and bury a cable, you might imagine that it could dig one up as well.'

Alex studied the image. 'How deep does it bury the cables?'

'Beyond accidental damage from trawling or stray anchors.'

'How hard might it be to get hold of a CBM?'

'Harder than a tractor, not as hard as a tank. It's basically a highly specialised robot. It operates tethered to a mother vessel, guided by cameras and sonar. If this was the method of attack, it wouldn't be discreet. It would be seen.'

Alex studied the yellow machine in the image. 'Could a successful attack be made, I don't know, by hand?'

'By divers?' The woman reflected for a moment. 'It wouldn't be my choice, if I wanted to disrupt the network. That is what we are talking about, isn't it? Disruption?'

Alex gave a small shrug. 'It's a legitimate concern when you consider the level of investment we'd be making.'

'What purpose would the disruption serve?'

'It might create commercial or political advantages,' he said.

Abruptly, Philippou killed the image-cast and stood. 'I'm so sorry. We're out of time. My advice, at this point, would be to consult with your own security services, Monsieur Panhard. Now, I'm afraid I have another meeting.'

Once the man she knew as Maurice Panhard was gone, Director Philippou sat for a moment in silence. She didn't like the way he had looked at her, his gaze far too innocent and trusting. Only someone determined to deceive would work that hard to give the impression he had nothing to hide.

She opened a drawer and took out a dedicated comms device capable of sending a highly encrypted message to someone she had never met, but with whom she shared a philosophy – a philosophy based on fire and destruction. A storm to sweep away and a clean slate from which to rebuild.

Before she sent her message, she reviewed the security footage from the moment Panhard entered the building to the moment she invited him into her office. She ran lip-reading software to catch incomplete fragments of Panhard's conversation with Tani Sakelliou. When she'd finished, she dictated fifty more words into the encrypted comms device, concluding with a terse question:

Action?

The next day, tired and sticky from his overnight flight out of Cyprus, Alex stood once more in his mother's spacious apartment. It was empty. Gloria was gone. Hours earlier, the med-centre had assessed her illness as notifiable and moved her into compulsory quarantine.

He opened the windows onto the boulevard, feeling guilty. Nelinha had done her best to clean the place, but the reek of vomit was still present in the room. An area of carpet was wet from scrubbing, discoloured by disinfectant. He was waiting for a professional disinfection service, but they were late and he was beginning to wonder if they would come at all.

Alex stepped out onto the balcony. An urban-farm team were tending to the apple trees. As he watched them, a message appeared on his watch. The cleaning company was postponing. The isolation clinic had told them to await further test results before entering the apartment.

So, it was serious.

He hoped Nelinha had been careful, and wondered about the wisdom of being in the apartment himself. Then again, two days ago, he had spent over an hour with his mother, drinking coffee.

He went back inside and spent a few minutes searching for a copy of the paper about 'Gerboise Bleue', the one she had asked him to read, but without success. It was striking, in fact, how few books and papers there were in the apartment. The home-diag was the only thing left on her desk.

He thought back to the day she had called him at dawn, the mess of papers everywhere. Had she tidied everything away? That would be odd, given how ill she'd been feeling.

He flipped open the screen on the home-diag and scrolled through the data, suddenly fearful that this might be his final memento of her – not a photograph or a tender message, but an impersonal set of medical parameters recorded by a machine.

He dropped it, furious with himself. He'd known when he left that there was what the analysts call a 'plausible risk'. Yes, he had taken steps, contacting the med-centre and asking a friend to watch out for her. He'd home tested and passed hygiene protocols at two airports and the data centre. But, yes, he'd got on a plane and left her alone.

He remembered his mother's good-humoured threat to call Professor Fayard, the head of the Internal Security service. Like Gloria and Poiret, Fayard believed in his ability to anticipate the future. But what use was that if he couldn't understand what was coming? He needed evidence, leads, suspects.

He needed his mother to be well.

As he began shutting the windows, he thought suddenly about the rundown shopfront round the corner – the headquarters of Tabula Rasa. It was unusual for an activist group to be allowed premises close to the centre of Paris. What were they? Pacifists? He made a mental note to ask Mariam what she knew. They would be an issue for Internal, not External. The idea dipped him back into a memory from initial training, in 2027, ten years ago.

'A defensive strategy,' said Professor Fayard, 'whether it's a secret service or a navy or an array of satellites, should be there "just in case", operating on a precautionary principle. It will often be costly, and the relevant threats may never materialise. Opponents argue that the precautionary principle makes policy reactive rather than active, that it's too expensive, that it inhibits the ability to improvise. Its supporters insist that the disadvantages of inaction are always outweighed by the downsides of overhasty action – the fear that, in the future, with the benefit of hindsight, what was done or what was not done will turn out to have been a catastrophic error of judgement.'

Fayard pressed a button on his lectern and showed a montage of media reports on the release of biological pesticides, all the projects having unexpected consequences, some trivial, some grave.

'There have been successes but, in the natural sciences, including environmentalism, the legacy of the precautionary principle is disputed. Was it useful to imagine the worst? To behave as if human ingenuity would have no scope for solving the problems created by human greed?'

Alex raised his hand. 'The first treaties signed into international law for the protection of the environment were all essentially precautionary. They created a purposeful framework for action.'

'Ah yes. The young are always so very keen on action.'

Fayard pressed another button, projecting a new montage. The screen divided into four equal frames. In each one was a rolling news report on displaced populations – people leaving their homes to escape war, famine, fire and flood.

'Do you understand the reference?' Fayard asked the hall.

Alex supposed he meant the four horsemen of the Apocalypse. Next to him, Amaury raised his hand, but Fayard went on without calling on him.

'In this, the third decade of the twenty-first century, the precautionary principle is often derided as populations starve, their food supplies disrupted by drought, disease, flood and war. Yes, global conflict has been avoided. Yes, economies in what we still call the developed world have continued, on the whole, to flourish.'

The professor activated a new slide that cross-dissolved into another and another – emergency wards all over the world, struggling to treat explosions of novel transgenic diseases.

'Doctors sign up to their own precautionary principle,' he continued. 'The oath to "do no harm". But what if that means doing nothing? That's giving up, accepting defeat. To give in is to collaborate.'

The word had an ugly sound. Alex assumed Fayard had used it deliberately. Because of the Nazi occupation of World War II, the idea of collaboration still had a special flavour in how the French state and people saw themselves.

He raised his hand again, speaking without waiting to be called.

'But who chooses? Where's the clear policy that can guide judgement and action?'

Fayard gave him a steely look. 'If that's what you need in order to do what is right, Monsieur Lamarque – a universal theory of everything – I can't help you. And if that is what you expect from this lecture, you are going to be disappointed.'

Alex's thoughts returned to the present, but with Fayard's words still in his head. No, there was no universal theory of everything.

He left his mother's flat, walked up the boulevard beneath the apple trees and crossed the enormous Bastille intersection using the foot tunnels. The isolation clinic was only ten minutes away, in a neighbourhood that, when he was a child, had been all furniture and musical instrument showrooms. He passed two medical facilities before finding the correct entrance.

He gave his name via a camera link and was admitted to a pristine foyer where a woman in medicals scrubs was on duty behind a large white desk. He completed a few administrative formalities, and she took a blood sample.

'When can I see her?' he asked.

She gave him a puzzled look. 'You can't enter the quarantined area.'

'Even if I've been tested three times in the last few days?' Alex looked at the locked doors that controlled access to the main part of the facility. It was more prison than hospital. 'Wouldn't she have been better isolating at home?'

'There are strong therapeutic arguments on both sides, but the priority must always be containment. The decision is never taken lightly. We understand the trauma of separation,' she said kindly. 'Are you in a position to care for your mother?'

Alex lowered his eyes. 'No.'

'In the clinic, we can control her environment to minimise every risk – to her and to others.'

Yes, thought Alex. The precautionary principle. It made sense.

'Can I at least speak to her remotely? Do I need to book a session?'

'Of course.' The nurse consulted her holo-screen. 'The earliest we can do is Sunday, three o'clock.'

Alex was taken aback. 'That's not for two days.'

For the first time she looked truly sympathetic. 'I'm sorry, it does sound like a long way off, but we are very busy. I promise we're taking excellent care of her.'

He understood the healthcare system was constantly over-stretched. But Sunday was too far away – not just because he needed to know she was all right, but because he thought Gloria knew something about what was coming. The thing he couldn't quite see in his mind.

'Is there no way to bring it forward?' he pleaded.

The nurse shook her head. 'We are currently caring for thirty-two isolation patients. Most will be able to return home in seven or fourteen days. They all have pre-booked video visits, but… ah, I see.' Her eye was scanning some clinical notes. 'Your mother is in one of our special rooms.'

A chill ran through Alex. 'What does that mean, exactly?'

'Enhanced atmospheric control, non-human treatment protocols.'

Non-human treatment protocols.

The words gave Alex an image of loneliness and desperation.

'She's being attended by robots?'

'Yes. And specially designated staff who interact under strictly controlled conditions of extreme isolation. She must have an unclassified infection.'

Alex wondered if there was a way to find Gloria and carry her out of this place. But all he said was, 'I assume you have internal cameras? Can you at least show me her room?'

'Of course.'

The nurse swiped her holoscreen and popped out a 3-D image. Gloria was sitting up in bed, her right hand moving, conducting an imaginary orchestra.

Something inside Alex eased, just a little.

'She's listening to music, I think,' said the nurse.

'Is there audio? Is there a two-way connection?'

'I'm afraid not. But I'll be on duty on Sunday so I can tell you how she's been getting on. Please don't worry. She seems like a lovely lady.'

'Thank you. She is.' He reached out to the holo-image. '*Sois forte, maman.*'

Be strong.

13

The next day, Alex's presence was requested for a briefing on the North-African republic of Cyrenia. It was to take place at the headquarters of External Security, housed in an untidy complex of buildings near the Père Lachaise cemetery. He arrived early and found a hot desk in a soundproofed cubicle on level minus four where he could finish his report on the Kofinou trip. Once that was done, he spent a moment thinking about Director Philippou's distinction between 'purposeful terrorism' and 'random acts of nihilistic violence'. That led him back to the investigation into the aborted attack on Bunker Martha.

The digital record told him that a local police officer had floated the idea of a third participant who had abused the naivety of the two students and incited them to make and deliver the bomb. The evidence for this was the fact that they were both dead – and the cut fence at the end of the alley.

So that would be me, thought Alex, wryly. The mystery man who cut the fence.

He scanned the students' identities and physical exams. Their IDs were in order, their health checks clear, their financial resources appropriate to beneficiaries of a charitable technology transfer scheme from Mali. There were a few stark photographs of their corpses and a note to indicate that the bodies had already been taken for incineration.

That was quick, Alex thought.

He checked the sequence of events – the digital paperwork was reproduced in the file. Crime scene, mortuary van, post-mortem, private storage, then signed out for disposal. He pinched out the signature – 'Charles de Gaulle.'

Was that someone's idea of a joke?

No, it wasn't a joke. The bodies had been disposed of in order to hide something.

He wondered what that something was.

He copied the images in the highest available resolution, then was interrupted by a soft chime from his comm-watch telling him the briefing was about to begin.

He shut down the workstation and made his way through the hot desks, out into the corridor to the lift lobby, travelling alone to the top floor. As he emerged, the automated diagnostic device gave him an all-clear. He slipped inside the meeting room and took a seat in the back row with his legs stretched out in the aisle.

The room was almost full. He counted four members of the General Council and eight operatives at his rank, maybe twenty more with less experience. Plus, there were at least a dozen analysts and administrators. Damien Gerest, the head of External Security – a very fat man with suspiciously black hair – had taken a seat up front.

Alex wasn't surprised. People liked to get important news in person, especially when there was a solid prospect of intervention on foreign soil. As he waited, he noticed an analyst he knew, a man with close-cropped red hair and an eager expression. He wondered what his particular interest was.

Finally, Poiret entered. She wore a khaki trouser-suit reminiscent of military fatigues, with shiny buttons on the cuffs and lapels. She walked to the lectern and checked her notes. On the screen behind her was External Security's coat-of-arms, with France at the epicentre of a network of interconnected lines. Beneath the emblem was the service's motto.

'*Partout où nécessité fait loi.*'

Wherever necessity makes the law.

'Thank you all for coming. My name is Claudine Poiret. I am speaking with the authority of the minister. Please interrupt if anything is unclear. In turn, I may ask you questions.'

The screen switched to a satellite view of the North African coastline and the briefing began.

'Cyrenia is a new nation with profound classical-era roots but a relatively tenuous contemporary status. It arose out of chaos and, at this moment, risks slipping back into chaos. A new pathogen has crippled Cyrene City, with mass hospitalisations leading to rising tensions. Our analysts are picking up other signs of unrest. It is imperative the government retains control.'

Alex thought he felt a change in the atmosphere in the room. Then he realised the change wasn't in the room. It was in him.

Poiret switched to a new slide comprising an image of a dead Libyan leader and a complex map with arrows for troop movements. Some people were nodding, indicating they had read the preliminary papers. Alex hadn't bothered. Experience had taught him that too much preparation clouded his intuitive judgements. And now he was thinking about the dotted line on the map of cables from Marseille to Corsica to the North African coast. Whatever Poiret was about to say, it was connected to Kofinou.

'Libya is a big place,' Poiret resumed. '*Was* a big place – most of it desert, insignificant were it not for the oil underneath. Civil War One began in February 2011. Muammar Gaddafi had been in power since 1970, an Islamic socialist with his own interpretation of politics and social justice. At the conclusion of Civil War One, Gaddafi was captured and killed. Civil War Two began in 2014. It left Libya barely a country; its infrastructure smashed, its economy compromised. The eastern three-quarters of the country ended up under the control of a new government and the army. The quarter to the west, including the capital Tripoli, was run by the rump of Gaddafi support backed by feral militias. I'm tempted to try and catch you out and ask you who else was drawn into the conflict.' Poiret smiled at them. 'But it would be quicker to ask who wasn't. UAE, Egypt, Sudan, Russia, Syria, Turkey, Italy, the USA, the UK – everyone was involved, including France. Who can tell me when Civil War Two ended?'

The man with ginger hair raised a hand.

'Chambon, André – analyst,' he said. 'Civil War Two lasted eight years.'

'*Voilà,*' said Poiret. 'After that, Libya fragmented, descending into in-fighting until finally, in 2032, Cyrenia was legally established with new borders and new institutions. Libya's neighbours, exhausted by the chaos, quickly recognised the new country. Despite being on the "wrong" side of the Mediterranean, Cyrenia was granted associate membership of the European Union. Who was the inspired architect of this transition?'

Poiret tapped a button on the lectern and an informal photograph of a woman with a wide face and heavy dark eyebrows appeared on the screen. The photograph had been taken in a wood-panelled room. She was sitting in a leather armchair, writing in a leather-bound notebook. Her long formal gown fell in smooth folds to the polished cedarwood floorboards.

'Prime Minister Souad Mourad. A woman of genius. And of her many remarkable political decisions, which one do we admire most?'

There was a pause. Alex had no idea. He was wondering precisely what the Ministry wanted from External Security.

'Would it be that she has refused to take on the role of president?' Chambon offered diffidently.

'Go on,' said Poiret, stepping back.

'Well, she maintains that her role is managerial, leader of the government, not the nation, balanced by a triumvirate council of three elected city mayors from Cyrene City, Benghazi and Tobruk. Between them, as the Presidential Council, they replace the role of president as head of state and provide balance in the new country's political institutions.'

'Precisely,' said Poiret, approvingly. 'A new-old structure, modelled to a certain extent on other presidential advisory councils – the Privy Council that traditionally advised the English monarch, the Councils of State in Ireland and Portugal and so on. How does the Presidential Council differ from these?'

'They take executive decisions themselves,' offered Chambon. 'They are, in effect, the president.'

A new slide showed the locations of the three most important coastal cities – Benghazi in the west, Cyrene in the middle, Tobruk to the east. Above the map were the faces of the three current mayors – men in their fifties or sixties, half-frowning, trying to give an impression of severe competence.

'The supposed authority of the presidential council is a dangerous fiction,' said Poiret, looking around the room. 'Aside from Mourad's charisma, real power in this unstable nation lies with the joint heads of the Cyrenia Military, General Al-Fathi and General Bader whose intentions are, at this point, unclear.'

A new slide pictured two men in uniform.

'To bring this summary up to date,' said Poiret, 'Cyrenia exists as a kind of historical accident, the unexpected result of a particular and unplanned set of pressures and principles, mediated by one woman's intelligence and force of will. Cyrenia is rich because it has most of the oil. Cyrenia is well-armed because so many developed and second-world nations are committed to its survival.' Poiret showed another slide – Prime Minister Mourad in full charismatic flow, addressing the European Parliament. 'Cyrenia is respected because its political structures and policies make it a safe haven for refugees. Who made all this possible? Mourad. Who is leading Cyrenia into EU membership? Mourad. All of this is at risk. She must be protected. Questions?'

Alex raised a hand, piecing it together. 'Protected from insurrection by her own people?'

'If necessary, yes,' said Poiret.

'So,' Alex persisted, 'you intend to ask the DGES to step in on sovereign foreign soil? Surely the Cyrenian Presidential Council would be the appropriate channel for such a request.'

There was a pause. It was unusual for an agent to challenge the Ministry's thinking.

'We have not yet received a formal request,' said Poiret, coolly. 'We will stand ready.'

'To do what, precisely?' asked Alex.

There was another uncomfortable silence. In his peripheral vision, Alex was aware that Director Damien Gerest was watching him with disapproval.

'There are many reasons why we would want to support and protect the democratic ideals Mourad stands for,' Poiret said. 'Protecting those ideals will, undoubtedly, mean protecting her.'

So that was it. thought Alex. Poiret was asking for a blank cheque. And she was getting it. There was nothing else to say. This was exactly the kind of unilateral action that had undermined his faith in the service.

As Poiret pressed on with the briefing, he checked out, allowing his mind to freewheel. Then he realised Poiret was wrapping up.

'Cyrenia has emerged as an alternative to the arbitrary lines in the sand drawn by the European colonisers of Africa. Perhaps there was no obvious need for Cyrenia until Libya fell to pieces. No distinct subset of humans could reasonably say, because of their unique language or heritage or ethnic characteristics, “This is where we are from”. It’s another set of made-up borders, lines on maps. But, because it exists, it creates an opportunity. It has the potential to become, very quickly and to the benefit of the whole region, including Europe, a kind of African Hong Kong – at least, what Hong Kong used to be – a place where business can be done with integrity and respect for the rule of law.’

She rapped with her knuckles on the lectern.

’How much of human life, over thousands of years, has been determined by whether some powerful person can demand you pay their taxes? Or abide by their laws? Or respect their church? The situation today is tense. Prime Minister Mourad maintains that her position is secure, her military commanders loyal. But her people may not agree. And Cyrenia’s status as a safe haven for refugees has made the management of disease extremely challenging. New populations take time to identify, triage and assimilate. With the emergence of the new pathogen, this has become a crisis. Mourad’s opponents want to pin the blame on her. The Ministry for Foreign Affairs believes some form of revolt or uprising may occur within months or weeks. Some additional catastrophic event could easily accelerate that timeline. In that case, the DGES will be called upon to act with speed and precision.’

There was more, but Alex had had enough. He slipped out but was stopped by a Ministry security officer in the corridor.

‘Madame Poiret would like to speak to you, Monsieur Lamarque. Her car is waiting outside.’

The rear cabin of the ministerial vehicle was like a small living room, everything plush and warm to the touch. The ride was almost silent, the hydrogen power unit inaudible, the soft suspension absorbing any imperfections in the road surface. Now and then, the bottles on the refrigerated shelf clinked together.

The car moved through the heart of the city towards the area cordoned off for official cars. Two steel bollards sank down into the cobbles to allow them through. There was a low hum as the air con began a new cooling cycle.

'Your mother is a believer,' said Poiret. 'She regularly attends Saint Paul's church. Do you go with her?'

'Never.'

'How sad for her,' said Poiret.

Alex wondered what she was getting at. They joined a small queue of official vehicles at a checkpoint on the bridge by Place de la Concorde.

'Her church is a very interesting one,' Poiret continued. 'Early seventeenth century, but the site dates back to the twelfth. Paul of Thebes spent a lifetime as a hermit in the desert. When he died, another saint, Anthony the Great, buried him. Two lions helped dig the grave. Isn't that charming?'

'Like most religious stories, it's only beautiful once you've decided to believe it.' The car inched forward and he didn't bother to hide his impatience. 'Look, if you want someone to interpret intelligence, why don't you recruit André Chambon?'

'But I have,' she smiled. 'Did you think it was an accident that he answered all my questions today? Also, did you read my preliminary notes?'

Alex considered lying but decided it didn't matter. 'No.'

'Tell me why.' Poiret looked more interested than irritated.

'Because I'm more likely to make connections if my mind is clear.'

A checkpoint officer came to the driver's window. The driver showed him Poiret's credentials and he instantly stepped back, motioning the driver to proceed. Poiret became brisk.

'As well as being a believer – which I am not – your mother is an individualist. Suffering from a notifiable illness, she irresponsibly went about her business, visiting shops, celebrating her religious fantasies.'

Yes, Alex thought. Gloria had acted not just irresponsibly, but illegally. This was how Poiret intended to pressure him.

He met her gaze. 'To what extent are we under surveillance, Madame Poiret?'

She didn't blink. 'To a necessary extent.'

'She hadn't been diagnosed—' he began, but Poiret cut him off.

'She did not *seek* a diagnosis.'

'She wanted to speak to me first and I was away. Now, she's in extreme isolation.'

'I know that,' Poiret replied, then added unexpectedly: 'We must see what we can do to help.'

Alex watched her warily. 'Help how?'

'Are you aware of the Rothschild Institute?' she asked. 'Pioneering work is being done there in experimental treatments.'

Alex was aware of it. The hospital was well known for looking after VIPs. If anyone could help Gloria, it was the doctors there. But Poiret wouldn't offer this for nothing.

'What exactly do you want from me, Madame Poiret?'

'It's not what I want, Monsieur Lamarque,' she smiled. 'It's your past coming back to haunt you.'

14

Later that afternoon, in the miserable Paris suburb of Aulnay-sous-Bois, the two fake undertakers pulled into a parking zone behind a decaying social housing block. The older man was driving, nosing the hearse into a garage lock-up. Once inside, he got out and leaned his hands on the roof, stretching his back and leg muscles, rotating his neck. His younger colleague jerked awake, unfolded his stiffened limbs, and hauled his huge frame out of the passenger seat.

'I'm hungry,' he complained.

'You're always hungry.' As he spoke, the older man read a message on his comm-watch.

'Any news?' the younger man asked.

'We're to have a word with our tame cameraman.'

The younger man nodded. 'The kid messed up. How do we find him?'

'He's chipped. He's close to home, in Montmartre.'

'Excellent,' said the younger man. 'Food first?'

'I don't think so. It's urgent.'

The young man the fake undertakers called 'our tame cameraman' was Luís Beira. He was small, with dark hair and a handsome face. He was sitting on some stone steps, his eyes closed, his face angled up towards the sun, like a lizard.

He knew he had made a mistake. He had dropped a lens cap and hadn't been able to find it. But that wasn't his fault. They'd hassled him, telling him to hurry up. Surely it wasn't an important mistake? He hadn't appeared on camera, had he? Oh, yes, there was that one moment when he walked in front of the lens. But that was only for a second. Then again, the film was online. Anyone could look at it with their special machines – machines that could work things out on their own.

It was silly to worry, he told himself. There was no law against filming in a church. There was no law against saying what was true, what everybody knew, that the world was a mess and the only way things would ever improve was to burn it all down and start again.

A wisp of cloud crossed the sun. The warmth on his face lessened momentarily, then returned. Without opening his eyes, he rubbed the tattooed letters on the backs of his fingers. It had taken him a whole evening with a pin and a bottle of old-fashioned ink, with whisky to numb the pain and disinfect the wounds. He was quite pleased with the result.

Yes, the cause was right. He was proud that he was taking a stand, alone among his classmates.

Thinking about his classmates, he regretted for a moment leaving college. They had been kind to him – the other students, the teacher who taught him to use the old-fashioned cameras, who told him he had talent. He realised he had felt at home there and now he was alone, detached from the world. And he hadn't been given anywhere near as much to do as he had anticipated, even though he had let them put the chip in his chest so they would always know where he was.

Didn't they trust him?

Abruptly, he realised a deeper shadow had fallen across his face. He opened his eyes and there they were. The younger one tall and fat, the older one short and very thin, bright sky behind them, making him screw up his eyes.

'Hello, Luís,' said the older man. 'How's it going?'

'Okay,' said Luís.

The younger man came very close, intimidating and oppressive. 'Up you get.'

'Where are we going?' Luís asked, as he climbed to his feet.

'Don't you want to have a walk with us?' the younger man drawled.

'We can't talk here,' explained the older man. 'We don't want to be overheard, do we?'

Luís composed his features, trying to look innocent and unconcerned. 'What do we need to talk about?'

'You've done very well.' The older man's voice was soothing. 'Everyone is very pleased with you.'

'That's good.' Luís relaxed slightly. 'I just wanted to do something worthwhile.'

The older man put a hand on his shoulder. 'And you have.'

'Are we going to make another video?' Luís asked.

'Hush, now. Let's not go blurting things out in the street.' The man's gaunt features composed into a smile. 'We want to give you some choices.'

For a moment, Luís began to believe that everything was going to be all right. Then the younger man prodded him in the solar plexus. 'You left something behind. And someone found it and soon they'll know who you are.'

Luís looked from one to the other. It was disconcerting. One was looking at him with an expression of sympathy, the other's eyes were as cold as stone. He took a small step back. 'I couldn't find it. It was dark when we finished. The power was out.'

'You should have taken more trouble,' said the younger man. 'On your hands and knees if necessary.'

'I did go on my hands and knees,' said Luís. 'But the priest came to lock up and—'

'Now then,' said the older man. 'There's no need to get upset.'

'You try to find a lens cap in the dark,' Luís told him, desperately. 'It must have rolled away—'

The younger man struck him across the face, a swift deft slap. The gesture was so quick, so economical, that it attracted no attention on the quiet street. Luís's eyes filled with tears.

'I feel very sorry for you,' said the older man.

'You made a stupid mistake,' said the younger man.

'I know,' sniffed Luís.

'Now you have to clear up the mess,' the younger man said.

'Yes, that's what I want to do,' said Luís. Then he sniffled. 'What mess?'

'Listen to him,' said the younger man, sarcastically. 'He doesn't know what mess.'

'Let's walk together,' said the older man.

They took him to a funeral parlour on the main road out of Paris, not far from where he lived with his widowed mother in a tiny narrow house wedged between two larger buildings. The funeral parlour had wide plate-glass windows that opened onto a gaudy display of coffins, urns, artificial wreaths and tombstones.

'What do you think?' asked the older man.

Luís was confused. 'What do I think of what?'

The older man pointed to a shiny black casket. 'Which one would you choose? How about that one?'

'Who for?' asked Luís.

'He's making me tired,' grumbled the younger man. He pushed Luís up against the glass. 'Look in the window and choose. Tell us what you want.'

'The black one,' said Luís, desperately. 'I like the black one, the shiny one with the silver handles.'

'Good,' said the older man. 'And what about flowers?'

'My mother likes flowers,' said Luís.

'There,' said the older man, pointing into the window at an impressive display of tall white blooms. 'Lilies. Do you like those?'

'They look expensive.'

'Yes, but do you like them?'

Luís felt hopeless. 'Yes, I like them.'

'Lilies are best,' agreed the older man.

'Why do I need flowers?'

The younger man put his heavy hands on Luís's shoulders. 'There you go again, asking questions that needn't be asked.'

'Now,' said the older man, 'you just stay here while I go inside and order.'

Luís watched him as he pushed open the door and went inside. 'What happens now?' he asked.

The younger man gave him a single white tablet. 'You put this under your tongue.'

'Do you have any water?' asked Luís.

'Put it under your tongue. Let it dissolve.'

'My mouth is dry,' said Luís. 'There's a water fountain over there—'

He made as if to move. This was his chance. If he could just slip away, he might run and run and never come back. But the man put a heavy, fleshy hand round his throat and pushed him firmly back against the window.

'Put it under your tongue and let it dissolve and you will feel much better.'

Luís's shoulders slumped. He did as he was told.

'It has to be lilies,' explained the younger man, 'because they mean that the soul of the deceased has been restored to the state of innocence.' He pointed at Luís. 'That's you.'

'What do you mean, me?' asked Luís hazily, as the drug began its work.

'You're the deceased.'

'Oh, yes,' said Luís vaguely. 'Everyone dies.'

He began to feel better. He began to remember that this was, after all, what he wanted, that there was nothing to worry about, that it was his destiny to be a spark to the flame, the tumbling pebble that starts the avalanche. Eventually, everyone would have to admit that he was somebody.

After another twenty seconds, he didn't feel anything at all.

15

On Sunday morning, as he made his way back to the med-centre, Alex was still angry about how Poiret was manipulating him. And furious that he was allowing himself to be manipulated.

When he arrived, the virtual visiting room was ready, comfortably appointed with a large screen and audio loop. Unfortunately, his mother's condition was worse. He peered at the screen, struggling to see her in the shadows. 'It's very dark.'

'The lights are kept low in her room,' explained the nurse. 'Her sensitivity to light.'

'Is it worse?' he asked.

'Yes.' The nurse's face gave nothing away, but her crisp medical sympathy made Alex anxious.

'Can you adjust the monitor?' he asked

The nurse leaned forward, tapped the screen and raised the brightness. Alex was shocked by his mother's shrunken sleeping form. How could she have declined so much so quickly?

'Will she wake?' he asked.

The nurse looked shocked. 'Of course she will.'

'I don't mean will she *ever* wake. I mean will she wake up now, before I have to leave?'

'Oh, I see.' Her face cleared. 'Perhaps not. She slept poorly last night.'

'Has she been eating?'

'Very little. Her throat is constricted.'

Alex stared at the small figure on the screen. The thing he kept circling back to was, how had Gloria become infected? She only went out to church and the shops. Where could she have acquired a novel infection so dangerous it required extreme isolation? It didn't make sense.

There was a pause and Alex realised the nurse was waiting for him to say something.

'*Merci,*' he murmured.

The nurse slipped away and Alex watched his mother's blankets rise and fall, his own heart contracting a little more with each weak breath.

Fifty minutes later, Alex's visiting time was over. His mother had barely moved and he took that as a good sign that she was at least resting peacefully. On the way out, he spoke again to the nurse.

'What would you do in my place?' he asked.

The nurse hesitated, her expression becoming evasive. 'I really couldn't say. Would you like me to request a consultation with the supervising doctor?'

'I mean, if she was your mother,' Alex persisted. 'Would you try to have her moved, to get her accepted on an experimental programme?'

The nurse shook her head. 'You can't expect me to answer that.'

'If she were transferred, could I be with her?'

'It's possible.'

There was a pause – Alex wanting more information, the nurse unwilling to commit herself.

'Okay, yes,' he said. 'Could you ask the supervising doctor to call me?'

'I'll do my best,' she assured him. 'It may not be today or tomorrow.'

Alex left the clinic, walking slowly. People died, of course – illness and accidents and old age. Gloria had said so herself. In his own line of work – bullets and explosions. Many times, he had prevented deaths. Many more times, he had been responsible for them. But this enemy was different. He had never before had to prepare himself to watch someone's inexorable decline over days or weeks or months, powerless to intervene.

In her office overlooking the esplanade of the Invalides, Claudine Poiret took a video call from André Chambon.

'Have you seen, *madame*?'

'Have I seen what?'

'There's been a vast explosion at the docks in Cyrene City. A huge perimeter has been reduced to rubble.' There was a pause. 'This is what you expected, isn't it?'

'Casualties?' asked Poiret.

'Thousands, at least.'

'I see.' Poiret tapped her smoked-glass desk with her screen-stylus. 'Prepare a preliminary briefing note, Send it on to Fayard at Internal as well.'

'Right away, *madame*.'

Lost in thought, Alex trudged through the relentless heat to Gloria's apartment. On the fourth floor, the hygiene team was there, deep-cleaning, so he went back downstairs.

Nelinha made him a cup of coffee and asked him to wait in the courtyard while she finished a piece of work.

Alex dragged an uncomfortable cast-iron chair into the shade, wondering what he ought to do. The offer Poiret had made was compelling. Whether to agree wasn't just a question of who he trusted.

Instead of resigning and 'disappearing into the undergrowth', as she put it, Poiret wanted him to agree to be redeployed from External to Internal Security. Also, should it become necessary, she wanted him to take the lead on the extraction of Prime Minister Mourad. That was why he'd been invited to the briefing.

If he did those two things, she would ensure no legal action would be taken over his mother's failure to notify her illness, and she would move Gloria to the Rothschild Institute.

He gazed up at a patch of blue sky between the buildings, slowing his breathing, trying to feel his way into the future, into the consequences of the decision he was about to take. Obviously, because of Gloria, he had no choice, but there was something else, another potential consequence, just on the edge of consciousness.

'Call Claudine Poiret,' he told his comm-watch.

She answered without preamble. 'So, we have a deal?'

He breathed out slowly, composing himself. Nelinha came out into the courtyard. He put a finger to his lips.

'Well?' Poiret demanded.

'We have a deal,' agreed Alex.

'Excellent.' There was a hint of triumph in her voice. 'We'll sort out the details later.'

There was no going back.

16

At the same time, in the sixth-floor conference room at the headquarters of the Directorate-General for Internal Security in Levallois-Perret, just outside the western loop of the Paris orbital motorway, Administrator Sabie had prepared a briefing for his boss, Professor Fayard.

They were seated in a nest of uncomfortable swing chairs beneath the enormous windows. Outside, streets radiated away through the nebulous suburbs. Sabie looked as he always did – small, grey, lean, self-possessed. Professor Fayard looked weak and tired.

'Am I mistaken, Sabie? This seems familiar to me.'

In front of them, a holoscreen carried a live news channel.

'There are several examples, Professor—' Sabie began, but Fayard interrupted him, his eyes closed in reminiscence.

'I want to say Tianjin, perhaps twenty years ago?'

'Yes, sir, in 2015. The blasts registered on seismographs as small earthquakes.'

'And Beirut, too?' Fayard asked.

'August 2020.'

'Of course,' said Fayard. 'You are a student of human disasters, Sabie. Why is that?'

'I suppose, sir, it's because they are moments of opportunity as well as loss,' said Sabie evenly.

'A brutal assessment.' Fayard swiped the holoscreen to switch to a written report on the disaster. 'Their use of water to douse the fires increased the ferocity of the conflagration?'

Sabie nodded. 'Where the active compound is ammonium nitrate, water is contra-indicated.'

'Could it have been spontaneous?'

Sabie made a vague gesture. 'In the presence of an accelerant – kerosene, for example. It's possible with damaged storage facilities, incompatible corrosive products, leaks and cross-contaminations.'

'But you judge,' said Fayard, 'that the explosion was contrived as a way to worsen the dangerous political situation in Cyrenia.'

'I do.'

'We were not involved?' Fayard mused. 'Our counterparts in External Security – might they have launched some unilateral action?'

'We have Madame Poiret's assurances to the contrary, sir. She has assigned Alexandre Lamarque to the extraction mission.'

Fayard gazed out of the window. 'For the time being, this is not our business. But it will become our business. If the extraction is successful, Prime Minister Mourad will become our guest.'

Sabie nodded. 'A facility has been chosen.'

'Good.' Fayard picked up his mahogany walking stick and rested both hands on the silver pommel. 'We must not jump to conclusions. There will be time enough.'

Sabie gave a slight bow. 'Yes, sir.'

Fayard leaned back and closed his eyes. Sabie watched him. The new infection was hitting him hard.

'Should I give Lamarque the standard induction on his return?' Sabie asked.

'Yes.' Fayard stood up, wheezing slightly. 'I must go.'

Sabie watched him slowly cross the enormous room, saw him put a hand on the wall for balance as he opened the concealed door in the bookshelves to step wearily through into the private rooms beyond.

The door closed softly on its mag-locks and Sabie re-woke the holo, scrolling till he found what he wanted – an eyewitness video of the explosion. It had no audio and began with a bride in a long white gown, a tiara made of flowers and a gauzy veil. She was climbing down from a carriage drawn by a bay horse. The bride embraced two older men who led her up three steps to the doors of a registry office. A small girl in pastel pink twitched at the folds of her train. Without warning the bay horse reared up, and the image shuddered and swung upwards before finding a cloud of dust and smoke billowing over the rooftops. Then the camera was in motion, running away from the wedding party, along the street, past children and adults all transfixed, gazing up into the sky.

The camera swung left and in through the gates of a park. There were twenty seconds of bouncing images of the grass going by under the videographer's feet, climbing to the summit of an ornamental rose garden. Then the image levelled out, found a view of the source of the explosion and became still. A vast column of smoke rose from the docks. Between two twisted cranes a fire raged. Dozens of buildings lay flattened and charred.

Sabie froze the frame. In left of shot was an enormous cedar tree, perhaps six metres round at the base and four hundred years old.

Sabie didn't need the video to tell him how big it was or what it felt like to stand beneath it. He could almost feel the bark beneath his fingers. He had sat beneath that same tree when he was a child, before his family fled the chaos and the civil war into exile.

With a jolt, he realised Fayard's face had appeared in a corner of the holo. He tapped to accept the call.

'What quantity of ammonium nitrate?' Fayard asked.

It was as if their conversation had never paused.

'The analyst says three thousand tonnes,' Sabie said. 'Ammonium nitrate is used as a fertiliser, but it is also one of the main components in mining explosives. Large quantities transit through Cyrenia, overland to the lithium mines in southern Mali.'

'Pollutants?'

'The chemicals produced by combustion should disperse fairly quickly in the air.'

'Enough to deter an insurrection?' suggested Fayard. 'To keep people indoors?'

'No, sir,' Sabie told him. 'In my judgement, an insurrection is now inevitable.'

Fayard cut the connection. Sabie packed up and crossed the conference room in the other direction, going out through the double doors and across the lobby to the lifts, pressing a button for the basement. He emerged in a narrow corridor, leading to the armoured door of his own office. With a swipe of his hand, he disabled the locks and went inside.

It was a crowded room, equipped with seven screens on a large, curved desk. The middle screen held a report on the 1947 Texas City Disaster. In that case, an ammonium nitrate explosion killed five hundred people and created a five-metre tidal wave. On two other screens were images of the other catastrophic events Fayard had mentioned, in Tianjin and Beirut. On the wall, a hyperreal kinetic artwork of the mushroom cloud of an atomic explosion rose and swelled in eerie slow motion.

Sabie opened his electronic calendar. Two dates were marked in bold. One was the anniversary of the Beirut explosion, the other the anniversary of the atomic bomb dropped on Hiroshima. Sabie looked from one to the other, counting the days.

Both anniversaries were coming closer.

A Foreign Ministry speakerbot popped up as a three-dimensional holo. Extraction had officially been offered to Prime Minister Mourad. Whether she would accept remained uncertain.

Sabie reconciled himself to not leaving DGES headquarters until it was over. Fayard might need him. He might need to take action himself.

He passed the message on to the base commander in Al-Jaghar, Latifah Bader. She had sufficient forces to do whatever needed to be done.

17

Later that evening, the two fake undertakers stood arguing in the lock-up in Aulnay-sous-Bois. The older one was angry.

'This is a problem,' he said.

Luís lay in a coffin in the back of the hearse – not because he was dead but because it was a convenient way to transport an unconscious body.

'What did you expect me to do?' The younger undertaker sounded defensive. 'He was going to run.'

'You over-drugged him,' the older man chided. 'You messed up the schedule. He has to do it himself.'

'Can't we do it for him?'

'No,' the older man growled. 'It's got to be him.'

He sighed. The job had seemed straightforward, at first. All he'd had to do was create a funeral business – a website, a fake history, a hearse, a fake address, fake corporate records, all that. Then recruit some muscle to be a kind of clean-up service. But now things had changed. The pace was accelerating and he didn't like it. And there was this stress on everything being 'seen'. It had become…

What would he call it? A kind of performance?

Who were these people anyway? Apart from Luís and the woman in the enormous dark glasses and the blond wig, he had never met anyone else. He'd had no chance to judge their motivation, how they managed to influence people, to push them onto paths of…

He wanted to say evil. It sounded melodramatic, but what other word was there?

The younger man gave him a strange look. 'You're standing there moving your lips, but you're not saying anything.'

The older man grimaced. 'I'm thinking things through.'

'If we have to get all the way to the Seine then make it back before curfew—'

'No one stops a hearse,' interrupted the older man.

'And he has to—'

'I know what he has to do,' he began, then stopped at a sound from the open casket in the rear of the hearse.

Luís opened his sticky eyes, wondering where he was. He ran his hands over the plush lining. What was this? Some kind of bed? Then it all came back to him. The funeral parlour. The shiny black coffin. Was someone about to close the lid?

He lurched up, striking his head on the roof of the hearse.

'What's happening?' His voice was thick, his words slurred.

The younger undertaker, the one with the hard eyes, leaned in. 'Oh, well, if you're awake, let's just do it,' he said.

They made him lie back down in the coffin as they drove somewhere else. He felt like he was navigating a dream. The narcotic was still in his system and events seemed to slow down and speed up without logic.

Finally, they let him out in a neighbourhood near the orbital motorway, a marginal quarter where time on the clock meant little and the days were just cycles of heat and cool, of light and dark, of want and sleep. It was only a couple of kilometres from where he lived but it was on the far side of the line that separated society from the Blanks, their homes made of waste wood, plastic sheeting and cardboard.

Incongruously, there was a playground with brightly coloured plastic equipment – a dinosaur to climb, a tortoise that small children could crawl inside, a snail on a rocking spring. Six or seven undernourished kids were enjoying the cool air, darting in and out of the shadows without adult supervision, creating their own rules, their own structures, their own goals.

The two undertakers explained that he must snatch one of the children, preferably older than three or four, but not so big that they might fight back or be difficult to carry.

'I know what to do,' Luís said.

They gave him an enormous bar of chocolate with which to entice his victim away from the others. Only when he looked at it did he realise he was hungry.

'Can I eat this?' he asked, hopefully.

The younger man rolled his eyes. 'No. You can't eat it.'

'Of course you can eat it,' corrected the older man. 'Just not all of it. And try to get one that we don't have to clean up.'

'Get one that looks innocent,' insisted the younger man, 'like it's a victim of an uncaring society, that deserves better.' He pointed. 'Maybe that one.'

The child was five or six years old, perhaps a boy, its front teeth missing and its dark hair tied back in a pony tail. He climbed onto the neck of the dinosaur and shouted in pidgin French that he was the king of the world. An adult voice called back from the collection of shanty dwellings, telling him not to make so much noise.

'If you run,' the younger man told Luís, 'we will find you and cut off your fingers one by one.'

'I'm not going to run,' Luís told him. 'You don't understand. I want to do this.'

It was true. He was the pebble to start the avalanche.

The older man gave him a curious look. 'Why?'

'It all has to burn,' Luís explained, 'so it can be reborn. So we can all be reborn.'

'You really believe that? That you will be reborn? What does that even mean?'

'Don't you know?' Luís was surprised. The older man looked angry and confused. 'Why are you doing this if you don't believe?'

The older man shook his head. 'Never mind.'

They left Luís at the entrance to the playground, peeling paper and foil from the chocolate. Almost immediately, two older children ran over to him, brazen in their misery. He put a square of chocolate in his mouth and watched them watching. One held out a wistful hand.

Luís broke off a square and threw it as hard as he could. The children shouted and ran after it. He watched them scrabbling in the dust. The other five children came over to see what was happening. He broke off another square, throwing it into another corner. They ran. A girl found it and stuffed it in her mouth. There was another shout for quiet from the adults in the shanty dwellings.

Luís ate a second piece but, nauseated by the after-effects of the drug, found it difficult to swallow. Then the children were back, all seven of them, avid for more, one of them licking her fingers. Luís looked at the boy with the ponytail, broke off the next two rows of the chocolate bar, separating them into twelve smaller squares.

'Ready?' Luís asked.

They nodded.

'Don't shout or someone will come and I will have to go.' They nodded again and he spoke to the ponytail boy. 'When the others run, you stay here.'

'I get chocolate?' asked the child in his pidgin French.

'Yes,' said Luís. 'But you must stay here. Do you trust me?'

The boy nodded and put his hands together in front of his breast bone, as if he was praying.

Luís hurled the twelve squares of chocolate. They scattered across the poorly lit playground, one or two of them striking the plastic toys. Six of the children dashed away, eerily quiet. The boy with the ponytail flinched but stayed where he was. Luís gave him a square of chocolate.

'Now come with me,' he said.

Docile, the child put the chocolate in his mouth and followed Luís around the corner to where the hearse sat parked in the shadow of a warehouse doorway. As they approached the vehicle, Luís gave the boy another square. He licked it, trying to make it last.

Luís looked at the fake undertakers. 'Is this the one you meant?'

18

The next morning, Alex received his orders just before dawn. He was already dressed, but he waited for the end-of-curfew siren before opening the hatch and stepping off the boat onto the cobbled walkway along the edge of the canal.

The air smelled clean. It was quiet enough to hear the electric buzz from a motion-triggered camera as he climbed the eighteen worn stone steps to the road. There, the air felt less damp, less loaded with summer mist. The light was perfectly balanced, the brightening dawn matching the intensity of the art-nouveau streetlamps. In less than ten minutes, the harsh day would take over and bleach away the subtleties of the night. But right now, it was beautiful.

Passing a bridge over the River Seine, he noticed two officers in hi-vis jackets erecting a temporary tent-like shelter in the shadow of the statue of Saint Genevieve, patron and defender of the city. He paused, curious about who they'd found in the water. Was it a crime, a suicide, an accident?

Summer hours meant a few cafés were already opening so he stopped for an espresso. The waiter took a break from preparing the outdoor tables and followed him inside.

'*Un serré, s'il vous plaît.*'

'*Tout de suite, monsieur.*'

He drank his tiny black coffee standing at the counter. An early bus went by, reflected in the mirrors behind the bar, not yet in service, rubber wheels humming on the tarmac, its hydro-cell engine almost inaudible. He tapped his comm-watch on a device by the till, heard the beep of acknowledgement and left. The whole transaction from ordering to finishing the drink to paying took less than ninety seconds.

A few streets away, a crowd queued outside a soup kitchen on the piazza in front of the Hôtel de Ville. Twenty or so people waiting impatiently for the canvas awnings to open. Six or seven more joined the line in the minute it took Alex to cross the square.

At the head of the Métro escalator, an automated diagnostic device scanned customers for symptoms. Alex followed a group of night-workers on their way home from the dark shift. Down in the cool concrete lobby, he merged with commuters making their way along air-conditioned tunnels to a platform lined with advertisements. He gazed at the illuminated kinetic billboards – health insurance, vitamins, entertainment channels, religion, gyms, more vitamins, more religion.

Nothing he wanted to buy.

A rapid arrived four minutes later, then it was twenty minutes of noisy steel wheels on noisy steel rails, allowing his mind to wander, before he arrived at Charles de Gaulle airport for more health screening, a metal detector, and two separate x-ray machines. Finally, an early civilian flight, sitting up front thanks to his security service credentials.

He leaned back and closed his eyes.

Alex emerged from Toulouse airport into thirty-two degree heat and scorching sunshine. An Air Force driver met him in a weary Renault Trafic daubed in camouflage paint – a kind of military minibus. They made good progress for a while, before grinding to a crawl. The driver made a wordless apologetic gesture at the sea of vehicles. Through the open windows, Alex could smell the carbon monoxide in the air. It seemed there were more petrol vehicles in Toulouse than in Paris.

'No air con?' he asked.

'I'm sorry, sir. It was the only vehicle available at short notice.'

After a few minutes, the driver swung onto a slip-road and headed south-west. Fifteen minutes later they arrived at the perimeter of Toulouse-Francazal airbase, Base Aérienne 101, about eight kilometres from the centre of the city. They pulled up behind a truck which was being checked by the security team.

'The checkpoint guys are a nightmare, sir,' the driver warned.

'Is the base on special alert?' Alex asked, watching the activity.

'Always,' replied the driver.

The duty officers were thorough. They ran face recognition on each of the truck's passengers, cross-checking with their records. Bags were opened and patience wore thin. Eventually an NCO arrived from somewhere inside the base and the truck was grudgingly admitted.

When Alex's driver pulled forward, the duty officers identified Alex and waved him through without another word.

They made for an isolated hangar on the eastern perimeter and parked inside, next to a stack of three Portakabin offices inscribed with Air Force insignia. The hangar doors faced west and the air inside was reasonably cool. As Alex climbed out of the van, a staff officer emerged from the Portakabin at the bottom of the stack.

Alex recognised her type. Reliable, punctilious, overlooked.

'I am instructed to inform you, sir, that there will be a delay while we await the arrival of the representative of the Ministry for Foreign Affairs. All personal comms should be offline.' He showed her his powered-down comm-watch. 'Would you follow me?'

She led him up an external staircase to the top Portakabin. The steps creaked as they reached the landing. She opened the door with a plastic card and stood back. 'After you, sir.'

Inside, an air-con unit whirred away, cold air falling in a cascade past the glass of the only window. The battered room held a low sofa with worn-out foam cushions, a cheap desk and an old-school computer terminal with a VR headset.

'You can log in with your DGES credentials,' the officer said. 'I'll come back when I have an ETA on your final orders.'

She left, shutting the door behind her. Alex went to stand directly in the cool draught of the air con.

Travel was tiring. Traffic was tiring. Heat was tiring.

Other people were tiring.

He counted to sixty, gazing out of the grimy window into the vast, nearly empty hangar where a couple of engineers were doing something to a helicopter. The truck he had seen at the checkpoint was parked in shadow at the far end, looking like a child's toy in the vast space.

He turned away from the window and checked the computer terminal, a flat LED screen networked by ethernet cable, probably to some kind of ring-fenced intranet. Military installations were a target for hackers. They were rightly paranoid.

The computer had no microphone for voice activation, so he logged in manually. It went straight to a DGES portal dominated by an invitation to access his specific mission parameters, but first he clicked on a newsfeed, collated and dragged in by web crawlers from a few officially sanctioned websites, updated every couple of hours from a massively encrypted external connection.

Thinking of the body he'd seen being recovered near the statue of Saint Genevieve, he searched for media references to recent drownings. Following link after link, he came across street camera footage of two more recent child murders, one in Tours on the Loire and another in Lyon on the Rhône. They had taken place in full view of remote surveillance, as if they wanted to be seen, like some kind of performance. There was no known motive for either crime and, perhaps because of that, there was considerable online debate about whether they were linked and what they might mean.

Alex sat back, feeling uneasy. Yes, the news reports were unsettling, but that wasn't it. He felt like something was being concealed from him, some alignment of events that concerned him, but that he didn't yet understand.

Or maybe the events hadn't yet begun?

Yes, that was it. Something was coming but it hadn't found him yet.

He searched the DGES database, looking for information not yet in the public domain. Sure enough, the Saint Genevieve victim was a child.

Then it came back to him – the corpse in the water of the canal basin when he returned from Norway. He hadn't remembered to find out what that was about. It took him no time to at all. The body retrieved from the canal basin was also a child.

He wanted to look into it further but needed to focus on the DGES portal with its invitation to consult his 'specific mission parameters'. He wasn't worried. The mission to extract Prime Minister Mourad would happen or it wouldn't. He would be successful or he wouldn't. Time would decide.

But this was the information that would keep him alive.

At the same time, in Paris, in a locked room in the basement of a building just to the west of the orbital motorway, someone was counting barrels and boxes, running wires between them, calculating the likely impact of the explosion, anticipating the extent of the impact zone, estimating the loss of life.

'Not enough,' they decided.

It took Alex a couple of hours to assimilate his briefing. The most useful element was the VR walkthrough of the parliamentary compound, exterior and interior. He concentrated on memorising the topography, seeing himself in a variety of virtual locations, visualising the real-world distances and angles. When his feet hit the ground, he wanted to feel he was somewhere he had been many times before. If the place seemed familiar, it would leave him greater mental resources for more important challenges.

Speed of incursion. Location of target. Peripheral vision. Perception of threats.

Staying alive.

He took off the VR headset, committing to memory the three-word code he would use to confirm his identity to the prime minister, a classic alliterative trio: '*constant – certain – connu.*'

Constant, certain, known.

A private message through the portal informed him that Prime Minister Mourad had not yet agreed to the extraction. The stairs creaked and he darkened the old-fashioned screen. The door opened to reveal the driver who had brought him from the airport, bringing him a sandwich and a bottle of water for lunch. He was a *mécanicien de maintenance aéronautique* – a flight engineer. His name badge said 'Sanchez'.

Alex found he was hungry. He'd had nothing since a protein bar he'd been given on the plane. When he'd finished eating, he went to stand in the huge hangar doorway, Sanchez was there, looking up. The skies were clear. Someone important was approaching.

'Could be your orders, Captain,' said Sanchez. 'I'll be with you on the transport, by the way.'

'Good,' said Alex, politely.

For sixty seconds the incoming plane was just a dot. Then, as it banked on approach, Alex recognised it. A Dassault Falcon, a 32 LX.

Silly, really. A civilian flight would have done just as well. The Falcon had a range of more than four thousand kilometres. It was for oligarchs and tech bosses, people for whom numbers had ceased to have any real meaning, for whom only time was a constraint.

And death, of course. Everyone dies in the end.

'How about that bird?' said Sanchez. 'I've worked on one of those.'

'Did you ever fly it?'

'Thirty hours in the simulator. I'm on the pilot training track,' he said, proudly.

The Falcon came to a stop and ground crew scurried towards it. On the tarmac, it looked almost resentful in its immobility. A motorised staircase was positioned beneath the hatch and a man in a charcoal-grey suit emerged – the security officer Alex had met at DGES headquarters. He was followed by a heavily built woman in navy blue.

Claudine Poiret.

The man went ahead, carrying a briefcase and a large document wallet. He got into the front seat of a waiting car. Poiret got in the back and they pulled away, heading for the control tower.

'Captain Lamarque,' said Sanchez, hesitantly. 'You're External Security?'

'That's right.'

'Did you pass the exams?'

'Yes.' Alex gave him a curious look. 'Why do you ask? Do you want to join the service?'

Sanchez grinned. 'Absolutely.'

Alex weighed him up. 'Tell me about yourself. Languages?'

'Arabic, some Spanish. French, obviously,' he added, as an afterthought.

'Add some English, some Chinese,' Alex advised.

'I try, sir. I watch stuff. But it's hard.'

‘Be systematic. Watch the news with the subtitles on,’ Alex advised. ‘Any weapons certification?’

Sanchez nodded. ‘Basic training.’

‘Find a way to do more. Explosives? Telecoms?’

‘The same. Do I have no chance?’ he said sadly.

Alex considered this. Once he moved to Internal Security, it might be useful to be owed a favour by someone new to DGES. ‘What’s your first name?’

‘Paul, sir.’

‘I’ll see what I can do.’

‘Really?’ the engineer looked thrilled. ‘Thank you, Captain.’

Back in the Portakabin at the top of the creaky stairs, Alex returned to the news pages. It was always worth knowing what was going on in the world. Where were the latest riots? What were scientists saying? Which travel corridors had reopened and which had slammed shut?

The sun began to sink. The perfect dome of blue became stained with pink and orange. Alex decided to revisit the mission parameters one more time, setting the VR to ‘night’. It could be dark on arrival in Cyrene City.

There was no such thing as too much preparation.

19

In a windowless basement beneath an undistinguished building just inside the perimeter of the parliament compound in Cyrene City, three men were cleaning their weapons. Two of them worked clumsily, the third with practised ease. The room smelled strongly of gun oil and sweat. An old-fashioned television set on a battered sideboard displayed silent images of the catastrophic destruction at the docks.

'At last, it has begun,' said Weasel, the leader, not for the first time.

'And to us falls the kill,' agreed Tariq, his naive companion.

The third man remained impassive. He was strongly built with short dark hair and hard eyes. Neither of the others knew his name.

'What do you say, brother?' asked Weasel, when he didn't speak.

Amaury slotted the sights onto his rifle with a sharp metallic sound, satisfying and precise.

'People are taking to the streets,' he murmured.

'They are,' agreed Weasel. 'The time has come. The nation will be rebuilt, at last.'

The building they were hiding beneath served as a dormitory for a team of gardeners. Amaury and his two revolutionary colleagues had not been discovered beneath the heap of organic mulch on Tariq's cousin's flat-bed trailer. Amaury could still smell it in his hair.

'The people are rising,' Tariq intoned.

'And we rise with them,' replied Amaury, like a religious response.

'Yes, brother.' Weasel smiled.

Could they possibly be as naive as they seemed, Amaury wondered. The two men believed that everything could be swept away in an instant; at worst in a weekend of cleansing violence. He wanted to ask them: 'And when we have killed all the politicians, who will be in charge? Who will clean the streets? Who will decide how many nurses the hospitals must train? Who will renegotiate the country's foreign debt? Who will have the authority to unite the inevitable factions?'

But he said nothing. Revolution was a childish dream – a belief that, if only the old order could be destroyed, something bright and perfect and new would emerge, as if by magic, to fix everything.

Stock footage of Prime Minister Mourad flickered on the TV screen – a reception in the sumptuous atrium of the parliament buildings, distinguished foreign visitors arriving by limousine at the foot of the ceremonial staircase and entering through impressive carved wooden doors.

'They flaunt their luxuries while people struggle for food,' snarled Weasel. 'For milk for their children to drink.'

'They have broken the nation and they will pay,' replied Tariq.

Again, the quasi-religious call and response.

Amaury wanted to school them in their own history. That the motherland they thought of as Libya had been invented between the two world wars by Italian fascists drawing lines in the sand. That 'Libya' was a Greek word that meant all of North Africa beyond Egypt.

'To you will fall the honour,' said Weasel.

The two men were both looking at him. Amaury realised he had disappeared into his own thoughts and missed his cue.

'Yes, brother,' he murmured.

'Because we may not get close,' continued Tariq, simply.

How earnest they look, Amaury thought. How driven. How sure of themselves.

'Speak,' said Weasel. 'Say you will kill her.'

Amaury nodded. 'I will.'

Weasel pointed to a paper plan of the parliamentary compound spread out on the cheap table. 'Even if we can penetrate the parliament building, we may not be able to get close.' His oily finger jabbed at an area outside the parliamentary debating chamber. 'She is the spider at the centre of their web of lies.'

'Would it not be better to take her prisoner?' asked Amaury.

Weasel gave him a surprised look. ‘Why?’

‘Well,’ Amaury said, as if thinking of it for the first time, ‘shouldn’t she be tried for her crimes?’

‘Perhaps,’ said Weasel, but his frown was doubtful.

This was the moment Amaury was looking for. He wanted access to the phone Weasel used to communicate with his superiors. But Weasel wouldn’t let him near it.

‘What would the leadership say?’ Amaury asked. ‘Should we contact them?’

‘Can we do that?’ Tariq looked at Weasel. ‘Can we ask for new orders?’

Clearly torn, Weasel didn’t answer. The phone was in a safe in the corner of the basement room. If Amaury could persuade Weasel to use it, that might be the moment to shoot them both between the eyes. Then he would use Weasel’s dead thumbprint to activate the phone. It would automatically dial and he would finally have a connection to someone higher up.

‘If she survives, she may escape,’ said Weasel. ‘If she escapes, she may return.’

Amaury pretended to consider this. ‘But if we put her on trial, her crimes will be spoken out loud.’

‘Yes,’ enthused Tariq. ‘All should hear her condemned and she must pay the price.’

Weasel glanced over at the safe. ‘We already have orders.’

‘True.’ Amaury picked up his gun. ‘But circumstances change.’

The television reverted to the pillar of smoke rising from the devastated port. Weasel began to pace the room.

’None but we can do this,’ he said. ‘No one else is inside the perimeter, but…’

He seemed torn. Abruptly, he squatted down at the heavy steel door, his hand on the dial of the combination lock. Very quietly Amaury removed the safety catch on his gun, shifting his chair on the cement floor and speaking to cover the sound.

‘If you are certain,’ he said. ‘If you are sure there isn’t a better path.’

Amaury left the thought hanging, as if it didn’t matter to him either way.

Weasel spun the dial. Amaury held his breath. But then, Weasel stopped. He stood up and looked Amaury in the eye.

'No. The army will defend her. Only we can act. You must kill her, comrade. That is your role.'

Amaury nodded slowly.

'I will do my duty.' He re-engaged the safety and lifted his hand from the gun. Weasel didn't seem to notice. 'No one will be able to say that I failed to do my duty.'

20

Only a few hundred metres away, Prime Minister Souad Mourad sat in a wood-panelled safe room, discussing the growing crisis with the three city mayors that made up the Presidential Council. Benghazi and Tobruk were on screen, speaking from offices in their home cities; the mayor of Cyrene City was with her in the room. They'd been talking for ninety minutes.

'Keep me updated,' said Mourad. 'I will remain in the parliamentary compound.'

'Yes, Prime Minister,' said Tobruk.

'Of course, Prime Minister,' said Benghazi.

Their screens became blank. Mourad stood up, smoothing her long formal gown, woven from traditional cloth – ivory silk with vertical panels of burgundy embroidery. She turned to the mayor of Cyrene City. 'You should return to City Hall. They'll be expecting you.'

He inclined his head. 'Perhaps that would be best.'

He left without another word, sketching a half bow on his way out. She followed him to the door and peered out into the vast lobby with its glazed atrium roof. Two generals in dress uniform were waiting their turn, accompanied by a female staff officer.

She motioned for them to enter.

The door to the safe room looked like a normal door – normal for a head of government's private apartment – heavy and intricately carved. But within the sandwich of timber was a cellular core of tempered steel, like a honeycomb, immensely strong and surprisingly light. When the three were inside, she sealed it in place and returned to her leather armchair with a brass reading-light over her shoulder. There were two more lamps at either end of the enormous cedarwood sideboard, a matching table and several mirrors set at different angles. The walls and ceiling were also designed to absorb the shock of any attack.

The staff officer used a hand-held computer to cast a news report to one of the large screens – the devastation at the port as seen from the ancient cedar tree in the botanical gardens.

'Do we have nothing but this footage?' complained Mourad.

'For the moment, Prime Minister,' said the staff officer, freezing the frame. 'Every camera within four hundred metres was destroyed.'

Mourad threw up her hands in frustration. 'How can there not be a single camera left on the dockside?'

'The radius of the blast was massive,' said one of the two men.

'All the same, General Al-Fathi, some of the cameras must have been sheltered by buildings.' Mourad said. 'We could analyse the footage—'

'Forgive me, Prime Minister,' interrupted Al-Fathi, politely. 'But there are no more buildings.'

Mourad fell silent. The reality of the devastating explosion was hard to comprehend from inside these four walls. But she didn't dare leave. Since the explosion, there had been constant riots in the streets.

General Bader cleared his throat. 'The insurrection is already taking advantage of the disturbance to come out into the open. It is beginning, Prime Minister.'

'Go ahead,' said Mourad. 'Play the damn recording.'

The video ran on, then cut to an interview with the bride and her husband.

'I was so happy, so happy to be getting married. My mother made my dress. For six months she has been sewing my dress. I was to look like a princess.'

The bride began to cry. The groom put his arm round her shoulders.

'There are no words,' he said. 'We were wondering, are we going to die?'

'It was supposed to be my happiest day,' sobbed the bride.

There was a pause as an inaudible question was asked off-camera.

'No,' said the groom, 'we went ahead. We are married after all.'

The bride nodded. 'My husband said: "We can't stop." I was like: "Okay, we continue." But the windows were broken all down one side of the room and, though my face was smiling, I could only think of the poor people. Many people must have died and I was having my happiest day.'

'It's no longer possible,' said the groom, 'to live here, in this city, in this country. I have cousins in France. I thank God we escaped unharmed. I thank God for His mercy.'

'Turn it off,' snapped Prime Minister Mourad.

The screen froze on the faces of the bride and groom, the woman like a disappointed child but with a flush of excitement in her eyes, the man determined, as if he had been presented with a challenge but knew himself strong enough to meet it.

'This is a disaster.' Mourad stood up.

The two generals followed suit. General Bader spoke apologetically.

'The explosion has been blamed on a stockpile of fertiliser stored in unsafe conditions. Fertiliser is well known as—'

Mourad glared at him. 'That's the best you can do?'

'Seventeen years ago,' Bader persisted, 'in Beirut—'

'Could it have been organised by Tripoli?' demanded Mourad.

There was a pause.

'It might,' conceded Al-Fathi.

'Investigations are ongoing,' said Bader.

Mourad turned back to the screen. Her life's work was falling to pieces in front of her eyes. The people she loved were turning on her.

There was a knock at the door. The staff officer opened the door just wide enough to take a message from a worried-looking civilian official. The safe room could not be penetrated by a bomb, but that same construction made wireless comms unusable.

'Well?' demanded Mourad.

'The central bank has been surrounded,' the staff officer replied, handing her the note. 'The road to the airport has been rendered impassable.'

'Marvellous.' Mourad turned to her generals. 'Well?'

'Should events move against us,' General Bader began carefully, 'it is uncertain how long we will be able to ensure your protection.'

The prime minister gestured to the image of the bridegroom. ‘So I should flee to France, like this imbecile?’

‘If your safety cannot be guaranteed,’ General Al-Fathi conceded. ‘It would be best.’

‘We must play a long game,’ Bader reminded her. ‘Much can be achieved in exile.’

Mourad drummed her fingers on the table as she contemplated her own banishment. ‘The parliamentary compound is secure?’

‘For the time being,’ Al-Fathi said.

‘You are uncertain of your forces?’

‘It is wise to be uncertain,’ he told her.

‘Uncertainty is wisdom,’ agreed Bader.

Prime Minister Mourad looked from one to the other. She wondered if they had escape plans of their own. Military authority could be a path towards wealth as well as power. Perhaps one or other of them saw himself as a new Gaddafi, the ‘strong man’ capable of reuniting the broken nation. The staff officer, on the other hand, looked worried. Mourad found that reassuring. If the woman was worried, surely she wasn’t a threat?

‘With the airport inaccessible,’ the staff officer said, ‘we’ll need an external extraction force. Should I contact Paris, Prime Minister?’

Mourad hesitated. That was her generals’ recommendation – extraction by French special forces and then exile. Mourad wondered about taking the staff officer with her. She would need someone at her side.

The brief silence was broken by the sound of a helicopter starting its engines, preparing for take-off.

‘Who is that?’ demanded Mourad. ‘This air space is restricted. Go find out.’

The woman staff officer hurried out. Mourad and the two generals listened to the sound of the rotor blades chopping the air. Al-Fathi raised his hand.

‘If you leave, Prime Minister, there should be a contingency for the passing on of power,’ said Al-Fathi, ‘a known chain of command, to prevent the creation of factions, in exile as well as at home. Might we know in advance what you have arranged?'

She looked from one to the other, wondering if either of them had already betrayed her.

'I hope I have arranged to survive.'

They all heard the helicopter leave the ground, beginning to gain height. The staff officer returned.

'It is the honourable member of the Presidential Council, the mayor of the City of Cyrene. No flight plan was logged.'

Mourad gave a dark smile. 'So, he's fleeing the sinking ship already.'

Suddenly, an explosion, muffled but quite close, shook the building. The thrumming of the helicopter ceased.

Mourad drew in a sharp breath. 'You told me the insurrection has no ground-to-air capability.'

'They do not,' confirmed Al-Fathi. 'But we have issued standing orders to bring down any aircraft.'

The prime minister stared at her generals. 'So, we just shot down one of our own,' she said, angrily. 'The situation seems to be escaping your control.'

'He was a traitor,' Bader reminded her. 'He was leaving the country.'

For a fraction of a second, the two generals exchanged a glance and Mourad caught a glimmer in their eyes. What was it? Satisfaction? Ambition? Not surprise, in any case.

Had they encouraged the Cyrene City mayor to take a helicopter and join one of the other Presidential Council members, perhaps forming an opposition government in Benghazi or Tobruk? Or had they advised him to defect entirely to the rump Libyan parliament in the impoverished former capital of Tripoli? And had they done this, knowing a ground-to-air strike would take him out?

And what of her? What plan did they have for her?

'What does Tripoli say?' she asked.

'That the will of the people is for a reunited Libya,' said Al-Fathi.

'Is it?' she asked.

'Absolutely not, Prime Minister.'

Mourad realised her hands were balled into fists. Bader stepped into her eyeline.

'Prime Minister Mourad, for the good of the state and its people, you must survive. Cyrenia is a young country. Guided by you, we have come far. You have the support of the French government. You withdraw to return stronger.'

Al-Fathi chimed in. 'The insurrection will exhaust itself. There is an imminent danger, but not a lasting danger.'

Mourad's logical mind turned over the possibilities. Even if her generals weren't behind the insurrection, they would try to profit from it. If she declined the extraction, she would be trapped by civil war. Military decisions would be taken out of her hands. Her authority would diminish. If the insurrection garnered support from Tripoli and beyond, the only way to appease the insurrection would be to promise change. As government figurehead, she could not offer change while remaining in place.

'France will provide air cover,' said Al-Fathi. 'This is for the best – for you and, therefore, for Cyrenia.'

The moment of decision had come. Mourad was forty-seven years old. From the age of twelve, when she'd first begun to understand that her own fate was intimately bound up with the fate of her fragile nation, her life had been leading to this moment. For years she had dreamed and studied and struggled and schemed. She had climbed to the pinnacle of political power and it was all about to end in abject failure.

Mourad's tone was decisive. 'I will leave and return stronger.'

'We all fervently desire it, *madame*,' said Bader.

Ignoring him, Mourad turned to the staff officer. 'Confirm the extraction with Paris.'

21

At DGIS headquarters, behind the armoured door to his basement office, Administrator Sabie sat reading a document forwarded to him by Professor Fayard. He wasn't sure why. Was it some kind of test? He hoped not.

Eusegnius Barnabas Sabie was thirty-seven years old, born into a Coptic Christian family two days into the new century. In early childhood, the family had benefited from living in Sabha, the celebrated home town of the Libyan leader. By the time Gaddafi fell in 2011, Sabie's family had already emigrated to France.

Life was hard. At first, they were undocumented immigrants, what people now called Blanks. Although they were ultimately granted refugee status, it was only when Sabie went to university that things really improved. Fluent in Arabic, French, Berber and Italian, he was fast-tracked into early graduation from one of the best schools in Paris, and from there into the Directorate-General for Internal Security.

The report on his screen was a history of missile sites in colonial Africa, all with a connection to France. The first section concerned Gerboise Bleue, a nuclear test facility in the Saharan wilderness of southern Algeria where the first French plutonium bomb was detonated in 1960. The next two sections concerned missile bases in Zaire and Kenya. The fourth concerned a ballistic missile facility built in the late 1950s near Jabal Hamzah, about sixty kilometres northwest of Cairo. After the 1979 Egypt–Israel peace treaty, Jabal Hamzah fell into disuse. In 2032, a French commercial space flight and telecoms company enquired about updating the launch site for satellite deployment, but Egypt's isolationist government vetoed the plan.

The next section concerned a more recent facility – part of a deal that had been struck by Prime Minister Mourad and France. It was located near the oasis town of Al-Jaghar, close to the Egyptian border. As Sabie pondered, not for the first time, its grandiose name, *Tahadath 'ila Al-Nujum* – 'Talk to the Stars' – a 3-D image of Fayard popped up from his comm-watch.

'Do we have confirmation from Cyrenia?' Fayard asked.

He glanced at the latest mission update. The transport plane was still on the ground.

'Not yet.'

Fayard made a sound of frustration. 'What is she waiting for?'

He paused, and Sabie waited, judging that he wasn't required to answer.

'There will be time enough,' said Fayard finally, before cutting the communication.

Sabie tapped his fingers on his desk. Was it worry for Alexandre Lamarque that had unsettled his boss?

Still, as long as the transport plane was on the ground, there was no reason to go hungry. Sabie locked his seven screens and set off for the canteen.

While he was eating, he noticed one of the junior operatives from the training cohort glancing at him. When he finished, he went to speak to her.

'Mademoiselle Cantor, I hope all is well?' he asked, formally.

'Thank you, sir.'

He was about to walk away when the woman squeezed out from behind her table, knocking into it, just rescuing a bottle of salad dressing before it fell to the floor.

'I have something to present at Forum,' said Cantor in a rush. 'Would that be possible?'

Sabie frowned. 'At Forum?'

'I happened to speak to Professor Fayard. He said he was interested.'

'Is that so?' Sabie pondered. 'Perhaps your team leader will be able to find a slot for you to present your intelligence.'

Before he could walk away, Cantor said, 'Except that would only be to the other trainees. I think it should be considered more widely. It provides a connection between several separate investigations. That's the purpose of the Forum, isn't it?'

Sabie considered the woman. He wanted to refuse the request. There was too much going on right now. But Fayard had expressed an interest…

'Send me a briefing of no more than fifty words,' he told her. 'If it seems valuable, I will see what I can do.'

Cantor beamed. 'Thank you, sir.'

By the time Sabie had reached his enormous desk and unlocked his screens, Cantor had already sent him a fifty-word note on an anonymous preacher and possible connections to a wider apocalyptic movement. He read it twice, noticing Mariam Jordane's slight involvement. That made him think about what Fayard had once told him about Alexandre Lamarque – that the young man had a kind of sixth sense, an ability to envision possible futures, like a chess grandmaster anticipating countless iterations of cause and effect.

Sabie didn't quite believe that. It sounded too good to be true, like a belief in magic or fairies. On the other hand, Fayard was seldom wrong. It was how he'd reached the top of the organisation, and stayed there so long.

'Thank you, Mademoiselle Cantor,' he dictated. 'I'll put your ideas forward, though it may not be straight away.'

Another message arrived, from an analyst at External Security, a man he vaguely knew called André Chambon.

Mourad is go.

22

Alex stood on the tarmac at Toulouse-Francazal, looking at a A430M transport plane. It was maybe ten years old and, according to the manufacturer, it was capable of landing in 'adverse' conditions, although Alex wasn't sure anyone had ever really put it to the test.

'We should have left earlier,' he said.

Waiting all day had made him tetchy. Too much time to think.

'The situation was unclear earlier,' said Poiret. 'Mourad was uncertain.'

She stood next to him, watching patiently as the team loaded equipment.

'How do we know Mourad is still alive?' Alex asked.

'We've heard nothing to the contrary.'

She seemed utterly relaxed. But then she wasn't about to board a plane and parachute down into a revolution.

'Will her own forces stand by her?'

Poiret kept her eyes averted. 'If you've read your briefing, you know as much as I do.'

Alex ignored the implied criticism and watched Paul Sanchez carry two gun-cases up the ramp into the belly of the plane. Poiret moved away to take a call on her earpiece. Her security officer stepped between them as a kind of privacy shield.

A truck arrived and four men in full paratroop kit unfolded themselves from the too-small seats, jumped out, and followed Sanchez on board.

The security officer stepped back as Poiret ended her call. She looked worried.

'What is it?' asked Alex.

'A detail,' Poiret said, frowning. 'A missing detail.'

'That doesn't sound good. If circumstances change, will we be updated in flight?'

'There's a satlink. If anything is unclear to you it will be because it is unclear to us. Assume any changes are for the worse.' Poiret seemed distracted, her gaze skating past his. Finally, she drew a breath and told him, 'The issue is our agent – our mole. He's gone quiet.'

'No mole is mentioned in the briefing,' said Alex, annoyed.

'His presence is classified.'

'Is he inside the parliamentary compound?'

She nodded. 'He's infiltrated the insurgency.'

Alex felt a shadow fall across the mission.

'So, we have a mole in the insurrection's assassination squad,' he said curtly. 'How will I know not to kill him?'

'Hopefully the circumstances will not arise,' she said shortly. 'In any case, I'm glad you took our deal. You'll be an asset to Internal. The Ministry has every confidence in your future success and thanks you for your service. Regarding your mother's care, I have delegated a senior physician from the Rothschild Institute to oversee her transfer. How is she?'

Alex knew Poiret was only interested in Gloria's health insofar as it provided her with leverage.

'Her condition has stabilised, apparently.'

'Good.'

The transport plane revved its engines and they turned away from the noise. Sanchez caught his eye and held up a finger meaning 'one minute'.

'Another thing,' Alex asked. 'Can we communicate with their air defences?'

'The M7s?' she said.

'Exactly.' Alex's tone was wry. M7s were among the best pieces of kit the French armed forces had ever deployed – infrared homing, proximity or impact triggers, capable of two-and-a-half times the speed of sound. And they'd shared them with Cyrenia. 'Do they know not to fire when we come within range?'

'We believe so.' Her tone did not inspire confidence. 'Good luck.'

She moved away, heading for her plush private jet. Sanchez waved to him from the utilitarian ramp of the A430M. Time was up.

Alex introduced himself to his team – solid paratroopers with impressive focus and experience. He used a device mounted on the fuselage to pop up a 3-D representation of the grounds, reviewing the terrain, showing them the route to the ceremonial entrance.

'It's the most direct approach to the safe room,' Alex concluded.

At that moment, the engines fired up for take-off and conversation became impossible.

The plane was fitted out for a medical evacuation with hospital gurneys down each side of the fuselage. Alex lay down on one of them. It had already been a long day. He thought he would just allow his mind to drift but, in the end, he slept. Unusually, he didn't dream.

23

Amaury heard the insurrection's small-arms attacks on the parliamentary compound just as the TV signal failed.

'Someone's disabled the transmitters,' said Weasel, angrily.

'Perhaps the insurrection destroyed them,' suggested Tariq, 'to stop the government spreading propaganda.'

Which would be stupid, thought Amaury. Control of information is control of the narrative.

'Or there could be a power outage,' continued Tariq.

'They have backup generators,' Weasel reminded him.

'What about the special phone?' Tariq shot a glance at the safe. 'Is it working?'

'I'll find out.'

Weasel crouched down in front of the safe and spun the dial back and forth. After a moment, the door swung open. He picked up the phone and pressed his right thumb to the security pad. The dumb phone booted up, the screen glowing green against his hand. He stared at it in disgust.

'No signal.'

Shame, thought Amaury, relaxing. He had a cute piece of kit concealed in the tongue of one of his shoes – a few centimetres square and little thicker than a credit card. He could have used it to locate the person on the other end of the call, but not if the mobile network was down.

'What do we do now?' Tariq's voice was brittle.

'We go out,' decided Weasel. 'We climb out of this hole where we hide like rats, and we fight our way into the parliament building. And we kill her.'

'What if we encounter other politicians?' asked Tariq.

'The hydra has many heads. We cut them all off until they can't grow back.' Pleased with his metaphor, Weasel squeezed himself into a black and grey camouflage jacket. 'Brothers?' he said, glancing at the two of them.

Amaury nodded. On balance, he would be better off outside than trapped in the basement.

'We rise up,' he said, providing the expected phrase.

'Yes,' Weasel smiled. 'We rise up.'

At that moment, the lights in the basement went out, plunging the windowless room into darkness.

'What is happening?' There was genuine fear in Tariq's voice.

'It's nothing,' Amaury assured him. 'A blackout makes it harder to target the government buildings from outside the perimeter.'

They groped their way upstairs. On the ground floor, they found the gardeners' dirty cutlery and plates on a communal table that appeared to have been rapidly abandoned. A carafe of water had been knocked over and the tablecloth was soaked through. Amaury opened one of the window shutters and peered out. Two hundred metres away, a Russian-made lightweight tank from the ageing Sprut series was crawling towards the perimeter.

'We should stay here for the time being,' he told them.

'No, we go now,' argued Weasel. He was hopped up on adrenaline, his eyes blazing.

'And then?' Amaury challenged him.

'We fight our way into the parliament building and…' He raised his rifle to his shoulder and made a 'pow' noise with his mouth.

'And how do we break into the safe room?' Amaury asked.

Tariq had the answer for that. 'We fire the mortar.'

Amaury gave him a level look. 'The safe room will be too strong for mortar attack, even if we make a direct hit.'

'So, she is out of reach. We have failed already.' Tariq sounded bewildered.

Amaury shook his head. 'Paris will send a team to extract her.'

'How can you know that?' demanded Weasel.

'It's her only option.'

Weasel banged a fist on the table. ‘Then we must move quickly before they get here.’

‘No.’ Amaury’s tone was steady. ‘The best moment is when they try to get her out of the building. When she leaves the safe room and is unprotected, that will be our chance.’

‘So, we don’t get to use the mortar?’ Tariq sounded disappointed.

‘Yes, we do,’ said Weasel before Amaury could reply. ‘We drive her out. We bring down fire.’

Right, thought Amaury. Another problem.

24

The safe room didn't allow wireless comms, but Mourad still had hard-wired contact with Al-Fathi and Bader in their command post. She was in her leather armchair, apparently focused on a printed intelligence service report on the forces working for her downfall. The power for her reading light came from batteries within the wall panelling. At the same time, she was surreptitiously watching the staff officer making her a cup of tea.

A shame, she thought.

'Would you like milk?' the officer asked.

'No,' said the prime minister. 'Sit down for a moment. I want to ask you something.'

The staff officer set the tea down in front of her and perched on the very edge of the second armchair.

'Where's my bag?' said Mourad. 'I have some sweeteners in it.'

The staff officer looked around.

'Oh wait, here it is.' Mourad reached down. The bag was tucked down between the cushion and the arm of the chair. 'How silly of me.'

Mourad put it in her lap and unclasped the gold fastening. She dropped two sweeteners into her cup and slowly stirred.

'Nothing is more important than to have a plan,' she said quietly.

'Yes, Prime Minister.'

'And these people…' Mourad waved a hand, indicating the insurrection beyond the walls. 'They have no plan.'

The woman's face remained blank. 'We shouldn't underestimate them, Prime Minister.'

'They think that, with my removal, an absence of organisation will create a void of power that a new and better order will fill,' Mourad continued. 'They give so little thought to what comes after.'

'Perhaps,' the staff officer agreed.

'They are idealists. They can already see the sunlit uplands. In my opinion, they will be sorely disappointed.'

'It is still in your best interests to leave, *madame*.'

'I have always had a plan,' Mourad continued, as if the staff officer hadn't spoken. 'This room, for example. I designed it myself. Tell me, what do you notice about it?'

The woman glanced around. Mourad stirred her tea, the silver teaspoon grating slightly against the fine china.

'It doesn't feel like a safe room. The light is so natural.'

'Yes, the backlit windows,' Mourad agreed. 'Regulated to the movement of the sun so there is no disturbance to circadian rhythms if one is obliged to remain a prisoner for any length of time.'

'Not a prisoner, surely?'

'To remain safe here, then.' Mourad went to drink then seemed to change her mind. 'What else do you notice?'

'Lots of dark wood, all handmade, I would guess. I'm no expert.'

'Anything else?'

The staff officer glanced at the teacup in the prime minister's hand. Mourad put it back on the table and looked for something else in her bag.

'Mirrors,' said the staff officer.

'Yes,' said Mourad. 'There are no dark corners, even though in reality it's little more than a cave.'

'It's very effective…'

Her voiced tailed off as Mourad took out her gun.

'That's right,' said the prime minister. 'Lots of mirrors. Do you know who I mean by Victor Hugo, dear?'

The staff officer didn't answer. The expression on her face had completely changed. No longer biddable and polite, her eyes were now hard and calculating.

'He bought a house on the island of Guernsey where he lived in a kind of luxurious exile. I suppose it made him paranoid.' The prime minister shook her head. 'What am I saying? It made him justifiably careful. He arranged a sequence of mirrors throughout his home so that he could see into every single room from the writing desk where he was accustomed to working each day.'

The staff officer's eyes darted round the room.

'Right again,' Mourad said. 'From this chair, where only I am accustomed to sitting, I can see every corner of the room reflected in a mirror, or in two mirrors, or in three mirrors. Tell me, why do you want me to drink poison?'

The woman slumped back in her chair. 'It doesn't matter.'

'Come now. I really would like to know. What exactly is your plan? Surely you must have one? It can't all be random, can it, just sweeping things away and hoping for the best?'

'You wouldn't understand.'

'No,' Mourad agreed. 'Perhaps I wouldn't.'

'Better times will come,' the officer said, as if it was an article of faith.

'Better times? How vague.'

'The future will prove us right.'

'You say "us". Are my generals in league with you?' Mourad asked. 'They seemed keen to see the back of me.'

'So are we all. Go. Run away. You are nothing.'

Mourad's eyebrows rose. 'I am nothing?'

'The people suffer and die. You do nothing.'

'You think I don't know they suffer?'

'You flaunt your luxury.'

'You speak like a child,' Mourad told her. 'You know very well that I live simply, but I also fulfil a role. I have no choice but to wear the trappings of power.'

'The expression of your ambition.'

Mourad paused, cocking her head on one side. She had hoped for some useful intelligence. But it looked like all she was going to get was nonsense.

'Tell me, who was behind the attack on the port?' she asked. 'Was it a provocation, or just an extraordinary accident?'

'You have kept an unsafe peace.' The woman's voice was venomous. 'You have failed to protect the people.'

'Was it designed to spark a revolution?'

'Of course,' she snapped. 'You refuse to protect us from foreign exploitation. We are playthings.'

'We are a tiny country in a very large and hostile world.'

'The explosion at the docks has woken the people from their apathy. You see, even a little destruction is a good thing.'

'A little destruction?' said Mourad, suddenly angry. 'We will be counting the dead for weeks.'

'That is something you are good at. When the new virus came—'

Mourad cut her off. 'When the virus came, we acted swiftly. No one could have done more.'

'How many have died?'

'Too many, but the measures we put in place—'

'They bleed from their eyes.'

'And many have recovered,' Mourad said defensively.

'They bleed from their noses.'

Mourad didn't know why she was arguing, but she couldn't seem to stop herself. 'Science is and always has been our best defence. The steady acquisition and application of knowledge—'

'Stories, that's all you are.' The officer spoke over her. 'You spin your stories, but you do nothing while people die.'

'From a virus,' said Mourad.

The staff officer made as if to stand. In a quick movement, Mourad extended her arm and shot her twice between the eyes. The first bullet took off most of the top of the woman's head, splattering tissue, blood and bone across the carved panelling of the wall. The second bullet lodged in the headrest of the chair. The noise echoed for two or three seconds, then the air was still.

Mourad picked up the telephone that connected her to the command position at the main gatehouse. The generals were not available, but the comms officer's report was satisfactory.

'What about the extraction?' she demanded.

'The transport and fighter support are inbound, madame.'

'ETA?' She listened, then nodded. 'Thank you.'

She put the phone down and stood up, smoothing her long formal dress over her hips, running the absurd dialogue through her mind.

What had she achieved by trying to debate with a traitor?

Nothing.

What had she learned?

Nothing.

She took a step forward and pumped two more bullets into the dead woman's heart.

25

At that moment, Amaury, Weasel and Tariq were just a few hundred metres away, on the far side of the parliamentary compound, concealed behind the slatted fence of a squalid bin shelter outside the gardeners' dormitory. Amaury was watching the two men struggling to assemble a lightweight mortar.

Tariq had dropped the mortar on the stairs while bringing it up out of the basement. It was an M6-895, British-made and obsolete. That was the nature of revolutionary conflict. Equipment was scavenged from all kinds of sources. That said, there was no reason the weapon shouldn't work. The device was simplicity itself.

The narrow barrel sat on a round base plate designed to spread the recoil and give stability. Inside the barrel was a firing pin. Drop the mortar bomb into the barrel and it would strike the pin, triggering the propulsive explosion. If the barrel was very upright it would fly only a short distance, falling vertically. If the bipod legs were spread wide, a flatter trajectory could achieve a greater distance.

What Amaury had told them was true. There was no real need for them to use it. An extraction force must, by now, be imminent. The real action would take place when Mourad attempted to leave her safe room. But Weasel and Tariq had other ideas.

As he watched them work, he wondered if Mourad might already be dead. If she was, his best option would be to try to hitch a ride with her extraction force himself.

Finally, Weasel and Tariq stood back and looked at the mortar with satisfaction.

'Where are the mortar bombs?' Weasel asked.

'I'll get them,' said Tariq.

They only had two, stored in a corner of the basement. Amaury had a brief vision of Tariq dropping them like he had the mortar. That would resolve the question of whether or not Amaury should kill them without, in the end, finding out anything useful about the hierarchy of the insurrection.

There would be no need. They would all three be blown to pieces.

'I'll help,' he said.

26

A change in engine note woke Alex from shallow sleep. Instantly alert, he sat up. Catching his eye from across the plane, Sanchez gave him a five-minute signal and indicated where he had laid out his kit – a parachute and two weapons. Alex walked over to inspect them.

The Hécate III was a beast of a gun that weighed nearly fourteen kilograms without its sights, with a range of 1,800 metres – if you had the strength to lift it.

He chose the second rifle as much more suitable for quick, mobile incursions – an FR-F2 with a ten-round detachable box magazine. It weighed just five kilos.

Alex packed two magazines of ammunition in a pouch of his fatigues, in addition to the one already in the slot. Sanchez helped him into his parachute, checking the free bag, bridle and bungee. When both he and Sanchez were satisfied, Alex found a window and looked out.

They had flown east, against the sun. Dusk had been replaced by night. Other smaller aircraft flew close at hand.

Fighter support. Good news.

The four paratroopers were already standing by. Alex figured he still had a couple of minutes. Sanchez helped him access the satlink at the screen on the fuselage. It stuttered and refreshed with an update on the progress of the insurrection.

Worse, thought Alex, reading the report. Definitely worse.

He touched another icon. A scanner on the bezel of the screen read his thumbprint and connected him to his messages. As promised, there was one from Poiret.

The attached image file rendered slowly, eventually revealing the face of the mole, the man who might be dead, whose presence might complicate things so much as to be dangerous, or who might be looking for extraction himself.

Amaury Barra.

Alex felt the future close in.

Poiret had to know that he and Amaury had trained and worked together. Was this some kind of game?

There was no time to think about it. The paratroopers were clipping the carabiners attaching their release lines to the rail. Alex went to join them. They stood aside as he stepped up to the threshold, his heart rate climbing as it did before every jump. Sanchez stood with his hand on the door release.

The paratroopers activated the cameras mounted on their chests. Alex did the same. Five tiny red tell-tales illuminated for two seconds as the cameras began recording, then went dark so as not to present a target.

Sanchez opened the hatch.

Night wind came buffeting into the plane, whipping at the webbing on the walls, tugging at the oxygen and saline lines, shaking the stands. Alex smelled dust and smoke and heat. Sanchez tapped his shoulder and held up one finger.

Outside the open door, the world slid woozily from side to side as the transport plane banked on its final approach. Below, the city was burning in a dozen places, the flames illuminating martyred highways and rubble-strewn streets.

A dark lozenge indicated the blacked-out perimeter of the parliamentary compound. In the centre of the darkness, Alex glimpsed a fleeting reflection of the moon in the dark glass of the atrium roof.

Then, as he watched, a sudden explosion sent flames shooting up the walls of the parliament building.

The perimeter is supposed to be secure, he thought. Where did that come from?

27

'That wasn't a bad attempt,' said Amaury. 'Not bad at all.'

'You said you knew what you were doing,' complained Weasel. 'You missed. We only have two bombs.'

'Should we adjust the angle of the barrel?' suggested Tariq.

Amaury nodded. 'I can do that.'

'And you will still destroy the entrance?' insisted Weasel. 'We have to get inside.'

'It's possible.' Amaury kept his reply vague, but Weasel wasn't having that.

'It must be done.'

'The second mortar bomb might not have the same performance as the first,' Amaury explained. 'They were made fifteen years ago. One might be in better condition than the other.'

'We are alone inside the compound. This is our mission. No one else can do this.' Weasel's voice was tight.

'I know,' Amaury said calmly. 'Do you want to adjust the aim or shall I? Aren't we all on the same side?'

'I ask myself,' said Weasel, angrily. 'Are we?'

He had a nasty look in his eye – a combination of excitement and panic. Amaury took a step away from the mortar and motioned for him to take over. 'Go ahead.'

They had anchored the mortar with two dinner knives, pushed through holes in the base plate into the turf. Weasel put his hands on the barrel of the mortar, a frown of concentration on his face.

'You know I don't know how to do this,' he complained.

Amaury glanced at the device. 'The trajectory needs to be slightly flatter.'

'How much is slightly?' snapped Weasel.

'A few degrees.' Amaury tugged the two knives out of the ground, pulling them up like tent pegs. 'It's hard to…' His voice tailed off as he heard the distinctive deep rumble of a transport plane coming in low overhead. He looked up. 'They're here.'

Tariq followed his gaze, but Weasel paid no attention.

'We need to find her inside the walls,' he said. 'While she's waiting for the plane to evacuate her.'

Behind the transport's engines was a different note. The transport plane banked and came directly overhead.

'You hear that?' said Amaury. 'Fighter support. Once the transport gets down to an altitude of about two hundred metres they'll jump.'

'When is that?' said Weasel.

'Soon.'

'Then hurry and help me,' said Weasel.

Amaury had a very clear sense of the schematics of the parliament and was fairly certain he could send the second – and final – mortar bomb into the parliament chamber, a corner of the building that was unlikely to be occupied. On the other hand, there was an atrium with a glass roof just alongside. If the mortar bomb fell into the atrium, it might block the exit from the safe room. Meanwhile, Weasel seemed to be getting suspicious when there was still a chance that Amaury might be able to infiltrate higher up in the insurrection.

'They've jumped,' shouted Tariq.

'Quickly,' Weasel urged Amaury. 'You must do it now.'

'Okay.' Amaury edged the base plate back about a hand's width.

'Send the second bomb,' Weasel ordered. 'Do your duty as you have promised and make us all proud in return for all we have suffered.'

'You must have the honour,' Amaury told him.

He stood back and covered his ears. Against the black of the sky, he could see five parachutes drifting lazily on the dusty air.

I wonder who they've sent, he thought.

Weasel picked up the shell and dropped it into the tube. Amaury felt the whump of the propulsion explosion close at hand, then took his hands away from his ears. He glimpsed the mortar bomb in flight, following its trajectory towards the parliament building. It fell square through the glass atrium and exploded inside the building, out of sight but audible.

'*Merde,*' he whispered.

Flames began rising through the shattered roof. The two revolutionaries were delighted. They raised their fists, shouting with joy.

Amaury picked up his rifle. He tapped Weasel on the shoulder.

'Come on,' he said. 'While the paratroopers are in the air.'

28

Even inside the cellular walls and ceiling, Prime Minister Mourad felt the safe room shake. The reinforced door stayed shut, but a cloud of dust was forced through the crack at the bottom and settled on the polished cedarwood floorboards.

Mourad walked to a console in the corner of the room. It had four screens connected to internal cameras. She needed to know what was going on outside but all four were dead.

She crossed the room, past the corpse of the staff officer slumped in the blood-stained chair. To the left of the door, at head height, was a small photographic print in a steel frame, a memento of her first election victory. It pictured her at twenty-two years old – serious, optimistic, determined. The frame was hinged on the left-hand side. She swung it open. Behind it, a peephole was set into the reinforced cavity wall.

She put her eye to the wide-angle lens, expecting to see the whole atrium lobby, but her field of view was obscured by some indistinct obstruction. Beyond it, she could make out that a fire was raging.

She hurried back to her desk, and picked up the hard-wired telephone connecting her to the command post at the gatehouse.

29

Alex hit the ground, rolled and glanced round for cover. The compound felt strange for only as long as it took him to gather up his parachute and harness. Then his VR prep kicked in – the formal driveway, the summer house, the domestic staff accommodation, the interlocking pathways, the rose borders.

Everything was right where it ought to be.

He set off towards the parliament building, knowing the other members of his team would follow, knowing it was not his business if they didn't, if they were already dead.

There was cover most of the way. He crouched behind a low wall and glanced back. Two of the paratroopers were nearby with their weapons ready. The other two were balling up their parachutes. Their weapons looked like FAMAS assault rifles, chunky killing machines capable of over a thousand rounds per minute.

Handy, he thought.

There was no one else close at hand. All the government troops and vehicles must have been moved to the perimeter, if they hadn't deserted altogether.

Movement up ahead caught his eye, near the main entrance to the parliament building – three unknown shadowy figures were disappearing inside.

Alex's mind turned over the possibilities.

The prime minister might have already been moved out by her own military, to some safe house, incognito. Then, perhaps, they would smuggle her to the coast for a fast boat to take her across the Mediterranean to Greece or to Italy.

No, that would have been made known on the satlink. If Mourad was already off-compound, the transport plane would have circled as a distraction then returned home.

Another option was that she had been abandoned by her defenders, left to fend for herself. But no, there was still fighting on the perimeter. The state forces had not entirely deserted their democratic leader.

Finally, there was his preferred option, that Mourad was being allowed to leave – that her generals wanted her out of the picture and were unconcerned about the fact that she might survive into exile.

He let the ideas settle. Yes, he was sure that was it – the third option. But then, who had launched the mortar strike?

Staying low, he ran along the wall to the foot of the stone staircase – twenty-five wide steps leading to a high-lintelled entrance and two mighty wooden doors. He met no opposition as he raced up the stairs, finding a small, undamaged service door which stood slightly ajar.

Three of his support team would wait outside, making sure the transport could land safely. Motioning for the fourth paratrooper to follow, he slipped inside.

30

General Bader was sheltering with his colleague, General Al-Fathi, inside the imposing gatehouse at the edge of the compound. They both had binoculars through which they were observing the flames rising from the parliament building.

'The explosion at the port was well judged,' said Al-Fathi. 'Was it easy to accomplish?'

'The explosive chemicals were already in storage,' Bader replied. 'Transit warehouses for the lithium mines in Mali. Badly maintained. Minimal security.'

'It has woken the people. Now, we must direct their anger.' Al-Fathi lowered his binoculars. 'This, however, is a mistake.'

'Allowing the extraction?' asked Bader. 'In the short term, perhaps.'

'In the long term.' Al-Fathi said. 'This moment is not the end, and she will have survived. By letting her leave, we create the opportunity for her return.'

Bader wondered if his staff officer had succeeded in her mission. All the same, he didn't want Al-Fathi to know what he had planned.

'By letting her leave,' he suggested, 'we can create the circumstances for a legitimate transfer of power. We show that we are not assassins.'

'According to whom?'

'In the eyes of the world. You know this.

A comms officer coughed gently to attract their attention, holding up a wired phone.

'The prime minister, sir. She wants to speak to you.'

Disappointing, thought Bader. If Mourad was on the line, his staff officer had failed.

'Tell her we are not available. Tell her to stay where she is.'

'She wants to know, sir, who was responsible for those two explosions,' the man persisted. 'How they got inside the perimeter.'

Gunfire rang out from across the gardens. In a single movement, the two generals raised their field glasses towards it.

'Tell her you don't know but you will keep her informed,' barked Bader. 'Tell her the extraction goes ahead as planned.'

'Sir.'

The comms officer moved away.

'How *did* the insurrection get inside the perimeter?' Al-Fathi asked Bader. 'The compound is completely encircled. The exclusion zone goes back beyond the walls into the first few blocks of the city.'

'Who knows?' Bader shrugged. 'Perhaps they were already hidden on site before we locked it down.'

'I told her we should have reduced the staff. There were always too many people within the compound. But she was determined to maintain appearances,' said Al-Fathi. 'Still, the French paratroopers are here now. I imagine they have the training to deal with amateur insurgents. Either way, dead or exiled, all will be well.'

Bader lowered his binoculars and looked sideways at his colleague. Al-Fathi thought they were at the heart of things here in the city, but Bader knew that they must soon fly south to Al-Jaghar. That was where the future would be shaped, for Cyrenia and for the world.

He thought about his sister, Latifah, the commander of the airbase. While the insurrection monopolised everyone's attention, she could be relied upon to advance the plan.

And then…?

Then it would be the turn of General Ramzi Bader.

31

In the safe room, Prime Minister Mourad sat at the comms console, writing quickly by hand on a pad of high-quality writing paper.

She had wondered, at first, if there was any point in sharing what might be her final observations, her judgement on her time in office. Paper could so easily be destroyed. But to write by hand was much better than typing. It was as good as signing every word, with the personality, the authentic presence of the author in every line, just as the identity of the greatest painters is incontrovertibly confirmed in every unique brushstroke.

As she completed each sheet, she photographed it with her hand-held, creating, she hoped, an enduring testimony.

She finished the final sheet and took the last photograph. Whatever happened next, there might be somebody loyal to her memory who would find the images and make the text public.

She sat back. It was strangely quiet in the safe room. The air was acrid, however, making her eyes run. The atmospheric filters must have been damaged.

Mourad straightened the stack of embossed sheets and folded them over twice, squeezing them into her handbag alongside the tube of sweeteners, her makeup and her gun. Then she walked back across the room to the peephole and peered out.

The partial obstruction had fallen away. The fish-eye lens allowed her to see the width of the atrium lobby. The fire was burning itself out for want of fuel. There was no movement, either in the lobby or up on the gallery leading to the public viewing area.

Did that mean that the French had decided not to send an extraction team after all? Surely they should be here by now? Perhaps everyone had been lying to her and the coded request had never been sent?

She released the heavy locks on the reinforced door, easing it inwards, just a few centimetres. There was no resistance from fallen debris but the thick smoke hit her in a hot wave. She reeled back, hastily re-closing it and setting the locks.

It was bad out there, but not as bad as it might be. She was alone but she was not trapped. When the French extraction force arrived – if they arrived – she could at least open the door and take her first steps into exile.

32

'We should go up to the gallery,' said Amaury. The staircase was supported by thick pillars with a decorative pattern like strands of woven concrete rope. He could feel the twisted shapes beneath his fingers. 'You go first. I'll cover you.'

Tariq grasped his arm. 'Why is no one else here?'

'They have deserted her,' said Weasel with satisfaction.

The two would-be assassins climbed the stone steps two at a time, making no effort to stay low. Amaury hung back, watching them playing at being soldiers.

His mission was a failure. Weasel and Tariq, he decided, were pawns with no real connections or authority. Perhaps they had never been important.

He watched them pause on the landing, scoping out their next steps in plain view. Amaury had only two remaining objectives: to eliminate the threat to Prime Minister Mourad and to make his own escape with the extraction team.

He leaned back against the concrete pillar and raised his rifle to his shoulder. He would have to be quick. Weasel and Tariq were about to disappear through a doorway onto the gallery.

Before he could shoot, a volley of automatic gunfire sliced through the air, deafeningly loud and close at hand. It came from the small service doorway to the left of the ceremonial entrance behind him.

Tariq jerked and twisted as he fell to the ground.

Amaury made himself small behind the pillar as Weasel got away, slipping through the doorway onto the gallery above.

Amaury swore softly.

From there, Weasel would have a clear shot down into the floor of the atrium and Mourad would be unable to leave the safe room without crossing right in front of him.

And Amaury couldn't chase Weasel for fear of being cut down himself.

33

A few moments before, Alex had crept into the lobby. It was darker than he'd expected. Smoke hung in the air like a curtain of fog.

He enabled his night vision and the space came to life in tones of green. All at once, he could see a spacious lobby with pillars like stone ropes, a low embroidered divan. On the far side, there were two men on the stairs, wearing a curious mix of civilian and combat clothing.

That had to be two of the three men he'd spotted as he crossed the grounds.

Another dark shape – the fourth para – slipped in through the service doorway behind him. There was gunfire, deafeningly loud. He recognised the distinctive note of his colleague's FAMAS weapon. One of the men on the stairs fell heavily, possibly dead. The other slipped through a doorway onto the upper gallery where he would have clear line of sight on the safe room.

Alex weighed his decision, his mind scrolling through possible outcomes. It took less than a couple of seconds, though it felt longer. He decided to push on. He was close to his goal.

Ducking low, he dashed to the double doors on the far side of the lobby. One was hanging askew, knocked loose in the blast. Crouching on the threshold, he contemplated the ruined atrium.

A fire was smouldering, smoke drifting up towards the remnants of the once-beautiful glass roof. He crept forward, keeping low, broken glass crunching underfoot. The brightness of the flames overexposed his night vision, making it hard to see.

An ominous cracking sound came from above and there was a whump of air as rafters and plate-glass crashed down only a few metres away. He jumped back, but something struck him around his left hip and he felt a stabbing sensation – a deep and sudden ache.

Without taking his eyes away from his surroundings, he reached down to explore the wound. He found the tear in the fabric of his uniform and felt blood on his fingertips. It wasn't serious.

In that moment, shots rang out from above.

He flinched back behind a column, peering up through the haze of smoke and dust.

The gallery ran along the far wall, about twenty metres up. That's where the shooter was.

He glanced left. He was on the same level as the prime minister's safe room. He could see it behind the smouldering fire.

Would Mourad stay safe inside, cowering out of sight, or would she come out and meet the challenge of fate?

The second, obviously.

Alex edged forward, half-concealed by the smoke. He heard another gunshot – a rudimentary, single-shot weapon. Its bullet hit the safe room door with a heavy punch, lodging deep in the carved timber. Alex knew the door was bulletproof. The man could fire at it all day and it wouldn't make a difference.

But, as he watched, somebody pulled it very slightly ajar.

Don't do it, he willed Mourad. Just stay where you are.

He shuffled round to get a better angle up into the gallery. The attacker was not taking any kind of cover, leaning his weapon on the balustrade.

Amateur, thought Alex.

He took a deep breath and time slowed as he prepared to act. The prime minister was safe, as long as she remained sheltering behind the reinforced door.

Then everything changed.

Above the broken struts of the atrium's glass roof, a capricious wind caught at the clouds and uncovered the moon. By its light, Alex saw a second man emerging onto the gallery in a half-crouch, his weapon raised ready to fire.

34

Ninety seconds earlier, huddled behind his pillar, Amaury had faced his own difficult decision. There was a soldier below, somewhere near the dark doorway, concealed by the smoke. Amaury had no way of knowing if it was a member of the French extraction team or Cyrenian army. In either case, as far as anyone knew, Amaury was the enemy, the threat to be eliminated.

He took a small mirror from a pocket in his jacket and used it to look round the pillar, trying to make out shapes in the darkness, keeping it hooded by his hand so it didn't reflect any light. He heard a crash from the far room and, in his mirror, he detected a movement of darkness on darkness – a human shape in black-and-grey camouflage gear. The sudden impact of the falling rubble had made them flinch, giving themselves away.

If they were a member of the extraction force, there was a chance Amaury might safely make himself known. Then again, they would almost certainly be highly alert to any kind of movement and would probably shoot to kill.

Either way, Amaury needed to get up the stairs and stop Weasel from getting a clear shot at the prime minister.

He steadied himself, and then swung around the pillar in a single smooth movement and shot four rounds into the wall. As his bullets slammed into the masonry, the man dove for cover. Simultaneously, Amaury jumped up and ran for the doorway at the top of the stairs, taking them two at a time. Then he slowed as he crept out onto the gallery, emerging half crouched, his weapon ready to fire.

35

The moon was almost directly overhead. The combination of moonlight and flames lit up the wrecked atrium like day.

Alex saw the shooter on the balcony turn in surprise to face the crouching figure. This was his chance.

Alex fired four shots, two double-taps. The first two took apart the shooter's head. The second pair were targeted at the other man as he rose from his crouched position, trying to regain the cover of the doorway. Alex thought one of the shots caught the man's arm. In any case, his weapon fell from his hands and clattered through the balustrade, down into the wreckage of the atrium.

Instantly, Alex knew – without knowing how he knew – that he had made a mistake. He felt it as an almost physical pain.

There was no time to analyse what had gone wrong. He refocused on his next task, edging forward towards the safe room door, and called out in a loud voice.

'*Force d'extraction française, madame. Le transport est prêt.*'

'Identify yourself,' came a woman's voice.

Alex gave the three-word code.

'*Constant – certain – connu.*'

The prime minister pulled the reinforced door wider. She was in shadow, but Alex recognised the dark brows and wide forehead. She wore a long formal gown, as she had in several of the photos in the preparatory dossier. She said something that Alex didn't catch and, seeing this, she reached out a hand and touched the bodycam on his chest.

'Lose that,' she said, very clearly. 'And let's go.'

36

Twenty-five minutes later, they were both on board the transport plane. Only forty minutes had passed since Alex had woken for the drop. The engines roared as the plane shot down the long driveway. The acceleration was shockingly abrupt.

Kneeling by the frame of Amaury's gurney, Alex barely noticed the plane leave the ground.

'Careful,' warned the medic. 'He's lost a lot of blood. He's sedated.'

Alex reached out, putting a gentle hand on the man's cheek. Without waking, Amaury turned his head – square features, dark brows, low forehead.

'How bad is it?' Alex asked.

The medic glanced at the padded bandaging round Amaury's right forearm, where his hand should be. 'Isn't it obvious?'

As he stared at the clean white bandages, Alex felt hollowed out. Lost.

'Will he wake up?' he asked, shouting above the noises of the engines. 'I need to talk to him. I have to explain.'

'There will have to be an inquiry.' The medic's voice was firm but not unsympathetic. 'It's protocol in the event of friendly fire. You may not talk with the victim.'

'I've known him for twelve years,' Alex explained, aware that this was futile but unable to stop himself. 'We graduated together. We're… friends.'

But the medic was unmoved. It didn't matter anyway. Amaury did not wake.

After a while, Alex stumbled away and sat on a gurney at the far end of the plane.

The wound on his hip throbbed, but he ignored it. He'd have it seen to when they reached France. It was nothing compared to what he had done to Amaury.

He glanced up to see Prime Minister Mourad across from him. She sat alone, saying nothing. He thought she was watching him but she might simply have been gazing past him, lost in her own thoughts.

The A430M banked to the west. He assumed the fighter escort was alongside once more.

The mission had been a success – the prime minister was safe. And yet, something was lost.

He'd made a terrible mistake.

Three hours later, they touched down at Toulouse-Francazal. Again, he was prevented from speaking to Amaury and was made to wait for medical treatment and initial debrief. Then there was a long delay before a seat could be found on a blended-wing body aircraft powered by liquid hydrogen. The BWB deposited Alex at Base Aérienne 117, the Paris military airport, and he was given a car for the journey into the city centre.

He arrived just after lunch. It was a normal summer day – hot and sticky, the streets crowded with people who hadn't just returned from a war zone.

He went for a walk, through the Marais and Saint-Paul neighbourhoods, down small cobbled streets and shadowy passageways between tightly packed buildings where he caught glimpses of cool courtyards.

He felt empty. As if all of his emotions had been left on that plane.

He got back to his boat around four and finally checked his personal comms. Among a dozen uninteresting messages there was one from Mariam. He answered straight away.

Come if you're free.

He fetched a green drink from the fridge, specifically tailored to his body's requirements, and forced himself to be practical.

He should sleep, but he still felt wired. If there was to be an inquiry, he wanted to get ahead of it. He dictated a first draft of his report via voice-recognition software. He kept it factual, unemotional. He didn't apologise or overexplain. He didn't talk about how it had felt. He simply put down, in the simplest possible language, what had occurred.

His watch vibrated with Mariam's reply.

Later.

Satisfied with the first draft of his report, he decided to wait until morning to check it over and submit it.

He retrieved the photographs of the two students who attacked Bunker Martha and studied them closely – the greyish tinge to their faces, the flaccid arms, the fingers of each hand lying half-curled on the wipe-clean mattresses. He sent the photos on to a DGES technician to see if enlargement and enhancement could provide any more clues.

There must be something, he thought. Otherwise, why had they been incinerated so quickly?

Fulfilling his promise, he sent a message to the head of DGES recruitment concerning Paul Sanchez, the young flight engineer, recommending him for promotion and transfer from his low Air Force position. He copied it to the base commander at Base Aérienne 101 and was gratified to receive an instant response. The man must have been at his desk, probably occupied with his own report on the extraction mission. The reply was brief but to the point.

Good choice.

Alex's eyes felt dry, his limbs heavy.

'Cabin, dark,' he said aloud.

The screen shut down and the cabin lights dimmed. He went through to the bedroom, touching the door frame with his fingertips for orientation. He lay down but, each time he closed his eyes, he saw again Amaury's right arm swathed in padded bandages.

'Lamp.'

He read for an hour – fiction, connected with nothing but itself.

At last, Mariam arrived. He lost himself in her, hungrily, gratefully.

Afterwards, they lay in the dark, listening to the hum of the on-board systems. In the hush, he told her what he had done.

'Oh, Alex. Not Amaury. Did you know he was in Cyrene City?'

'I found out a few minutes before we jumped. I knew I'd made a mistake the second it happened. But, in that moment, he was just a second shooter, about to fire on the prime minister.'

'How bad is it?'

Alex paused. ‘I think his hand was completely destroyed.’

‘Poor Amaury.’ She brushed the hair back from his forehead, her touch gentle. ‘I’m so sorry.’

Alex fell silent, imagining speaking to Amaury, making his apology. It was, after all, a random event. All kinds of different outcomes had been equally possible.

‘There will be an inquiry,’ he said, ‘an investigation.’

‘But it wasn’t your fault. You didn’t send Amaury in there unprotected. They did. They can’t make you take the blame.’

‘Blame no. Responsibility, yes.’ He sighed. ‘I did what I was supposed to do.’

He knew he sounded defensive. Mariam must have heard it, too.

She squeezed his hand. ‘Should we be worried?’

‘About what?’

‘About us.’

She was right. The investigation might uncover details of his personal life and the fact that he, currently an External Security operative, was in a relationship with someone who worked at Internal.

‘Perhaps,’ he conceded.

There was another pause, a gap between them as each thought their own thoughts.

Then he moved some more and she moved some more and the gap between them disappeared and time passed until, finally, they slept.

37

The next morning, Alex discovered he had been placed on compulsory leave from all DGES operations. Despite that, using his false identity as Maurice Panhard, he audio-called the data centre in Kofinou, asking to speak to Tani Sakelliou, but she was unavailable. Because he still had the nagging feeling he had missed something, he asked for Director Philippou.

'I don't understand why you're calling me,' she told him flatly.

'Has anything happened, anything out of the ordinary? My investors are interested in the new undersea connector to Cyrenia, but with the insurrection there—'

'I do not run this data centre on rumour or suspicion. Frankly, I'm astonished that's the way you conduct your business.'

Alex felt he was on the verge of compromising himself so he ended the call, disappointed.

Another message told him he was expected that morning at the headquarters of Fayard's Internal Security service for induction. Before leaving the boat, he checked in with the clinic. Gloria's condition was slightly improved. He requested a new appointment to visit her and, straight away, received a notification that Gloria's transfer to the Rothschild Institute had been approved.

Good, he thought. Poiret was making good on her promise.

Because the message didn't say when, he rang Poiret's office, looking for more details, but there was no one who could help him.

He dressed and went outside, crossing the street to avoid the spray from an insect control team. Masked and gloved, he took the Métro, heading west to Internal Security headquarters at Levallois-Perret.

Alex wasn't sure what form the 'induction' would take. He had been ordered to wait in the sixth-floor lobby. There a window looked out over the streets below, where life went on and no one knew that he had shot one of his own colleagues, that his mother was in quarantine.

Beyond the lobby was a large conference room behind semi-glazed doors. A meeting was in progress – a dozen junior members of Internal Security, barely filling a quarter of the long table. He looked at their eager faces, a woman with flame-red hair on her feet, in full flow.

Trainees, he thought, about to graduate.

He accessed the news on his comm-watch and let a pop-up 3-D avatar tell him about the latest from Cyrenia – Mourad's exile, a statement from General Al-Fathi, a calming of the tension, a ceasefire, a curfew. An invitation had been issued by the government in Tripoli to immediately embark on talks for reunification between 'the authentic Libyan state' and 'the illegally seceded province of Cyrenia'.

This was his doing. He had followed orders and this was the result.

He cut the connection with a hard swipe of his fingers.

He was thirty-two years old and life had taught him only two things worth knowing. First, that a darkness was coming and there was nothing much left to believe in. Second, wherever he went from here, he wanted Mariam to be with him.

The meeting in the conference room had ended, and he watched the young trainees emerge and disappear into the lifts. No one came to greet him, so after a few minutes he went inside. The only person left in the room was a small grey man, very lean and self-possessed.

'Welcome, Monsieur Lamarque,' he said cheerfully. 'My name is Sabie. Take a seat, please.'

Alex crossed the room and sat down. They faced one another across the long conference table. Between them were two manuals, official guides to the structure, policies and procedures of the two state security services, External and Internal.

'This induction meeting is for the purposes of comparison,' Sabie explained. He was wiry, with a genial manner. 'It is a formality, but necessary.'

'I appreciate the trouble you're taking,' said Alex.

The administrator began turning the pages of the two manuals in sync, pointing out the differences between DGES and DGIS regulations and practice. His voice was calm and measured, as if he had made this speech many times before.

'I could read this myself,' Alex interrupted, after a while.

'You could,' replied Sabie, with the ghost of a smile. 'But would you?'

'Perhaps not,' Alex conceded.

He took care not to let the other man notice, but his attention wandered. He had never read the External Security handbook so he didn't really see the benefit of Sabie pointing out to him all the things he would now have to make an effort to forget. The administrator was either taken in by Alex's acting or was so absorbed by his own performance that he didn't need an audience. Finally, the two books were closed and Sabie smiled.

'Thank you for your attention.'

Alex found he was beginning to enjoy this funny little man with the grey face and fussy manners.

'Thank you for yours,' he replied.

The administrator brought out an unusually heavy laptop, almost the size of a briefcase. It had a built-in scanner and extra-wide slots for external drives.

'Put your right thumb here, please.' The scanner took a print of Alex's right thumb. 'Now the left. One moment.' The administrator pushed a USB stick into a one of the slots. 'This drive will be biometrically coded to your thumbprints. Only you will be able to access the information therein.'

'What information?' Alex asked.

'The information you are designated to receive.' The administrator looked up. 'Did that sound abrupt? Please don't take offence.'

'You're a model of courtesy,' Alex assured him.

The administrator looked pleased. 'If the drive is inactive for more than fifteen seconds, your thumbprint will be required to regain access.'

'Understood.'

The USB stick slid out of the slot. Sabie handed it over. Alex put it in the breast pocket of his shirt.

Sabie's eyebrows rose. 'You don't want to examine it?'

'I choose to believe you know what you are doing.'

That faint smile again. 'You "choose to believe". Excellent.' Sabie stood up, gathered his manuals and laptop into one neat pile. 'Activate the drive any time you are in this building and the calendar and data will automatically update.'

'Thank you.'

Alex began to stand up, but Sabie stopped him.

'You have a second meeting,' he said. 'It is Professor Fayard who will decide, ultimately, if your transfer is approved. Officially, you have not yet joined our service. After today, you will remain on probation until the professor says you are not.'

'And if I fail to integrate?'

'Then, I imagine, we will never meet again,' said Sabie.

Plain-speaking, but not unfriendly, Alex thought.

'Shall I wait here?'

'*S'il vous plaît.*'

38

As he waited for his second meeting, Alex got up and went to contemplate the suburban landscape beyond the window. The room was quiet enough for the clock above the water cooler to become audible. Finally, he heard faint, dragging footsteps.

Fayard entered from a door Alex hadn't noticed, recessed in a set of bookshelves. He wore dark glasses and moved slowly, giving the impression that he had, until recently, been leaning heavily on his stick.

A woman wearing a driver's uniform watched him from the doorway. She took care not to meet Alex's eye.

Mariam.

He saw her wait until Fayard was seated in an uncomfortable swivel chair in a carpeted area near the windows, then closed the recessed door and left them alone. Alex sat down opposite, surprised to discover how closely she worked with his old mentor. Fayard placed the palm of his thin right hand over his heart.

'My dear Alexandre.'

'Professor Fayard,' said Alex, smiling.

'This is a pleasure.'

'For me, too. I have very fond memories of your lectures.'

'I'm glad to hear it. And yet you chose a different path from the one I recommended.' The old man didn't give him a chance to respond. 'But never mind that now.'

Fayard picked a remote control up from the coffee table and darkened the glass in the window. 'The light is oppressive. At least, I find it so.'

His hand trembled as he set the control down. Alex searched his face.

'How are you, Professor Fayard?'

'As you see.' The old man removed his dark glasses. His eyes were rimmed with red. 'Thank you for making this sideways move to work with us.'

Alex wondered if Fayard knew Poiret had blackmailed him into the transfer. ‘You mean career-wise?’

The old man shook his head. ‘That is for you to decide.’

Alex worked out what he meant. The old man had always enjoyed wordplay. ‘Ah, you were being literal.’

Fayard inclined his head. ‘Sideways across Paris, from the east to the west, from External to Internal, from one set of beliefs and priorities to another.’

‘From one ethos to another?’ Alex asked.

‘I like to think so. Is there a feeling still at External?’

‘A feeling?’

‘DGES headquarters was an internment camp in World War Two. Does it reek of collaboration still?’

‘Oh,’ said Alex. ‘That was a very long time ago.’

‘All the same, the reek of treachery,’ the old man murmured.

‘I’ve never heard it mentioned.’

‘Treachery casts a long shadow.’

There was a pause. Fayard’s hand was in his jacket pocket. Alex could see the fingers moving slightly, like someone running the beads of a rosary between thumb and forefinger.

‘Do you know how old I am?’ he asked, unexpectedly. ‘Most people in your position might have taken steps to find out.’

‘I’m not most people.’ Alex realised he sounded abrupt. ‘I’m sorry, Professor. I thought this was my induction before starting my new duties. Inactivity doesn’t suit me.’

‘Nor me. At least, it didn’t suit me in my youth. In my comparative youth. Twelve years ago, when first we met, you and I.’

Fayard looked at the floor. Alex realised he was regathering his energies. It made an unhappy contrast with his memories of the professor’s powerful lectures at the École Militaire. Finally, he spoke.

‘I’m glad you have requested to join our family but, if I was asked to describe your approach, Alexandre, I would not necessarily talk about your inability to tolerate inactivity. I’d put it another way. I’d say you do just enough.’

‘Is that right?’ Alex’s tone was polite.

'I don't mean that you fail to prepare. When I say just enough, I mean sufficient, but also selective. Do you understand?'

'I believe intelligence is the ability to make good choices.'

'I expect you do.'

Alex was beginning to worry. Fayard seemed so different from how he'd been the last time they'd met.

'Should I be concerned about the inquiry, Professor Fayard? The friendly fire—'

'Poor Amaury. A terrible accident. I remember him well. You always sat together, though he didn't have your insight.' Fayard shook his head. 'The inquiry will take its own course. This meeting is an opportunity for you to get to know me once more.' He gave Alex a critical look. 'You haven't made any serious attempts to research me, even something as straightforward as my age?'

'No, Professor.'

'Because you assume your own…' He searched for the perfect word. 'Your own intrinsic qualities will carry you through.' He smiled. 'Oh, yes, you have an exemplary record and you have achieved this by undertaking every mission with a thorough understanding of its parameters, but with a careless disregard for anything else.'

There was no point arguing.

'Yes,' said Alex.

'You are politically incompetent.' There was no rancour in his tone.

'My strategy,' said Alex, 'leaves my mind clear.'

'Free to be influenced by your subconscious impulses.'

'Something like that,' said Alex.

For almost a minute, neither of them spoke. Alex could hear Fayard's laboured breath. Then the old man said, 'I will attend the inquiry. I will be called upon, as your new commanding officer.'

He began coughing and couldn't seem to stop. Alex brought a glass of water from the cooler beneath the clock. Gradually the coughing eased, but he looked weaker now.

'Could you tell me why you requested a transfer?' Fayard asked, his voice rough.

'You have my reasons,' Alex said.

'I know what you wrote in your transfer request.' Fayard waved a hand. 'Shall I tell you what I think? I think you have lost your neutrality. You can no longer follow orders without *judging* your orders. Am I right?'

Alex didn't want to answer that. 'What else do you think?' he asked.

'You hope that Internal's mission will turn out to be nobler, perhaps more honest than External's.'

'Why would I believe that?'

'Fighting back is unimpeachable. Pre-emptive interference less so.'

'If I say you're right, will that be more evidence of my political incompetence?'

Fayard's red-lined eyes watched him closely. 'In other circumstances, yes, but not in conversation with me.'

'Does any of this make a difference?'

'Not officially. Not on paper.'

'And unofficially?'

Fayard glanced out the window. 'How can I predict? Time will tell.'

'Do I have orders, Professor?'

Alex heard the chirp of an electronic device – perhaps an alarm on a watch. Fayard fished in his jacket pocket and brought out a silver pill box.

'I think we will do very well,' said the old man. 'Come to the Forum tomorrow. Then, you may consider yourself part of the family.'

'Thank you, Professor.'

Fayard put a pill in his mouth. 'You are dismissed.'

Alex glanced back as he left. The old man looked small and weak, swallowing his medicine with the dregs of his water, sitting back in relief and closing his eyes.

39

The woman in the blond wig was finishing another speech. Luís was trying to concentrate but he was thinking about the moment he'd thrown the boy with the ponytail into the Seine. He'd been having nightmares about him. It was a necessary sacrifice, wasn't it?

Abruptly, the woman stopped declaiming. Luís pressed a button on the side of the camera to end the recording.

'*Isso é bom,*' he said.

All good.

The woman climbed down from the pulpit and swept past him, out of the doors of the church.

This building was much smaller than the Church of Saint Genevieve. Luís knew they blamed him for the fact that they'd had to search out new premises. But how had it been his fault? Anyone could drop a lens cap. Did that make him a bad person?

Never mind, he thought. None of that matters now.

The drugs in his system were ebbing. He supposed they would hold off giving him more until he finished editing the new video.

He played back the beginning of the speech. He didn't think it was as good as the last one, but that wasn't his business. All he had to do was crop the opening so that it began tight on the woman in the pulpit, losing the few seconds of focusing and composing the shot. He manoeuvred the timeline on the touch screen, finding the perfect frames.

'All good,' he said again.

This time someone did answer, the older of the two fake undertakers.

'Shall we go, then?'

'Take this,' said the younger one, holding out a white pill.

'I'm fine,' said Luís.

'Take it.' The younger undertaker's big fleshy hand closed over his jaw, pushing the tablet between his lips. Luís closed his eyes, feeling the faint effervescence on his tongue, then the familiar sense of chemical well-being.

Was it time, he wondered dreamily, to crop the last few frames of his life?

The woman in the blond wig made her way home by a complicated route, first locating a camera shadow where she changed her appearance. By the time she reached her building, the video had already been posted. She used an encrypted connection to watch herself on screen.

She was not particularly pleased with her performance. It seemed a little stilted, lacking the energy and passion that she could usually summon.

It was probably because she was distracted. At first, it had seemed like an advantage, that she should be so well connected. Now, not so much. Key players in the coming darkness were too close to her, perhaps even beginning to suspect her.

She believed she had done nothing to excite suspicion, acting in secret, receiving instructions only over a highly encrypted link. The boy Luís always posted the videos without any possibility of them being traced back to her.

She made a cup of coffee and took it out into the courtyard. Her eyes went up to the perfect window of blue sky, framed by the buildings, standing still for so long that the sun crept into the gap between two roofs and dazzled her.

She felt a rush of adrenaline. She hoped her own sacrifice could wait. She was desperate to be there at the end.

40

The next day, Alex was to visit his mother at the clinic. Before doing so, he used his comm-watch to try to access the 'Gerboise Bleue' document in Gloria's cloud storage but couldn't connect.

That's odd, he thought.

The clinic visit wasn't face-to-face, but used remote video room with two-way audio. Alex was pleased to find Gloria sitting up, alert, thinking about her work and her houseplants, looking forward to returning home. As it happened, she wanted to know if he had read the 'Gerboise Bleue' research and he explained that he hadn't been able to access the shared drive. Had she changed the password?

The question seemed to confuse her. 'Perhaps,' she said vaguely.

This worried Alex. His mother had an excellent mind and a sharp memory. But he didn't want her to know he was concerned.

'Well, I suppose it will have to wait until you are home, and we have your thumbprint,' he said. 'I'll read it then.'

Again, Gloria appeared perplexed. 'Why can't you use your thumbprint?'

Alex wasn't sure what to say. Only his mother could have altered the settings to exclude him.

He changed the subject, and they chatted for a little longer. By the time he was preparing to leave, she looked weaker, grey with exhaustion.

Alex's brow furrowed as he watched her struggle to adjust her pillows. 'Are you sure you feel better? You're not just saying that so they'll allow you home?'

'Don't be foolish,' she said, with a touch of her old hauteur. 'As if I would do such a thing.'

But you would, he thought to himself.

'You know,' she said, 'Nelinha's parents were in touch before I became ill, from Portugal, you know, and I forgot to tell you. They're worried.'

'Why are they worried?'

'They said she insisted on them going away, and now they're stuck. The travel corridor has closed.'

'She told me they love it in Portugal.'

'No, she had to insist.' Gloria shook her head. Alex remembered Nelinha being evasive. 'Perhaps you can help them.'

'I'll see what I can do,' he promised. 'Don't worry.'

He left and crossed the city once more, heading for the DGIS Forum that Fayard had mentioned. The wound on his hip irritated him. It was slow to heal.

He checked in to Internal Security headquarters with the biometrically encoded thumb drive, then followed signs to a large meeting room on the fourth floor. He counted about forty-five people in the audience and two at the front, getting ready with their digital slideshow and handwritten notes.

For Alex, connections between things were more important than the individual nuggets of information. Unfortunately, the first presentation seemed connected to more or less nothing, just detailed reports of completed investigations without wider significance – closed cases with no loose ends, no follow-ups. Alex began to regret attending.

As the second presentation got underway, he grew more alert. The delivery was punchy, covering several topics that interested him – disruption to communications from stolen network infrastructure, causing breakdowns in the distribution and supply of legitimate medicines, creating opportunities for unlicensed suppliers; organised crime and its role in the resale of stolen kit and in the supply of drugs.

Alex wondered if there might be a connection to his investigation in Kofinou but couldn't see one.

The conference broke for coffee and he realised the audience had grown by another couple of dozen. Perhaps it was normal for DGIS staff to dip in and out. What was more, he was struck by the atmosphere. No one seemed to be in charge. The pattern of the Forum seemed to emerge organically. It felt very different from the top-down structure at External Security.

After the break, the mood changed with a formal speech from the DGIS's head of government relations, a man with cropped grey hair and a very smooth manner. Alex paid little attention until the question of the competing philosophies of Internal and External Security came up.

'There is a growing recognition in government – and among the more informed sections of the public – that our record is superior, our goals more honest. It is important that we maintain a reputation for effective, well-directed interventions, outperforming our sister service, extending our influence both operatively and politically.'

A few people applauded.

'Informal meetings, such as this one,' continued the government-relations man, 'without senior officer supervision, have been shown to be the most potent and fruitful method for making imaginative and unexpected connections. It might even be said to be our speciality – out-performing the algorithms.'

There was more applause and a few cheers.

Here, too, thought Alex, there are people who've had enough of the hyperconnected world.

The government-relations speaker didn't elaborate on any particular cases or investigations. There were a few more paragraphs of corporate guff so Alex zoned out, waiting for the next substantive contribution. That, too, was disappointing – another closed case – so he got up from his seat, smiled vaguely to the people around him, slipped out into the lobby and down the stairs to the street.

A few electric vehicles were waiting behind a delivery truck that was having trouble reversing into the DGIS goods entrance. There was a Blank, huddled against the wall, sheltering in a tiny patch of shadow. The driver – a tall fat man in an incongruous dark suit – wanted her to move but didn't want to touch her.

Alex walked on, east towards the city centre, clinging to the shade of the buildings. It was very hot and the sunlight was harsh. Sensible people were indoors – if they had an indoors. The Blank was right to take shelter.

After a while, he came to a shanty of two dozen improvised dwellings on a stretch of road reclaimed from traffic – waste timber and plastic sheeting, a few repurposed tents. Someone was collecting water in a bucket from a 500-litre plastic cistern on a low metal platform. The shanty was in direct sunlight. The water from the cistern – for washing and cooking and drinking – would be warm.

Alex thought about the journeys he had recently made and the things he had seen. He hadn't travelled for his own pleasure, but he had been places, seen things, broken the monotony of the curfewed city. Not like the inhabitants of the shanty settlement that was little more than an improvised prison, albeit one without fences or guards. When would any of them travel more than a few kilometres from where they slept?

What would it be like, he wondered, to live in a plastic shelter between stone buildings where your neighbours – regular citizens with IDs and tax statements and travel vouchers and up-to-date vax status – could close their shutters, watch their entertainment screens and look forward to the cool of the night without fear?

The Blanks were the end of the chain of exploitation, paying the costs of environmental degradation, the burden of transgenic diseases, miserably persisting, with no hope of improvement or relief.

Alex walked on, ignoring the appeals to buy, to give. A short distance away, he stopped by a fenced park crowded with fruit trees – well-watered apples, pears and cherries, all protected by nets. Gazing through the bars, he realised that two magpies stood close by on the pavement, about five metres away, doing exactly the same thing.

I have been too passive, he thought, waiting for the darkness to come to me. I need to go out and find it.

At just that moment, someone else took an elevator to a basement storeroom to which only they had access. It was stacked with barrels and boxes marked '*comestibles*' – foodstuffs. There were several new containers, recently delivered from an unmarked delivery vehicle.

It took only a few minutes to connect them all to a small transmitter with a single function – the destruction of sixteen square blocks of innocent Parisian suburb, with an epicentre in the headquarters of Internal Security.

41

In Fayard's private quarters, Mariam was watching a new video, shot in a different church or chapel. It was more of the same – a combination of apocalyptic threats and promises of renewal. It looked like the same woman – the same build, the same wig – but the performance was less fiery, as if she'd had less time to prepare.

Mariam waited for the algorithmic intelligence to identify the location. With the authority of Fayard's terminal, the confirmation appeared almost at once – the Church of Saint Helen in northern Paris, on the far side of Montmartre, on a road called Rue du Ruisseau. It was another ugly, late twentieth-century building, more like a defensive bastion than a spiritual centre.

Mariam asked Camera Control to look back through its archive of images, cross-referencing with those from the Church of Saint Genevieve in the previous video. While she waited, she frowned, thinking of the lens cap she'd sent to forensics. What had happened to that?

A slideshow came through from Camera Control – a sequence of still photographs of the woman in the blond wig leaving the church and taking the narrow street alongside. At the end of the street was a park, Square Sainte-Hélène. The woman entered through a gate in the tall railings, then was lost beneath the trees.

Mariam requested all the images from the subsequent ten minutes from all around the small park, scrolling them across Fayard's screen. There were seven camera positions that gave her a kind of perimeter.

Unlike the continuous video feeds in the wealthy centre of the city, the images were only taken every three seconds and assembled into a kind of jerky stop-motion animation. Mariam saw no one who seemed exactly like the woman in the blond wig, though there were five people of similar build who might be her in different clothes. One was walking with a wheeled frame, another held hands with a small child, another carried a heavy suitcase, another was jogging, another used a long white cane. Any of those actions might be sufficient disguise.

Just before she gave up, the camera caught two undertakers accompanied by a young man in a suit. Their hearse was parked outside the gate so there were only three images between the moment they left the park and their disappearing inside their vehicle.

The grouping struck her as odd – the undertakers with a young man, his head angled to the right, as if watching someone leave, perhaps the figure with the long white cane?

Mariam tilted her head, as if she could change the angle of the two-dimensional image. Was this important? She wanted to talk to Alex, ask him what he thought. But, now he was moving to Internal, would their relationship be an even more serious breach of the rules?

She heard the door open in the bookshelves behind her, and Fayard walked in.

'The president's office wishes to discuss Prime Minster Mourad,' he told her. 'We must go.'

'At once, Professor.'

'Anything of interest?' he asked, glancing at the screen.

'I've identified the church. It's not far from the first one, in the eighteenth. But I wasn't able to track the woman. I'm not sure how important she is.' Mariam closed the searches and stood up. 'She was less impressive in this recording.'

'I thought so too,' he said, turning away.

42

That evening, back on his boat, Alex wasn't sure who he was working for any more. There was no word about the inquiry. Amaury remained in hospital, unreachable, recovering from his wounds.

No, not recovering, thought Alex. It wasn't the sort of wound you recover from.

He decided to interrogate the Camera Control archive, looking for information about the drowned body he had seen just before leaving for Toulouse. The search led him to something more recent. Something that, on its own, made no sense.

Because it was from the very centre of the city, the footage was continuous, though grainy, and Alex could watch the entire incident play out in real time. It had happened late the previous evening in a sudden downpour. A young man in a shiny suit had thrown himself from a bridge, down into the dark waters of the River Seine, shouting some unheard slogan into the night. Like some kind of grotesque performance.

The incident had been reported, and the body recovered and identified.

It was probably not important. There was likely no connection at all to the dead children whose bodies had been found in the same water.

All the same, despite the fact that he was suspended and had no authority, Alex set off to investigate.

By the time he got there, the sun had set, although there was still light in the sky. The city air was hot and close, suggestive of another downpour.

He was close to the northern edge of the city, at the gate of an odd-looking house, wedged in between bigger buildings, with two cramped floors and some wiry grass in front. As well as the unwelcome buzz of biting insects, there was the sickly perfume of two dozen lilies in two plastic buckets either side of the front step. The door stood open, like an invitation. He went inside.

He found more lilies in the hallway, in a vase on the floor. In a niche over the doorway into the front room, where there should have been a plaster saint, they lay on their sides, tied in a bunch. On the wall was an embroidered motto in Portuguese.

'*Deus abençoe esta casa.*'

God bless this house.

He could hear a kind of murmuring. He went through, composing his features in an attitude of sympathetic grief.

The front room was bare, aside from four dining chairs pushed back against the walls and a gaudy black coffin balanced on trestles. Above it, the shade on the ceiling lamp was draped with gauzy black fabric. The coffin was open and he could see the dead boy's face.

At the far end of the room, a woman in black was perched on the edge of a straight-backed chair, running a rosary through her fingers. Apart from her murmured prayer, there were no other sounds, just the murmur of the city sliding in through the open window – territorial cats, a hum of traffic, someone singing.

He sat down beside her and waited for her to notice he was there. Time took a breath as he listened.

'*Ó Deus, a Quem unicamente compete dar o remédio após a morte, fazei, Vos pedimos…*'

Each time she reached the end of the ritual prayer for the dead, she began again, reciting it like a round, under her breath. At the third cycle, she stopped.

'*Quem é você?*' she whispered.

Who are you?

'Don't be afraid,' he told her in Portuguese.

'*Por quê você está aqui?*'

Why are you here?

'I knew your son.'

It was a lie. He didn't enjoy deceiving her, but he would get on quicker if he could persuade her to trust him.

'You knew Luís,' she said, like a waiter repeating an order, so as not to forget. Then, as if trying to convince herself: 'He wasn't a bad boy.'

He reached out a consoling hand. 'Are you alone, keeping vigil?'

She nodded and her eyes filled with tears.

'Will anyone else come?'

'Who would come?' she asked, helplessly. 'Who else is there?'

A properly conducted vigil should last all night, through until dawn. The woman was already exhausted.

'It's a beautiful casket,' she said.

Alex looked at the showy black finish and the vulgar fittings and found nothing to say in reply.

'What is your name?' she asked.

He thought quickly. 'Call me Joao.' He paused, and then said, 'You must be exhausted. I will sit with him. Why don't you go upstairs and rest? Perhaps it will be cooler.'

'You speak very good Portuguese. Where are you from?'

'From here. Go,' he encouraged, softening his voice. 'Luís won't be alone.'

She was too tired to argue. The woman hooked her rosary through one of the coffin handles, crossed herself and left the room.

Alex sat quietly, listening for her tread on the stair and then her footfalls directly above his head. There were so many parts of the story that didn't seem to fit together. Lilies were expensive. She didn't look like someone who could afford cut flowers. Certainly not so many of them. And what about the gaudy, expensive coffin?

Alex went to the open window. The silence had become complete, she must be asleep. He closed the curtains and twitched the scrap of black cloth from the pendant light, waiting a few moments for his eyes to adjust to the brightness.

Luís had a square, handsome face with mid-brown hair, combed wet across his forehead. The closed eyes were at rest, the mouth composed, the jawline firm. He was dressed in a shiny grey suit and a lemon-yellow shirt with ruffles down the front, like a gigolo in an old-fashioned film. He looked about nineteen.

Alex activated lidar on his comm-watch, bouncing an infrared signal round the room to take a 3-D scan, and began his search.

The suit and the lining of the coffin were damp and there was a trace of rigor in the neck. He examined the coffin lining, finding only soggy synthetic padding. He searched the pockets of the trousers, then ran his hands over the dead meat of the legs and arms and either side of the torso. He slid his hands under the boy's back and felt his skeleton through the flaccid flesh. He tried the wet pockets of the jacket – nothing. There was a speck of blood on the ruffled shirtfront. He undid two buttons and discovered a small incision in the chest.

That was all.

Would it help to remove the body completely? Or was this just a corpse in a box in a house of mourning? Perhaps Luís wasn't even connected to anything important, simply collateral damage. Someone unlucky enough to stand in the way of forces he couldn't hope to control.

But then, there was the way the way the body had been plucked so quickly from the water, and the shiny black coffin, so out of sync with the miserable little house on the far side of Montmartre.

And the lilies, the absurd overabundance of lilies.

Alex heard a creak of floorboards. Ten minutes had been enough for Luís's mother to realise she didn't want to lie alone in an upstairs room while a stranger kept vigil over the corpse of her dead son.

Quickly, he killed the lidar scan and straightened the wrinkles in the shiny grey suit. He just had time to re-drape the scrap of black cloth over the pendant lamp and take the boy's left hand in his as she appeared in the doorway. He bowed his head, silently moving his lips.

'You pray for Luís?' Her voice trembled.

'I do.'

She stood across from him, taking her dead son's other hand in hers. 'Shall we pray together?' she asked.

She recited the *Pater Noster*, the *Our Father*, in Latin, but with a Portuguese inflection, in the singsong voice people use for something learned by rote. Alex joined in, enjoying the cadence of the language. As they spoke the

'Amen', the black fabric slipped from the shade and landed softly on the dead man's chest. Alex hadn't had time to secure it properly.

'I should have used a pin,' the woman sighed, and went off in search of one, her soft footsteps the only sound.

The hand she had released lay across her son's chest. Alex realised he had missed something. The backs of the fingers were tattooed. He hadn't seen before because the dead hands had been curled into fists. He lifted the hand closer to the light, expecting something commonplace – perhaps '*amor*' and '*ódio*', Portuguese for 'love' and 'hate'. But that wasn't it at all. There were five letters, clumsily inscribed, one for each finger and thumb: U D S M C. He wished he had time to photograph them, but the mother was back in the doorway once more, holding a safety pin in her fingers.

Alex helped her attach the black cloth more securely. Then she unhooked her rosary from the coffin handle and looked at Alex for the first time with an air of challenge.

'Are you here because you are guilty? Be honest with me. Are you here to atone?'

'No.' His voice was firm.

'Why else would you come? I've never seen you before. Never.'

'I told you. I was his friend.' The lie came more easily as he repeated it.

'I suppose I must believe you,' she said, with a kind of despair.

'I saw him pulled from the water. I recognised him.'

That, at least, was partly true.

'If you saw him pulled from the water, then you were there. You know what happened. You don't know why he…'

Again, she couldn't bring herself to say the fatal word.

'Why he died,' said Alex.

She corrected him without raising her eyes. 'Why he was killed.'

Alex said nothing, but she was wrong. Her son had thrown himself into the river. No one else had been near.

He took his leave. On his way back to the centre of the city, he dictated a voice message for Fayard – what he had seen on camera, what he had found in Montmartre. The reply was almost immediate.

Meet me where it happened.

He increased his pace.

43

Two hours later, the impatient calendar in Alex's head clicked round to a new day. He was standing on a bridge overlooking the Seine, beneath the statue of Genevieve, patron saint of Paris. He'd walked all the way from the house of mourning, climbing from the northern suburbs up to Sacré Coeur, then down through increasingly smart right-bank neighbourhoods to the river and its islands, the ancient heart of the city.

Fayard's car pulled quietly alongside. The driver emerged, a woman with a symmetrical face and an athletic build.

Mariam, again.

She helped a frail figure climb awkwardly out of the rear seat, then stood back.

'Good evening, Alexandre.' The old man looked up at the statue of Saint Genevieve. 'What a dreadful piece of work. Don't you think so?'

Alex glanced up – it was twenty-five metres tall and towered over them. He had no strong feelings about it.

'You responded very quickly,' he said.

'I trust your instincts. Tell me, why is it important?'

Yes, thought Alex. That's the most important question.

'I was reviewing the surveillance archives. I'd seen a body collection team here a few days earlier, the morning I left for Toulouse. A child was drowned – an almost theatrical murder, not an accident.'

A discreet alarm sounded. Fayard checked his comm-watch, sighed and took out his silver pill box. Mariam brought him a glass of water from a dispenser in the car. He gestured to the statue.

'It must have been reassuring to have a patron saint, don't you think? Your poor corpse could have done with one. But the odds are never fully in one's favour. Who was it who said that?'

'Damon Runyon,' said Alex. 'All of life is six-to-five against.'

'That's right.' Fayard swallowed his pill.

'Sounds clever, means nothing,' said Alex.

'For every five times you win, you lose six. Eventually your stake dwindles to nothing.' Fayard coughed. Mariam made a movement to help, but he waved her away, still gazing up at the statue. 'Genevieve lived in the period after the fall of the Roman Empire, when Visigoths, Ostrogoths and Huns were picking over the spoils of imperial decadence. She starved herself into having visions of angels and saints. She gave the people of Paris the courage to endure. Each July, she would pray for rain to fatten the harvest. Each September she would pray for sunshine so the harvest could safely be brought in.' He smiled. 'Have you ever been in the Luxembourg Gardens?'

Alex was starting to wonder what those little pills could be, but all he said was, 'Access is restricted to people with business in the Senate.'

'In the old days anyone could swan in and pull up a green metal chair, prop their heels on the edge of the fountain and waste an afternoon watching other people waste their afternoons, too.' Fayard turned to Mariam. 'There's a lovely classical sculpture of Genevieve in the Luxembourg Gardens, my dear, but she is depicted without her attribute. Do you know what an attribute is?'

'An object associated with a saint,' said Mariam, 'in her hagiography.'

Fayard gave her an approving look. 'In Genevieve's case, a candle. When she rose in the night to pray, to torment her and test her faith and courage, the Devil would sneak in and blow her candle out.'

He coughed again.

'Are you seriously ill, Professor?' Alex asked, bluntly.

'I thought I was quite recovered. Now, I am unwell once more, but still active, as you see.' Fayard straightened. 'Genevieve is positioned here because fifth-century threats came from upriver, from the east, where Attila's marauders were in the field.' He turned to Mariam. 'Come closer, my dear. Lean out and look up.'

Alex watched her put her hands on the parapet, angling her face up towards the statue, feeling her presence acutely, just a pace or two away.

'As we stand here on this bridge after midnight,' the old man continued, 'Genevieve faces away from us. She protects a small child. Perhaps you can just see her hands are on his shoulders? She will ensure he comes to no harm.'

Alex felt an unexpected shimmer of connection. Something Fayard was saying was familiar, but he couldn't place it. He wanted to be alone to think, but the old man had not yet finished.

'Wait for me in the car, my dear,' Fayard told Mariam.

She went back to the vehicle, got inside and shut the door. Alex heard the air con humming to life. The old man stood with his eyes closed. Alex thought about Saint Genevieve, how she had done nothing to protect Luís who drowned beneath her stone feet – nor all the other children. He looked down into the black water. There ought to be some kind of echo, some awareness of the violence that had happened here.

'Tell me more, Alexandre,' Fayard's voice broke in. 'Your voice message was intriguing but perhaps incomplete?'

'I wasn't looking for anything in particular, but I began to sense that there was something waiting to be found.'

'And you followed where it was leading. How?' Fayard watched him with interest.

Alex looked down into the water. 'It might have been a coincidence.'

Fayard shook his head. 'There is no such thing as coincidence.'

The half-hour siren sounded and a police officer came by on a bicycle, calling out: 'Twelve-thirty. I hope you don't have far to go.'

'Not far,' Alex called back.

The officer cycled away, calling the same message to a few pedestrians on the far bank.

When he'd gone, Alex pointed to a device mounted on an ornate art-nouveau streetlamp. 'I saw the recording from that camera. There was a cloudburst.'

'There was no audio, but you thought he was chanting some kind of slogan? In your message, you said "one weak voice against the night".'

'His mouth moved.'

'Might there be something in the shapes his mouth made?' suggested Fayard. 'Could he be lip-read, from the camera footage?'

'I ran the DGIS software,' Alex said. 'The angle wasn't good enough, the image too poor. It wasn't even clear if it was Portuguese or French.'

'Go on.'

Alex pointed at a spot nearby. 'He climbed up onto the parapet and put his hands to his face.'

'A natural gesture,' Fayard suggested, 'or something else? An expression of shock or surprise?'

'I'm not sure. He was only just in shot.'

'Could he have been raising his hands in prayer or crossing himself?' Fayard asked. 'Or putting something in his mouth? Poison, perhaps?'

That was an interesting suggestion. 'It's possible he put something in his mouth,' Alex said. 'In any case, he turned and fell.'

'He fell or he threw himself?'

Alex pictured the scene, replaying it in his mind. 'He let himself fall, hitting the water on the flat of his back.'

'Yes, how did you put it? "Inert, like a sack of wet sand." So very tactile.' Fayard glanced at him. 'How does it work, Alexandre? How does it seem to you that you are there?'

'It's a state of mind,' said Alex quietly. 'My imagination involves me, somehow, until I feel… Until I seem to know what has happened, what is happening, what will happen.'

'There must be a gap between imagining and knowing,' Fayard said.

Alex shrugged. 'Not for me.'

Fayard smiled. 'Think what we might achieve together, if only we had time,' he said with emphasis. 'What happened next?'

Alex gestured. 'There are cameras all along the riverbank. The system is designed to track movement. The AI passed him on from camera to camera on the current, face up in the water.'

'Already dead?'

'In my judgement, yes.'

'The poison pill he swallowed, if there was a pill?'

'Perhaps.'

'And then?'

'I saw him picked up by a river patrol, beneath the buttresses of Notre-Dame. They hooked him with a gaff, pulled him alongside and heaved him on board. Eventually he flopped onto the deck like a landed fish and they scanned his ID. I used the clearance Sabie gave me to connect to the central DGIS database and thirty seconds later I had the name and address. And…' Alex stopped. What did he want to say? 'It's a feeling I have learned to trust.'

'You needed to follow up.'

'I expected a grieving family, but also evidence of some kind, some indication that the dead man was important, worth my time.' Alex activated the almost-complete 3-D scan of the room and coffin from his comm-watch. It hovered above his wrist. 'There was the mother, grief on the way to acceptance, but also the irreconcilable elements – the miserable dwelling, the expensive vulgar coffin, the lilies.'

'And the river patrol?' Fayard prompted.

Alex nodded. 'Almost as if they were waiting for him, as if they were stationed there, ready to pull him from the water.'

'What will you do next?'

Alex killed the 3-D holo. 'I can't talk to the river police. I have no authority while the Cyrenia panel is pending.'

As he spoke, someone hurtled past them on the bridge. The suddenness of the movement was shocking. Instinctively, Alex stepped out so that he was between the old man and the pounding footsteps, but it was just a jogger, racing to get home before the one o'clock curfew. He checked the time.

'I have to go. Your government car won't be stopped but I will be.'

But Fayard paid no attention. 'There is no such thing as coincidence,' he repeated thoughtfully. 'Humanity would get along much better if everyone understood that and acted accordingly. What did Heraclitus say?'

'Although reason is common to all,' Alex quoted, 'most people live as if they have a private understanding of their own.'

'The philosopher of change. The Greeks knew a thing or two about human behaviour.' Fayard gave him a smile. 'What a bonus that you had a classical education. Doubtless your mother's doing. Now, take my arm. This day has gone on long enough.'

Alex opened the door and helped him into the back seat. The waft of cool air from inside was delicious.

'I agree there is something in this,' Fayard told him decisively. 'Go back. Question the mother further and retrieve the body. I want to bring the post-mortem into the family.'

'Of course,' said Alex. 'First thing in the morning.'

But morning would be too late.

44

Alex jogged back home, running along the right bank of the river, letting his thoughts wander. He greeted the guard in the hut above the lock gates that separated the canal basin from the Seine, and made his way down the worn stone steps to the water, reaching the houseboat just as curfew began.

Inside, he opened the door to his fridge and pulled the lid off a green drink, wondering if the special composition really did him any good. As he drank, he unbuttoned his damp shirt. He was still thinking about one of the old man's apparently inconsequential remarks.

'What a bonus that you had a classical education. Doubtless your mother's doing.'

How well, exactly, did Fayard know Gloria Lamarque?

He sat down at his holo. 'Wake.'

The display came to life, showing the last few apps he'd used. The camera feed from Notre-Dame was still active. He watched it for a few seconds, contemplating the untroubled flow of river water between the cobbled embankments.

A notification appeared. He opened the message and saw that the first session of the Cyrene inquiry had been convened for that afternoon.

He felt conflicting emotions – glad that things were moving, guilt at what had happened, hope that he could somehow put things right.

'Search,' said Alex. 'Open quotes, U D S M C, close quotes.'

He took a sip of his drink. In a few milliseconds, the search produced a list of results. A Seventh-Day Adventist church. A union of amateur music clubs. A professional Minecrafter. Something to do with rarefied gas dynamics: 'Unstructured DSMC'. He made a mental note to find out what that meant.

He'd expected to turn up a stack of gang references. Surely that was the most likely explanation for the finger tattoos? He tried the search again, specifying Portuguese results.

Nothing of interest.

He put down his bottle and sat back, turning things over in his mind. Was he certain that Luís had been shouting a slogan on the bridge? A political affiliation would help to identify his importance. And was the river patrol there for a reason, waiting to retrieve his body?

Yes, no, maybe.

He set about cross-referencing as many details as he possessed – name, address, gender, age, ethnicity, community, religion, distinguishing marks, educational record, licences to drive or carry weapons, medical status, drug use and so on. He used multiple platforms, his DGIS thumb drive connecting him to almost every government database. For security reasons, public information was kept in separate silos. Sabie had told him he had been building an unrivalled master database of the entire French population by crawling and downloading data from multiple state agencies.

'Is that legal?' Alex had asked.

'It is justifiable,' Sabie had replied, without elaborating.

Alex saved the data to his biometric drive. It was nearly two in the morning, and he had to be up at dawn to return to the house of mourning in Montmartre.

'Sleep.' The screen went black. 'Cabin dark.'

The lights dimmed. Alex undressed, leaving his clothes where they fell, went through to the sleeping cabin and lay down. A combination of the hull stabilisers, the air purifiers and the temperature controllers gave him a faint backdrop of white noise. On the edge of deep sleep, he dreamed.

The light was oblique and low in the sky, a kind of cold sun. The buildings were grey stone, unwelcoming, inhuman, a grand boulevard lined with unhappy trees. There were no people. Despite the emptiness and the cold twilight, he had an impression of suffocation, of being choked by something he could not see.

Then, abruptly, he was indoors in a huge room – a ballroom in a nineteenth-century palace, gilt and plaster falling from the stonework of the walls, paint peeling from the decorated ceiling. At the far end, a woman was trapped in a cage, smoke and flames rising around her, but he was unable to move, stuck in some viscous substance that would not let him save her.

He almost woke, turning over under the lightweight duvet, then dipped back into unreality.

The cage and the flames were gone, the disintegrating ballroom merged with the horizon to become a frozen sea. He walked out onto the ice, metal crampons on his heavy boots biting into the surface, small cracks scurrying around him, tinkling and whispering. Then he fell, as if the ice had disappeared and the water was air, into cold. And everything closed over his head and he would remain there for ever in the frigid darkness, friendless and frozen.

Alex sat up with a start, shocked out of the nightmare. There was someone on the hull.

He waited, wondering if it might be some nocturnal creature, but the movement rocked the boat slightly on its mooring, more like the weight of a person.

The canal basin was a good six metres below the level of the street and relatively dark. It wasn't unknown for burglars to think the boats tethered to the quayside between the Bastille and the Seine might be an easy target. But if this was a burglar it was a particularly incompetent one, moving clumsily, unable to disguise their presence.

'Lights, ten percent,' Alex said softly.

The sleeping cabin became discreetly lit. The effect was gentle, and wouldn't be seen through the closed shutters.

He stepped through into the main room. The boat's AI tracked his movement and brought up the same intensity of light in the cabin.

Alex spoke quietly to his holo. 'Wake.'

In the few moments it took to boot up, he pressed the edge of the dressing on his hip. It was trying to curl away from his skin. He heard another scuffle on the hull as the screen came awake.

'Exterior cameras.'

The screen split into six frames, stacked two-by-three.

'Enlarge four.'

The frame in the bottom left expanded.

The figure was crouched, facing away from the lens, looking back towards the quay, as if that was the direction from which danger would come. They moved slightly and a flare of light hit the camera lens, momentarily bleaching out the image.

Alex's left hand hovered over the defence panel. He could activate an electric current sufficient to throw someone off the hull into the water, as long as they were in contact with an appropriate portion of the deck, holding a rail, for example, or with a hand on the hatch.

The flare of light faded and the image recomposed. He thought it was a beam of light reflected from a streetlamp. Reflected by what? The dial of a watch? A weapon?

'Activate defence.'

The panel beneath his left hand came to life.

Then the figure turned toward the camera, reached out and tapped on the lens with a fingernail.

Alex smiled.

'Deactivate defence.'

'He seems to believe I can see the future,' said Alex.

Mariam pulled the dark balaclava from her head. 'Can you?'

'Enough to know we should be worried.' He watched her smooth her dark hair. 'You shouldn't take so many risks, you know.'

She smiled. 'What risks?'

'You might be arrested for breaking curfew.'

'I might become ill tomorrow. I might die tomorrow. I'd rather know that I'm alive today.' She sat on the floor, her back to the low cupboards. 'So, it's all agreed?'

'The transfer to Internal? I assume Poiret has spoken to Fayard.' Alex frowned. 'I think he might have been in touch with Gloria, too.'

Why was that important?

'But there's something wrong?' said Mariam. 'You can sense it?'

'Something I can't see clearly because, whatever it is, it hasn't yet begun.' He stopped, wondering why his intuition was so clouded. Then he sighed. 'I don't want to do any of this any more – manipulation, doing what my country needs to be done, regardless of law or justice. I thought I could walk away, but I can't, because if I don't do what Poiret asks my mother won't get the best possible treatment and may even be prosecuted for non-notification of illness.'

'You really think she'd go that far?' Mariam sounded sceptical.

'Without question,' Alex said. 'She pushed me into writing a transfer request to Internal. And Internal is run by Fayard, who is my old professor, who knows an awful lot about me and about my mother too, apparently. Personal things that shouldn't be at the top of the file they keep on every operative.'

He thought again of his dream – friendless and frozen.

'Come back to what you sense,' suggested Mariam. 'You know it's there, but it's not yet begun. Is that it?'

'The different elements aren't yet connected. Whatever it is, it's happening in more than one place.'

Saying it out loud made it seem more real, but Mariam looked puzzled.

'You mean several sequences of events are in train, but they aren't yet… what exactly?'

'They don't yet mean the same thing,' he explained. 'Similar events being planned in many places, but the time has not yet come.'

'I understand that,' said Mariam.

He waited, giving them both time to think.

'You know him better than I do,' said Alex, switching back to Fayard. 'Should I trust him?'

'Yes.' Her answer came without hesitation.

'Because?'

'Because you have no one else,' she told him. 'Poiret is completely without principles. She would send your sick mother to jail.'

'Fayard calls the DGIS a family.'

She gave a low laugh. 'I believe he means it.'

All the same, Alex couldn't shake the feeling that he was being manipulated – not by Mariam, not necessarily by Fayard, and not solely by Poiret. But by someone. Some collection of forces that knew more than he did. That was stronger than he was.

He opened the fridge. Mariam pulled off her dark sweater, revealing much lighter clothes beneath.

'I'm so sorry about Gloria,' she said. 'I hoped she'd be better by now.'

He passed her a chilled glass, watching her take it, seeing the sympathy in her eyes, but she didn't say anything else. What was the point? Illness was like an earthquake – it wasn't a battle you could decide to win. You just had to hope for the best.

She sipped the drink and gave a smile. 'Always the vodka. In this case…' She hesitated. 'With cranberry and lime?'

He nodded. 'Right again.'

She wiped her mouth with the back of her hand. 'Tell me more about this evening, before we met you on the bridge.'

He gave her the whole story – the young man, Luís, throwing himself into the Seine, fished from the water, the odd little house on the far side of Montmartre. And the fact that the first session of the inquiry would convene later that day at two o'clock. She told him about the Tabula Rasa speaker in the church, the two videos the old man had shared with her.

'Could all that be connected as well, do you think?'

'I don't know,' he said. 'I'd like to work the case but right now I'm nobody.'

'You aren't nobody.'

'I'm suspended,' he reminded her. 'That isn't what they call it, but it's true.'

'You'll soon be Internal. You're just inactive pending the panel.'

'Which may go against me.'

'I don't think it will.' Her voice was confident.

'Because?'

'Fayard will support you. And, if there's something she wants from you, Poiret will too.'

'Then I'll owe her even more,' he said, and changed the subject. 'You could use a special knock. That way you wouldn't run the risk of me activating the electric defences and throwing you off into the canal.'

Mariam didn't smile. 'There was a security officer up on the boulevard.'

'Doing what?'

'I couldn't see. I just heard a voice. Making a report, maybe.'

'Poiret told me I was under surveillance "to a necessary extent",' Alex said. 'Did they see you?'

'I don't think so.'

'Or they saw you and had orders not to intercept?'

She shrugged. 'Perhaps.'

'Why do you like taking risks?'

'Would you prefer I didn't?'

There was a slight sheen of sweat on her forehead and shoulders. With two human bodies on board, the climate control would have to work a little harder. He stood up to adjust the setting on the panel on the wall.

'You should fix that dressing,' she told him, glancing at his hip.

'I know.'

'Where's your medikit?'

'In the morning,' he said. Then he asked her: 'You'll be here in the morning?'

She peeled off the light-coloured top.

'I will.'

45

In the narrow house of mourning in Montmartre, Luísa Beira – Luís's mother – didn't quite keep vigil until dawn. A hearse arrived just before the sun.

The two fake undertakers came inside without waiting for an invitation. They spoke to her and she did her best to answer in broken French, to ask them questions, but she didn't understand their replies. She sat on one of the straight-backed chairs and watched them close the casket, hiding her son's face for ever from her eyes and those of the world and from his incomprehensible fate.

For a moment she was still, then suddenly everything seemed wrong and she decided she had to stop them.

'*Pare.*'

Stop.

They shook their heads and carried the casket out of the house.

She followed, trying to explain that it was not yet dawn, that this wasn't right. They paid no attention and she stood appalled on the front step, between the two plastic buckets of lilies, watching them load her son into the rear compartment of the hearse, sliding the coffin across the built-in rollers. The short thin tired one seemed to take pity, and said something sympathetic – she could tell from the intonation and the expression on his face. She shook her head and tried to smile and failed.

'*Pare,*' she said again.

She was sick of the flowers she had never asked for and the awful shiny suit Luís had never owned, that someone she had never met had dressed him in. She was sick of the loneliness and the mystery. She understood nothing about why her son had been taken from her and was abruptly furious. She snatched a bunch of lilies out of their plastic bucket.

'*Quem mandou todas essas flores?*'

She genuinely wanted to know who had sent all these flowers. She bent down to the second bucket, lifting out another dozen sodden stems. The discoloured water ran down her arms and into her sleeves.

'There are more inside,' she continued in Portuguese. 'I don't know who sent them.'

The undertakers mimed incomprehension, turned away.

She stumbled down the path, following them. To an outsider, she knew, she must look deranged. What did she even want? For them to take the flowers as a kind of offering, a kind of penance?

The tall fat youthful one waved a finger at her and she thought he was telling her to go back inside, that she was breaking curfew. She pushed the lilies at him. He shook his head and tapped the watch on his wrist. She shook her head, thinking about how she hadn't heard the siren, but she didn't care. She dropped the lilies on the ground and took hold of the lapels of his smart black jacket in her wet hands, asking where they were taking him.

'*Aonde está levando ele?*'

He pushed her away and she stumbled back, tripping on the edge of the path, landing on her backside in the wiry grass. She knew he was swearing at her, recognising two unkind words, words she had heard before. She pulled herself upright on the gatepost.

'*Por favor, aonde está levando ele?*'

The short thin tired one caught at his colleague's sleeve. 'She has no idea what's happening, what we're talking about. Let it go.'

'She mussed my jacket.'

The woman closed her eyes and began to weep. The tall fat one kicked at the flowers around his feet.

'What was she saying, anyway?'

'How should I know? Asking who we are, where we're taking him. Wouldn't you want to know?'

The younger undertaker waved a fat hand under the rim of the rear hatch. It silently descended. 'I'd be wondering how I had made such a loser of my son.'

'Perhaps that's exactly what she's thinking,' the older man said.

The younger man got into the driver's seat. The older man sighed. He looked at the bereaved woman. She had stopped crying and seemed to be in shock. He took out his wallet and held out a food voucher, wanting to do something for her, however insignificant. The woman's gaze remained blank.

'Hey!' he shouted.

She looked up slowly, a question in her eyes. He twitched the voucher in his fingers.

'Buy yourself a bottle of wine. Buy yourself a steak.'

He mimed eating. She didn't move.

It was hopeless. She seemed to have no idea what he was trying to say. He had no idea either.

Eventually, she let go of the gatepost and took a step towards him, holding out an uncertain hand. He leaned in, making an effort to smile with his eyes above his mask.

She spat in his face.

He drew back his fist and punched her square in the jaw. She staggered away, clasping her hands across her face. He tore off his mask and threw it on the ground. It lay with the voucher among the sodden lilies.

'What did I do to you?' he demanded. 'What's wrong with you?' He had a dim awareness that he might have managed things better, but now it was over. 'This is just a job,' he told her.

She lowered her hands. The tips of her fingers were bloody.

He sighed and climbed into the hearse. 'Let's go.'

The younger man gave him a sideways look. 'What happened?'

'It doesn't matter.'

The tall fat youthful one engaged drive and the electric hearse pulled away.

The short thin tired one opened the glove compartment and took out a medikit. He found a sachet of antiviral wipes and, slowly and methodically, cleaned his eyes and nose and mouth.

The journey was brief because the roads were clear. The two fake undertakers saw the sun come up in glimpses between six-storey residential buildings. It would be another scorching day.

They drove for fifteen minutes due north, across the orbital motorway and out into the social housing estates of the northern suburbs. They crossed the vast valley of the mainline railway tracks, then the tower blocks gave way to another traditional neighbourhood. At a four-way junction they saw two cafés, their doors open, waiters unwinding security cables from tables and chairs left outside overnight, getting ready for business.

The older man took a new mask from a cardboard dispenser between the front seats, and hooked it over his ears as they branched right, following a dark green canal to a vast industrial lot.

'Left-hand lane,' he said.

'I know.'

They showed their fake credentials at an automated checkpoint. It was early, so there were only a few trucks queueing to unload. They joined a line beneath a banner marked 'organics'. They waited.

'How long will this take?'

'They'll bump us up,' said the older man confidently.

A frowning attendant in a hi-vis vest came over carrying an ID scanner. She completed formalities on a food-waste lorry spattered with dried garbage, glanced up, recognised them for what they were and beckoned them forward.

'I told you,' said the older man. 'Human waste won't wait.'

The younger man twitched the hearse out of the line and crawled forward to a broad turning circle twenty metres from the building's huge maw – a dark mouth with a filthy conveyor belt as its tongue, constantly running, dragging waste into the incinerator. The frowning attendant came to the driver's side window.

'Open it up.'

The younger man popped the rear hatch and watched her in the rear-view mirror as she leaned in and lifted the coffin lid.

'What a shirt,' she called out.

He watched her hold her ID scanner against the corpse's chest, searching for a signal. He saw her frown deepen.

'What's the matter?' he asked her.

The older man turned round stiffly in his seat. 'What's she doing?'

'There's only something wrong, isn't there,' said his colleague. 'Because we removed his chip.' He leaned out and called out to the incinerator attendant. 'It doesn't matter. He's no one.'

She said something in reply, but not loud enough to be heard over the rumble of an idling lorry. The driver had revved his powerful engine, indicating impatience.

The older man got out of the hearse with his hand-held and came round to the rear.

'Is there a problem?'

'Do you have his ID?' the frowning woman asked.

'We removed his chip for forensics, but I can show you who he is.' He tapped through a couple of screens – found nothing. 'That's weird.'

'What's weird?' she asked.

He refreshed the database, trying to find the official record of the identification of the corpse. Nothing.

'Come and look at this,' he called to his colleague. The younger one got out and came round. 'He's been deleted.'

'Without identification,' said the attendant, 'I can't accept this corpse.'

The three of them looked warily at one another.

'Nothing good can come of this,' said the older man.

'Who are you two?' the attendant asked.

'It's written on the vehicle,' said the younger man.

He pointed to the branding on the side window of the hearse. Discreet gold lettering eight centimetres tall. A name. A city. A year of incorporation.

The older man took out his wallet and showed her a rectangle of plastic with an embedded chip, a business card for the fake undertaking company.

'Scan it,' he told her.

The attendant did so. The chip held a sum of money equivalent to a week's wages.

'So?' she asked. 'What's the story?'

'The story,' said the younger one, 'is you don't ask for the story.'

The attendant chewed her lip. 'Is this going to come back to bite me?'

The impatient trucker sounded his horn. She waved back at him, asking for patience.

'He used to be somebody but now he's a Blank,' said the older man.

The attendant looked from one to the other, undecided. Finally, she pocketed the card.

'All right, turn it round.'

The fake undertakers got back in and crunched a three-point turn over the uneven ground. They reversed up to the dark maw, the conveyor belt leading to the heart of the incinerator.

The woman spoke through the driver's window. 'None of this ever happened.'

'Obviously,' the younger man replied.

She went round the back and, with unexpected strength, pulled the coffin out across the built-in rollers and onto the moving belt. She stood back as it trundled away, swallowed up by the vast industrial shed with its towering chimney.

As soon as the rear doors were shut, the hearse pulled away and it was done. Inside the incinerator, Luís's body was already becoming heat and light and smoke and memories.

Only the memories would be dangerous.

46

Alex woke early, unaware that it was not early enough.

He and Mariam left separately. She walked home to change. He took an autodrive taxi to Montmartre. But he arrived to find Luís's body gone and his mother dead, lying on a blood-soaked mattress in the little bedroom above the parlour.

He went across the road to the bakery and showed his credentials to a woman with strong masculine features, standing behind a Perspex hygiene shield. He asked her how well she knew the mother and son who lived in the little house opposite. She wiped her hands on her floury apron, shaking her head sorrowfully, speaking in a thick accent.

'She come to me after morning siren. I sorry I not do vigil. In life, not everything is possible.'

Alex looked round the sparse bakery. 'You work alone?'

'Before sun, even in summer, heat from ovens.' She mimed wiping her brow. He wondered where she was from. The accent was Romany, he thought. 'If I awake, I working. If I not working, I sleep. That is business alone.' She looked him up and down. 'You do not know this. This not your life.'

'So, you didn't join her vigil. Did you go across this morning?'

'No, she come to me. She come to me with voucher, all wet and…' She mimed scrunching something up. 'I tell her: "Clean it, please." She wipe it on sleeve. I clean it better later.' The boulangère waved an arm. 'She buy this.'

To the left of the counter was a rack with two dozen bottles of wine. Alex wondered if alcohol sales meant more to the business than bread and pastries. It was harder to obtain an alcohol licence than it was to sell food with alcohol on the side.

'She bought a bottle of wine?'

'No, three bottles for dirty voucher and no change.' She gestured to a sign by the till. 'No change given.'

'And then she went home?'

'I guess.'

'Then you went back to your ovens and you saw no one.'

'I see everything. I have cameras.' She pointed to a closed-circuit video camera over the counter and another in the top corner of her street window. 'I watch world go by.'

Alex studied the angle of the camera. It would catch anyone going into the house opposite. 'I'll send someone to take a copy of your recordings.'

'No recordings. Live camera relay,' she said.

'Never mind,' Alex sighed. 'Tell me. Who did you see?'

'I do not know them.'

'Them?'

'Two men, young one tall and fat, old one and short and thin. In black car, one car for dead bodies.'

'A hearse?'

'Yes. Say again please?'

He repeated the word.

'Hearse,' she tried it out herself, committing the word to memory. 'Yes. Then they leave and she sit on ground. I load oven, not looking. I come back. She on ground. I mix new dough. I come back. She get up, slowly, slowly. I am sad for her.'

'Then she came in?'

'Then she pick up dirty mask and put it on, then another thing.' She put her head on one side. 'The voucher, I think.'

'How did she seem?'

The boulangère looked at him as if he was an idiot. 'She seem like Portuguese lady from across the street.'

Alex hid his frustration. 'Happy, upset, frightened?'

'Her son dead. Her face behind dirty mask from street.' She threw up her hands. 'What you think?'

'How was her voice?' he asked evenly.

'She sad. Her voice sad. Quiet and sad.' She glanced over her shoulder. 'I empty oven now.'

She bustled away to the kitchen in the back room.

'Thank you,' he called after her. 'You've been very helpful.'

Alex went back to the sad little house. The buckets by the front door were empty. A dozen lilies lay crushed on the step next to a mask with what he thought was blood on it, almost certainly the one she had worn and discarded on her way back inside.

He picked it up with an evidence bag turned inside out and went through the unlocked door. The trestles were still in the front room, slightly askew.

He went upstairs and stopped in the bedroom doorway. Luís's mother's body was lying pale and still on the rickety bed in the quiet bedroom overlooking the street, with only flies for company, laying eggs in her blood. The three wine bottles the boulangère had sold her were on the floor. Two were empty but the third hadn't been needed and remained unopened. A mean-looking serrated kitchen knife lay at her side on the bedspread. The damage was ragged, the flesh torn and ripped by the metal teeth.

She'd slashed both wrists, one after the other. The rosary trailed from her dead fingers.

Was it possible someone had faked the suicide? Alex visualised the scene. The wounds were angled, just as they ought to be if self-inflicted. There was relatively little visible blood because it had soaked into the bedclothes and mattress. But then there was the split lip and bruising about the width of a fist on her face.

'I don't believe you ever knew anything,' he told her, softly. 'I don't believe anyone needed to silence you.'

Alex sent a message with a location pin to police headquarters for the 18th arrondissement, and followed up with a request to Camera Control for the algorithm to identify the hearse and track it away from the area.

The scene was real, he decided. She had killed herself from grief.

He went to the window and looked down. People were out and about. A woman came by with a pushchair. The child reached out for the flowers spilled across the pavement and cried when its mother wouldn't let her touch them.

A police officer arrived. Alex showed his credentials then went on his way, leaving her to scan and seal the house. For the second time in two days, he hurried home from the far side of Montmartre.

47

Alex went straight to the isolation clinic but Gloria was worse again and slept through his visit. As he watched her blankets rise and fall, he found himself thinking about the information she'd wanted to give him.

Why had she changed her passwords? What had been going on in her life in the days before she became ill that made her suddenly cautious?

On the way out of the clinic he ran into the nurse he'd met on his first visit.

'Should I be worried?' he asked. 'She's not better.'

The nurse scanned her notes. 'I don't think so. Her stats are stable, and yesterday she had a good chat with her visitor.'

Alex was surprised. 'She had a visitor?'

'Yes, in the morning. She's usually more alert first thing.'

Alex's mind flicked through a checklist of people who knew about Gloria's condition.

'Who was this visitor?'

'I beg your pardon?'

'You must have a name.'

The nurse looked troubled. 'I'm afraid I can't release that information.'

'But I'm her son.'

'It's a question of confidentiality.'

There was a pause and Alex changed tack. 'I understand. But I would love to talk to them, to know what my mother might have said.'

The nurse hesitated. He could see her wavering.

'Please,' he said. 'It might be important.'

She glanced around to make sure no one was looking, and began to turn the screen so he could read the details. Alex leaned forward. Just then, though, a senior physician in a dark suit approached. Blanching, the nurse twitched the device back.

'I'm sorry,' she mouthed, silently.

Alex left the clinic with no new information, only more questions. He found himself walking to his mother's apartment.

The flat felt stale and dusty, already sad and uninhabited. He opened the curtains and windows, throwing back the shutters. In the fresh air and the better light, he looked around.

'What were you up to?' he whispered aloud.

He searched the desk for anything that might suggest who she had recently been in contact with. He found nothing.

He walked down to the little flat on the ground floor. He could see Nelinha through the obscured glass, working at her kitchen table. He knocked and watched as she removed her oversized headphones and opened the door.

'While I was away, before she became ill, did Gloria have any visitors?'

'No one as far as I know. I told you the other day – I've barely seen her. Why do you ask?'

Alex made a vague gesture. 'Someone visited her at the clinic.'

Nelinha frowned. 'I thought you said it was hard to get an appointment.'

That was what he should have asked, he realised. Not who the visitor was, but how they managed to jump the queue when he had to wait.

'It must be someone she's been in touch with recently,' he said. 'Maybe it was to do with the transfer to the Rothschild?'

Nelinha opened a new window on her holo. It gave access to the management software for the building, including security cameras.

'There's a camera on every landing,' she explained. 'Fixed, but quite a wide angle. What day are we talking about?'

He counted back and Nelinha scrolled the dateline on her screen.

'I'll copy you the whole of that week. If you don't find what you're looking for, we can go back further. It will be the feeds from all the cameras, one on each of the six floors.'

'Thank you.' Alex looked over her shoulder at the screen. 'Do you have some kind of reminder of my mother's passwords, in case she forgets? There's some research she wanted me to read.'

'What is it?' she asked.

'Something called "Gerboise Bleue".'

'Oh.'

Alex gave her a curious glance. 'That means something to you?'

'It was a nuclear testing site in the Sahara. It's been kind of fetishised by people who are interested in destruction.'

'In what way?' Alex asked.

'People who think we've gone too far – centralised control, hyperconnection, structurally embedded inequality, all that.'

Something about the way she said it struck him.

'Is that what you think?' he asked.

She held his gaze for a moment, a question in her eyes. What was she asking him?

But then she turned back to her holo. 'I don't think anything. I'm just trying to make a living. Now, I need to get back to work. I'll forward the videos.'

By the time Alex got back to his boat, Nelinha's security footage was already on his system. He opened it and found the screen split into frames. He scrolled the timeline to the day he'd discovered Gloria unwell and asked his new Internal Security software to scan for movement.

It was laborious work. Every time there was a flicker of someone on the stairs he had to stop and try to identify them. Several times, he saw Nelinha dusting, vacuuming and delivering parcels. Monsieur Labidie, the downstairs neighbour, went out and in at the same times each day. The couple from the top floor went up and down with their baby in a carrycot.

Finally, he found someone he didn't know on the fourth-floor landing. He clicked the icon for full screen. The resolution was so poor that whoever it was became almost a blur against the pale walls, but he saw the apartment door open and someone he knew must be his mother appeared. The two grey smudges greeted one another, briefly embracing. Or was it that his mother took hold of her visitor to help them across the threshold? Then, they disappeared into the apartment and the door closed.

Alex let the video run on, waiting for the visitor to leave. Then the timestamp in the corner of the screen seized at11:00, the image went black and there were two or three seconds of stuttering as the system rebooted. Then the clock indicated 13:02, two hours later.

Alex accessed the power company website to check load-shedding records. Sure enough, on that very day there'd been a two-hour brown-out from eleven o'clock. Whoever his mother's visitor was, they had slipped away while the cameras were down.

Was it deliberate or accidental? Was any of this important?

He decided to take a break and put on his running gear. In a couple of hours, he would have to get ready for the panel of inquiry.

He headed west, downstream along the pedestrianised right embankment of the Seine. Beneath each bridge he skirted shanty dwellings erected in the shelter of the shadows. He thought about his mother's career as a historian and how her patterns of thought had shaped his own – the analysis of continuity and change. He thought about how change used to be a neutral concept. Now all change seemed to be for the worse.

After a couple of kilometres, he doubled back, crossing to the left bank. On the riverside, close to the water, he sprinted four hundred metres until he came level with the statue of Saint Genevieve, then jogged on as far as the botanical gardens. There, he found a quiet bench near a century-old lime tree and paused, allowing the heat of the day to dry the sweat from his clothes.

The river ran quietly, greenish-brown, quite low between the stone embankments. Now and then a piece of paper or a twig floated past, making its way towards the sea at Le Havre, two hundred kilometres away. He felt passive, like those fragments of flotsam, swept on the flow of events to some distant destination without purpose or meaning, just a dispersal into the vastness of the future, a great formless incoherence, like the sea.

Eight years before, on this very spot, he had faced death – not for the first time.

It was a quiet Sunday evening and he had recently graduated in the top six out of his intake of over a hundred. He'd gone out with the other top graduates to a celebratory dinner at the Tour d'Argent, a famous restaurant in a lovely nineteenth-century building overlooking the left bank of the Seine.

It was tradition that graduates should order the house speciality, 'pressed duck'. Each time the signature dish was served, it was accompanied by a numbered certificate. Alex hadn't kept his, but he remembered being told that the US wartime President Roosevelt had received a certificate numbered around one hundred thousand, that Charlie Chaplin had been around a quarter of a million, an ageing ex-Chancellor Merkel of Germany around 400,000.

The ceremony depressed him. Nothing he had ever experienced had so clearly brought home to him the magnitude of human exploitation of the natural world – a single restaurant on the banks of the Seine serving nearly half a million plates of pressed duck.

At this point, he and his colleagues were simply military graduates rather than undercover operatives, so each brought a date. He had chosen to bring Nelinha. They'd sat with Amaury Barra and his younger brother, who was twelve at the time and completely blown away by the luxury of the room.

Alex had spent much of the evening in conversation with one of the other candidates' guests, a woman with a very symmetrical face and an athletic build. He learned that she had qualified to attend the same programme, but had been prevented from finishing by her responsibilities as a carer.

'I'm sorry,' he remembered saying more than once.

The woman left a little before everyone else, finally telling him her name because, eventually, he'd thought to ask for it.

Mariam Jordane.

It was tradition for the newly graduated operatives to finish the meal alone with speeches, toasts and declarations of ambition and purpose. Soon after, Nelinha and Amaury's brother left as well.

'I couldn't be prouder of you, *amigo do minho*,' Nelinha told him, her eyes shining.

When the evening broke up, Alex found his way to the banks of the Seine where he sat alone beneath a lime tree thick with leaves on a bench in deep shadow, at the darkest midpoint between the narrow throws of two streetlamps. He watched the river running, waiting for the half-hour curfew warning.

Suddenly, he heard running feet – four people fleeing clumsily along the cobbled quayside, Blanks probably, poorly dressed and shambling, being chased. They reached a dead end where the walkway met the pillars of a bridge. Trapped, they looked at one another, the message of desperation clear on their dirty faces.

The two men pursuing them did not notice Alex in the shadows. They carried metal canes about half a metre in length. One of them jabbed the parapet over the water and the end sparked. They were shock sticks, like cattle prods – high voltage, low current, to maximise pain. The Blanks cringed and clung to one another as the men swished their weapons and laughed – bullies, thugs, doing evil for sport.

Alex drew in a breath. He was unarmed and felt unsteady from the wine at dinner, so he stayed quiet, allowing the men get within a couple of metres of the Blanks so he could approach them from behind. One of them, a terrified old woman with a scarf drawn across her face in lieu of a mask, only her eyes visible, glanced at Alex just as he reached the first man. He put a finger to his lips for her to be quiet, but she cried out.

'Help us, please.'

The man swung round. Purely by chance, he jabbed the shock stick into Alex's thigh as he tried to dodge away. The pain was instant and disabling, as if some wild animal had just bitten a chunk out of his quad. He stumbled, only managing to keep his balance by leaning his hands on the concrete parapet over the water.

Together, the two men advanced on him, the shock sticks extended.

Putting all his concentration and energy into a single movement, Alex lunged at them, curling his right hand into a claw, scratching at the side of the first man's neck, simultaneously slamming his left fist into the man's chin. His head snapped back and he stumbled as Alex shouted at the Blanks to run.

'Call for help.'

They shambled away, wailing at the night.

The second man, slower to react, jabbed forward. His aim was poor but the shock stick caught Alex a glancing blow on the shoulder. All the strength went out of his arm and he staggered back, his heels hitting the parapet. The first man got up, his nose pumping blood.

'You're going to pay for this,' he spluttered.

Alex was torn. He wanted to keep the two men busy until the Blanks were safe, but his position was helpless.

Just then, he heard shouts from the road above the pedestrian embankment, followed by footsteps thumping down the stone steps towards the river.

'Police, stay where you are!'

Alex's two assailants exchanged a glance. They knew they should run but they wanted to make Alex pay first. They closed in.

There was no reason for Alex to stay where he was. The Blanks would now be safe.

He hurled himself backwards, falling two metres into the dark water, disappearing beneath the surface, pulling strongly with his one good hand and kicking with his one good leg. When he broke the surface, he was thirty metres away, his right fist tightly shut to protect the DNA evidence under his fingernails.

A vibration from his comm-watch snapped Alex out of memory. Camera Control had replied to his request for information about the hearse. The vehicle had entered the city limits well before dawn, from the west. It had travelled to the far side of Montmartre, then it had been on-camera but stationary for seven minutes.

Seven minutes, Alex thought. That was all the time it had taken to remove the coffin and the corpse and destroy a mother's life.

The hearse had then driven into the northern suburbs, across the main railway lines and through a residential neighbourhood, where it had disappeared from view for nine minutes. Finally, it reappeared and drove on, beyond the ability of Paris Camera Control to track its movements.

He forwarded the details to the National Network. It was possible he could find some hint of its final destination, but the regional camera network was less dense than the one that surveilled the capital.

He popped out a holo-map, looking at the neighbourhood where the car had gone off camera for nine minutes. He swiped and pinched out, centring and recentring, until he found the hearse's destination.

Makes sense, he thought. That's what I would do.

Incinerators. The deadest of dead ends.

48

That same morning, in the courtyard of the seventeenth-century church of Val-de-Grâce, alongside the much newer buildings of the military hospital, exiled Prime Minister Souad Mourad of Cyrenia contemplated the statue of Dominique-Jean Larrey.

Larrey was a French military surgeon of the Napoleonic era, the first person to conceive the idea of battlefield triage, treating wounded soldiers in order of need rather than in order of allegiance or rank. He created the first mobile ambulance services to accompany armies into the field. In 2011, the North Atlantic Treaty Organisation's highest medical honour was named after him.

The sculpture, cast in black-green bronze, undersold the man. It was created in 1843, soon after his death. It made him look squat and fat, swaddled in his uniform and cloak. Mourad wondered if that was deliberate, so he shouldn't appear greater than his commanding officer and emperor, Napoleon Bonaparte. Of course, by 1843, Napoleon himself had been dead more than twenty years, succumbing to stomach cancer, a prisoner on the isolated South Atlantic island of Saint Helena.

And now here I am, in exile, she thought.

During his long imprisonment, Napoleon wrote a book about one of his great heroes, Julius Caesar. Mourad had never read it but she was, of course, aware of the Shakespearean legend of the great Roman emperor three times refusing the title. She had been accused of doing something similar for the purposes of PR.

And what a stupid decision that was, she reflected bitterly.

Was that the reason for her downfall? A reluctance to consolidate political authority with military power? But why should a prime minister need military alliances within her own nation, her own administration?

Now, though, would it be wise to re-establish direct communication with her armed forces? France would support her. So would Italy, their neighbour across the Mediterranean. Also, the other nations of North Africa, fearful of renewed chaos on their borders. Cyrenia would once more be a beacon for a better future. But which general should she choose?

Both had their flaws. Al-Fathi was cautious, slow to act. It would be hard to convince him to take decisive action. Bader was stronger-willed and more likely to take a leap of faith. Whichever she chose, she knew what she could hold out as a reward – the mayoralty of Cyrene City and the empty seat on the Presidential Council. Surely that would satisfy their ambition, at least for a while?

She looked around the courtyard. Two army officers were in attendance, ostensibly paying her no attention. Were they her jailers or were they there to keep her safe?

Some people believed Napoleon was poisoned by the copper arsenite in the wallpaper of his lodgings on Saint Helena. Was Val-de-Grâce where she would die, like the Vietnamese emperor Bảo Đại? Or would she be deliberately infected with some intractable transgenic pathogen, cared for pointlessly, isolated tenderly, expiring in the midst of the most sophisticated medical technology?

She glanced at the insignia on the shoulder of one of the lurking officers.

'Lieutenant,' she said, 'what is the date today?'

He told her.

Yes, she ought to be four thousand kilometres away, preparing to celebrate the official opening of an extension to the Great Solar Array just outside Al-Jaghar. The array had been financed by the European Union and by several private infrastructure investors. She had negotiated the deal when her international partners became reluctant to buy Cyrenian oil, the primary resource she had been banking on for economic development. They had insisted on clean energy instead, and she made that happen. The site would soon be connected to the European energy grid. The perimeter at Al-Jaghar had been pushed thirty kilometres out into the desert, even beyond the border with Egypt. Despite its fierce, isolationist rhetoric, impoverished Egypt had no choice but to cede to Cyrenia a tiny sliver of its territory in return for preferential energy contracts.

Mourad thought about the paper testimony she'd drafted in her safe room. She'd devoted two pages to Al-Jaghar – the aeronautical campus, including a rocket launch pad and factories for aircraft construction, missile defence and space exploration. The site was called *Tahadath 'ila Al-Nujum* and was the jewel in the crown of Cyrenian development. But, since the insurrection, the launch site was also of enormous strategic importance. The fighter squadrons stationed there were a force in their own right.

She thought again about Al-Fathi and Bader. Al-Fathi could be persuaded to any course of action that satisfied his inflated sense of his own worth. Bader, she thought, was more pragmatic, but there was also something unpleasant, almost inhuman, in his calculations.

She frowned. No, neither could be entirely trusted. It would depend on the deal of the cards. And now that the insurrection had thrown the entire deck high into the air…

Something had to be done.

'I need to speak to Claudine Poiret,' she said abruptly to the lieutenant. 'And with my embassy in Paris.'

49

Alex arrived at the first session of the panel of inquiry at two o'clock that afternoon. It was in a seminar room at the Palace of Justice on the larger of the two islands at the heart of the city.

The assessor tapped her microphone and spoke aloud, confirming her presence.

'Senior Assessor.'

She gestured to the other five participants. They each spoke the call-sign letters that had been assigned to them.

'Alpha,' said Alex.

'Bravo,' said Fayard.

'Charlie,' said Amaury.

'Delta,' said the representative of the office of the French president.

'Echo,' said Claudine Poiret.

It was the first time Alex had seen Amaury since Toulouse-Francazal airbase. Amaury had been brought in last, once the others were seated at the table, and they hadn't been able to speak. For his part, Amaury kept his eyes averted and his hands in his lap, under the table.

The assessor resumed.

'This panel,' she began, 'is convened under Chaland Rules. There will be no written report. The encrypted video record will be available for consultation at a level of clearance yet to be defined.'

She looked round the room. Alex followed her gaze. The other participants were focused on their individual screens, recessed in the tabletop in front of them. In the upper bezel, a tiny camera and a condenser microphone recorded the participants' actions and speech. It was the only tech in the room. They had all handed over their comms on the way in.

'In the course of this hearing, you will refer to one another only by your designated letters. There will be no mention of places or dates. If you need to specify a location, you will use the code names indicated on the outline map on your monitors.'

Fayard, designated Bravo, raised a thin hand.

'Might we lower the lights? Perhaps I am not alone in finding them overbright?'

The assessor moved a slider control on her screen. The room dimmed and Fayard took off his dark glasses.

'Alpha, your actions are under investigation. This panel will determine whether this challenge must lead to a court martial, other disciplinary action, a civil tribunal or no action of any kind. Do you understand?'

'I do,' said Alex.

She turned to Fayard.

'Bravo, the operation was carried out according to DGES protocols under the authority of the Minister for Foreign Affairs, but Alpha has since transferred to Internal Security and is, therefore, your responsibility.'

He nodded. 'Agreed.'

She turned to Amaury.

'An inquiry is mandatory in friendly-fire incidents of this kind. In this case, Charlie was the victim.' Amaury acknowledged her with a nod. 'You must speak out loud for the recording.'

'Present,' he said.

She turned to the fourth participant, a small woman with an air of diffidence and discretion.

'Delta is present as an independent witness, representing the of the office of the president.'

'Good afternoon.'

Finally, she turned to Claudine Poiret.

'Echo will provide background on behalf of the Ministry for Foreign Affairs.'

'Agreed,' said Poiret.

'If you need to refer to me, please use the designation Senior Assessor.' The assessor looked at her assistant. 'Stamp your encryption with date and time and we will begin.'

After that, an hour passed mostly in silence as the participants read confidential documents that could not leave the room. When they'd all finished, the assessor spoke again.

'Let us proceed to the direct evidence.'

Delta raised a tentative hand. 'Before the inquiry proceeds, the office of the president requests an adjournment.'

'For what possible reason?'

'The president apologises,' said Delta, 'but wishes it known that he is keen that the position of Prime Minister Mourad should be resolved before the panel concludes.'

'Seriously?' The assessor sounded displeased. 'But I will not let this inquiry drag its feet. We will examine more evidence tomorrow and, in the meantime, I will speak to the president's office myself.'

The meeting was adjourned. They were to reconvene the following day, Saturday, at twelve o'clock.

Alex asked to speak to Amaury, but was refused. He was required to stay seated while 'Charlie' was ushered out of the room. By that time Fayard, also, had left.

On his own way out, Alex retrieved his comm-watch and found a message from Sabie with an attachment that would not open without the encrypted memory stick back at the boat. At the main exit, he joined a queue of witnesses, court officers, police officers and lawyers, before being allowed down the wide ceremonial staircase that led to Place Dauphine and the Seine.

The sun was beating down. He went to find shade by the exit from the underground car park. A colony of giant ants was scurrying in and out of a crack in the paving. Then the metal shutter rolled up and an ancient ambulance emerged – petrol driven, noisily climbing the ramp in low gear. As Alex turned away from the fumes, he wondered if it was carrying Amaury back to some rehabilitation centre.

He heard voices and turned to see Professor Fayard creeping down the ceremonial staircase, moving painfully slowly. A police officer came to his aid. They took the steps one at a time, planting both feet on each stone tread before lurching awkwardly to the next. Alex ran halfway up to meet them and took Fayard's frail arm.

'There is a disabled exit to the basement car park,' said Alex. 'With a lift.'

'I will not use it,' said Fayard, his voice breathless but firm.

Alex didn't reply until they reached the pavement.

'Your symptoms are worse, Professor.'

Fayard waved that away. 'No. Overall, no. This is a merely a bad moment.'

Alex watched him tap his watch to send a message to Mariam to bring the car. 'What did you think of the meeting, the delay?' he asked.

'The president wants Mourad's position resolved first,' said Fayard, 'what she might try to do, what assistance she might request from France. That seems reasonable.'

'And, until she decides, I am suspended and may not speak to Amaury?' Alex's tone was bitter.

'Nor he to you. But he is a professional.'

Fayard made it sound like this explained everything.

'Have you seen the extent of the injury to his hand?' Alex asked.

The professor looked away. 'That will emerge from tomorrow's session.' There was a pause, and then Fayard asked, unexpectedly: 'How is your mother?'

'They tell me her stats are stable but she isn't improving. I'm not sure what happens next.'

The shutters from the underground car park rolled up again and Alex watched Fayard's official vehicle climbing the ramp. Again, he found himself wondering whether Fayard was aware of his deal with Poiret, Gloria's transfer to the Rothschild Institute. He thought about his mental checklist of visitors to his mother's apartment. Should Fayard be on that list? After all, hadn't Gloria been threatening to call the professor when she first became ill?

Mariam parked, got out and came around to open the rear passenger door. Still, Fayard made no move to get in. Out of the professor's view, Mariam caught his eye and almost smiled.

'What do you think will happen with the inquiry, Alexandre?' he asked.

'I did my duty, within the limits of the options available to me,' Alex answered simply.

Fayard's smile was thin. 'That's all right, then.' Mariam took his arm, leading him towards the car. The professor lowered himself slowly into the back seat. 'Though the inquiry is perhaps an opportunity for someone to attack me through you.'

Alex hadn't considered this possibility. 'As you told me, I'm "politically incompetent". But, in the meantime, I can't do my job.'

'And yet, already something has come up to entertain you.' Fayard leaned back in his seat, his eyes closed. 'Follow up on the Portuguese youth. I will instruct Administrator Sabie to make your transfer official. There will be time enough.'

Mariam shut Fayard's door, jogged round and got in. The electric vehicle pulled away with almost no sound, just a dull clunk as the drive engaged, then the tyres hissing faintly as they crossed the hot tarmac.

In his basement office at DGIS headquarters in Levallois-Perret, Administrator Sabie's eyes tracked across the largest of his seven screens, the one in the middle, showing real-time images of Al-Jaghar. Atmospheric conditions were good, with only low-level dust to obscure the view. He watched a heavy transport helicopter come in to land and could just make out a fork-lift truck being used to assist in unloading.

The clean energy installation was a triumph, but what about the airbase? A launch site for satellites was good business for a new country with a need to establish a sense of national pride. And it was a sound method for enhancing and cementing diplomatic relations. The isolation of the base on the edge of the Great Sand Sea provided what might be called 'natural' security. Proximity to a weak neighbour nation – the isolationist Egyptian Republic – minimised geopolitical threats.

He thought about the historical analysis that Professor Fayard had sent him. Could it be the old man believed that the Al-Jaghar site was intended for some kind of novel weapons testing? Even nuclear weapons testing? In the era of transgenic illness, basically since 2025, the nations of the world had found an unusual consensus, and the futile nuclear arms race had been sidelined by the need for international cooperation to combat microscopic adversaries that invaded and mutated without warning.

Was that what the old man was getting at? That history was no longer driven by military conflict?

A corollary of the transgenic age was isolationism. All frontiers were, in effect, closed. Tourist travel corridors were narrow and time-sensitive, liable at any moment to be slammed shut if clusters of novel infections arose. Wasn't that the case in northern Portugal right now?

Sabie opened a dictation program. Fayard had asked him to put his thoughts together in three hundred concise words. He did so and, as requested, copied them to Alexandre Lamarque with the historical paper as an attachment. If Lamarque was as perceptive as the old man seemed to believe, perhaps he would see through the fog.

Just before he shut down his screen, Sabie saw a second helicopter come in to land at Al-Jaghar – much smaller, perhaps only five or six people on board.

So, they are going ahead with it, he thought. Good.

50

As the sun struggled to pierce the desert dust that hung in the air like mist, the small but rapid helicopter carrying General Bader and General Al-Fathi, a staff officer and two pilots arrived in Al-Jaghar. Both generals were on edge.

Earlier that day, in a seminar room in an undamaged portion of the Cyrene City parliamentary compound, they had officially promoted a new staff officer from General Bader's team. They were on their way to Al-Jaghar to speak at the official opening of the extension to the solar array – and perhaps stay on for the launch of a new rocket a week later. Each had their own reasons for attending. Al-Fathi wanted to look important on the news. Bader wanted to secure the gateway into space.

'This should not be a purely military event,' Al-Fathi had said.

'What do you suggest we do?' Bader had asked.

'To maintain a fig leaf of democratic oversight, we should invite the members of the Presidential Council to accompany us.'

'The mayor of Cyrene is dead,' Bader pointed out.

'Then we should invite the remaining members, Benghazi and Tobruk. Tobruk is almost on our route. We can offer to bring him with us. Meanwhile, we can send a message to Benghazi to join us there.'

Bader shrugged. 'If you wish.'

Al-Fathi had turned to Bader's newly appointed staff officer, a young woman with a permanently worried expression.

'Noori, the food and drink for the feast?'

'On board the heavy copter, sir,' said Staff Officer Noori. 'We follow in the X3.'

'Good. Via Tobruk. Log the two routes with ground-to-air defence.'

'Yes, sir.'

They had taken off less than an hour later. The X3 had a sharp nose, a two-person cockpit and a small passenger compartment. Propellors either side of the fuselage counterbalanced the torque from the top rotor, meaning it had no need of a tail rotor to stop it spinning round on itself. They also gave it exceptional acceleration and top speed.

As it gained altitude, they were able to see the remedial works already under way. A new solid roof was being erected to replace the shattered atrium.

They had travelled east to Tobruk and were met at the airport by the mayor, a cautious man chosen by Mourad for his technocratic abilities rather than his inspirational vision. He refused to accompany them.

'There is much to do here if we are to re-establish order,' he said.

'Tobruk has been quiet, however,' Bader observed.

'And will remain so only if I stay.'

'You have an elevated sense of your own qualities,' said Al-Fathi.

'It is not personal. It is the visible presence of a civil authority.'

'The mayor of Benghazi is to join us at Al-Jaghar,' Bader lied.

'He may or he may not,' said the mayor of Tobruk. 'His concerns are as mine.'

'Then you are both making the same mistake,' Al-Fathi snapped.

The mayor sighed. 'I am an administrator, a functionary. I simply tell you that peace is better than war and talk is better than bullets. I understand you have priorities that are not my own. I trust you will always keep what is best for the Cyrenian people uppermost in your thoughts.'

'You would have preferred the prime minister not to have fled?' Al-Fathi suggested.

'That was the decision we reached when last we spoke,' said the mayor. 'We all had confidence at that point – at least I thought we did.'

'Confidence?' asked Bader.

'In the integrity of the armed forces, of the military perimeter around the compound. Only the mayor of Cyrene spoke against it. He was keen the prime minister should make her way to safety. But then, he was a small, frightened man. Frightened for himself and frightened for her, perhaps.' The mayor of

Tobruk shook his head. 'I am a small man, too, in the great scheme of things, but I will not let myself be led by fear.'

They left him and a message came through as they were re-crossing the tarmac.

'The Mayor of Benghazi regrets,' said Staff Officer Noori, 'that he is unable to attend the ceremony at *Tahadath 'ila Al-Nujum.*'

They paused. The mayor of Tobruk was a hundred metres away, standing alongside his modest official car, politely awaiting their departure.

'We should force him to come with us,' Al-Fathi said. 'It would be a mistake to allow anyone to suggest that this is an overthrow of democracy. Cyrenia must remain unsullied – as an idea as much as a reality. The world must believe that Mourad is in exile for her own safety, not because you and I have replaced her.'

'Who else is there?' Bader made a sweeping gesture with his arm. 'These men are not leaders.'

'They don't have to be. They need only to provide the window dressing.'

Bader wasn't convinced. 'To force this small man to come with us would be worse.'

'Perhaps,' acknowledged Al-Fathi, after a pause.

'We will both speak at the ceremony,' said Bader carefully. 'We will frame our words in such a way that we are seen—'

'We will speak with the authority of guardians of the nation,' interrupted Al-Fathi, 'not as generals.'

'Exactly.'

The X3 had taken them due south at low altitude. From time to time, they could see the frontier with Egypt and the remains of the extraordinary folly of the barbed-wire fence built by the twentieth-century Italian colonists, all the way from the Mediterranean. Every so often they glimpsed an Egyptian Republic border post, sad and dusty, poorly equipped, no more than a token barrier.

Landing in Al-Jaghar, they both felt the unique atmosphere of the old oasis settlement. It wasn't simply the cognitive challenge of seeing the busy military campus and the date plantations in the midst of endless sands. There was an odd stillness in the air – perhaps because the oasis was below sea level – and, when all human activity was paused, a special quality of silence.

'You have a little over an hour to prepare,' Staff Officer Noori told them. 'The banquet will begin at the conclusion of your speeches celebrating the extension to the Great Solar Array.'

'Good,' said Bader.

'Show us to our quarters,' said Al-Fathi. 'We will not appear in uniform.'

An hour and a half later, Bader and Al-Fathi each spoke in turn, praising international cooperation, native ingenuity and national pride to an audience of engineers, scientists and Air Force personnel at three long outdoor tables. The word 'Cyrenia' was not pronounced, but neither was the word 'Libya'. Each person was free to think of themselves as a citizen of either Gaddafi's post-colonial state or Mourad's independent secession.

Bader and Al-Fathi both wore knee-length tunics over loose trousers, embroidered waistcoats and a traditional 'jard', a single length of hand-woven fabric, knotted on the left-hand side and wrapped over the head and shoulders like a hood.

Bader spoke second and, as he reached his climax, he took Al-Fathi's hand and raised it high above his head, as Al-Fathi had asked him to do, in order to reveal the honourable scar that ran the length of his left forearm.

'Together we will confront the challenges of the future,' Bader declaimed, 'strong in the traditions of our past. Change is coming. Change is good. Change is our opportunity – to refresh, reinvigorate and renew, to begin again, better, stronger, leaving the mistakes of the past behind, a clean slate.'

Bader dropped Al-Fathi's hand and there was polite applause, then the staff began serving the feast – an exceptional meal provided by the local kitchens, supplemented by delicacies from the heavy copter. As the many small courses progressed, senior members of different departments came to pay homage at Bader and Al-Fathi's table. The chief executive of the array wanted to know if a further extension was anticipated and if new staff would be provided, if new accommodation would be built to house them. Bader told Staff Officer Noori to schedule a meeting in three days.

‘You will still be here?’ asked the chief executive.

‘Oh, yes.’ said Bader.

The scientist responsible for a planning a solar tower wanted to know when building would commence, bombarding them with statistics, clearly demonstrating – or so she claimed – that her installation would be more efficient than the traditional photovoltaic arrays.

‘I will be happy to take a tour of inspection, said Bader. ‘Schedule it with my assistant.’

‘Gladly, gladly,’ said the scientist.

The base commander of the Air Force fighter squadron joined them, a woman with thirty years of service. Staff-Officer Noori had been expecting her arrival and stepped back, saluting smartly. Bader stood up to greet her.

‘Sister,’ he said, embracing her.

‘Brother,’ said the woman.

They embraced.

Latifah Bader remained at their table for an hour, assuming almost equal status. The three of them greeted more members of staff, like a receiving line at a wedding, with Noori as usher. Finally, protocol was complete. Bader nodded in satisfaction.

’Enough,’ said Al-Fathi, passing a hand across his brow.

’I’m glad you will remain for the launch,’ Latifah told her brother.

‘We will,’ said Al-Fathi.

Bader frowned, irritated at his interruption. ‘A great day is coming, sister,’ he said. ‘Is everything ready?’

‘The testing sequence is under way,’ Latifah replied.

Bader smiled. He and his sister stood and embraced once more. Then Latifah gave a curt bow to Al-Fathi and turned on her heel, heading back to her own secure Air Force compound.

The two generals retired to their VIP accommodation – a prefabricated bungalow decorated with hand-woven rugs.

‘Noori, the bottle,’ ordered Bader.

Staff Officer Noori brought in an unopened bottle of champagne and ostentatiously uncorked it, showing them its untampered seal, then stepped discreetly away to stand beside the door. Bader brought in two glasses.

'You prefer ice?' he asked.

'Always,' said Al-Fathi.

Bader turned away to add it, before passing the glass back to his brother-in-arms. They drank.

'I still maintain it was a mistake to let Mourad leave,' Al-Fathi said. 'She is in Paris. They'll protect her.'

Bader shrugged. 'As far as they are able.'

Al-Fathi emptied his glass and held it out for more. Bader refilled it and gave a toast.

'To the future.'

Al-Fathi smiled. 'The future.'

They drank, then Al-Fathi rubbed the long scar along his left forearm.

'The wound troubles you, General?' asked Bader solicitously.

'No more than usual.'

'I envy you,' said Bader. 'Scars are better than medals,'

Al-Fathi unwound the jard from over his shoulder. 'The air is heavy. Do you not think so?'

'This oasis is below sea level,' Bader said, as if this explained everything.

Al-Fathi clenched and unclenched his fist.

'I have a cramp,' he began.

'Yes?' Bader looked concerned.

'My fist…'

'Your fist?'

Al-Fathi looked at Bader. His breathing was becoming shallow. 'What have you done?'

'Perhaps not the climate,' said Bader, softly. 'Perhaps not the bowl of the land.'

'What have…' Al-Fathi whispered.

'No, the neurological poison in your wine.' Bader stood up and poured himself another glass of champagne. 'In the old days, the jard was used in many ways – as clothing, as bedding, as a tent for shelter. Your jard, my dear colleague, in other circumstances might have draped your coffin.'

'What poison…' Al-Fathi whispered, then turned his head towards the door. 'Help me.'

Staff Officer Noori did not acknowledge him.

'Today,' continued Bader, 'the jard is worn only at festivals and on special occasions. You know why I tell you this?'

Al-Fathi tried to answer but found that he could not.

'The right hand,' said Bader, 'is exposed, but the other is concealed within its folds.'

He withdrew his left hand from beneath the coarse fabric and showed Al-Fathi the empty phial. Al-Fathi moved his lips but his eyes were becoming glazed.

'I knew you would ask for ice.' Bader said. 'I gave you something else as well.'

Bader watched Al-Fathi dying, his body stiffening, bending. Falling forward onto the floor, incongruous on the hand-woven rug. He could hear noises from the party outside – people mingling, talking, dancing. Finally, once he was sure that Al-Fathi was no longer breathing, Bader instructed Noori to remove the body.

'Take it far out into the dunes and leave it there, naked,' he said, 'for carrion birds to shred.'

51

Staff Officer Noori's considerable authority derived not from her middling rank, but from her association with Cyrenia's supreme command. That authority brought with it a single unshakeable imperative – to follow orders.

Noori knew when she was appointed that she would see things, hear things, that might put her in danger. For example, the body of her predecessor carried out of the prime minister's safe room, half of her head blown away, a massive cavity in the area of her heart.

Her only protection was unswerving loyalty to whoever was in charge.

All the same, she hadn't immediately obeyed the order to strip Al-Fathi's body and dump it on the sand.

She didn't disagree with the order. She, too, wanted the vultures and other carrion-feeders to make the problem go away. But the campus at Al-Jaghar was busy with the aftermath of the celebrations and with preparations for the upcoming rocket launch. And it was, after all, a facility with military checkpoints, a place where everyone, at all times, needed a reason to be where they were, to be doing what they doing.

As a short-term solution, she stripped Al-Fathi's body of its loose trousers, tunic and waistcoat and wrapped it in the jard, like a shroud. Then she concealed it in the luggage compartment of a small electric vehicle called a Pratique, borrowed from the Air Force. She put the Pratique on charge with the air con at maximum. Even so, she was worried the corpse would soon start to stink.

As the sun began to set, the base became quieter. Noori made her way back towards the charging points, not far from the accommodation units. She noticed a woman, an insignificant labourer, Egyptian in origin from her clothing, reading a paper book on the small veranda of her prefabricated dwelling. Noori introduced herself.

'I am personally attached to General Bader, supreme commander of the Cyrenian army,' she said. 'I have a job for you, on the general's orders.'

'I've already finished my shift,' the woman informed her.

'This is extra. There will be an additional payment.'

The money did the trick. The labourer closed her book. 'I will be pleased to be of assistance.'

'The task is confidential. I'll need you to be discreet.'

'Of course,' the woman replied.

'There has been a breach of security. A terrorist has penetrated the campus. Fortunately, he was apprehended and killed. General Bader himself orders us to take the body out into the sands to be disposed of discreetly, so as not to create uncertainty or panic. Do you understand?'

The woman nodded. 'Panic is in nobody's interest. Discretion is always the best path.'

'Good,' said the staff officer. 'You are Egyptian?'

'Confirmed refugee status. I've applied for Cyrenian citizenship.'

'What is your name?' Noori asked.

'Sanaa Wasi,' the labourer lied.

The labourer's real name was Zeina Yaseen, but she knew better than to share that. She also knew better than to take at face value the implausible story the staff officer had told her. But she had no choice. The woman had the authority of the supreme commander of the Cyrenian army behind her and she carried a pistol in the holster on her belt.

Zeina indicated her sandals. 'If we're going into the desert, I need to put on better shoes.'

Leaving Noori outside, she went into the small but tidy room and looked around. Was there anything valuable that she would be unwilling to leave behind? Access to her small savings was controlled by the identity card and plastic bank credentials in the belt she wore under her clothes. Likewise, her old-fashioned smartphone was in a pocket of her loose-fitting jellabiya.

Was there a small chance she was overreacting?

No, of course not. Once they had dumped the body out in the endless sands, Zeina knew she would have outlived her usefulness.

She took a short paring knife from the kitchenette and tucked it in a side pocket of her rucksack, leaving the zip open, then put three bottles of water and the paper book she had been reading in the main compartment. It had been her grandmother's favourite novel and was her last true memento of home.

Pushing her feet into her boots, she called out.

'Just coming.'

When she went back outside, Noori was looking west towards the setting sun.

'Where would be a discreet location?' she asked. 'We need somewhere no one ever goes.'

'I have an idea,' said Zeina.

Because she knew the way, Zeina took the wheel of the Pratique. They were stopped at a checkpoint at the entrance to the array. Zeina showed her ID to the guard, making sure that Noori couldn't see her real name.

'The officer would like to visit the array. I am ordered to show her my section,' she explained.

'Which officer?' said the guard.

Noori leaned across, showing her face and the insignia on her tunic. 'I'm with General Bader.'

'Excuse me,' said the guard, stepping back. 'Go ahead.'

After leaving the accommodation campus, Zeina forked left, around the perimeter of the launch site, heading out into the rocks and sand.

'The array has more than three million square metres of photovoltaic panels,' she said as she drove. 'My section is at the southern end. No one else ever goes there.'

'Is there any barrier, a fence or a wall that would stop jackals disposing of the bones?'

Zeina shook her head. 'We're so remote it isn't considered necessary. But there are motion sensors.'

'In the sand?' Noori asked.

'You can see them all around from the array. There's one there, on that post. But no one approaches across the Great Sand Sea.'

'The Egyptian border isn't so far away.'

Oh, yes, thought Zeina. I'm aware of that.

She cast about in her mind for something to talk about while she formulated a plan of escape.

This is an excellent plan, thought Staff Officer Noori. Out to the very southern end of the array. Leave the body on the sand. No one to know what had happened except this biddable Egyptian peasant.

'How long does it take for a body to decompose?' asked the labourer, unexpectedly.

'Why do you ask?'

'I'm just preparing myself,' said the labourer, reasonably.

'In this heat, the internal organs will begin breaking down within a day or two. Bloating begins maybe three to five days after death. A corpse inflates from internal decomposition after eight or ten days.'

'This terrorist will not be bloated?' the woman asked.

'Not yet. It has only been a few hours.'

The woman glanced over her shoulder. 'He's behind us, in the luggage compartment?'

'He is.' Noori had a moment of doubt. Bader had given the order in the heat of the moment. 'You are sure the desert animals will strip it well before the wind covers it with sand?'

'Yes,' said the labourer. 'Jackals and vultures will break the bones for the marrow within.'

'Good,' said Noori.

Zeina wasn't afraid. The harshness of her life – seeing livestock die under her father's knife at their failing farm in the Nile delta, the terrible decline of the Egyptian economy, her flight into exile, the awful human misery and desperate competition of the refugee camp – all of this had hardened her. She fully expected Noori to try to kill her and leave her body out in the sands alongside that of the alleged intruder. But she wouldn't go down without a fight.

Zeina suspected the duties of a staff officer weren't conducive to maintaining peak physical fitness. She thought she might prove stronger in physical combat. On the other hand, Noori was armed, and the leather flap of her holster was buttoned down over the hilt of her pistol, making it impossible to snatch.

She turned the vehicle south along the perimeter access road. The motorised array cast a long shadow. Zeina wondered whose body really was in the luggage compartment at the back of the Pratique. What did those in authority always say if they wanted to create a smokescreen to cover something up?

The harvests are failing.

Terrorists.

The air is polluted.

Terrorists.

The electricity supply is inadequate.

Terrorists.

They reached the southern tip of the array and Zeina drove a little further onto a pan of rough rock. They got out of the car and walked to the rear. Noori raised the hatch.

There was the corpse, loosely wrapped in a coarse, light-coloured fabric. The left arm was exposed, greenish in colour with a long scar along the inside of the forearm. Zeina recognised it from the moment at the end of the ceremony when Bader had raised Al-Fathi's hand towards the sky.

This is very bad, she thought.

Zeina pretended to feel sick. 'Excuse me, I must just get some water.'

Noori nodded. Zeina ran to her rucksack and grabbed the paring knife. She tucked it into her sleeve then opened a water bottle, drinking from it on her way back to the trunk. She immediately saw that Noori had undone the leather flap on her holster.

So, Zeina thought, this is how it will end.

'Can you do this?' Noori demanded, one hand near the gun.

'Yes, I can.'

'Good. You take the shoulders. I'll take the feet.'

Noori leaned in to wrap her arms under the knees of the corpse. As she did so, Zeina stabbed the paring knife into the side of the woman's neck. The blade disappeared up to the hilt. With her other hand, she caught hold of the woman's hair, overbalanced her and pushed her face down into the ground, working the knife violently back and forth until she felt the tip grating against bone. Noori's arms and legs flailed desperately as the blood gushed out of her severed carotid into the hot sand.

Time slowed as Zeina knelt on Noori's back, waiting to be sure the woman was dead. The low sun dazzled her eyes. It felt like she was trapped in a loop of horror in a nightmare. She tried to make her guilty, unconscious mind understand that she'd had no choice, that the alternative had been her own death.

Finally, it was done. The staff officer was no longer a person, merely an object.

Zeina sat back on her heels, breathing deeply, waiting for the surge of adrenaline to subside, aware of the thumping of her heart, thinking about the day her father had taught her to bleed a goat.

A few wisps of cloud crossed the sky. On the back of her right hand, blood dried to a crust. It took all her strength to lift the dead woman into the trunk, on top of the body of the general. When it was done, she looked for her bottle and used the tepid water to wash her hands imperfectly clean.

A little later, Zeina drove past a motion sensor on a post not far from the dusty road that ran east towards the Egyptian border. She knew it would send a ping to the control centre back at Al-Jaghar, but she didn't care. The die was cast. Twenty minutes later she stopped and got out. The sun had set and the cool of the evening felt shocking after the heat of the day.

She opened the luggage compartment and dragged out the body of Staff Officer Noori, stripping her of her clothes and equipment, removing all identifying objects, checking for identification chips under the skin by the torch on her old-fashioned smartphone. She found one lodged in the flesh that covered the pectoral muscle, about five centimetres below Noori's left collar bone. She prised it out and used the point of her knife to damage it beyond readability. Then she threw it into the sand beside the road.

Zeina got back into the driving seat and pulled away. She had no plan, beyond making her way to the Egyptian border. There, perhaps, in her homeland, she could gain some advantage from what she knew – and from the body of the murdered general still slowly decomposing in the trunk.

52

In Paris, earlier that afternoon, Alex had left the Palace of Justice and returned to his boat. He opened Sabie's message with the biometric thumb drive and was immediately transported back in time to his mother's living room and her untidy desk. It was the research she had wanted him to read, the paper on Gerboise Bleue. He checked the message headers and saw that the attachment had been forwarded to Sabie by Fayard.

Why on earth would Fayard have had his mother's document?

Something clicked.

So, it had been the professor at his mother's door on Nelinha's video.

But the realisation raised even more questions.

Had Fayard infected her? If he had, was it deliberate or accidental? Had Gloria let him in because he was unwell, or had he insisted? Had she given Fayard the research or had he taken it? Was it Fayard who had taken all evidence of his mother's current academic preoccupations from the apartment? Alex had searched and found no scraps of paper, no notes of spontaneous ideas, no drafts written by hand – nothing.

He slowed himself down. He needed not to get carried away with supposition. The best thing would be to confront Fayard, looking him in the eye, before the panel resumed the following day.

He turned his attention to the attachment. As Nelinha had mentioned, Gerboise Bleue was the codename for the French nuclear test site in the Saharan wilderness of southern Algeria. Gloria's paper also explored French nuclear testing in the South Pacific and missile bases in Zaire and Kenya. There was a detailed chapter on a ballistic missile facility built in the late 1950s near Cairo and a section on an abandoned complex in southern Libya. The final section concerned the airbase at Al-Jaghar in Cyrenia and was marked for particular study.

Seeing this, Alex felt the pieces of his investigation shifting. Why was that important? Was it the connection with Prime Minister Mourad?

He thought about when precisely Gloria had asked him to read it. Just after the debacle at Bunker Martha, when he'd come to see her in the midst of his self-indulgent existential crisis. At least, that was what he'd thought at the time. Now, he knew, there was more to it – a dawning awareness that a catastrophe was coming.

He remembered the phrase he had used then: 'a vast absence'.

He still didn't know what that actually meant. Events had overtaken it all – Norway, Kofinou, Cyrenia. The dead Portuguese youth in Montmartre.

He opened the digital file he'd downloaded on Luís and his mother. The young man had died at the age of nineteen with little to link him to anything beyond his neighbourhood circle. He was, more or less, nobody. But then, why the gaudy coffin and the lilies?

The downloaded data informed him that Luís had been a reasonably good student – earnest, committed, with a gift for self-expression, an affinity with cameras. Alex made several audio calls and, finally, spoke to the headteacher of the college Luís had attended. He didn't need to provide a false identity to get the man to talk.

'Yes, that's right, Luís Beira. I was so very disappointed when he dropped out to take a job, apparently to support his mother. I understand she is a widow with limited resources.'

'Do you know what this job was?' Alex asked.

'No, but Luís spoke of it as a great opportunity. I got the impression it would allow him to further his talent with cameras. He insisted that he couldn't share details. I told him I was pleased for him, then he said something odd.'

'What was that?'

'He said the job would make people take notice of him.'

Alex's eyebrows rose. 'Were those his exact words?'

'I think so. "People will have to take notice of me." Something like that.'

'What do you think he meant?'

'I've wondered that myself,' the headteacher answered. 'I must say, I didn't like his tone. It was very out of character. He was always very polite. His mother brought him up mostly alone, you know, after his father died. A police officer, and quite the hero. Perhaps you already know what happened – a terrorist outrage, the wrong person in the wrong place at the wrong time.'

'The cause?' Alex asked.

'The terrorists' cause?' The teacher sounded surprised. 'I have no idea.'

Alex let it go. The information would be in the files.

'You said just now that you didn't like his tone?' he said.

'No,' the headteacher replied. 'To be honest, he seemed shifty, almost secretive, but conflicted. It was as if he wanted to tell me something, but he knew he mustn't.'

'And what did you say?'

He could almost hear the man's helpless shrug. 'I wished him well.'

After ending the call, Alex turned to another database where he discovered that Luís's mother, Luísa Beira, had come to France when the Portuguese medical system began to fail. This was after financial support from Angola, a major oil exporter and an ex-Portuguese colony, dried up with the move away from fossil fuels. The husband had been a French police officer of Portuguese heritage she'd met in Paris. But the records indicated he'd died in an armed robbery – not terrorism at all.

Why, he wondered, had Luís lied? Teenage self-aggrandisement or something more sinister?

Luísa Beira had never integrated, remaining isolated within her Portuguese-speaking community. Contrary to what the headteacher believed, she received a modest state pension every month. The idea that the boy had left the college to support her might also be a lie.

Consulting another part of the dossier, he saw that someone at DGIS had worked hard to enhance a sequence of street surveillance shots of the hearse provided by Camera Control. In doing so, they had been able to decipher the name, home city and date of incorporation of the funeral directors, written in fancy gold lettering on the side window of the vehicle. Alex followed this new lead and discovered the funeral company was just a façade.

Another dead end.

Despite his frustration, there was one more lead he could follow up – the blood-stained mask he had retrieved outside the house. It might carry traces of the mother's DNA. Of course, it might also have belonged to someone else, someone yet to be identified, for example one of the undertakers.

It reminded him to copy the DNA record for Luís. He instructed the computer to retrieve it and found zero results. He re-ran the search, specifying the address as well as the name and date of birth.

Nothing. According to the official records, Luís Beira didn't exist.

Worse, he had never existed. In the twenty-four hours since Alex had downloaded his life story, the boy had become a Blank.

Alex re-ran the searches for the tattooed letters on the boy's hands. The results were exactly as he remembered them – the Seventh-Day Adventist church, the union of amateur music clubs, the professional Minecrafter, Unstructured DSMC. He ran a further search to find out what that last one meant, pinning it down to a computer modelling technique used to simulate hypersonic gas flows, for example over the nose of a missile. Because of the Al-Jaghar launch site, he wanted to fit this new information about air turbulence into some kind of pattern, but he couldn't see it. Maybe it was a coincidence?

Fayard wouldn't agree. Fayard maintained there was no such thing as a coincidence, just undiscovered patterns of cause and effect.

Alex yawned. It was still relatively early, but he had several short or broken nights to make up for.

He was about to silence all his comms for sleep when his watch vibrated with a message from Paul Sanchez. It contained an embedded 3-D video that his decryption software had to quarantine before it could be played – an earnest to-camera monologue of respectful thanks.

It made good sense. If Sanchez was now DGES, the obvious deployment for him was Base Aérienne 117, the Paris military airport.

53

Outside in the real world, it was Saturday, 1 August 2037 and the sun was almost up. In the sleep cabin on board his boat, Alex was half-dreaming. Or, rather, he was remembering something that had happened, recreating it in the slippery fantasy of a dream.

It was late at night, after curfew. The streetlamps were out. He and Mariam were lying on the deck of the boat, looking up. In the absence of light pollution, they could see countless pinpricks of light, most of them still, some of them moving across the blue-black sky. Somehow, in the dream, he was also looking down on himself and on her. He heard her voice in his head, as if from far away.

'How many of them are satellites, do you think?'

He didn't hear his own voice in the dream. He only thought his answer.

'I don't know. Can you see satellites from Earth?'

The perspective swung round. The feeling was uncomfortable, woozy. He was looking up, out of his own eyes. Then the sky seemed to dip, to come closer, and the dream faded as his consciousness began to rise up from sleep.

He turned over in his bed, forcing himself to remain submerged, dipping back into darkness. Mariam's voice sounded again in his memory.

'*Quand le soleil brille, on n'a point besoin d'étoiles.*'

Then he woke and it took him a few moments to realise he was alone.

'Stars,' he said out loud, not wanting to lose the thought. He went to his screen. 'Wake,' he ordered.

'Stars,' he said again, thoughtfully. 'Or satellites.'

The software transcribed the words. He looked at them, his eyes vague. Then it came back to him as a true memory, no longer a dream – he and Mariam lying on their backs, looking at the sky. He had turned his head and she had done the same, gazing into his eyes.

‘You are home,’ he told her. ‘For me, you are home.’

She smiled.

‘*Quand le soleil brille, on n’a point besoin d’étoiles.*’

‘What’s that?’

‘My grandmother’s saying,’ she told him. ‘When the sun shines, there’s no need for stars.’

Then the moment was gone, the memory faded and he was alone in the cabin of his boat, listening to the hum of the climate control.

He shook himself and refocused, fetching a green drink from the fridge and pacing the small cabin. He hadn’t thought of that conversation in months. There had to be a reason he’d dreamt about it now.

What if the coming darkness had nothing to do with undersea cables, with Bunker Martha, with the Norwegian lab, with Prime Minister Mourad? At least, nothing directly to do with any of them?

He had a mental checklist of all the moments that had troubled him – words spoken, actions he had witnessed, details learned from interviews and research. The answer would be found in the pattern. It always was. But, before he searched the pattern, he had to find out about those tiny specks in the night that had no light of their own and could only be seen as reflections of the sun and, counterintuitively, only when the sun had left the sky.

Because he’d slept well and woken early, Alex had plenty of time before the inquiry reconvened at noon. He put the blood-stained mask inside an envelope and addressed it for Sabie’s attention, before leaving a voice message requesting that it be sent to forensics for DNA matching. He spent the next hour on the embankment, running, trying to think.

When he got back to the boat, the courier was waiting. He handed over the envelope, then showered and changed before checking his holo. All his previous searches were still live. Hoping Fayard had done as he’d promised and given him professional privileges, he messaged Sabie with a request for a report on the current state of all observational and communications satellites in Earth orbit.

Including strategic analysis.

The answer was immediate.

I will find you something within the hour.

While he waited, he went back to his searches, reconfiguring them without the sequence U D S M C, simply specifying 'death', 'fingers', 'tattoos', and set the date parameters to the last two weeks. The top result was brand new. It came from that very morning and seemed utterly inexplicable – another gratuitous but horrible crime, in Calais.

He messaged Sabie again to ask the administrator to book him a car from the DGIS pool. Within seconds, the authority to travel from Paris to Calais was on his comm-watch.

He left the canal basin and climbed up to the boulevard. The day was pleasant, not too hot, a veil of thin cloud trapped in the bowl of the Paris basin, filtering the sun. He had plenty of time to walk through the city and find something to eat – perhaps a last meal before his life changed for ever.

After all, he had no idea what the conclusion of the inquiry might be.

On the Cyrenia-Egypt border, the sun was already approaching the zenith.

Zeina Yaseen understood that the Egyptian border guards had no real idea how to respond to the situation they found themselves in. She had driven up to the bedraggled remnant of the old barbed-wire frontier between Libya and Egypt, and opened the trunk to display the corpse of a sixty-year-old man with a scar running the length of his left forearm. She told them he was General Al-Fathi of the Cyrenia high command, that he had been murdered by…

Well, she couldn't say for sure but she suspected it had something to do General Bader, whose sister was the commander of the Air Force base and launch site.

Zeina decided she wouldn't share the whole story. In any case, for the two border guards, it was clearly too many names all at once, too many ideas, too many questions.

She persuaded them to send a radio message to the nearest local authority, a more important road crossing point about 140 kilometres away. Then they put her in a mud-built holding cell, telling her there would be a delay, that they would refer the question up the chain of command to the OC Western Frontier.

Could he be contacted straight away?

No.

Then when?

Soon – he would be contacted soon.

At the Ministry for Foreign Affairs, Claudine Poiret was conflicted. She'd just endured a ninety-minute meeting with André Chambon, the ginger-haired DGES analyst, attempting to devise a new strategy for France in relation to Cyrenia.

A waste of time.

Chambon's mind was an encyclopaedia but he had no ability to synthesise. He could recognise every fragment of colour in the kaleidoscope, but the patterns escaped him.

Still, it had been a useful meeting in another respect. Questioning Chambon had been a good way to interrogate her own thought processes.

The extraction of Prime Minister Mourad had been a success, as far as it went, but the beacon of democracy that Cyrenia represented had now been compromised. Significant European and, above all, French state investment was in jeopardy. And those investments had been made in good faith on commercial terms – generous commercial terms, but motivated by profit as well as philanthropy. The office of the French president wanted to know how the situation could be resolved, promoting the idea – without putting forward any kind of plan – that Mourad should be repatriated and reinstated.

Poiret had already thought of that, and had presented a report with a possible scenario to make it happen. She wondered if the report had been read and, if it had, whether it had reached someone with the clearance and political influence to make it happen.

In any case, before she took action, she needed to speak to Mourad in person.

Mourad would by now have understood that she was being held at Val-de-Grâce not only for her own safety, but also as a prized asset – a chess piece of high value that Poiret would only allow to rejoin the game when it was useful.

Manipulating her would not be easy. The woman was a brilliant politician, a charismatic leader, a skilful exploiter of people and opportunities.

Poiret knew herself well enough to recognise when she might be out of her depth. She was not an intuitive person. She could never be confident of seeing behind the veil of other people's words and actions to their deeper motivations.

Alexandre Lamarque, on the other hand…

She had reviewed his file a second time. It was truly remarkable to see how many times his analysis of circumstances and strategy had been proved correct.

And, right now, according to Professor Fayard, he foresaw disaster.

Poiret didn't want to believe it. On the other hand, she was one of very few people aware of the danger above their heads.

For decades, France had considered placing nuclear warheads in orbit. She and others had argued against it, suggesting the risk was far greater than any dissuasive or tactical benefit. But the hawks in the Defence Ministry had persisted and, over time, a kind of compromise had been worked out.

The deployment they'd settled on didn't contradict the letter of international law – in particular, the 2031 update to the Outer Space Treaty. But it was clearly against its spirit.

Instead of nuclear weapons, France had placed three platforms in orbit, each carrying dense tungsten rods – heavy yet aerodynamic objects that, if deployed, would accelerate to hypersonic speeds and hit the ground with the force of a nuclear blast. They would penetrate much deeper than a ballistic missile ever could, but would cause no radioactive contamination.

As long as their orbiting platforms were under control, the tungsten rods posed no threat. Remove that control and they became devastating and indiscriminate accidents waiting to happen.

They called it '*Tonnerre de Dieu*' – God's Thunder.

Was this the disaster Lamarque feared?

Poiret ordered an assistant to progress the plan she had put in place for Gloria Lamarque – a transfer to the Rothschild Institute, a facility only available to those connected to the heart of power. By helping his mother, she would keep him onside. She had a feeling she was going to need him, maybe to accompany her at a meeting with Mourad. But how would she explain to the deposed prime minister the presence of a soldier who reached out a hand to draw her out of the burning parliament building and fly her away to an exile that was, for the time being, little better than prison?

She would find a way.

Her decision made, she sent a message to both Lamarque and Mourad and ordered a car to take her to the Palace of Justice.

54

By the time Alex reached the Palace of Justice just before noon, the sun beat down harshly. He climbed the great stairs and entered the building, fulfilling the hygiene and security protocols, handing in his comms, being escorted to the appropriate part of the building. Again, it was impossible to speak to Amaury who was led into the seminar room via a different entrance.

The assessor announced that the first part of the session would be spent on seven aspects of the mission: the briefing given to Alex's paratrooper support; the flight plan across the Mediterranean; the approach to Cyrenia; fighter support; ground-to-air defences; the parachute drop itself; the plan of action on the ground.

None of that had a material impact, so Alex let it wash over him. Eventually they broke for coffee. Amaury was led into a private room. Alex followed Fayard into the lobby.

'The room is too cold. Is that your doing?'

'I have a touch of fever,' Fayard explained. 'A cooler room is more comfortable.'

'Did you visit my mother two weeks ago?'

Alex thought the professor looked taken aback, but it lasted only an instant.

'Was it the cameras in the stairwell?' he guessed.

'So, you did visit her?' Alex insisted.

'Yes.'

'Why?'

'At her invitation,' Fayard said simply.

'For what reason?'

'Because she was worried about you.' The professor paused, his red-rimmed eyes searching Alex's face. 'Ah, I see that surprises you.'

It was what Gloria had jokingly threatened. She had been trying to help.

'She wanted to talk to you,' said Alex, seeing it all in his mind, 'to ask if you would give me a job.'

Fayard gave a faint smile. 'Gloria told me External wasn't your natural home, had never been your natural home. We met several times during your training – receptions and so forth. Her work as a historian was always of interest to me. Of course, I agreed with her.'

'She sent you her research?'

'She did. I asked Sabie to send it on to you,' Fayard said. 'What did you think of it?'

This was not how Alex had intended the conversation to go. He felt caught off guard. How much should he tell Fayard? How much did the old man already know?

'It's interesting. But everywhere I look there's a suggestion of a pattern but no pattern,' he said. 'Just ideas that lead nowhere, dead ends.'

Fayard touched Alex's sleeve. It was an oddly intimate gesture. 'Your conscious mind begins not to trust me, but I implore you to follow your instincts instead. Your instinct says we're on the same side, doesn't it?'

Alex weighed up the question but, before he could answer, a clerk approached.

'They want you inside,' he told them.

A few kilometres away, in an almost-deserted forensics laboratory at Paris-Descartes University, a tired technician was working overtime, applying the most modern technology to the extraction and analysis of DNA retrieved from a bloodstained mask. The technician was tired. Short of money, he had worked three double shifts in the last seven days.

This job was an unusual one – not in its technical challenges, but because it had no case file allotted to it, no crime number. The technician didn't care. It was simply another routine task in a life of routine tasks.

He blinked his reddened eyes as the results came through, labelled with the name he had been given. He added a second reference, the one he had discovered by cross-referencing with the national ID database: 'Luísa Beira, widow.'

He sent the results on, rubbed his temples, sat back in his chair and yawned.

Because he was tired, he didn't also discover that 'Luísa Beira, widow' had given birth to a male child. Had he been paying closer attention he might have asked himself how the woman could have a son, yet there be no separate ID record for that child. He might have discovered that the child, despite its officially documented entrance into the world, was a Blank.

He wandered off in search of coffee.

Moments later, the information about 'Luísa Beira, widow' arrived in Sabie's inbox. He read it and forwarded it to Lamarque. He had no choice. Fayard would monitor it, he knew. The old man was convinced that his protégé could see connections where no one else could.

That might be true. It wasn't important. Time was almost up.

Mariam was sitting in Fayard's official car in the subterranean garage beneath the Palace of Justice when her comms alerted her to a new message. There was very little light, just the emergency exit sign glowing pale green over the door to the pedestrian stairs. She had the windows open because the air underground was pleasantly cool.

Before opening the communication, she remembered she hadn't replied to Alex when he messaged that he would be away on Sunday.

Have a good trip.

The device took a few moments to connect, struggling with a weak signal, giving her time to re-read her words on the screen.

What a miserable message, she thought, and added something she hoped would appear more affectionate.

Stay safe.

Finally, she opened the official communication – an automated ping from forensics. The AI had found a match – in evidence analysed at the forensics laboratory at Paris-Descartes University – for the biometric evidence she had retrieved from the Church of Saint Genevieve. She followed a trail of click-throughs and an official login until she finally found the original technician's report.

The details were straightforward. There was no record of the fingerprints taken from the lens cap, but the human hair had yielded a result. It wasn't a result for the hair itself, but for a connection to another investigation.

Mariam half closed her eyes, thinking about when she had sent the lens cap for analysis. It was like the response from Camera Control, trying to identify the woman in the wig – another long delay. She sent Alex another message.

Is there a problem at forensics? There seem to be a lot of delays.

She looked back at the screen. The genetic connection to the unattributed hair sample was pinged on the strength of a shared mutation in both her sample and another in analysis. Further study of the two samples had shown shared DNA on the X-chromosome. They were either mother and son or, less likely, grandmother and son.

If my sample is the son, she thought, he is the one who handled the lens cap.

She clicked through three more screens, ending up at the ID record of the mother, Luísa Beira, a widow, domiciled in Montmartre, deceased just a couple of days ago. There was also a date-of birth listed for a child, 1 July 2018, and a name, 'Luís'. But when she tried to access the ID record of the child, she found nothing. There was a record that the woman had given birth, the name of the father, but no record for the child.

She frowned, thinking of the story Alex had told her. The youth had existed. Alex had seen the body. How could the woman have given birth to a child that had no record?

She clicked through a different pathway to find out where the pinged DNA sample had come from, what investigation it was connected to.

The top-level authority for the forensic analysis was DGIS, meaning the request had come from someone at headquarters in Levallois-Perret. The authorising signature was Administrator Sabie, but that didn't mean anything. Sabie would be called on to authorise all kinds of investigations. The interesting thing was the absence of a crime number and, in its absence, the designation someone had decided to use.

Request for forensic analysis: Lamarque.

55

After the pause for coffee, Alex sat back down at the shiny table with its recessed screens. The assessor asked Echo – Claudine Poiret – to run the video.

It was a shaky night-vision recording, all in tones of green, with a poor-quality, crackly audio – Alex's bodycam. They watched the lurching point-of-view move through a sumptuous lobby – massive pillars wound like gigantic ropes, low embroidered divans, probably red and gold but in night-vision it was impossible to say. The camera came to a stop at a double door, hanging askew on massive strap hinges. Gunfire could be heard, tinny and unconvincing.

The bodycam ducked down to knee height and crept forward, pushing one of the doors out of the way. Then the angle eased up to take in the vast debating chamber. Part of the roof was missing and debris fell in fine pieces.

Alex glanced round the participants in the inquiry. It was an odd experience. Everyone else was gripped by the events unspooling on their screens. He, of course, was watching it for a second time, remembering how the moon had emerged from behind clouds, adding its pale white light to the flickering of the flames.

How it had felt to be blackmailed into a situation where death was almost as likely as survival.

The bodycam angled down to reveal Alex's smoothly efficient hands connecting the sights to his lightweight sniper's rifle, checking the magazine, raising the gun so the camera pointed along the barrel and became still.

Alex looked away. He heard the two double-taps – the first pair at the terrorist, the second at his friend.

Amaury lifted his arm onto the desk and pulled back his right sleeve, revealing an ugly rubber prosthesis.

'This is the result of those shots,' he said quietly.

'Wait for the end of the evidence,' the assessor told him sharply.

The bodycam video lurched up and bounced across the space. Then Mourad appeared in the doorway in her long ivory and burgundy gown.

In the underground parking garage, Mariam felt her mind beginning to spiral, trapped by her own desire for secrecy, her need not to be pitied. However close she and Alex had grown, she was determined to maintain her distance, to keep her secrets. But was that distance the reason why she had now begun to suspect Alex of working against her?

Was he senior enough to delay forensics and, having done so, to then cover his tracks? No, that was ridiculous. But, if he had, was it possible that Sabie had found out and left a clue for others by putting 'Lamarque' on the case?

She knew that Alex was Fayard's chosen one, the agent he had sought to bring into the family for over a year. Perhaps Sabie knew this too. Perhaps even Sabie was wary of going against the old man's wishes and judgement.

She thought about their conversations, when they were alone in the darkness of the cabin. Was he that good an actor? Had he deliberately curated his mood of disillusionment to draw her in? Was he using her to get closer to Professor Fayard? Was she being played?

She thought back to their first meeting at the Tour d'Argent eight years before, and remembered the immediate emotional connection between them, despite her grief at her mother's death and the realisation that her life would, henceforward, be dominated by her sisters' care. Had he known her history already and used it as a way to… To what?

To seduce her?

She shook her head. This was absurd. Alex was honest. He loved her. And she had never told him she loved him in return.

After the dinner at the Tour d'Argent, their odd courtship had begun with her helping him track down the thugs who attacked the Blanks on the riverside path. The DNA evidence collected from beneath the fingernails of his right hand had been enough to convict one of them. The second man had confessed under interrogation.

Mariam frowned, remembering the idealism of their shared determination to bring them to justice. She wasn't naive or trusting. She had never outgrown the scepticism of adolescence, the belief that everything was a mess, that the world had been irrevocably screwed and the purpose of existence was simply the passing of time with the least possible heartache, the least damage done to others.

No. If she was being played, it wasn't by Alex.

But, if it wasn't Alex, who was it?

She began to look at it the other way round. What if Fayard had groomed her as a conduit to Alex? It was Fayard who found her a job – almost invented a job for her, making sure that she was at the heart of DGIS operations without ever having to leave Paris.

Whoever it was, Fayard or Alex, they must have been playing a very long game. Was that likely? It would mean all her instincts were at fault. But, she had to admit, it was possible. Who knew what other cards they might have to play – cards they had been preparing over many years? Was she just one of their options?

'Their'?

Mariam frowned.

Surely that was the most ridiculous idea of all – that they were in league, had been in league all along.

She thumped the dashboard in frustration. There seemed no way of finding the truth.

The video ended. For a few seconds the conference room was quiet.

Fayard spoke first. 'It seems clear to me. An exemplary mission.'

'Thank you, Bravo,' said the assessor. 'Do you have anything to add, Delta?'

'I have nothing to add,' said the anonymous civil servant from the office of the president. 'The events are outside our jurisdiction. We will abstain from judgement.'

'Alpha is transferring to DGIS and will be under your chain of command,' objected the assessor.

'All the same, our position is non-interference in the affairs of subsidiary departments. And the mission took place on foreign soil, under the auspices of External Security.'

'Alpha is currently inactive,' observed Fayard. 'If we follow Delta's lead, Alpha is therefore outside of the competence of this hearing and the inquiry is void or, at the very least, moot.'

Amaury's unconvincing prosthesis went halfway up his forearm. He tore off three noisy Velcro straps and removed it, revealing an angry-looking red stump.

'This isn't moot,' he said angrily.

The room felt suddenly small. All eyes were on Amaury's wound – all except Alex's. He spoke directly to his colleague and friend.

'You shouldn't have been there, Amaury,' he said. 'The situation was under control.'

'Address your remarks though the chair, Alpha,' said the assessor.

'Charlie shouldn't have been there,' Alex insisted. 'He should have hung back. It wasn't his mission.'

'I was about to take out the shooter,' Amaury spat. 'I didn't know you were going to be there. The mission planning was negligent.'

'Not everything can be controlled or foreseen. You know that.'

Even as he said it, Alex felt heartsick. He wanted this conversation – the one he had waited so long for – to go differently.

'Address me, Alpha,' insisted the assessor.

Alex made himself look at her. 'Charlie was supposed to maintain his cover. I took out what I thought were two hostiles. There was no way to know one of them was Charlie.'

'The hostile was barely capable of hitting the door,' Amaury's voice rose, 'let alone a moving human target. You knew my cover was being part of their assassination team.' He looked accusingly at Poiret. 'Your briefing was clearly completely inadequate.'

'Through the chair,' barked the assessor.

'Knowing Charlie might be there, I fired to disarm,' Alex said. 'The shot should have taken his weapon.'

Amaury laughed, a horrible mirthless sound.

'But it didn't, Alpha,' the assessor replied. 'It took his hand.'

There was a pause.

'The circumstances,' Fayard interjected, smoothly, 'were borderline. Alpha was under severe pressure. The shot was a good one, albeit twenty centimetres too far to the left. Twenty centimetres over thirty metres. That's a very narrow tolerance.'

The assessor nodded. 'Thank you, Bravo.'

'Zero point six recurring per cent,' Delta clarified. 'I mention it for information only. The president has no opinion.'

'Thank you, Delta,' said the assessor drily. 'Anything else?'

No one spoke.

She stood. 'Then that will be all for today. We will reconvene after review by the president's office.'

'When will that be?' asked Alex.

'That is not under my control,' said the assessor.

Amaury looked away, his face hard.

'I need to speak to Amaury.' Alex corrected himself, 'I mean, to Charlie.' Before she could stop him, he turned to his friend. 'You know it was an accident,' he pleaded.

Amaury glanced up and Alex felt something shift, as if some faint message of sympathy or solidarity had passed between them. Then it was gone.

'It was a failure of briefing and planning,' Amaury said bitterly, 'and I'm the one who has to pay.'

The assessor grew brisk. 'Court recorder, book the room, please. Shall we say in seven days?'

Alex frowned, certain that seven days would be too late.

56

Once more, Alex was detained while Amaury was hustled out and Fayard went with the assessor. He made his way out through the corridors of the Palace of Justice feeling helpless.

He retrieved his comms and saw three messages from Mariam waiting for him.

Have a good trip.

Stay safe.

Is there a problem at forensics? There seem to be a lot of delays.

He sent a brief reply.

I'm not sure. Ask Sabie? When can we speak?

At the bottom of the wide ceremonial staircase, Fayard's car was waiting. Mariam was at the wheel, the rear passenger door open. Fayard followed him down on the arm of a police officer. Alex waited for him, and picked up the conversation that had been interrupted by the resumption of the inquiry.

'What support and treatment will Amaury get? It should be the very best available.'

'I agree, but that is out of my hands.' Fayard touched Alex's arm. 'Amaury has his own plan, I'm sure.'

Was that right? Alex wasn't convinced.

'You say my mother showed you her research, the paper on African launch sites,' he said.

Fayard nodded. 'She gave me a copy that day I visited her.'

'There's nothing left in her apartment now,' Alex said. 'Did you take her other papers?'

'Nothing left at all?' Fayard looked puzzled. 'I took only the information she gave me.'

'So where's it all gone?'

'Might they have been destroyed by infection control?'

'I don't know. Perhaps.'

Alex hadn't heard of papers being destroyed for reasons of infection. He'd have to ask the nurses. Fayard was stepping towards the car when Alex asked the question he'd been holding back.

'Did you infect her?'

Fayard hesitated just a second too long before speaking. 'If I did, it was not intentional,' he said. 'I will send my results to the clinic and ask them to give a definitive answer.'

Alex couldn't argue with that. It was fair enough, if he could trust the results.

He gazed at the opaque lenses of the professor's dark glasses. 'When you visited her to discuss my career, what did she say about me?'

'That you were worried by the future,' he said.

'Yes, well, who isn't?'

'More than that, more than just someone having their private doubts,' Fayard said. 'She told me that, when you came back from Norway, you were… what was the word she used? "*Désabusé.*" That you no longer believed.'

Alex hesitated, studying Fayard's impassive expression. Was any of what he said likely to be true? Or was he being told what he wanted to hear?

'She told you that?'

'She did.'

Alex looked around – at Fayard's official car with Mariam in the driver's seat, the dusty tarmac, two lawyers eating sandwiches on the parapet above the river, a brazen seagull watching them from only a metre away. He couldn't shake the feeling that he was being manipulated. And not just by Poiret. By some other force he couldn't bring into focus.

'Alexandre,' said Fayard gently, 'what do you see?'

He didn't know want to say. What if Fayard challenged him to provide this evidence? What did he really have? Nothing.

'I see an absence.'

'An absence?'

'A darkness.'

'I see,' said Fayard. 'Or rather I don't. What exactly does that mean?'

Alex didn't answer. Under the pressure of Fayard's questioning, the pieces were beginning to form a more recognisable shape.

He wondered what he should do. He could decide to trust Fayard and share his ideas. Or shut him out and, more than likely, be confined to his home. If the panel went badly, he might be prosecuted. Without Fayard's support, the odds were six-to-five against, as always.

'What is it, Alexandre?' Behind his dark lenses, Fayard searched Alex's face. 'You suspect something.'

'Thank you for giving me privileges. I've asked Sabie for a car,' he said finally. 'I'm going to Calais tomorrow morning.'

'Why Calais?'

'There's a connection there,' Alex said. 'I'm sure of it.'

Fayard nodded. 'Good. Go find your connection. You may not entirely trust me, but I have complete faith in you.'

Fayard turned away and let himself fall back in the rear seat. Alex came to a decision.

'I'll tell you what I find,' he said.

Fayard smiled and Alex thought he looked relieved. Mariam came round to shut the door and shot him a quick, unreadable glance, then walked back round to retake her seat in front.

Alex heard the car's drive engage. He watched the electric vehicle pull quietly away, its tyres sticky with the heat, leaving him alone, searching his mind for clues.

Mariam drove smoothly along the embankment, stopping at the junction with the Pont Saint-Michel. She glanced back at the old man, framed in the rear-view mirror.

'I feel I might be able to walk a little,' Fayard announced unexpectedly. 'Let's find somewhere quiet where I won't get in the way as I cripple along.'

'Somewhere secure, also?'

The old man sighed. 'I suppose so.'

'The Luxembourg Gardens?' she suggested.

Fayard sat back, impenetrable behind his dark glasses as Mariam turned right over the river.

'What is this trade-off we must always make between security and freedom?' murmured the old man, as if to himself.

A few minutes later they parked in a designated bay, their DGIS credentials giving them authority, and were ushered through a checkpoint into the park. Fayard managed two circuits of the large pond then went to sit on a bench close to another statue of Saint Genevieve.

'It is interesting how she keeps turning up, don't you think?' he mused. 'The church dedicated to her where that intriguing video was shot. The modernist statue on the bridge where we met Alexandre. You remember? So different, that simplified monumental representation from this classical design.'

He gestured to the city's patron saint, carved in stone, her arms gently crossed, a scroll of stone paper held loosely in the fingers of her right hand.

Mariam studied her boss doubtfully.

'Was there something you wanted to say to me, Professor?'

'I asked you to leave your communication devices in the car. I have done the same. This area is a designated data shadow, to preserve the privacy of any senators who might exercise in the gardens. To be perfectly honest, I don't know how it's done. Some kind of technical wizardry. All the same, it is never a bad idea to take precautions, just in case.'

Mariam's brow furrowed. 'Just in case?'

'In case anyone is watching, listening.'

'Who might be listening?'

Fayard put his head on one side. 'Your tone is abrupt. It is most unlike you.'

Mariam blushed. 'I'm sorry. I was thinking of something else.'

He pointed at a metal seat nearby. 'Pull that over and sit down.'

The chair rattled across the gravel as she dragged it closer to him. The light filtered pleasantly through the leaves of a chestnut tree. She wondered if she ought to share with him about the ping from forensics but decided to hold the information back until she knew more about what he wanted.

'Would you tell me, my dear, about your illicit relationship with our new family member?' He smiled. 'I want to know about you and Alexandre Lamarque.'

57

At the same time, in a plain, mud-built cell on the Cyrene-Egyptian frontier, Zeina was bored. It had only been one night and, now, one interminable day. The frontier guards were, apparently, still waiting for a response from the person they called 'OC Western Frontier'.

She thought about how she'd arrived at the border post with the Pratique's batteries about to expire, thinking that the corpse of General Al-Fathi would be a kind of passport to acceptance. But the frontier guards had responded by putting her in detention with a jug of water and a loaf of stale bread. There was a hole in the ground to relieve herself and a bag of sand to cover it up. That was it.

What would come next, she wondered?

There was no official diplomacy between Cyrenia and Egypt. The government in Cairo was so wedded to neutrality and isolationism that it had withdrawn its diplomatic missions worldwide and, at least in public, took no active interest in the breakaway Libyan republic.

She heard the swish of footsteps in the sand, then the door was pushed open, allowing the superheated desert air to come rushing in, stirring up the dust. She pulled her headscarf over her mouth and nose but made sure to smile with her eyes.

'Have you confirmed my identity as an Egyptian citizen?' she asked hopefully.

He looked apologetic. 'Not yet. We don't have access to digital records. Would you come with me?'

Zeina went outside, blinking in the brightness of the sun. It was understandable that they didn't bother to lock the door to the mud-built cell. There was nothing but rocks and sand as far as the eye could see.

'Al-Fathi is important,' she insisted. 'Something is happening at Al-Jaghar. Something very important.'

'I know. You said. We are doing our best.'

The guard led her to the frontier post building, about thirty square metres of cheap temporary accommodation, covered in corrugated aluminium siding slowly roasting in the desert sun. Inside, the temperature was close to forty degrees. Instantly Zeina felt herself begin to sweat.

The border guard gave her a bottle of water.

'Thank you.'

A second man was seated at an old-fashioned radio set with a hand-held microphone. He gestured to her to come forward. Zeina felt like she'd stepped into the past. This was the analogue technology she remembered from childhood. But then, this was Egypt, a nation where living in the past had become a way of life.

Cautiously, she picked up the receiver and pressed it to her ear. It was warm against her skin. 'Hello?'

The voice at the other end spoke with a strong desert accent. 'The OC will speak to you.'

There was a pause, then a new voice, bored, irritated. 'Well, what is it? Be quick. I don't have much time.'

Zeina told her story. Gradually, the distant, crackly voice became more alert.

'And all of this happened in the last twenty-four hours?'

'More or less.'

The OC Western Frontier asked three more incisive questions then concluded: 'Do nothing. I will be in touch.'

The line went dead.

Still holding the receiver, she looked up at the second guard inquiringly. He looked as relieved as she felt.

'Would you like to wait with us,' he asked her, 'until they call back?'

'No, thank you,' she replied. 'I'd like to go back to the mud-hut. It's much cooler.'

Back at the airbase beside the solar array at Al-Jaghar, General Bader was in his sister's office at the top of the control tower. The wide windows had a view across the runways to the huge metal gantry beside the launch pad. The rocket was tethered in position with a jeep, a pick-up truck, and five small figures in conversation at its base. Technicians were working halfway up its fuselage.

'Still?' said General Bader, feigning anger. 'What is this incompetence? The launch cannot be brought forward?'

'No, brother,' said Commander Latifah Bader. She was dressed in desert uniform, sand-coloured fatigues, sitting in a leather swivel chair at a cedarwood desk. 'Do you think these things are easy?'

'Of course not,' he scowled, shaking his head. 'Are you not impatient, too?'

'The schedule is unaffected. Don't worry. The moment will soon come.'

'I am not worried.' He turned away, not wanting her to see his expression. 'Are you certain the countdown will be respected?'

'Technically, this isn't a delay. It's a normal sequence of tests and checks.'

'But the plan is time sensitive,' he reminded her. 'It must happen on a particular day at a particular time.'

She gave him a puzzled look. 'Why are you repeating all this to me? Did I not bring you into the movement?'

He nodded. 'You did.'

'And are we not united?'

'We are.'

'Then why aren't you confindent?' she asked. 'Nobody can stop us. The base is isolated in the desert for a reason.'

He contemplated her expression. Her eyes shon with zealotry. He admired her fervour. She never had the slightest doubt. He, on the other hand, had become unsure.

'I know that.'

'Right now, all attention is on Cyrene City and the insurrection. No one is looking at us. We are free to act, to bring on the darkness.'

'I hope you are right,' he told her.

'We must be patient and allow the engineers to ensure that everything goes according to plan,' she continued. 'Would you rather the rocket exploded on the ground?'

'Of course not.'

'Then let the experts do their jobs.'

'Experts,' grumbled Bader.

'Experts who will also take the blame,' she said.

Bader smiled. 'That, I agree with.'

'It will be all we have dreamed,' she told him. 'I feel it.'

'As long as the timeline is respected,' he replied, aware that he was repeating himself.

To avoid his sister's penetrating gaze, Bader went to fetch water in a paper cone from the cooler and tried to calm himself down. He was beginning to think the plan might already be off course. He'd said nothing to anyone, but he hadn't seen Staff Officer Noori in more than twenty-four hours. She wasn't answering her comms.

'It was unwise to kill Al-Fathi,' said Latifah, as if she had read his mind. 'Are you certain the body won't be found?'

'It's far away, out in the sands.' His voice sounded more confident than he felt.

Latifah got up from her swivel chair. 'Why did you do it?'

'He was insisting we convene the Presidential Council,' Bader said. 'He would eventually have persuaded them to let him take charge in Mourad's absence. He was a stronger candidate than I.'

'To become leader of Cyrenia?' She looked surprised. 'But there will be no more Cyrenia, brother. No more anything.'

He felt himself shudder and hoped she hadn't noticed. He nodded vigorously to cover the truth.

'Good, yes. This is the endgame.' He walked over to the window and looked out at the rocket.

'The clean slate,' she replied, her eyes blank, her mind focused on a vision of the future that he no longer shared.

Was this truly the only way? Now that his chance had come, his chance to step into the space left by Mourad's departure, were destruction and darkness now inevitable?

'You are right, sister,' he said, hoping he sounded convincing. 'Of course you are right.'

58

The next morning at nine o'clock sharp, Alex collected the DGIS pool car from an unmarked underground car park near Bastille. The attendant told him that overnight load-shedding meant it hadn't completed its charge cycle.

'Will it have enough range?'

'Probably not.' The attendant's shrug said it wasn't his problem.

Alex set off through light Sunday traffic. It would take nearly three hours to get to Calais. Time to think back over everything he had not yet understood, the threats he sensed but could not see.

The first important moment had been with his mother, discussing the botched attack on Bunker Martha. Then, later, with Mariam, aware of the impending threat without knowing what it was. Then there was the trip to Norway – a mission that began with sleep deprivation and developed into an awareness that he was messing with people whose only wish was to do good and to share that good with the world.

Back in Paris, the meeting with Poiret had forced him to articulate how his desire for a life of action had led him into compromise and guilt. Then Gloria became ill and everything changed. He had left her alone while he travelled to Kofinou, where Tani Sakelliou, the data manager, had shared two important ideas: 'Who is to say that satellites are more stable than undersea cables?' Then she had quoted Director Philippou: 'For each of us, one day will be shorter than all the rest.'

He still felt he'd missed something in Cyprus, so he dictated a message asking Sakelliou to call, using his alias as Maurice Panhard, commercial investor.

Next, he remembered returning to Gloria's apartment and his fear that the cold data on the diag might be his final remembrance of her living presence, leading to a flashback to Professor Fayard's lecture on the precautionary principle and then his mother looking small and weak at the clinic. The two things were related but he wasn't sure how.

He drove on for a while, his mind still. What was next? Yes, the moment in Poiret's briefing when he momentarily lost focus, visualising instead the unfinished undersea cable linking Marseille to Cyrenia. Later, at Toulouse-Francazal, reviewing the news feeds, finding the theatrical infanticides on the Loire and the Rhône. Before that, the temp-shelter on the bridge over the Seine, concealing a body – again the body of a child. Likewise, the corpse in the water of the canal basin on his return from Norway.

The memories were coming out of sequence and he wondered why. What actually had happened next? The runway and the transport plane, talking to Poiret about Amaury and the Cyrenian ground-to-air defences. Paul Sanchez. The extraction of Prime Minister Mourad – important but, he thought, without hidden meaning.

Amaury's injury.

Also, Amaury's anger. That had been unexpected.

For a while, Alex was distracted by a sequence of lorry overtakes, swapping positions on a climb. Once he was through the traffic, he re-engaged cruise control.

Next was the DGIS Forum with its interconnected investigations and lauded ability to find 'unexpected connections… out-performing the algorithms'. In that room too, there were people who had lost confidence in the hyperconnected world. Then, the odd little house in Montmartre, searching a stranger's corpse without knowing what it was he wanted to find, the tattoos he knew were important but couldn't understand. Had the records not been deleted, he was sure he would have learned that Luís drowned with a fast-acting poison in his bloodstream.

And that was another thing. How had the boy's ID been deleted? Who had the power to do that? Did it matter?

Yes. It mattered.

Traffic grew heavier as he neared the port, and the car's battery was nearly empty. Alex adjusted the position of his seat, looking for a fast-charge point. A vibration told him he had a message from Kofinou. Tani Sakelliou was not available.

He pulled off at the final service station before Calais, taking advantage of the pause to attend to the dressing on his hip. As he waited for the charge cycle to complete, he found one more memory – Mariam's grandmother's proverb, a fragment of rural wisdom reminding the listener how easy it is to travel by daylight, while knowledge and experience are needed to successfully find one's way at night.

'When the sun shines, there's no need for stars.'

There it was again, surely – the coming darkness.

At the energy and data interchange at Kofinou, in Director Philippou's electronic calendar, Thursday, the sixth of August was marked as an anniversary, a day of remembrance. It wasn't popular or widely respected like Greek Independence Day on the twenty-fifth of March. It didn't have the idiosyncratic charm of the twenty-eighth of October, the 'Day of the No' when the Greek nation stood up to the Italian ultimatum of 1940. But it was important to her and to all those who believed that renewal would follow destruction, that the new dawn could only arise out of chaos and darkness.

She touched the screen, and an embedded link took her to a gallery of images – photographs of the martyred streets of Hiroshima, the plane that delivered the bomb, the bomb itself, the one they called 'Big Boy', the mushroom cloud photographed with fetishising symmetry.

But she had a moment of doubt. The destruction was unsatisfactory, incomplete. The aftermath of Hiroshima was untidy, the landscape strewn with burnt-out wreckage. It offended her notion of renewal. In her mind was a vision of something much neater – a true clean slate, a Tabula Rasa.

Philippou shut the images and thought about the Frenchman, Maurice Panhard, the supposed representative of foreign investors. She thought about Tani Sakelliou. She thought about how 'Panhard', if that was his name, had rung and asked about her.

She had been right to tell Tani how much she was valued and liked. She had been right to invite Tani to go for a drive and a picnic, into the hills along the coast, as recognition for Tani's excellent work. She had been right to push her from the edge of the cliff down onto the rocks, where the sea sucked her into its undertow and she drowned. The solution had been admirably tidy.

No, nothing must be allowed to distract from what was coming. It was so close, now. But she felt uneasy, too, as if other forces – contrary forces – were closing in.

She received a message. The timeline might have to be brought forward, apparently. It might not be possible to wait.

She sent a terse reply.

'Understood. All is ready.'

The Channel Tunnel terminal, with its profusion of pylons and overhead high-voltage lines, reminded Alex of Kofinou. The directions on his comm-watch led him to a parking space outside the offices of Border Control. As he got out, he felt the ground tremble with the rumble of a train disappearing into the northbound tunnel towards England. A border guard in a worn blue uniform came to let him in.

'I've prepared a viewing room. It's pretty gruesome,' said the guard.

They climbed a narrow flight of stairs to an overwarm room on the first floor with a small conference table surrounded by six chairs. The blinds were closed against the sun. On the end wall was a large screen.

'Ready?' asked the guard.

'Go ahead.'

The footage was clear enough. An adult male, carrying a large black holdall, struggled up a grassy embankment and onto a service bridge about fifteen metres above the railway lines. He opened the holdall, heaved it onto the handrail, levered out the floppy body of a smallish, unconscious child, and tipped it over the edge.

'Can we pause?'

The guard froze the image. 'Like I said, gruesome.'

'How was the footage compiled?' Alex asked.

'An algorithm tracks the movement across the cameras and stitches the shots together automatically.'

'Reliably?'

The border guard shrugged. 'I guess.'

Alex thought about the first two child drownings he had discovered, on the Loire and the Rhône. Those had also happened in full view of surveillance camera, like a kind of performance – one designed to shock and disturb.

'Okay, go ahead,' he said. 'Show me the rest.'

From the waiting room at the on-site medical facility, Alex holo-called Fayard in his private rooms at DGIS headquarters.

'Abducted child, maybe six or seven, unconscious, carried in a holdall up onto a bridge and then dumped on the railway line. There was a train incoming.'

'That was the cause of death?'

'That must have been the intention,' he said, keeping his voice level, 'but the kid's head hit a stanchion and it kind of knocked him away from the lines. The head injury was traumatic and, ultimately, fatal.'

The 3-D image of Fayard wasn't looking directly at the lens. Alex thought it was because the old man shared his fury.

'And the perpetrator is also deceased? There's nothing to learn there?'

'Jumped down after his victim. Avoided the stanchion. Met the train. I'm waiting for the morgue right now.'

'So, suicide,' mused Fayard, 'like the young man who threw himself from Saint Genevieve's bridge. Any identifying marks?'

'You mean the hands? I'll let you know.'

'Thank you,' Fayard said, his face still averted. 'One more thing. There was no audio, I know, but did he shout before he jumped?'

'Yes,' said Alex. 'I think he did.'

The 3-D holo of Fayard nodded with what looked very much like satisfaction and the old man ended the call.

59

'Is this facility permanently staffed?' Alex asked.

'Has to be. We get more than our fair share of death,' said the mortuary attendant. He used a swipe card to open a pair of swing doors from reception into a long, antiseptic corridor. He wore latex surgical gloves dusted with talc and had raw skin in the creases of his wrists from eczema.

Alex followed him, half-closing his eyes against the bright LED downlights. 'Do you have an ID on the victim?'

The man waved a lazy hand. 'Police wouldn't necessarily tell me straight away.'

'And the perpetrator?'

'Chipped. English citizen. But they don't share with us. Not since 2027.'

The mortuary attendant slid his card through another reader and they entered a stark room that reeked of the medicalisation of death, the far wall made up entirely of refrigerated hatches – a sealed indoor space that had never seen the sun. In the centre were three stainless-steel examination tables, dished to collect bodily fluids and channel them to a drain in the tiled floor. On one of the examination tables lay a small body bag, zipped up tight. On the other two tables lay pieces of the perpetrator. Alex began breathing through his mouth instead of his nose.

'You were saying the perpetrator was chipped. Chipped like a criminal?'

The attendant nodded. 'Exactly, meaning he probably did time in an English jail.'

Alex thought back to the incision in the chest of the Portuguese boy, Luís. He had been chipped but the chip had been removed.

The attendant went to a desk at the far end of the room and sat down behind a large-format holo, stripping off his gloves along the way and dropping them into a bin.

Alex approached the tables. The perpetrator's body had been torn into seven or eight pieces. On the video he had seen it struck a glancing blow by the train that spun it over upon itself, before it was snatched under the wheels. He assembled the pieces in his imagination. There seemed to be quite a lot of body parts missing for an accident that happened on a closed site with a solid security perimeter.

'You only have the left hand?' he called.

The attendant peered past his screen. 'Pardon?'

'You don't have both hands? The right hand is missing.'

'There's an official record of body parts on the clipboard under the exam table,' the man said. 'We shade the missing parts in black.'

Alex found the clipboard hanging on a hook – an outline of a human form. The shaded areas were a chunk of the right thigh, a chunk of the torso, most of the right arm and hand, the right-hand side of the head.

'And you couldn't retrieve these missing pieces?' he asked.

'We're close to the sea, here,' said the attendant, as if that explained everything.

Alex worked it out for himself. 'Gulls. They scavenged the missing body parts before they could be retrieved.'

'Exactly,' the man said.

That hadn't been part of the video.

Alex put back the clipboard and studied the pieces of broken human. The left hand was still attached, though the limb was twisted like a rope of liquorice.

'How did this happen?' he asked.

'Caught on something moving, maybe,' said the attendant, half-hidden behind his screen. 'Rotational forces. I don't know.'

'Would you turn it over for me?'

With a sigh, the attendant pulled on a new pair of latex gloves. He approached the table and straightened the arm. Alex heard the grating of pieces of bone.

'Anything else?' the man asked.

'Uncurl the fist.'

The attendant unwound the hand and pressed it out flat, like a tailor smoothing a piece of cloth. There they were. Five letters. Alex photographed them with his comm-watch.

'You said you get more than your fair share of deaths,' he said. 'What did you mean by that?'

'People pass through the terminal. Some of them die. It's the law of averages. Put enough people in the same place, some of them will pass while passing through.'

He seemed pleased with his turn of phrase, but Alex didn't smile. 'So that would be your fair share, but you get more. How come?'

'Poor people. We have a lot of poor people – in the third-class transport, standing room only, close proximity, hot. And the refugees, all around us, living rough, living on waste. Unsanitary. Not the macrobiotic, vitamin-enriched diet that you and I enjoy. Am I right?'

'Okay. I get it.'

'And then there's violence,' the man continued. 'Those people are living on the edge, I mean literally on the edge, of Europe – political Europe, not geographical Europe – and on the edge of their ability to endure. They scrap like rats in a sewer.' He shook his head. 'Don't get me wrong. Rats are noble creatures, survivors. Maybe so are the Blanks, every one an individual, but they know they're superfluous, gutter-people. They do what they must to survive.'

'These tattoos on his fingers,' said Alex, abruptly. 'Do they mean anything to you?'

The attendant's expression became guarded. 'No.'

'Are you sure?' Alex pressed. 'Look carefully.'

'I've looked. I've never seen anything like them before.'

'Certain?'

'I have to get on. The doors will open for you on the way out.'

Alex went back outside and found his car. The cabin was superheated by the scorching sun. He set off the for the city centre with all the windows open, video-calling Fayard on the windscreen display. The signal was mediocre. Fayard sounded weak and distant.

'Yes to the identifying marks,' said Alex.

'On the backs of the fingers?' asked Fayard.

'Like Luís Beira, clumsy enough to be home-made. A pin from a sewing kit and a bottle of ink.'

'But still U D S M C?'

'O D W B S.'

There was a pause. He saw Fayard writing it down.

'Thoughts?' the old man asked.

'Some kind of code?' Alex suggested. 'Or a rank? If these two individuals are connected, could they be defined by a five-letter code within their organisation? Or is there something in it being different languages? The boy in Montmartre was Portuguese and the murderer was an English citizen.'

'How do we know he was English?' Fayard asked.

'Chipped. Served time in an English prison. I've copied the data. Sabie will have to make a decryption request to the English police. Maybe if I'd stripped Luís, I would have found other tattoos elsewhere on his body.'

'Which explanation do you prefer?' asked the old man.

'None as yet.'

There was a pause.

'Something else is troubling you, Alexandre?'

'The mortuary guy, the attendant, he gave me a spiel about the many reasons people die and get brought to his mortuary. He got carried away, and he was…'

Alex paused. What was it he wanted to say? He waited for the idea to present itself in words, but it wouldn't come.

'Is this a direct link or a lateral connection?' Fayard prompted. 'Are mortuary attendants generally *sympathiques?*'

'When I asked him about the tattoo, he was too quick. He said he'd never seen anything like it before. I didn't believe him.'

Fayard spoke to someone out of shot and a fragment of memory tugged at Alex's consciousness – untwisting the corkscrewed arm, the surprising tenderness. It reminded him of another morgue and the two Malian students from the attack on Bunker Martha – the greenish tinge to their dead faces, the flaccid arms, the thin fingers. He remembered sending the photographs to a DGES technician for enlargement and enhancement but he hadn't yet received a reply.

'And then what?' asked Fayard.

'He shut me down and wanted me out of there in a hurry. It felt wrong.' Suddenly he knew what he wanted to say. 'Something bad is going to happen here.'

'In Calais?' Fayard asked.

'Yes, in Calais.'

'U D S M C and O D W B S,' the old man mused. 'What is your next step?

'I have an appointment with the investigating magistrate.'

'Excellent. Please keep me informed.' Fayard paused. 'I should tell you that I have spoken to Mariam Jordane.'

He didn't need to say what about.

'Our relationship has no bearing on our work,' said Alex quickly.

'Of course, it doesn't,' said Fayard. 'No action will be taken.'

'Thank you, sir.' Alex was relieved but unhappy. Mariam was a very private person. This might be enough to push her away. 'I appreciate it.'

Fayard coughed and the coughing quickly became spluttering. Alex saw someone in the background bringing a glass of water – a very big man with long black hair. Fayard took the glass, waved his spare hand and cut the connection.

Alex quickly reached his destination, parking in an official bay outside the police station. Before getting out, he sent a message to Mariam.

How are you? I spoke to the old man... Good news, yes?

The reply was both immediate and disappointing.

Busy just now. Later?

He sat for a moment, feeling an unwanted rush of adrenaline, of fight or flight, as if something very bad was coming, and he was too late to stop it.

60

The mortuary attendant at the tunnel terminal didn't like wearing gloves. They were a necessary part of his job, but he suffered from eczema and the gloves exacerbated his symptoms.

He thought about Lamarque, the DGIS investigator from Paris. He had taken off his gloves to log the man into his computer system.

That had been close. What if Lamarque had seen the tattoos on his own fingers? Had he given himself away? He didn't think so, but he had talked too much. Yes, in his anxiety he had definitely run on a bit.

What had he talked about? Oh, yes. Death.

He shook his head. 'You're an idiot,' he told himself aloud. 'An idiot.'

On his desk in the mortuary was an old-fashioned paper calendar, a square of tear-off paper for each day. He found the sixth of August, where he had doodled a fist with letters on the fingers and thumb: U J S P C. He had shaded clouds and hills behind it. Then he had taken an eraser to smudge out some of the pencil marks at a cleft in the hills, giving an impression of a tiny ray of light, perhaps a sunrise.

What if Lamarque had seen that?

It was still four days away, but he had been told to stand ready. Events might have to be brought forward.

That would be a shame, he thought.

He removed the calendar page and tore it into tiny pieces, then flushed them through the grate in the centre of the mortuary's tiled floor, into the drain that carried away the bodily fluids released by dissection. He took a deep breath, imagining a brighter future, scoured of hypocrisy and deceit, a new start, a cleaner, more honest tomorrow.

'Tabula Rasa,' he murmured.

He went back to his desk and applied some soothing ointment to the stress eczema on his wrists.

Alex put his car on charge and entered the police station. It was a little after five in the afternoon. If he was lucky, he would be back in Paris for a late dinner.

Or he could stop halfway, find a quiet auberge and stay the night. Get up early the next day and play a round of golf. Enjoy life.

As if, he thought.

He was met by an assistant, a woman with wary eyes and uneven yellow teeth. She led him to an interview room and ushered him inside to meet the magistrate – an exceptionally tall man with a pronounced stoop.

They all took a seat, the assistant on a chair in the farthest corner, making a discreet recording. Alex looked round pointedly to make sure that both the assistant and magistrate knew that he knew. The magistrate began swiping at an oversized tablet.

'So, the dead child was not from the refugee camps?' Alex prompted.

'The displaced-persons camps,' the magistrate corrected, keeping his eyes on the screen. Then he looked up, smiling, as if remembering his manners. 'I'm sorry, would you remind me of your name?'

'Lamarque.'

'Lamarque. Thank you.'

The magistrate sank back into his chair with one knee drawn up almost against his chest. He reminded Alex of a paper clip.

'When was the child first reported missing?' he asked.

'Oh, straight away. The child – he, a boy-child, in fact – belongs to a distinguished local family. A caring, attentive family.' The magistrate glanced at his tablet. 'You have read the report?'

'I have,' said Alex. 'The family was having lunch and their seven year old was out of sight for how long in a busy mall without them noticing?'

'They were aware of his location. They thought he was exploring. They were never more than a few minutes away. Or he was never much more than a few minutes away from them.' He coughed apologetically, as if he was about to commit some kind of social *faux pas*. 'They could see where he was at all times, you understand?'

Alex understood. 'The kid was chipped.'

The man nodded. 'Yes.'

'Like a dog.'

The magistrate looked uncomfortable. 'Like anything valuable that one might want to keep track of.'

Alex heard himself becoming sarcastic. 'And this distinguished local family, what were they doing as they glanced, now and then, at their comm-watches to see where their kid had got to?'

'There are two or three better-quality establishments…' The magistrate's voice tailed off. He glanced at his tablet. 'The child-chip is legal—'

Alex didn't let him finish. 'The chip reassured the parents that the child was nearby but out of sight. They must have received a warning he was injured or drugged when he was put in the holdall.'

'The use of certain narcoleptics provokes a response very close to sleep,' the magistrate explained.

'So, your friends assumed the child was sleeping. Where?'

'In the public conveniences,' said the magistrate unhappily. 'It seems the cameras in the rest rooms were disabled; the lenses obscured. Although there is footage of the child going in, there is no evidence of him coming out.'

'But there is footage of someone coming out with a heavy black holdall?'

'Yes.'

Alex considered. 'Then, the chip told them their child had left the mall and they reported him missing to civilian security. Then, what, fifteen minutes later, the chip told them he was dead on the railway line. Is that a fair summary?'

The magistrate bowed his head. 'The location of his demise was indicated. Both police and Tunnel security were notified. An investigation was instigated and officers despatched.'

'They're friends of yours, these parents?'

The magistrate gave him a level look. 'No one could have predicted any of this.'

'All right. I get it,' said Alex harshly.

He could see clearly what was going on. The magistrate had nothing for him but was trying to protect the parents from an accusation of neglect. Chipping children was not illegal, but it enabled kids to be parented by surveillance instead of in person. Children's rights groups had a lot to say on the subject.

He was about to leave when he realised he could hear tinny, low-volume audio coming from the magistrate's tablet. It sounded like a news channel.

'Do you want to show me something?' he asked.

'The parents are about to make a public statement. Are you able to indulge me and wait just a few minutes? The family is closely connected to the office of the mayor. They run the local water supply.' The magistrate held out the tablet, turning it so Alex could see the screen. 'Here it is.'

It was a live news broadcast. The magistrate turned up the volume. A florid man with a rim of red hair like a monk's tonsure was leaning on a small, sharp-faced woman. The man looked slightly absent, his eyes vague. The woman had composed herself to address the camera.

'Words cannot express the horror and shock that this unexplained, unprovoked and undeserved attack has wrought upon us, upon my husband and me, upon our family.'

The husband nodded and looked as if he was about to cry.

'Our dear son,' the sharp-faced woman continued, 'has been taken from us. Seven years old. His sister, just a year older, wonders where he has gone. What shall we tell her? How can we explain this gratuitous crime? How can she – how can we – ever trust again?' She paused to take a shaky breath. 'We beg of you, please, leave us in peace with our grief.'

She turned away. The camera panned to a reporter and the magistrate turned down the sound.

Alex sat back on his hard office chair. He wanted to hate the couple, but their grief struck him as genuine. And yet the crime was so bizarre. Ostentatious even, like some kind of public humiliation.

'What about the perpetrator?' said Alex. 'Do you have any idea why he kidnapped a kid from the shopping centre and dropped him on the railway line, then threw himself in front of a train?'

Involuntarily, the magistrate glanced at his assistant. Alex realised the magistrate wanted to tell him something else. What was preventing him? Was it the assistant with her recording? Alex turned towards her.

'Could you please fetch me a bottle of water?'

The woman hesitated. 'There has to be someone here.'

'I know it's the rule that you record the meeting. Leave the device on the chair and get me a bottle of water.'

Reluctantly, the woman did as she was told. As soon as she was out of the room, Alex popped out his comm-watch's virtual keyboard and typed a silent message. He leaned in to the desk and showed it the magistrate.

Anything you send me will be encrypted at the very highest level of security. Only I will be able to read it and only when connected to DGIS servers. Do you understand?

'Absolutely,' mouthed the magistrate, the words making no sound. 'Thank you.'

Alex touched his watch to the man's tablet to share contact details, then deleted the message without sending it.

The assistant re-entered the room, breathing quickly, as if she'd rushed. Alex took a sip from the bottle, then stood up.

'I will wait to hear from you,' he told to the magistrate, 'through the usual channels.'

The man unfolded his contorted limbs and got out of his chair, an expression of grateful relief on his face – relief mingled with trepidation.

'*Merci, infiniment.*'

Alex left them. To avoid setting off in the rush hour, he went to find something to eat. While he was eating, he visualised the tattooed letters on the hands of Luís Beira and the dead English citizen.

U D S M C

O D W B S

How had the mother described the crime? 'Gratuitous', done without reason or purpose.

If only, thought Alex.

And, at last, he began to understand what they must mean.

61

On the Cyrene–Egypt border, night had fallen. Despite the chill, Zeina Yaseen stepped out of her mud-hut prison into the calming silence. Thirty metres away, a square of warm electric light spilled from a window. The sky was clear and bright, studded with countless stars.

The door of the prefab border-post swung open and one of the two frontier guards emerged.

'I was coming to fetch you,' he said. 'We thought you might be cold.'

'I am,' she admitted, with a smile.

He motioned for her to follow. 'Come inside. There's a chair you can sleep in.'

At a more important border post, 140 kilometres away, a senior Egyptian officer was becoming harsh with impatience.

'Can you not get through?'

The radio operator shook his head apologetically. 'I have a connection to the international relay now, sir. Soon I will have Tobruk.'

The officer's title was OC Western Frontier. Like his nation, he had seen enough of the hyperconnected world to be persuaded that the only secure future was in isolation and self-determination. Egypt took no part in the affairs of other sovereign nations. Egypt would neither hinder nor help, even its neighbours.

But there was also pragmatism to consider.

Since the secession of Cyrenia, Egypt had no longer had to cope with a conflagration on its western border. If it was true that General Bader was responsible for killing General Al-Fathi, that would inevitably relight the fire. And that was on top of the insurrection and the flight of Prime Minister Mourad. The situation risked becoming dangerous for Egypt once more.

The OC Western Frontier had no affection for Prime Minister Mourad. He considered her a showboating politician, motivated by narcissism and thirst for power. But his role had brought him into contact with a Cyrenian official he did respect – the mayor of Tobruk, one of the members of the triumvirate Presidential Council, an honourable man, a technocrat without personal ambition.

'We are through, sir.'

The connection was poor, disrupted by static. The OC Western Frontier had to repeat himself several times to get his message across.

He didn't know it, but the fact he was speaking over analogue radio was important. It was a channel no one had thought to monitor.

In Paris, dusk was just beginning to fall. Professor Fayard was alone in his private rooms, concealed behind the bookshelves that separated him from the top floor conference room. He'd dismissed Sébastien, his Sunday bodyguard. He felt weary but he was pleased to have spoken to Alex. He had been worried about losing the young man's trust.

He heard the backup generators kick into life, sending a reassuring hum through the building. Brown-outs were becoming more frequent, load-shedding a problem that more and more people had to manage. It was direct evidence of the failing state and yet people seemed to accommodate themselves to it, like a driver whose vehicle is falling apart who forgets why they never use third gear.

Energy technology, however, was one of the great success stories of the age. Generation and storage had been transformed over a single generation, at a pace of change unequalled since the early days of the industrial revolution. There was only one other area of human endeavour that had advanced as quickly – the healthcare applications of gene-sequencing and their extraordinary impact on disease prevention and control.

Not for everybody, however. The diseases themselves seemed to know they were in a fight to the death and were working equally hard to maintain their slender lead. In some circumstances – poverty, exclusion, co-morbidities – their significant lead.

He lay back in his motorised therapeutic chair. Alongside sensitivity to light, another of his symptoms was low blood pressure, leading to dizziness. He walked with a stick because his brain sometimes lacked oxygen and made him prone to falling. He had not yet broken a wrist or a hip, but he feared doing so.

No, that was the wrong word. He didn't fear injury or death, but the idea infuriated him. He had so much left to do.

At the same time, watching her most recent video, a woman was combing her blond wig. It had been made available on the internet, introduced by an image of a fist against a background of storm and destruction, a wave of darkness covering the burning land.

'Governments are in distress, crumbling and afraid. Good. Let the fear come. They are irrational. Good. Let the madness thrive. They live on lies. Good. Let the stink of hypocrisy tear them down. They are paranoid. Good. Let them lash out. Violence will hasten their demise.

'Fear is our weapon. Distress is our weapon. Desperation is our weapon. The curtain must be ripped aside, the constant under-hum of distraction – the rotten entertainment channels; the force-fed never-ending elite sports where a final champion will never be crowned; the rolling catastrophe of the infotainment industry where the worst thing that happens anywhere on any given day must occupy the front page, if only for twenty minutes. It must all be silenced. And the silence is coming, and so is the darkness, because only in the darkness can the faintest glimmer of light be perceived, nurtured, fanned into a flame, a conflagration.

'It is good that governments are afraid, just as they have tried to make us afraid. It is good that they do not know who to trust, as they have told us to trust nobody but them. It is good that they have become a criminal class themselves, wrapped in a national flag or in a cloak of good works, the fiction of the common good, while they work only for themselves. But not themselves as a class. Each as an island, separate and self-protective. And their actions form a pattern, like putrefaction forms a pattern, all the separate organisms working independently but, from the outside, appearing sentient, striving for a common goal.

'So, good. Only when the beam is fully rotten will it fall. Only when the palace of corruption and deceit has crumbled can a better one be built in its place.'

Better than I thought, she reflected.

She packed the items essential to her disguise and went out dressed in her own clothes, wearing her own hair, picking up the rapid transit network, out past the edge of the city, beyond the orbital motorway where the cameras were fewer. She had received new instructions and, apparently, it had to be done today. The same venue was going to be used.

She followed late Sunday walkers on a meandering route, losing herself from potential observation, changing her appearance in a camera shadow. Then she queued at a bus stop that would take her anticlockwise round the city to the northern edge of the 18th arrondissement.

Earlier that day, having made her regular Sunday visit to her sisters, Mariam wandered away past the Luxembourg Gardens, reflecting on how she and Alex had, in this last week, seen less of one another in private but several times in public, unable to acknowledge each other's presence. It was a relief to know that Fayard promised to take no action against them.

She carried on into the pedestrianised heart of the city, across the river then north. As she walked, her purpose became more certain – over the hill of Montmartre and down the other side, past the tiny house wedged between taller buildings where Alex had interrupted the Beira vigil, past the Church of Saint Genevieve where the first video had been filmed. Finally, she reached the second one, closer to the city's edge, dedicated to Saint Helen.

From the analysis of the videos, she knew it had been filmed at dusk. Without planning it, her long walk had coincided with the setting of the sun. Perhaps she would come across the woman in the blond wig or, maybe, the two undertakers. She was sure they were connected.

Mariam thought back to that moment in Fayard's private rooms, studying video footage on his screens. She had been on the verge of connecting several strands when Fayard interrupted, summoned by the office of the president. She had been trailing the woman in the blond wig using Camera Control. There had been a young man in a suit between two undertakers, just outside Square Sainte-Hélène.

Could it be the youth Alex had told her about, the Portuguese boy who'd thrown himself into the Seine, the mysterious deleted son of Luísa Beira?

Eventually, she found the place – a few reasonably prosperous streets bordering a derelict area dominated by shanty dwellings for Blanks. Close by, there was a playground with brightly coloured plastic equipment – a snail on a rocking spring, a dinosaur, a tortoise.

Mariam approached the gate. A handful of children were dodging back and forth, playing tag. She heard a shout and a dirty-faced woman in ill-fitting clothes came quickly towards her. Mariam stepped back. The woman grasped the gatepost. There was blood at the corners of her bitten fingernails.

'What do you want?' she demanded.

'Nothing,' said Mariam.

Two more Blanks came to join them, an older woman and a man who leaned on an improvised crutch.

'What do you want here?' the first woman repeated.

'I am on my way to the Church of Saint Helen. There is an evening service.'

The three Blanks spoke together in a language Mariam did not understand. She noticed a piece of tattered cardboard tied to the fence with twine – an improvised appeal for help. A child had gone missing.

Mariam gestured to the poster. 'When did this happen?'

'You are not welcome here,' the woman told her angrily.

'I might be able to help.'

The three Blanks surged out onto the pavement. Mariam took another step back.

'Go,' the first one shouted.

Mariam held up her hands. 'I don't mean you any harm.'

They paid no attention, coming at her in a shambling, disorganised rush, tormented by the loss of a child, not knowing where or how to find revenge. The first woman drew a short knife from some fold of her awful garments and lunged.

Mariam swayed a little to her left, grasped the woman's wrist and twisted it back and up. The woman cried out and the knife clattered to the ground. Mariam pushed her away.

'Don't do this,' Mariam warned them. 'I don't want to hurt you.'

The man swung his improvised crutch at her head. She dodged it easily, bending at the knees as it whistled past her shoulder. She shot out her left foot, thumping the sole of her shoe into his hip and sending him tumbling against the railings.

'Stay down,' she ordered.

The third Blank remained out of reach. She, too, held a knife – much longer and viciously serrated.

'Don't do this,' Mariam repeated, trying to calm them. 'I'm not your enemy.'

The man with the crutch was pulling himself upright. The first woman was scrabbling on the ground for her blade.

'Why are you here?' the second woman asked.

Mariam kept her empty hands raised. 'I was simply walking, like I told you.'

The second woman indicated the improvised sign. 'You were not surprised,' she said, 'to see this.'

'No,' Mariam admitted.

'Why?' the woman demanded, the knife still gripped in her hand.

The other two Blanks were on their feet. They wanted to surround her. They thought they were strong, that together they would have an advantage.

Mariam shook her head. 'I will have to hurt you,' she said, enunciating the words very clearly in case the man's French was not good. 'I want to know what happened to the child. Tell me what happened, and I will try to help you. I have connections. There are things I can find out.'

The three Blanks looked at one another.

'Why would you help us?' the man asked.

'Because you have lost a child,' said Mariam simply. 'And you are not the only ones.'

As she spoke the words, Mariam remembered what Alex had told her.

'Similar events are being planned in many places, but the time has not yet come.'

What if he was right? What if she had stumbled on the truth, that this was not the only child?

'What can you find out?' The first woman waved her short knife, taking in the other two Blanks, the playground and the shanty dwellings on the far side. 'The child had no identity. None of us exist.'

'He was not our child,' interjected the second woman. 'He was an orphan, the parents dead. But he was one of our children and the police do nothing.'

'I understand. I see that.' Mariam made her tone gentle. 'Just tell me everything you know, and I will make the police do their duty.'

The two fake undertakers were in position, parked two minutes from the church, side by side in the synthetic leather seats.

'Why are we back here?' said the younger one.

The older one shook his head. 'I don't know.'

'I have a bad feeling.'

'So do I,' said the older one.

'We should get a new disguise.'

The older man didn't think this was such a bad idea. They'd been undertakers for a long time. 'What do you suggest?'

'I don't know.'

'Builders?' asked the older man.

'No, something where you don't get your hands dirty.' The younger man frowned in concentration. 'I know. Flower delivery. If we were florists, we would always have access to lilies.'

'For the state of innocence,' said the older man, smiling. 'Yes, that would be nice.'

The heads-up display bleeped into life. They contemplated the image on the windscreen, the person they were instructed to kill.

'Oh,' said the younger one. 'That's interesting.'

'Isn't it?'

'This is the endgame.'

The older man pondered his answer. Was it, though?

'Almost,' he decided.

62

The woman in the blond wig paced quickly along the pavement, the echo of her heels bouncing from the quiet buildings. She felt hot, aware that she might be pressed for time to change her disguise and make her way home before curfew. She would need to take a direct route, something she didn't normally do. Safety lay in never repeating oneself.

The two fake undertakers waited inside the Church of Saint Helen. They'd broken the lock to gain entry and now sat patiently alongside one another in a rear pew. They had left the door ajar and could hear footsteps in the street outside.

'That's her tread,' said the older man.

'Agreed.'

The younger man got up and moved behind a pillar, out of sight. The older man picked up three small books and moved towards the door, composing his features into a smile.

The woman in the blond wig was surprised to find the door of the church standing open, the lock damaged. She went inside to see the undertakers waiting for her.

'What is happening?' she asked. 'Has it begun?'

The older man smiled. He was standing in a pool of coloured light from a streetlamp, filtered through stained glass, yellow and blue and red. He held out a little parcel of books. Without thinking, she took them, glancing at the spines – a Book of Common Prayer and two hymnals.

'The time has come,' he quoted, 'for the stars of the heavens and their constellations will not give their light and the sun will be dark at its rising.'

The woman in the blond wig recognised the quotation from Isaiah 13:10. Then she realised a number of things almost all at once.

That this would be the one day in her life that was shorter than all the rest, but not by much, the time being already so late.

That the older undertaker had handed her the parcel of small church books to occupy her hands, to make her slower to react.

That her parents would never know why she had sent them away into safety, to a distant corner of northern Portugal, where the coming darkness would leave them safe.

That the quick footsteps behind her belonged to the other man, the younger one with the unkind eyes.

That she had dropped the Book of Common Prayer and the two dusty hymnals too slowly.

That the wire he had looped around her neck was already disappearing into the flesh of her neck, constricting her windpipe.

That her desperate fingernails would find no edge, no way of relieving the awful pressure.

That it would soon be over.

She was disappointed that it had come just a little too soon, because she had believed that she might persuade Alex to join their cause. Hadn't she almost told him outright?

'People live, people die. The darkness is always on the horizon, *amigo do minho*. However much money you make, nothing can change that.'

He had been so wrapped up in the discovery of his mother's illness that he hadn't noticed the appeal in her eyes.

And he hadn't seen her apology either, for being the source of the virus.

The yellow and blue and red from the stained-glass windows all faded to grey, lack of oxygen turning the world black and white. Nelinha felt sad that she would not be alive to witness what she had worked so hard to bring about.

Then she felt nothing at all.

It took a while for Mariam to fulfil her promise, summoning a police officer from the 18th arrondissement, making the investigation into the lost child official business. Then she left the playground and the Blanks and headed towards the church. When she came close, she heard heavy footsteps, two sets, pounding away down a side street, out of sight.

She stood in the entrance, uncertain of what to do. Should she follow the sound and see who they were, where they went, or should she look inside?

The door of the church was ajar, damage visible around the lock. She chose the second option and slipped inside.

The place was quiet. Light from a streetlamp shone through a window of red, blue and yellow stained glass, casting a pattern of colours across the flagstones, across the corpse, across the blond wig that lay a little askew, revealing the dark wavy hair beneath.

Alex returned the pool car to the underground garage just after eleven. He messaged Mariam and received an immediate breezy reply.

Hope you are well. Speak tomorrow?

She's putting me off, he thought. She doesn't want to talk to me.

It was what he had feared. Fayard bringing their relationship out into the open would, inevitably, destroy it.

When he got home, he sat on the roof of his boat with a metabolically appropriate green drink in his hand, looking up into the sky. The lights of the city were reflected by a haze of smog, casting an orange-brown veil between him and the stars. Time passed and another explanation for the out-of-character message presented itself – a much more sinister one.

Before he could think it through, he was interrupted by footsteps descending the eighteen worn stone steps – a big man in a charcoal-grey suit. Poiret's security officer. Alex climbed off the deck and went to join him on the towpath.

'Madame Poiret wonders why you haven't replied to her messages?'

Alex frowned. 'I haven't received any messages.'

'In the absence of any reply, I took the liberty of checking with your previous employers at External Security. I found this.' The bodyguard held out an official A4 envelope containing at most a few sheets of paper or card. Alex took it. 'Also, I am instructed to inform you that your mother has been transferred to the Rothschild Institute, as per your agreement.'

Alex felt the words like a release of tension. At last Poiret had done her part. 'Thank you.'

'A senior clinician will contact you in the morning with an update. Later, Madame Poiret requests you to join her at four o'clock tomorrow, at Val-de-Grâce.'

'Because?'

'To meet with Prime Minister Mourad.'

This was a surprise. Why would Poiret want him at a meeting with the exiled prime minister?

'I'll be there, 'he replied.

The big man turned on his heel and climbed up the stone steps. Soon his footsteps were lost to the night. Alex went back on board, the motorised hatch closing almost silently behind him.

'Lights.'

The envelope was from a DGES technician. It held a massively enhanced close-up of one of the perpetrators of the failed attack on Bunker Martha. It was a superb piece of work. The technician had searched for distinguishing features and had found tattoos on the back of the fingers. The tattoos could be clearly read. They consisted of five letters: U J S P C.

Alex woke his holo and spoke the three sequences into voice recognition. They appeared above one another on the screen.

U D S M C

O D W B S

U J S P C

It was quite obvious, once you saw the pattern. He had suggested it to Fayard – or something like it – but, at the time, there hadn't been a reason to pursue the idea. Now, he had two strong connections that tied everything together.

The first was the letters and the seemingly pointless deaths – in fact, the wish for death.

The other was about the stars.

Mariam notified the police about the body in the Church of Saint Helen, then took an autodrive straight to DGIS headquarters. She made her way to the sixth floor and the old man's private quarters. She told him the whole story, starting with the Blanks.

'Why did you not simply leave them?' Fayard asked.

'Alex told me about the mother and son in Montmartre, the shiny coffin, the lilies. He thought he saw a connection. Once I had their trust, I called an officer from the eighteenth arrondissement and used her credentials to show them the mortuary photographs of the child recovered from the Seine. They identified him straight away.'

'Not wishful thinking?'

'No. I questioned them closely for distinguishing features before showing them the images.'

'What sort of distinguishing features?'

'Dark hair tied back in a pony tail, top two front teeth missing.'

Fayard gave a nod of approval. 'And your conclusions?'

'Alex was right. The child murder is connected to the death of Luís Beira.'

'In what way?'

This was the part that bothered Mariam.

'Perhaps it's a kind of sacrifice? It sounds foolish, I know. But Alex told me that there's a pattern yet to reveal itself, of similar actions in many different places. What if he's right? So, I checked on the officer's comms and found a spike in abductions, all about the same age, female and male.'

Fayard pondered. 'What possible reason could there be?'

'To create distress?' Mariam suggested.

'And Alexandre expected this – or something like it?'

'Yes.'

As she said it, it struck her that she hadn't heard from Alex all day. She checked her comm-watch. In fact, he'd been out of touch longer than she'd thought. Nearly two days. She'd been too busy to notice.

'Should I message him? I think we need him in on this,' she said.

'He may not yet have returned to the city,' observed Fayard. 'He went to Calais to investigate what might be another element in your pattern.'

They were both silent for a moment. Eventually, Mariam spoke.

'I left the Blanks and went to the church,' said Mariam. 'That was my intention all along, in case there was another video being made. I found the corpse of the woman in the blond wig. She had been garrotted.'

'Was she carrying ID?' he asked.

'I recognised her. It took a minute to come back to me, but I'd seen her several times in passing. Her name was Nelinha Costa, the daughter of the concierge at Alex's mother's building.'

'Gloria's concierge,' said Fayard, quietly. The old man's eyes unfocused and he hunched forward in a gesture that Mariam knew took pressure off his lungs. 'One moment…' he wheezed, drawing in a painful breath.

'I shouldn't have disturbed you so late.' Mariam heard the rattle in his chest. 'It's after midnight. You need to rest.'

'Yes, perhaps I do. Thank you. Go home, my dear,' he told her, wearily. 'There will be time enough.'

After Mariam left, the pain eventually eased but Fayard found he could not sleep.

To tire his body and still his mind, he slowly paced his private rooms, leaning heavily on his stick, before sitting at one of his three holoscreens to solve a sequence of numerical puzzles from an app that he used for this exact purpose. Afterwards, he spent over an hour watching night patrols on the feed from Camera Control. It calmed him to see them moving sedately through the curfewed streets.

At about three in the morning, he ate some fruit and a protein bar and was promptly sick, a symptom of this new illness that he hated. Emptying his stomach made him more comfortable, however, and he read for an hour or two from one of his favourite authors, an English writer of historical fiction whose work celebrated ordinary people caught up in extraordinary events. Finally, as the sky outside his window began to lighten, he tried again to rest, lying back in his motorised therapeutic chair, his head a little lower than his chest, his chest lower than his hips, his hips lower than his feet. The position raised his arterial blood pressure and improved the oxygenation of his brain.

As his weary body, racked by illness, teetered on the edge of sleep, a memory blossomed on the edge of consciousness, a conversation from several days before.

'You are a student of human disasters, Sabie. Why is that?'

63

Administrator Sabie was in his office behind the armoured door on the basement floor of the headquarters of the Directorate-General for Internal Security. He had sent several encrypted messages, warning his associates that the date might have to be brought forward. Now, he was monitoring multiple streams of information at once.

There were many processes in motion, some within his control, others not. For example, he had been watching a small red dot, blinking its progress across a map of Paris, from a six-storey townhouse on Boulevard Henri IV to the Church of Saint Helen. Then the dot had blinked out, indicating that Nelinha Costa was dead.

Good.

He was interested – even surprised – to see that Mariam Jordane had barely used her personal login for a couple of days. That was a fact worth remembering. He knew she often worked at the terminal in the old man's private quarters, the only one to which Sabie had no access whatsoever. That was a reasonable explanation, unless something else came along to disprove it. For example, that she knew herself to be under surveillance.

He saw only one flaw in his management of the information allowed to Fayard's driver. It was the way he had felt obliged to slow down the results provided to her by Camera Control and by forensics – the name and location of the church in the first apocalyptic 'sermon', for example. Then there had been the DNA match from the hair caught in the lens cap. How long had he delayed that?

It didn't matter. She seemed to have made nothing of it.

Sabie was also monitoring communications from Amaury Barra. His inbox contained only notifications about the Cyrenia inquiry and his medical appointments, the most recent concerned with a first fitting for a more sophisticated prosthesis. Was it plausible that Barra had neither sent nor received any other messages? Perhaps yes. The man was convalescing, after all.

Sabie was aware that someone was looking into the child that had been sacrificed by the Portuguese boy, Luís Beira. An officer in the 18th arrondissement had accessed the information. Geolocation told him that the access had been requested at the very place from which Luís had abducted the child.

Sabie was pleased with the child abductions. They destabilised. They created distress and panic. They were risky, however, because they were, of necessity, high-profile, but they helped to prepare the ground for what was to come when everything would burn.

Sabie turned to the screen monitoring Alexandre Lamarque. Sabie still wasn't sure why Lamarque had been at the Marseille data centre where everything began. It didn't seem to matter, though. He hadn't understood what he'd seen. All the same, Sabie had deemed it best to shut down all Lamarque's comms after his second call to the old man from the terminal. Between them, Fayard and Lamarque were getting too close.

The situation in Calais was evolving quickly. It had been necessary to exert pressure on the couple whose business controlled the Calais water supply. Now that was done and the follow-up ultimatum had been delivered. To protect their remaining child, they would do anything they were told.

The idea was, of course, that everything happened at once, for maximum effect, maximum destruction and maximum distress. He smiled, glancing at Director Philippou's admirably terse message from Kofinou:

All is ready.

The precise location of the undersea connectors had been transmitted to an old-fashioned bucket dredger, moored a little way along the coast. When the time came, the dredger would move into position, run its immensely powerful diesel engines, sending the conveyor belt of heavy steel buckets into the shallow silt, chopping the data cables into pieces, disrupting communications between Africa and Asia and Europe. Then it would adjust position slightly and destroy the power cables that linked Cyprus and Europe with renewables from across the other two continents.

Sabie was sure of Director Philippou. She was, like him, a person of fixed ideas. He was not so sure of the operatives he had recruited in Tahiti and Long Island. They were less senior, which brought its own complications, and his communications with them had been more difficult. Fortunately, the destruction of the undersea network was not fundamental to the first shocking moment of darkness.

Sabie tapped on the desk, feeling uneasy.

Lamarque in Marseille, Lamarque in Calais. Why?

He put the thought out of his mind. Coincidences were a fact of life, whatever the old man had to say about them. He checked another strand of his web – a news feed from Cyrenia.

His plan required a tide of emotion and, wherever and however the flood of distress occurred, he would surf that tide, taking advantage of raised emotions to accelerate the destruction. It would have been better if the insurrection in Cyrene City could have been delayed. But it was important to remember that not everything could be controlled.

Almost everything, though. In policy meetings in Paris, it was he who first mooted the extraction of Prime Minister Mourad, judging that her absence would create a vacuum that could only lead to conflict. Someone, inevitably, would try to step into that space, almost certainly his tame general, Ramzi Bader.

He glanced at the recent communications from Al-Jaghar, written by the general's sister, Latifah Bader. Her messages told him that Al-Fathi was dead, that the launch sequence could begin when instructed, that the final checks were under way.

He answered, not expecting a reply before morning.

What is the earliest possible moment?

He pondered. If the final climax was approaching, should he sleep now, at least a little? He would have four or five hours before Latifah Bader woke.

Logically, Sabie knew that his hatred of the new Cyrenian republic was irrational, a flaw in the logic of destruction that guided his plan. He knew it arose out of his own childhood, his alienation and exile. He knew that Mourad's policies of inclusion and tolerance had become an *abcès de fixation*, the counterargument to his own nihilistic vision. Where he saw a world stripped of hyperconnection, able to make a new start out of chaos, she represented a utopian vision of an integrated humanity.

It had been quite easy to use the novel pathogen made possible by the information stolen by Alexandre Lamarque from the Norwegian laboratory. Bader's staff officer had introduced the pathogen into the refugee camps on the edge of Cyrene City, destabilising the situation and priming the insurrection. Nelinha Costa had infected Lamarque's mother. He had infected Fayard.

Sabie smiled. The intricacy of the events pleased him. But his favourite part was yet to come.

Yes, it would be satisfying to destroy several nodes in the international network of undersea communications, but the rocket launch from Al-Jaghar was much more important. It would put into orbit a sequence of shrapnel explosions, sending 100,000 fast-moving pieces of metal into the midst of the constellations of communications satellites, causing a chain reaction of destruction, exponentially multiplying into a vast impenetrable field of debris into which no new devices could be launched, sealing Earth off from the stars and casting the planet into a communications blackout. And it would precipitate the launch of the novel French weapon God's Thunder, laying waste to vast tracts of the Earth's surface, provoking tsunamis and myriad desperate new wars.

That was the crisis that would bring down death and destruction, a clean slate, chaos and the prospect of a new dawn. That was the meaning of the coming darkness.

Sabie enjoyed the irony of Mourad's vanity project, largely financed by the French government, being used to reap destruction. He liked the fact that he would take its vainglorious name, *Tahadath 'ila Al-Nujum*, 'Talk to the Stars', and twist it to his own design. It would be a dozen generations before enough debris fell out of orbit to burn up in the atmosphere such that the sundered peoples of the Earth could again talk to one another across the sky.

Sabie took a breath. He was getting ahead of himself, celebrating too early.

For some time, Lamarque had not used his encrypted biometric USB. It might not be significant, but Sabie filed the fact away, waiting for a reason to slot it into a pattern. It was the encrypted USB stick that had provided a back door through which Sabie had taken possession of Lamarque's whole life, even including his thumbprint. He had removed that as a permission for access to Gloria Lamarque's cloud storage, then created his own feed, designed to convince Lamarque that he was still connected, still in touch with the world, when in fact Sabie had taken complete control.

It was a risk. The messages Sabie allowed Lamarque to receive were bland, sufficient to give the impression that the wheels of life were still turning, but no more. They were generated by an algorithm that processed past traffic and used it to devise new content, but the process couldn't go on for too long. The lack of imagination and spontaneity would, eventually, arouse suspicion.

If Sabie had been a different sort of man – a man with a creative imagination, rather than a fixed logical purpose – he might have supplemented the work of the algorithms. But he was not, and he knew it. The clock was running on his deception.

He checked the progress of Gloria Lamarque's treatment at the Rothschild Institute. Her transfer had gone well but they would only be able to help her if they managed to trace the infection back to the genetic data stolen from the Norwegian lab. If they managed that, someone might then connect it to Sabie himself.

But there was no reason why anyone would. Lamarque's mother was dying – slowly, but inevitably.

Sabie looked back at Lamarque's most recent comms. The spy-software had logged the keystrokes, even though Lamarque had not sent the message.

Anything you send me will be encrypted at the very highest level of security. Only I will be able to read it and only when connected to DGIS servers. Do you understand?

It had been some time before Sabie knew why Lamarque had typed those words. The answer had come a few hours later when he intercepted a message to Lamarque from a magistrate attached to the Calais administration, a close family friend of the couple who owned the local water supply company. The magistrate told Lamarque that the family was being blackmailed. Their son had been killed as a warning. Their daughter would be taken if they did not allow an unknown stranger to gain access to the city water supply.

Lamarque would never receive that message. He would not know that the 'unknown stranger', Sabie's agent, the mortuary attendant, was even now making his preparations. In its first wave, the novel pathogen would infect around 1.2 million people in northern France. Within six months it would propagate to a likely 25 million. The death rate might be as high as two-thirds.

Sabie opened his private electronic calendar. In two days, it would be the fourth of August, the anniversary of the 2020 port explosion in Beirut, an event that had given him one of his very best ideas for disruption. Bader's staff officer had done well. The Cyrene City explosion had done an excellent job destabilising the population and sparking the insurrection.

Two days later would be the sixth of August, the anniversary of the atomic bomb that fell on Hiroshima. He would have liked to wait those two extra days, but it was no good fetishising the past. The symbolism of parallel dates was pleasing, but not essential. Events should now be allowed to take their course, whatever the timeline. He would ride the wave, not try to control it.

He thought about Lamarque for a final time.

In order not to create suspicion, Sabie would – as Fayard had requested – make sure Lamarque attended the Forum the following morning. He would watch him not understanding what was in front of his eyes. Lamarque's failure would bring its own delicious satisfaction. The pre-eminence of logic over imagination, the inevitability of destruction, the primacy of darkness.

At that moment, he received a reply from Al-Jaghar, from the base commander, Latifah Bader. 'What is the earliest possible moment?' he had asked. The answer was brief and to the point.

Twenty-four hours, perhaps a little more.

So, thought Sabie, let it be early morning on the fourth of August. The symmetry was pleasing, after all.

64

The next morning, Alex woke later than he'd intended, his body catching up on lost sleep. Remembering the visit of Poiret's security officer, he called the clinic at the Rothschild Institute.

'Ah, thank you for responding,' came a voice.

'Responding?'

'Just thirty minutes ago. Did you not receive a message?'

Alex looked at his comm-watch. The pattern was confirmed. 'Never mind. Go ahead.'

'Will you be able to visit this morning? Doctor Labeur will make himself available.'

'How is she?'

'This is administrative services. We are not provided with clinical information.'

He sent Fayard a message before taking a shower. By the time he was ready to leave, the old man had still not replied.

Alex weighed up his options. He was supposed to go to the Forum meeting at DGIS headquarters. Fayard had invited him and Sabie expected him to attend. Not to go would arouse suspicion and he didn't yet know enough to let that happen. He was obviously under some kind of surveillance. Anything he did or said through electronic means could be intercepted. Mariam's most recent messages didn't sound like they'd come from her.

He decided to compromise. He'd make a flying visit to the Rothschild and speak to the senior clinician Poiret's security officer had mentioned, then arrive late at Forum.

For speed, he rented an electric mobike from an automated stand on the north side of the Bastille. Twelve minutes later he was outside the hospital – a beautiful late-nineteenth-century building with a profusion of twentieth- and twenty-first-century additions, new wings that sprouted like tumours in coarse concrete and cheap red brick. Alex made for the rehabilitation department, and asked for Doctor Labeur. He was directed to a sleek office overlooking a shaded courtyard, where a man in a bright white doctor's coat with close-cropped grey hair sat behind an untidy mahogany desk.

'She's doing reasonably well,' said Labeur.

'Is she eating?'

'She's intubated. She can't eat.'

Alex nodded, closing his eyes. 'Of course. She was sedated for the transfer.'

'Madame Poiret requested I try to speak to you in person,' the doctor said politely, 'before she was moved here, but you were unavailable.'

'I have some connectivity problems,' Alex told him. He looked at the floor, trying to organise his thoughts. Worry made it hard to focus. 'Why is she in the rehabilitation department?'

The doctor smiled. 'We're a specialist centre in physical therapy. The benefit of—'

'I understand,' Alex interrupted. 'Can you please show her to me?'

The doctor swiped a tablet on his desk, navigating through a sequence of commands. 'Here she is.'

He turned the tablet round. There was glare on the glass, but the camera was good quality. Gloria looked tiny under regulation blankets in the wide hospital bed, a mask over her face, a tube connecting her to a ventilator, encouraging oxygen into her lungs. Alex watched her breathe.

'How worried should I be?'

Labeur chose his words carefully. 'A truly effective treatment will require understanding at the genetic level.'

The doctor excused himself to take a call. Alex turned away, letting the words echo in his mind – 'at the genetic level'.

That was it. That was the connection he had been searching for.

Fayard hadn't infected Gloria, either by accident or design. And Alex hadn't himself accidentally brought back a novel pathogen from the genetics lab in Norway. Surely someone had used the information he'd stolen from the lab to synthesise a novel pathogen and, for reasons he did not fully understand, deliberately infected his mother.

The odds were better than six-to-five against.

And what were the chances that the same pathogen had been used against Fayard? He displayed the same symptoms of compromised breathing, nausea and sensitivity to light, though less severely because he was already being treated for a prior infection. Alex remembered him darkening the plate-glass windows at DGIS headquarters, asking for the lights to be turned down at the Palace of Justice. As Fayard always said, there was no such thing as coincidence.

Alex also calculated that whoever had done this must be someone with immediate access to the data. And to his comms. And Mariam's comms.

There was, truly, only one candidate. But Alex had no idea how he would find the proof he needed to expose him.

Doctor Labeur finished his call. Alex leaned forward and told him the truth about who he was. Then described clearly and succinctly where he believed the infection had originated.

'If you're right, this could change everything,' the doctor told him.

From memory, Alex wrote Director Genmis's details on the doctor's notepad. 'You will need to contact this man.'

Seeing what he'd written, the doctor raised his eyebrows. 'You have well-placed friends.'

'I believe this pathogen originated in the GFU lab,' said Alex. 'Given what you know, do you think it could be used to infect a public water supply?'

The doctor looked horrified. 'Yes, but who would do such a thing? The impact would be—'

'Devastating,' Alex said. 'I know.'

While Labeur dictated a personal message of introduction to Director Genmis, requesting an urgent call, Alex wondered what else he should do. Alongside the potential biological attack, there was a connection he thought he now understood to the airbase at Al-Jaghar, something equally catastrophic.

Knowing anything from his own devices could be intercepted, Alex borrowed the doctor's tablet to message Paul Sanchez.

Whatever happens, do not leave BA 117. Prepare the Falcon. Lamarque.

65

Alex left the doctor's office and made his way downstairs. To his surprise, Amaury was standing in the lobby, waiting for a lift.

Of course, he thought. The Rothschild was the top government rehabilitation centre.

'Amaury,' Alex said, reaching for his arm. 'Can we speak?'

Amaury looked momentarily pleased to see him, then his face darkened and he sneered: 'Get away from me, you bastard.'

'Amaury, it's just us here. Be reasonable,' said Alex. 'You know I didn't mean to hurt you. It was a mistake.'

'It was my mission,' said Amaury loudly. 'I had everything under control.'

'Nothing was under control. It was a war zone.'

'Fuck off. I have nothing to say to you,' said Amaury, but as he spoke, he shot a quick, telling glance up at the surveillance cameras in the ceiling. 'Get it?'

Alex looked from Amaury to the cameras to the people around them.

Just then, a team of paramedics and a doctor crashed through a pair of swing doors with a gurney. The hallway became crowded and chaotic. Amid the noise, Amaury leaned toward Alex and hissed: 'Follow me.'

Alex followed his old friend through a small door onto a dingy landing, then down a service stair to a basement corridor where equipment was stored – dusty ultrasound scanners, wheelchairs. Alex relaxed his mind, trying to see what was about to happen. The image that came to him was soft, like regret.

Eventually, they reached a fire exit that opened into a gloomy formal garden. Outside, the air was surprisingly cool. They were in deep shadow beneath the concrete cliff of one of the hospital extensions.

'So, you don't want to fight me?' he asked.

Amaury embraced him with his one good arm.

'I always want to fight you, you idiot. I want to beat you every time.' He took a step back. 'Didn't you know?'

'I'm not sure what's happening,' said Alex, cautiously.

Amaury waved his left hand in a vague circle. 'No cameras, no microphones, no surveillance.' Amaury's right arm was in a sling, held tight against his chest, the stump up at the level of his collar bone. He saw Alex looking at it. 'It hurts less if I keep it elevated,' he explained.

'I see,' Alex said, with a flashback to the moment he fired his weapon and caused the damage.

Amaury laughed. 'This is great. I've been wanting to talk to you. Did you know I'd be here today?'

'No, I'm here for my mother.'

'Gloria's ill?' Amaury's expression grew serious. 'What's wrong with her?'

'They don't know, but she's…' Alex stopped. 'Look, we shouldn't be speaking, but I need to say this. I had no choice. As far as I was concerned, you were an enemy shooter.'

'I know that,' Amaury said. 'You don't have to tell me.'

Alex searched his face. 'So why did you make them convene the panel?'

Instead of answering, Amaury took out an analgesic vape with his uninjured hand.

'Fast delivery, straight into the bloodstream.' He inhaled and let out a cloud of steam. 'You told the senior assessor you fired to disarm me. That made no sense.'

'I had to say something. Civilians have no concept of the speed of events. Your reactions were too quick. It was an accident. I might have missed you entirely.'

'I know that,' said Amaury, patiently. 'Come on, Alex. Work it out.'

Suddenly, Alex understood. Fayard had seen it from the start. What had he said?

'Amaury has his own plan, I'm sure.'

Amaury needed expensive care for his injury and continued employment at External Security. He would have a better chance if he could show that the friendly fire was someone else's fault. Alex realised that he'd had it all wrong. Amaury wasn't angry at him. He was trying to keep his job.

'You need DGES to be negligent,' he said.

Amaury grinned at him. 'They won't pay for state-of-the-art treatment unless you or the mission commanders made a mistake. Otherwise, I'll be on the scrapheap with a lump of dead rubber for a hand.'

Alex sighed. 'I can't believe I didn't figure it out before.'

'Well, you were busy,' Amaury said, drawing on the analgesic vape again.

In that same moment, Alex realised something else.

'*Merde.*' Amaury shook his head. 'There's that look, Alex.'

'What look?' Alex asked.

'The look in your eyes when you've seen something that mere hard-working mortals can't.' Amaury laughed again. 'Damn it, can you even imagine how it feels to work long hours, reading, taking notes, studying. And then Alex sits back in his chair and gives you the answer out of thin air? It's very annoying.'

'Well,' Alex gave a slight smile, 'I need your help now. Tell me how it played out over there. I need to understand it.'

In the shadow of the modern building, Amaury told Alex the story of his infiltration of the insurrection in Cyrene City and Weasel's special mobile phone link to the hierarchy.

'I spent the whole time hoping to reach someone higher up, someone with more authority. The organising intelligence for the insurrection. Then, as soon as we were inside the parliamentary compound, I lost contact with HQ. It was a mess.'

'The whole thing was a fiction,' Alex guessed. 'There was no hierarchy. They were being played by someone they'd never met.'

'There it is again.' Amaury shook his head. 'I was with these guys twenty-four seven, painfully inching towards that discovery, and you see it in a single moment of clarity. But can you tell me why?'

A different voice suddenly broke in. 'What's going on? You can't be here.' A hospital security guard stepped out of the doorway.

Because he thought he knew why, Alex was slow to react.

'I felt faint,' said Amaury, showing the guard his stump. 'I came outside for some fresh air.'

The guard recoiled at the severity of the wound, but recovered quickly.

'Fine,' she said. 'But you need to go back upstairs. This space is for clinical personnel only.'

'Sure,' said Amaury soothingly. He turned to Alex. 'Let's go.'

Alex nodded, trying not to lose his train of thought. He had no new answers, but he had an important new question. If the Cyrenian insurrection was a distraction, what was it distracting them from?

Just before they stepped through the door from the service stair into the reception area, Amaury spoke quietly, close to Alex's ear.

'We should meet again. I'll contact you.'

'Call Mariam, too.'

Alex recited her contact number. Amaury nodded and was gone.

By this time, Alex was running late but he wanted to know whether the surveillance he was under would allow him to contact Nelinha. His message returned an 'unknown number' autoreply.

'Strange,' he mused.

He remembered Gloria suggesting Nelinha had sent her parents to Portugal – that her parents hadn't really wanted to go. Why would she do that?

To keep them safe, far from… From what?

From danger, of course.

He dictated another message for Mariam, asking her to call. The reply came almost immediately.

Can't speak now. Later?

Alex scrolled her three previous replies.

Busy just now. Later?

Hope you are well. Speak tomorrow?

Hi there. How are you?

They were all of a piece. Each one, taken on its own, might pass. But all four, one after another?

He looked at his other comms. He had enough experience of algorithmically generated messages to know what was happening. Just then, he received a message from Sabie.

Monsieur Lamarque, vous arrivez?

Are you coming?

Alex considered. It seemed odd that no one else could spontaneously contact him, only Administrator Sabie. He remembered something Fayard had told him that ought to have given him pause.

'Such men are easily overlooked. They shouldn't be.'

Yes, Fayard had been right.

He spoke his reply, the comm-watch transcribing it as text, his mind reconfiguring what he knew, recasting Sabie as an enemy, not a friend.

Twenty minutes.

Finally he knew where to find the intelligence at the heart of the spider's web.

At that moment, another notification appeared on his watch, sent peer-to-peer, without transiting over a network. The sender's details were unknown, the message brief, evoking a shared memory.

Pressed duck. Siren.

66

Sabie was in the smaller Forum conference room on the fourth floor at DGIS headquarters, listening to a presentation on rural resettlement plans, thinking about his own vast project and the foolishness and impotence of the intelligence that surrounded him.

Were they all blind? Were they all stupid?

They were both. They were stupid because their optimism made them blind.

He received an automated notification telling him that Lamarque had received a peer-to-peer message that his surveillance software had been unable to prevent.

Pressed duck. Siren.

Sabie frowned. Discreetly, he tapped and swiped the screen of his hand-held. It didn't take him long to return a reference to the Tour d'Argent, a restaurant that made a speciality of pressed duck, that had served more than half-a-million portions of the dish.

So, he knew where.

The top reference from 'siren' was the thirty-minute curfew warning.

He knew when.

If Lamarque was going to meet someone at the Tour d'Argent at half past midnight, Sabie would send someone as well. Two people, in fact. And half past midnight would be thirty minutes into a new day, Tuesday the fourth of August, the anniversary of the Beirut explosion.

Soon people would be obliged to give the date a new name.

The Day of Darkness.

Thanks to the electric mobike rental, Alex made it across town in time for the Forum coffee break. He slipped in at the back of the conference room and caught sight of Sabie talking to a junior operative – fresh faced, enthusiastic, flame-red hair. A few moments later, Sabie came to join him.

'All is well, I hope?' asked the little grey man.

Alex smiled. 'Do you know why the professor wants me to hear this presentation?'

'Perhaps he thinks you will see connections where others do not?' said Sabie.

'He overestimates me,' said Alex.

Sabie returned to his seat near the front. To polite applause, the young woman with red hair stepped onto the low dais in front of the screen. Alex recognised her from the day he had come to DGIS headquarters for his induction.

Was that the day Sabie had taken control of his comms?

'Human history is punctuated by catastrophists,' the woman began. 'People who believe that everything must be torn down in order for us to begin again. They believe there is creativity in destruction, opportunity in disruption. We might call them clean-slaters. Once the slate is wiped clean, something better can be constructed in its place. Traditionally they, the catastrophists, would be at the heart of it, but somehow unharmed. The destruction would stop at their doorstep and they would, one way or another, survive and direct the next chapter, the next phase, the next turn of the wheel.'

She paused to reference a few on-screen graphics, taking too long, making the mistake of describing to her audience what they could already see. At the same time, Alex felt his pulse rate climbing. It felt like a provocation.

Surely Sabie didn't know what he thought he knew?

Finally, the woman moved on.

'The leaders of these organisations have – again traditionally – a dangerous amount of knowledge, enough to seem smart without actually being that smart.' The presentation showed live footage of a plane exploding in the air. 'But you will all remember how, in our grandparents' day, airline companies never checked the hold baggage, thinking no one on board would want to blow themselves up. As long as every item of hold baggage was associated with a human being who was seated in a numbered seat on the plane, it must be innocuous, safe. But it turned out that wasn't true. There were people who were willing to die for causes most of us wouldn't understand – for promises of redemption or paradise, or for material rewards for the people they left behind.'

There was another long digression, at the end of which the woman shuffled her notes.

'Okay, I'm going to skip ahead. I don't want to run out of time.'

She brought up a new slide, showing the tatty repurposed shop front round the corner from Gloria's building.

'The key is this. They seem unimportant, but groups like Tabula Rasa believe there are historical cycles and that the natural pattern of cycles can be accelerated by human action. They are essentially death cults who believe we are close to a cyclical catastrophe, and they want to make sure it is of sufficient depth to provoke a proper reset. They call it *ekpyrosis* – Greek, meaning "image of fire" and that fire might be a civil war, a revolution, or a pandemic – or all three at once.'

She switched to a sequence of slides giving examples from her list. In case Sabie glanced his way, Alex feigned boredom, letting the deranged ideas wash over him – old order, degeneracy, false dawn, regeneracy, new dawn, new order.

Time ticked by, then the amber light flashed indicating ninety per cent of the woman's time was up. She spoke quickly.

'If people who believe in these cycles gain power, they won't try and keep it. They'll put in place policies liable to foster a crescendo of conflict. That's bad, obviously. Worse, although they believe in the prospect of renewal – and this is the thing –they don't care if they survive the disaster. They don't need to see the renewal. They just want to lay waste and let the chips fall where they may. Maybe there will be no green shoots of recovery at all and that will be the end.' She paused. 'Because these people – the ones who seek destruction in order to wipe the slate clean – they don't care if they die bringing it.'

The light went red.

Breathless, thought Alex. And kind of mad. But mad because infected by the madness of the idea, not because the research was mad.

'Thank you,' said the woman, her voice faint because the microphone had been muted. 'I had a lot more.'

There was a polite smattering of applause as the Forum session broke for lunch. Alex saw Sabie approaching.

'Professor Fayard wondered if you might speak to Mademoiselle Cantor?'

'Of course,' said Alex, 'but surely we don't think there's anything in this? There's a reason organisations like Tabula Rasa aren't proscribed. Their hysteria is harmless.'

Sabie nodded. 'You may be right.'

Alex took the stairs down to street level and stood in the shade beneath the steel-and-glass canopy over the front door, watching the traffic, breathing the overheated air, thinking again about Mariam's fake messages.

She, too, was in danger – but he couldn't contact her without giving away what he knew.

The junior operative stepped out into the bright sunshine. What was her name? Cantor, that was it.

'Alexandre Lamarque,' Alex introduced himself politely. 'Thank you for your presentation. Administrator Sabie invited me to attend.'

'What did he say?' she asked eagerly. 'Did I do okay?'

'He just said I might find your work interesting. And I did.'

The woman looked disappointed. 'I went totally off track. I had to miss the part about symbolic meanings, like lilies meaning that the soul of the deceased has been restored to the state of innocence.'

Lilies.

Alex thought about Luís Beira's house. He knew there were two cameras over the entrance, that Sabie would be watching, so he kept his expression neutral.

'Well done, anyway.'

He smiled and turned away, calculating how long it would take to walk back across town to meet Poiret at Val-de-Grâce. He wouldn't take the mobike. Networked vehicles were easy to trace. No one else knew where he was going, and he wanted to keep it that way.

Sabie watched the conversation with Cantor on one of the screens in his basement office. He had just confronted Alexandre Lamarque with everything he needed to know, given him every opportunity to demonstrate his superior insight, and he had understood nothing.

Lamarque was a fool, he thought. And Fayard was a fool to trust a fool.

Around an hour into his journey, Alex came to a brasserie that he liked, where the dome of the Basilica of Saint-Augustin cast the terrace into shadow. If he took his time, Sabie would perhaps become bored watching him.

He ordered a cold drink and sat down. The waiter was soon at his side with a can of cold lemonade, a straw, a packet of nuts and an antiseptic wipe in a foil packet.

Sabie watched the feed from the street camera.

What was Lamarque doing? Eating peanuts while the world prepared to burn.

Inside, Alex was furious with himself. Only one person could take an organisation like Tabula Rasa and maintain it as a legal entity. Only one person could delay replies to Mariam from Camera Control and forensics. Only one person could intercept his own messages.

He leaned back in his chair, making sure to present an attitude of unruffled relaxation. Perhaps he would learn more when he met with Poiret at Val-de-Grâce?

For a moment, that gave him pause. Why had Poiret's invitation not been intercepted? Then he remembered that the message from Poiret hadn't come via comms. It had been delivered in person, by Poiret's security officer.

Did that mean that Poiret knew what was happening, and was trying to avoid surveillance?

No, she'd sent her security officer because she'd messaged him and not got a reply. And that was because her attempts to contact Alex had been blocked.

Alex finished his drink and stood up. He knew this brief moment of quiet couldn't last, that he was in the eye of the storm.

He paid and set off south, towards the restricted zone at the heart of the city.

There were only two things certain about history, he thought. One, it has not yet been written. And two, no one really wants to die.

On both counts he was wrong.

67

On the Mediterranean coast of Cyrenia, the mayor of Tobruk, one of the three members of the Cyrenian Presidential Council, appeared to be a small nervous man. But this impression was misleading. A skilful diplomat and an assiduous student of political history, he had learned, very early in his career, that as a British minister of the twentieth-century once remarked: 'It is never wise to appear cleverer than you really are. It is often better to appear slightly less so.'

Prime Minister Mourad had never underestimated him. She'd made sure he was promoted to the pinnacle of civilian authority, knowing he would commit his considerable intelligence and energy to the cause of the new republic. She could not have known, however, how crucial a role he would finally have to play. When all was said and done, there was always the question of chance and the law of unintended consequences.

There was probably no one else, for example, who would have taken the trouble to nurture relations with the Egyptian OC Western Frontier.

It was all very well dismissing the inertia and isolationism of the ancient empire of the pharaohs, but was it wise? Who knew what tomorrow might bring? And tomorrow – or rather yesterday – had brought an analogue radio message, meaning he was one of very few people to know of the death of General Al-Fathi. His conundrum was what to do with that information.

He thought back to the scene at the airport, when Generals Bader and Al-Fathi had tried to browbeat him into accompanying them to Al-Jaghar. Of course, he had known why they demanded his presence. They wanted him to provide a fig leaf of justification for the coup they were planning. If he hadn't refused, it might also have been his body lying naked, stretched out on the baking sand.

The mayor had no idea what was happening right now in Al-Jaghar, but it worried him. The fighter squadrons there were entirely outside of civilian control. The base commander, Latifah Bader, was sister to a man he now knew to be a murderer. The only authority to whom he – an unarmed mayor without so much as a city militia to support him – could reasonably appeal was in Paris, in exile, perhaps under diplomatic house arrest.

Still, free or not, he would contact her. Cyrenia had an embassy in the French capital, didn't it? An embassy staffed with diplomats who shared Mourad's vision, who were at least loyal to the fact that their own careers had risen with her own? The Cyrenian ambassador to Paris was another Mourad appointee. She could be relied upon to act with energy and integrity.

'Do we have a facility to contact our embassy in Paris by radio?' he asked his assistant.

'I beg your pardon, sir?' She looked astonished.

'By radio,' he said. 'I need analogue communications.'

There was a pause and then she said hurriedly, 'I'll find out, sir.'

Bader and his sister were in Latifah's private apartment on the top floor of the control tower at Al-Jaghar.

'They are sure, Latifah?' asked Bader. 'The checks have been carried out? The technicians are satisfied?'

'Yes. brother,' she replied. 'No more delays.'

'After midnight?'

'Early morning, August fourth. The darkness, at last.'

He recognised the gleam of fanaticism in her eyes.

'There's nothing you would not do to safeguard the plan, sister. Isn't that right?' he asked, concealing his doubts.

She smiled. 'Nothing.'

'You would pilot the rocket yourself if it was necessary.'

'I would. And die among the stars.'

She had such an expression of crazed delight that it was hard to look at her.

'Your commitment has always been an inspiration to me,' he said.

'Thank you, brother.'

He broke away. 'If it is not until after midnight, I'm going to return to the scientific campus and take the promised tour.'

Her smile faded. 'Is that necessary?'

'It's important that I show my face. It will help to allay any suspicions that may have arisen over the disappearance of Al-Fathi.'

'Well, perhaps,' she said. 'If you think it best.'

He still had not told her that his staff officer, the one to whom he had delegated the disposal of Al-Fathi's body, had disappeared. He knew she would be furious at his incompetence, but what difference could it make now?

He made a fist and touched it against his heart. 'I will return before you know it.'

'Don't be late,' she said. 'I want us to share this moment.'

'So do I, sister,' he assured her. 'So do I.'

About thirty kilometres east of Al-Jaghar, a diesel vehicle arrived at the border post with two dull-looking relief frontier guards. Zeina watched the new team unpack their gear, together with supplies for two weeks of isolation on the edge of the desert.

Fine. It was out of her hands. She was grateful to be out of the loop. All that was left was to put as much distance as possible between herself and these unfathomable events in which she could only ever be a victim.

She walked over to the border guard who had invited her indoors when the temperature had fallen. His kit bag was packed and lay in the sand at his feet.

'You are leaving?' she asked.

'Yes, that's right.'

'Where will the diesel transport take you?'

'The barracks at Marsa, on the coast.'

Zeina nodded. From Marsa to her old family farm in the Nile Delta was only three hundred kilometres on a single highway along the Mediterranean.

'Is there room for one more?'

The border guard looked surprised. 'Really?'

'Please.'

'Where are you headed yourself?' he asked.

'I don't know,' she lied, 'but I can't stay here.'

There was a moment of hesitation while he weighed up his decision. 'It's not up to me,' he said. 'But I'll go and ask.'

As he walked away, she found herself smiling, imagining the shabby rooms of her old family home, the central courtyard where there was always somewhere to sit that was either warmed by the sun or cooled by the shade.

But that was just a dream. Zeina knew what she would really find there – the untended crops struggling with the salination of the soil. But where else could she go? Home, after all, is the place where, when you have no choice but to go there, they have to let you in.

The border guard called her name and she turned to look at him. He was standing with the driver of the diesel transport truck, giving her a thumbs up.

Zeina sighed with relief.

Whatever happens next at Al-Jaghar, she thought, I want no part of it.

68

In a quiet street close to the Val-de-Grâce Hospital, Alex came across Claudine Poiret's security officer, the heavily built man in a charcoal-grey suit, half concealed in the shade of a lime tree.

'There's a change of plan,' he said, opening the door to an innocuous grey car. Poiret was in the rear seat. 'Would you…?'

'I'm being observed,' Alex warned him, quietly.

The security officer shook his head. 'Madame Poiret made that deduction when you didn't reply to her messages. Don't worry. We're in a camera shadow.'

Alex got in.

In the courtyard of the Val-de-Grâce Hospital, Prime Minister Mourad received the news of Al-Fathi's death with genuine shock. It had been brought to her in person by the Cyrenian ambassador to Paris, a woman with steel-grey hair and a fixed expression of bland indifference. As with most of Mourad's appointments, appearances were deceptive. She knew the ambassador was immensely shrewd, fiercely determined and completely loyal.

'How do we know this?' Mourad asked.

'It came through an analogue radio transmission.'

'Extraordinary.'

The woman nodded. 'It is. I think you must prepare to return.'

'Yes,' agreed Mourad. 'And, when we win this battle, we will reward Egypt's OC Western Frontier with…' She paused. 'Do we have an honour that we can award a foreign national?'

'Not yet,' said the ambassador. 'But it will be your right to create one.'

'Good, and then…' Mourad stopped. 'Had I asked you to choose, ambassador, who would you have expected to betray me, to betray Cyrenia?'

The woman didn't hesitate. 'Bader.'

'But Al-Fathi was the more impulsive.'

'Bader's sister, Latifah, has enjoyed an exemplary career of distinguished service,' the ambassador told her. 'But I knew her when she was younger. She was always unstable. She should never have been given access to power.'

Mourad gave her a curious look. 'And you think Bader is unstable, too?'

The ambassador weighed her words. 'Not exactly unstable, but he's definitely under her influence.'

Mourad looked at the ground. 'I thought I might control them, both of my honourable generals.'

'Diplomacy is made up of degrees of control, Prime Minister,' the ambassador said. 'It is never absolute.'

The French army lieutenant approached. 'Prime Minister, come with me, please.'

The ambassador took a deferential step back. 'Would you like me to leave?'

'No,' Mourad said. 'We'll receive them together.'

In his basement office at DGIS headquarters, Sabie logged into the smart controls for building services. It was time to get started.

He accessed the management system for the lifts and for the power and lighting on the sixth floor. He initiated a lock-down of Fayard's room. All power would be cut off and the door would be held shut by immensely strong magnetic catches. The emergency electrical supply would not kick in to release them because the building thought it was quarantining an infectious disease.

Then he could get on with his work, uninterrupted.

Having waited well beyond dawn for sleep to come, Fayard didn't know that it was the clunk of the mag-locks that woke him the following evening. He was aware in his weary bones that many hours had passed, but uncertain of what exactly the time might be. He pressed a button for the therapeutic chair to right itself, but it failed to move. He pressed the button again. No response.

With a painful effort, he hauled himself over the armrest, landing on his hands and knees on the polished wooden floor. He struggled to his feet, stumbling in his haste to reach the door concealed in the bookshelves.

It was locked, solid like a wall.

Fayard turned to look around the room. The only light came from the west-facing window, the sun dipping towards the horizon. He tried a light switch, no longer expecting it to work. He opened the door to the cooler-cupboard where he kept fruit and protein bars and health drinks. Though the shelves were still cold, no light came on. Moving to his desk, he found his screens were dead. Not even a tiny tell-tale to indicate that there was power.

Of course, he thought. Shutting down the electricity supply was the only way it could be accomplished.

His data connections to the outside world were secure, unshared with the rest of the building. The design of his rooms prevented wireless comms. Without power, he was isolated. Whoever had done this was inside the building. Someone who knew how to disconnect his private quarters from the backup generators.

What was the thought that had been on the edge of his consciousness, just before he slept? A conversation, from several days ago.

'You are a student of human disasters, Sabie. Why is that?'

'I suppose it's because they are moments of opportunity as well as loss.'

Fayard's shoulders slumped.

Finally, he knew who his enemy was, but he was too late to do anything about it.

69

Instead of meeting with Claudine Poiret at Val-de-Grâce, as promised, Mourad and her ambassador had been escorted to a battered police van and driven, complaining at the 'excessive speed', to the Paris military airport, Base Aérienne 117.

Alex and Poiret had followed in Poiret's official car with her security officer up front. The journey had lasted long enough for them to share a good deal of what they each knew.

Poiret, Alex realised, was extremely astute and had only been a few steps behind his own deductions. Yes, she'd callously exploited Gloria's illness, but she was, in the end, a politician with different priorities from his own.

As soon as they reached the airbase, they made their way to the sparse military equivalent of a departure lounge, a bare room close to the runways. Mourad recognised Alex as the soldier who'd escorted her from her safe room in the burning parliament building and became furious.

'I'm sure Monsieur Lamarque is a fine officer and does credit to your republic,' Mourad told Poiret, 'but that does not explain this kidnap—'

'Forgive me, Prime Minister,' began Poiret, her hands held out calmingly.

'This is an extremely serious derogation from protocol,' said the ambassador.

Alex had a horrible sensation of time running out, like he was trying to carry water in his hands. He wanted Mourad on board the Falcon as soon as he could make it happen.

'Madame Prime Minister,' he told her, 'I'm here to brief you on what is happening right now at Al-Jaghar.'

'What are you talking about?' Mourad's intelligent gaze swung from Alex to Poiret. 'What is this?'

'Madame Prime Minister,' Alex insisted, 'You are not in control of these events. Will you please be quiet and just listen to what I have to say?'

The was a deathly pause. Mourad looked even angrier. On the ambassador's face, however, he thought he saw evidence that she had recognised the note of authenticity in his voice.

'You forget yourself, Captain Lamarque,' said Mourad, with icy calm.

'I apologise,' said Alex.

'Prime Minister,' said the ambassador, hesitantly, 'perhaps you should listen to this.'

'You should,' agreed Alex. 'I need your help if I'm to stop what's about to happen.'

Mourad's eyes were hard, like stones. 'And what might that be?'

'The plan, as I understand it, is chaos, destruction, turning back time, erasing the last fifty years of human progress.'

Mourad exchanged a look with her ambassador, and then turned back to Alex. 'You are serious?'

'I'm afraid I am.'

Before he could continue, there was a polite knock and Paul Sanchez entered from the runway, looking flushed.

'Is the Falcon ready, Paul?' Alex asked.

'Yes, Captain.'

Alex turned back to the prime minister. 'There is no time. We must leave immediately. We're going to fly to Al-Jaghar and try to prevent the launch. Only you can do this. I'll explain everything once we're in the air.' Without waiting for her response, he turned to Sanchez. 'Paul, show the prime minister to the plane.'

'Yes, Captain,' Sanchez nodded.

Mourad looked from Alex to Poiret to her ambassador.

'I think you should trust him,' her ambassador said.

'Do I have any choice?' Mourad asked, looking at Poiret.

'Captain Lamarque will answer every one of your questions,' Poiret told her. 'But you must leave now.'

Mourad took just a moment more to decide.

'Fine. Let's go.' She turned to her ambassador. 'If anything happens to me, you know what to do.'

'I do.'

Sanchez led Mourad out onto the runway. Poiret asked her security officer to take the ambassador to her car. Once they were alone, she turned to Alex. 'Do you think you can get there in time?'

'I hope so,' he replied. 'I can only try.'

'I have to make you aware that the president has declined to authorise your mission. I've chosen to trust you, against his advice.'

'I appreciate your faith in me,' he said.

'The odds are against you,' she told him.

'They always are, but perhaps a single civilian jet can make it through. We should have the support of the authorities in Tobruk, at least.'

'And we cannot launch an immediate massive assault?'

'It wouldn't be quicker than the Falcon and it would give away that we were coming. It might precipitate the disaster.'

There was a moment's pause as they each took in the magnitude of the challenge.

'Lamarque, two things,' Poiret finally said. 'I will do everything I can for your mother. And, when you return, if you return, I will no longer oppose your resignation.'

Alex inclined his head. 'For the resignation, let's see. As far as my mother's illness is concerned, I believe I have that covered.'

She looked surprised. 'You do?'

Alex nodded. 'I think so. But I need you to make discreet contact with a magistrate in Calais. I've written down the details.' He handed her a piece of paper. He was getting used to writing things down by hand. 'Many thousands of lives depend upon it.'

'I'll take care of it,' she promised.

'Perhaps millions. Also, there is serious risk to the data centre in Kofinou. Maybe also Long Island and Tahiti,' he warned.

'What kind of risk?'

'I'm not certain. Some kind of sabotage, probably at sea or where the cables come ashore. You will have to move quickly. And you'll need to find a way to communicate without being intercepted.'

'I understand,' she said. 'And there's something else you need to know.'

She looked unsure of herself, for once.

'Go on.'

'What I'm about to share is classified, well above your clearance.'

Alex listened, appalled, as she told him about *Tonnerre de Dieu* – God's Thunder.

'*Merde,*' he whispered, when she'd finished. 'Why would anyone do that?'

'Strategy,' she said simply, with no apology.

'Where are they aimed?' he asked. 'How are they controlled?'

She held out her hands. 'Does it matter? If the Al-Jaghar rocket detonates, they will fall out of the sky, accelerating to hypersonic speeds and—'

'No one knows where they will hit,' Alex finished the thought. 'So, Armageddon. But none of this makes any difference. It merely accelerates the timeline of obliteration if we fail.'

The Falcon's engines were firing up on the runway outside. They were out of time.

'You need to check up on Professor Fayard and…' Alex had to force himself to mention Mariam, the habit of secrecy was so deeply ingrained. 'Let me write down another address, near the Panthéon, the home of Mariam Jordane. She, too, is under surveillance and she might not be aware. I don't know where she is, if she's safe. Please find her and tell her what's happening.'

The security officer in the charcoal-grey suit returned from escorting the Cyrenian ambassador to the car. Poiret nodded in his direction.

'Don't worry. I have just the man.'

70

The top-of-the-range Falcon, piloted by Paul Sanchez, was carrying just two passengers – Captain Alexandre Lamarque of the French Directorate-General for Internal Security and Prime Minister Souad Mourad of the independent republic of Cyrenia. Nobody else could know where they were going or why. The plane was capable of over a thousand kilometres per hour and they were making good headway. If all went well, they would arrive soon after midnight, local time.

If, that is, Mourad could be persuaded to radio the mayor of Tobruk and instruct him to stand down the Mistral M7 air defences that would, otherwise, blow them out of the sky.

'So, Captain.' Mourad raised her voice to be heard above the engines. 'I believe you have something you wish to tell me, about a plot?'

He gave her a drink from the well-stocked fridge. 'I'll start at the beginning.'

She gave the drink a dubious look. 'What is this?'

'Vodka, cranberry, lime. You may need it.'

She handed it back. 'I don't drink alcohol.

He put it aside and sat down in one of the six plush armchairs that lined the luxurious cabin, composing himself.

'It began very early one Sunday morning,' Alex began, 'between midnight and one o'clock, outside Bunker Martha, an international data station in a converted U-boat dock in Marseille…'

Amaury Barra sat in a waiting room on the third floor of the rehabilitation wing at the Rothschild Institute, waiting for the third adjustment of his new prosthesis. Since talking to Alex, he'd been there all day, overdoing the analgesic vape because he had nothing else with which to dull the pain from his stump.

A technician came out of the 3-D printing room.

'I'm very sorry it's so late. There was an interruption to the mains current. The generators kicked in, but it caused a hiccup in the print process. We had to start the cycle again.'

'How long will that take?' Amaury asked.

'We're nearly there,' the man said. 'But maybe you'd prefer to come back tomorrow?'

'Oh, I'll stay,' said Amaury, with a smile. 'I have nowhere else to be.' He showed him the vape. 'Do you have any painkillers I can take alongside this?'

The technician shook his head. 'I'm afraid I can't offer non-prescribed drugs.'

With that, he disappeared back into the printing room. Amaury glanced up at the clock on the wall. He had plenty of time before he had to meet Alex at the Tour d'Argent.

He leaned back in the armchair, trying to make himself comfortable. Perhaps, for a short while, his wound would allow him to sleep.

Sabie sat in his basement office, studying his array of seven screens.

Via the internal camera network, he could see the sixth-floor conference room and the door concealed in the bookshelves that gave access to Fayard's suite. Sabie had no access to Fayard's comms but then, neither did Fayard.

Through a private connection, he had a view of the basement storeroom with its payload of kerosene and ammonium nitrate, posing as 'foodstuffs', wired to create an explosion that would flatten twelve blocks of innocent suburb. The transmitter-detonator sat ready on his desk, a red safety guard covering the button.

Via a street-cam, he could see the entrance to Val-de-Grâce Hospital. Nobody had approached the building in hours, aside from a battered police van – not the sort of vehicle the French government would use to transport a visiting prime minister.

His third screen monitored comms between the various subjects in whom he took in interest: Alexandre Lamarque, Mariam Jordane, Amaury Barra, Director Philippou, Latifah Bader, several others. He would have liked to know exactly what Claudine Poiret was doing, but her rank at the Ministry for Foreign Affairs meant she was out of reach. In a separate window was the highly encrypted app he used to message his associates, including his 'clean-up' team, the two fake undertakers, thugs recruited from the underworld of organised crime.

His fourth screen showed a news feed from Cyrene City. Unfortunately, the army seemed to have the situation under increasing control. He'd been counting on the insurrection gathering momentum, for the violence to increase, not level out.

The fifth screen was divided into four. It showed satellite imagery from Kofinou, Tahiti, Long Island and Marseille. Of course, the Marseille attack had already failed. But the other three data centres would all fall, he hoped, a little after midnight. It wouldn't be the end of the network of undersea cables, but it would constitute three damaging amputations – like cutting the nerves that linked the brain to the hand or the foot, leaving great swathes of the network impotent, inert.

Sabie felt his heart rate rising.

The sixth screen showed the entrance to the water purification and pumping station that served the Calais region. Soon, he would see the arrival of the official van, in the livery of the family company whose child he'd had kidnapped and murdered. The mortuary attendant from the terminal would need only a few minutes to introduce the pathogen into the pumping system.

Then chaos would spread.

The final screen, the one in the centre, was a night-vision view of the launch pad at Al-Jaghar. The sky was clear, the moon high and bright. He could see incredible detail – vehicles and people moving around, like small insects against the pale sand.

This was the centrepiece of his plan. It was all so fragile. So easily destroyed.

Once the satellites were smashed into a cloud of fragments, planes would not immediately fall out of the sky, water supplies would not immediately fail, communications would not be completely silenced. But the connections – the hyperconnections – would be cut. And then, he hoped, in the absence of overarching information and authority, all the little wars might join hands. A drone squadron overflying some territory in conflict might lose direction and, orderless, tumble from the sky. Commanders on the battlefield, without political instructions, might succumb to confusion as mistrust blossomed. Pre-emptive attacks might be launched while civilian aircraft struggled to find routes through the mapless skies, their fuel running low, unable to stack around the major airport hubs, leading to crashes and collisions – just like the constellations of satellites in orbit round the Earth, one crash provoking another in a chain reaction of destruction.

In the world's most isolated places, fishermen, explorers, farmers and the rural poor would be cut off – not just their comms but also geolocation. Mobile commerce in the unwired world would crash because they were no longer connected to the virtual vaults that store the world's imaginary money. Without satellites, the global positioning system would fail and standardised global time would disappear. Clock-controlled systems in water treatment and supply, in the global network of power interchanges, would fall out of sync. And, if no one quite knows the time, then the world's digitised financial instruments would no longer have any meaning. Who bought first? Who sold first? When, exactly? And at what price?

Sabie flexed his hands.

Yes, it was happening. It was almost a fact, this chaotic future where no one will even know what the weather will be like in the next few hours or days or weeks because the weather satellites will have gone. Storms will go unpredicted. Hurricane pathways will surge into catastrophic existence without warning.

And at last, Sabie thought to himself, the Earth will breathe out and reassert itself. The planet, wrongly reduced to a global village by instant networked communications, will sigh and expand, becoming vast once more, atomised, almost alien.

And so, the cleansing chaos will begin.

Amaury flexed his new prosthetic hand without effort.

'Extraordinary,' he marvelled. 'It responds to my thoughts.'

‘Not exactly,’ the technician corrected him. ‘The muscles in your stump are responding to your thoughts. The prosthesis interprets those impulses and turns them into grab or poke or stroke. It’s going very well. You’re a natural.’ The technician set a tennis ball in the middle of the table. ‘Try that. Pick it up and squeeze.’

Amaury reached for the tennis ball, closing his artificial hand around its soft surface. He felt nothing beneath his fingers, but the hand curled obediently.

‘Got it.’

The tennis ball slipped, and the technician caught it before it rolled onto the floor. ‘You’ll develop more control as time goes by.’

‘Let me try again.’

He put it back in the middle of the table. Amaury reached out and picked it up between the tips of his artificial fingers and thumb.

‘It’s like a miracle,’ he said.

He used his left hand to push the ball deeper into his prosthetic palm, squeezing it and wincing.

The technician shook his head. ‘Careful, now. Your stump is nowhere near fully healed.’

‘How strong is it?’

‘Immensely strong,’ the tech told him. ‘Stronger than your original hand. Less dextrous, of course. But in terms of grip, between the thumb and the fingers, like a vice.’

Amaury squeezed his fingers and released them, almost flattening the ball.

‘I can imagine that being useful,’ he said.

71

As the hour neared, General Bader was on a tour of inspection of the scientific compound, spreading convincing but insincere confidence and bonhomie. Behind his smile, he was now certain that he'd been a fool to trust his sister.

For years, he'd known about her dark rages, her obsessions. Of course, he'd known. He'd witnessed her disregard for human life – in particular in the dirty war of secession that broke Cyrenia away from the rump of Gaddafi's Libya. He'd always believed he could control her and use her position in the Air Force as a prop for his political ambition. Now, too late, he saw that her fanaticism was well beyond anything he had imagined.

'Why,' he'd asked her tonight, 'must we destroy everything?'

'Everything must burn,' she told him, that fanatical glint in her eye. 'Nothing can remain.'

'Tabula Rasa,' he replied, careful not to show his doubts.

'Exactly.'

The tour of inspection moved on. He nodded sagely at an engineer who was explaining the method by which the solar mirrors tracked the sun, but he heard none of it. Instead, his mind was looking for a way out of the danger he'd helped create. Was there a way to retrace his steps, to turn back time?

If challenged, he could find a plausible explanation for Al-Fathi's disappearance. By now, there would be no evidence of the crime. The jackals and vultures would have disposed of both flesh and bones. Only he and Staff Officer Noori knew exactly what had happened.

But where was Noori? Had she actually carried out his orders?

'Shall we join the reception?' asked the engineer, finishing his briefing.

'Please,' said Bader, politely.

He had no appetite, but he would have to eat two dozen tiny culinary fantasies, receive half-a-dozen flattering toasts, and give a fatuous speech in reply, congratulating everyone on their heroic labours in the service of the new republic, this beacon of tolerance and harmony for the world.

Then he would have to return to the airbase to face his sister and decide what was best for him to do.

Not best for Cyrenia, nor even for the planet.

What was best for General Ramzi Bader.

Aboard the Falcon, Alex finished his story with a description of the probable consequences of the rocket launch, the chain reaction of destruction, Earth sealed off from space by a ring of shrapnel, debris and junk – and the multiple catastrophic impacts on the Earth's surface from God's Thunder.

'You do realise this sounds like fantasy?' Mourad told him.

He gave a sad smile. 'I wish it was.'

She paused to think. 'What did you call this organisation?'

'Tabula Rasa. Clean slate, in plain language.'

'And you think Sabie has manipulated this organisation to his own ends?'

'I do,' Alex said. 'But he is not alone. There are many others who believe as he does, all over the world.'

'Director Philippou in Kofinou, for example. What will Poiret be able to do about that?'

'I don't know.'

'And the Calais water supply?'

Alex thought of the investigating magistrate, the only person he had been able to suggest that Poiret might call upon. The man didn't inspire confidence.

'We have to hope,' he said. 'Poiret is very capable.'

'Approaching Cyrene airspace,' called Sanchez from the cockpit. 'I have Tobruk on the line.'

'On what line, Paul?' asked Alex, sharply.

'On analogue radio,' Sanchez clarified.

Alex turned to Mourad. 'Prime Minister, it's time. You must convince them to stand down the Mistral M7s.'

She unlocked her seatbelt and stood. 'The mayor of Tobruk is a personal friend,' she said. 'At least, a personal appointment. I think he'll listen.'

'I hope you're right,' Alex said.

Mariam had spent the evening with her sisters, sitting quietly by their beds, watching them sleep. It was late when she left, walking down past the Luxembourg Gardens where she had, perhaps, destroyed her career by admitting to Fayard that she and Alex were having an affair, that they habitually shared confidential details of operations, that they were laying themselves open to blackmail or worse.

She turned right, heading for home.

Everything she'd discovered, everything Alex had told her, came flickering through her mind. She remembered the desperate Blanks defending their children's playground. She imagined what Alex had seen on the cameras – the Portuguese boy hitting the water and then the police officers pulling him from the water.

But were they police officers?

She thought about what he had said after interviewing the baker who lived opposite the little house in Montmartre, about the undertakers who came before dawn to take away the body for incineration. What if the death of the Portuguese boy was staged? What if it was the same undertakers – the ones she had seen leaving Square Sainte-Hélène with the young man in the suit that she was sure now must have been Luís Beira – who retrieved the body from the water beneath the buttresses of Notre-Dame?

She thought about the delay in the DNA match with the hair she had retrieved from the lens cap.

She thought about the body of Nelinha Costa in the church. Why had she been killed? Were her apocalyptic sermons prophesying destruction no longer necessary?

Something is about to happen, she thought.

She tried again to get in touch with Alex, but there was no reply. She tried to reach Fayard, but his devices were offline, too. She tried to search the DGIS directory to find a contact number for Sébastien, Fayard's relief bodyguard, but couldn't get through. That was when she realised the problem was her, not them. She had no connection of any kind.

A feeling of dread washed over her.

DGIS communications were prioritised, the most protected, the most reliable. Yet she was cut off.

Her only option was to go to Fayard in person. She didn't want to do this unarmed, but automatic sensors would prevent her from taking a projectile gun into DGIS headquarters. Maybe the sonic immobiliser she kept at home would pass the scanners?

A few minutes later, she reached her building. In the doorway, a big man in a charcoal-grey suit stood waiting.

'Mademoiselle Jordane?' He spoke quietly, only just loud enough to hear.

Instinctively, Mariam prepared to fight. 'Who are you?'

'Madame Poiret will be glad to know you are safe.'

He told her about Sabie and about Alex's desperate plan to stop the attack. With every word, her dread grew.

'Professor Fayard is in danger, too,' she said.

'As I understand it,' he replied, 'we are all in danger.'

Amaury knew nothing of Mariam's intentions, nothing of Alex's flight, nothing of Sabie in his basement office behind an armoured door. He knew nothing of the imminent launch from Al-Jaghar. For Amaury, life was good. Despite the rawness of his stump, he had a powerful new hand.

He decided to walk to the Tour d'Argent. He'd been stuck at the rehab centre all day, and needed to stretch his legs. Using his anonymous throwaway phone, he sent Alex a message.

On my way. All good?

When, after a couple of minutes, he'd received no reply, he thought back to that morning when he and Alex had separated at the Rothschild Institute, when he had sent his original message.

Pressed duck. Siren.

He'd received no reply to that either.

Amaury paused beneath a streetlamp at the corner of a busy intersection. Why had Alex not responded?

Two possible reasons.

First, he could be under such close observation that he couldn't do so without giving them both away.

Second, he was caught up in something that was absorbing his entire attention.

Or both at once. That was possible, too.

Amaury reached behind his back to un-pop the holster concealed beneath his jacket. Like Alex, he carried a regulation Heckler & Koch .45-calibre pistol, equipped with a sound suppressor on its threaded barrel. Unlike Alex, he felt no hesitation about using it. If someone was coming for him, he'd take them out.

There was a problem, of course. He was right-handed. Unfortunately, he no longer had a right hand.

And, in the brief trial he'd carried out on the shooting range at DGES headquarters, he'd discovered that his left hand was a terrible shot.

72

General Bader returned to the Air Force base by electric buggy. The night air refreshed his senses after the rich meal. He had avoided alcohol, but the atmosphere had been oppressive and the conversation loud.

He parked at the foot of the control tower. He went inside, acknowledging an Air Force officer's salute.

'The lift is there for you, General,' the man told him.

He stepped into the narrow cubicle and pressed the button for the air-flight control floor, the penultimate level, the one beneath his sister's apartment and offices. The lift rose smoothly, then the doors opened.

Latifah was sitting at a wide console, watching closed-circuit camera feeds from the launch gantry. Around her, five flight controllers were busy with their screen-based tasks, but Latifah maintained an extraordinary stillness.

He looked round the consoles. None of this would endure. The entire control room was digital, dependent on satellite technology, on connectedness. Though he could not see Latifah's face, he could imagine the intense gleam of concentration in her eyes – an insane fixity. Did she really want to destroy all this?

Did he want to destroy all of this?

He knew the answer to the second question. He did not want it all swept away. He should never have got caught up in this madness. He wanted life to go on, for humanity to keep on muddling through, making the best of things, especially him, making the best of his opportunities. Becoming prime minister. Even unifying the presidency one day.

Feeling his gaze upon her, Latifah turned and smiled, and he saw in her eyes that there could be no turning back, that she would never be diverted. The darkness was coming and he and his sister, for better or worse, would be at its heart.

'Twelve minutes,' called Paul Sanchez from the cockpit.

The mayor of Tobruk had listened to Mourad and shut down the ground-to-air defences. Two Mistral M7s had launched automatically, but they had been detonated without endangering the Falcon.

Mourad also prevented an alert being sent to Al-Jaghar about their presence in Cyrenian airspace.

For the moment, no one knew they were coming.

It was ten past midnight in Paris as Mariam got out of her autodrive taxi. The ID on her comm-watch gave her access to the building. In her jacket pocket was her non-lethal service weapon – a son-imm with a range of fifteen metres.

In the lobby, all was quiet. Sébastien – the big man with long black hair who looked after Fayard on Sundays – was on duty at the desk.

'Sébastien, have you seen the professor?'

He gave her a surprised look. 'Should I have?'

She didn't have time to explain. 'So, he's alone?'

'I guess,' he said, looking puzzled. 'What's going on?'

'I wish I knew.' She went round to his side of the desk so she could see his holo. She spoke into the microphone. 'Sixth-floor conference room.'

The system showed her the huge space. All was quiet but gloomy.

'No trouble there,' said Sébastien.

'You don't think it's odd there are no lights on?' She leaned in, pinching out the image around the bookcases. There was no narrow gleam at the foot of the concealed door. 'Try to call him,' urged Mariam.

Sébastien jabbed the icon.

'No connection,' he told her, a new concern in his eyes. 'I've never known that to happen – not in six years of working for him.'

'Lift lobby,' Mariam ordered.

The system switched feeds. The landing was dark, with just the pale green of the battery-powered emergency exit signs over the doorway and two tiny red tell-tales indicating that the surveillance cameras were operating on battery power.

Mariam knew why the cameras were still functioning while all other power was out – because someone was keeping an eye on what was going on.

Sébastien swiped through two more screens. ‘The lifts are out of order. All of them.’

‘Show me the basement,’ said Mariam, tersely. ‘Administrator Sabie’s office.’

Sébastien looked shocked. ‘I have no access. No one does.’

Mariam made an impatient gesture. ‘The corridor outside, the lift lobby, anything.’

He tried, but not a single basement camera would respond. It was all she needed to know.

‘Sébastien,’ she told him, ‘Sabie is in his office. I need to get in there, but I will do it alone. You have to go up to the sixth floor. Fayard is in trouble. Break him out of his rooms. Do it with maximum force. Make as much noise as possible. Perhaps it will draw Sabie out.’

Sébastien took a moment. ‘Because?’

‘Because Sabie is a traitor and, if I don’t get to him, we are all dead.’

There was a pause as Sébastien reorganised his worldview. But they knew each other well. He trusted her.

‘Okay,’ he said. ‘Smash the door in. I can do that.’

‘Do it fast,’ Mariam told him.

Sébastien ran for the main stairs. He was heavy but he was fit. Six floors wouldn’t take him long.

Meanwhile, Mariam activated her son-imm and headed for the basement.

Sabie paced his room, glancing at each of his seven screens in turn, his eyes wide. As zero hour approached, it was becoming too much – his attention split between too many strands of information, all evolving simultaneously.

He stopped for a second in front of the screen that gave him a permanent feed from Al-Jaghar. The area around the launch pad had been cleared. It might have been a still photograph, were it not for the slight vapour haze rising from the rocket engines and the countdown displayed in the corner of the screen.

Latifah will not let me down, he thought to himself, trying to calm his nerves.

He glanced left and right along his semi-circular array. He felt no sense of irony that his plan was only possible because of his mastery of the hyperconnected world. Had he thought about it at all, he would have admired the symmetry of using the very tools he hated to bring about their destruction.

Movement flickered on one of the screens. He saw a large shape moving across the gloomy sixth-floor lift lobby, in through the double doors to the conference room. Sabie tapped the image and it expanded. He recognised the man straight away, with his broad shoulders and long black hair. The man moved towards the wall and, when he turned back, he was carrying something cylindrical.

Just at that moment, with his mind preoccupied by so many other questions, Sabie couldn't imagine what it might be.

The two fake undertakers were in position, close to the water, on the pedestrian walkway a few metres below the level of the embankment road. They didn't know it, but they were sitting on the same bench Alex had used after his graduation dinner at the Tour d'Argent, when he'd confronted the thugs with the shock sticks.

'How long?' the young one asked.

'Those footsteps up on the road, that could be him.'

'Good, I'm tired.' The younger man stood up, a heavy shadow in the night. 'The sooner the better. You draw him close. I'll take him from behind.'

'Like the preacher-woman,' the older man agreed. 'It'll be easy. He thinks he's coming to meet a friend.'

The young one glanced at him. 'Not dangerous?'

'Once, perhaps.' The older man popped out a 3D image of Amaury from the Rothschild Institute, his right arm in a sling. 'Now, not so much.'

Moments earlier, Amaury had arrived outside the Tour d'Argent restaurant. From there, it was no distance down the stairs to the pleasant pedestrian walkway alongside the river and Alex's favourite bench – the one in the almost-shadow between two dim streetlamps. It was not long until the twelve-thirty warning siren.

Amaury's heels echoed on the stone steps. When he got to the bottom, he saw someone waiting. It should have been Alex, but the shape was wrong. Too stooped. Too small.

Amaury released the Velcro straps on the sling that strapped his new prosthetic to his chest. With his left hand, he drew his .45 from the holster concealed beneath the tail of his jacket and released the safety.

73

Four thousand kilometres away, Alex was explaining to Prime Minister Mourad how he had worked out the significance of the tattoos.

'The letters – I was really very stupid about the letters. They were, I think, for allegiance, a kind of badge of honour for minor players, like membership of a secret website. There must be one, somewhere on the dark web, for the dissemination of orders, for evangelising new recruits.'

'How could they have believed this madness?'

'We shouldn't be talking in the past tense,' said Alex. 'Most of these people are still out there. If we survive this mission, there will still have to be a massive reckoning.'

'Of course. And we will not shrink from it. But the letters?'

'The first ones I saw were on the fist of the Portuguese boy, Luís Beira. It took me a ridiculously long time to realise they were Portuguese initials for a set phrase, "*um dia será mais curto*". Then, a few days later, I saw the corpse in the morgue at the Calais tunnel terminal, the English murderer, with O D W B S on his hand – "one day will be shorter". Because of the different languages, I missed it.'

'There was no reason to see it. Four of the five letters are different.'

'No, it was my mistake,' Alex insisted. 'I was too focused on my mother's illness and the child murders. That was part of the plan too, of course. Distress was used to take attention away from more important parts of the plan. It worked.'

Mourad looked disgusted. 'Grotesque.'

'In a way, infecting my mother perhaps wasn't an attempt to kill her. Just another distraction. Her research would lead anyone with eyes to see to the desert airbase in southern Libya.'

'Southern Cyrenia,' Mourad corrected him, firmly. 'And this Professor Fayard, the head of your Internal Security, he also is sick?'

Alex nodded. 'Probably the same infection. Essentially a kind of small-scale trial of the pathogen Sabie hopes to introduce into the Calais water supply. The surge in infections at the refugee camps outside Cyrene City may well have been from the same source.'

'Monstrous,' said Mourad.

'Fayard and my mother will both die unless the director of the laboratory in Norway can come up with a treatment. Fayard was better protected because he was already on palliative medicines for a prior infection.'

'Three minutes,' called Sanchez from the cockpit.

'Was there another clue?' asked Mourad, calm in her seat.

'The enhanced photograph from Bunker Martha. It was delivered to me by hand, otherwise Sabie would have intercepted it.'

'And it was the letters in French?' she guessed.

'Exactly. U J S P C – "*un jour sera plus court.*" Again, "one day will be shorter", a kind of crazed celebration of death.'

Mourad nodded. 'And the connection to your friend Mariam and her grandmother's proverb?'

'Ah, yes – "when the sun shines, there's no need of stars".' Alex smiled. 'There was no connection. It was the only aspect of this whole story that seems to have been genuine coincidence, without cause or meaning. Everything else has been intricately connected. She just happened to mention it.'

'I have visual on the base,' said Sanchez.

Amaury was an experienced operative with eight years of distinguished service in External Security. When the man came towards him, his arms outstretched, a vague smile on his face, palms out indicating surrender, he was not taken in. He swung the .45 from behind his back and sprayed eight rounds in the man's general direction, his weaker left hand struggling to absorb the recoil.

The man fell to the ground, groaning.

Amaury sensed a presence behind him, then a garrotte tightening around his throat. Instinctively, he dropped the gun and scrabbled at the thin cord with the fingers of his left hand, but it was already cutting into the flesh of his throat.

'You shot my friend,' came a surprisingly young voice, 'so this may take me some time.'

Amaury's training made it possible for him to control his instinctive panic. He managed to draw just a little air in through the tightening garrotte. With his prosthetic hand, he reached back and grasped his attacker's right wrist.

He squeezed. Because it wasn't really his hand, he heard rather than felt the carpal bones splinter beneath his grip. Then that sound was overwhelmed by squeals of agony.

The pressure on Amaury's neck released and he managed to half-turn. His attacker – a large man in his early twenties – wrenched himself away with great force, pulling the prosthetic clean off of Amaury's stump, causing it to bleed. The prosthetic hand stayed locked onto the man's crushed forearm.

'Worth it,' said Amaury.

He stepped in and drove his foot against the side of the big man's knee, hard against the joint. He fell to the ground and Amaury launched another kick against the side of his head. The man's mouth lolled open as he fell back, stunned.

Up on the sixth floor at DGIS headquarters, Sébastien had been as good as his word. By the faint orange glow from the streetlamps, he'd found two fire extinguishers hung on wall brackets. The smaller one contained some kind of foam for electrical fires. The other was larger, full of water and fire-suppressant chemicals. It was at least twice as heavy.

He'd crossed the huge room to the concealed door. It took him a couple of moments to clear the books and remove the shelves, then he raised the fire extinguisher over his right shoulder and brought it down with a crash against the frame.

Down at basement level, in a dark corridor, Mariam had no idea what was happening anywhere else in the building. She hoped Sébastien was in position, that he would make a lot of noise, a lot of mess.

From the other side of the armoured door to Sabie's office she thought she could hear movement. It struck her that she'd never noticed how different Sabie's door was from every other room in the building – almost as if Fayard's most trusted collaborator had something to hide.

How had she not realised sooner?

But then, she'd had almost no contact with Sabie, being only rarely involved with day-to-day operations.

How had Fayard not realised sooner?

He'd been unwell, of course.

All the same, what fools they had been.

On the far side of his armoured door, Sabie felt cold.

What was happening on the sixth floor? Had he been found out? What should he do?

He checked the relay from Al-Jaghar.

All was well.

He checked the message screen.

There was a notification from Latifah Bader informing him the countdown was under way.

Just minutes, now. Good.

But Sébastien was on the sixth floor, battering at the concealed door into Fayard's rooms and Sabie realised he had made a mistake. Because the big man with the long black hair and punctilious manners was only on duty with Fayard when Mariam wasn't available, he had neglected to monitor and control Sébastien's devices.

Was it important? Was there anything Fayard could do to stop what was coming?

Perhaps, there was, if he got access to comms.

And Sébastien would be able to provide them.

Sébastien had completely destroyed the catch and the handle, but the door would still not open. As he took a breather, he heard Fayard's weak voice from inside.

'Magnetic catches top and bottom. You'll have to break the timbers away. They won't give.'

'We'll see about that,' said Sébastien.

Alex had taken control of the Falcon and was sitting in the pilot's seat, while Paul Sanchez donned a parachute and strapped Prime Minister Mourad to his chest, preparing to jump in tandem.

'Go now, Paul,' Alex called, 'before the fighters get off the ground.'

'Are you ready?' Sanchez asked Mourad.

'Do I have a choice?' she answered

'Now, Paul. It's time,' Alex commanded.

'It's been an honour, Captain,' Sanchez shouted.

The Falcon lurched as Sanchez opened the door, destabilising the flow of air around the fuselage. Alex gripped the controls tightly.

Alex glanced over his shoulder, briefly meeting Mourad's eye. He saw her mouth move, but the rushing of the air was too loud for him to hear what she said.

Then she and Sanchez were gone and he and the Falcon were alone between the rocket on the launch pad and the crowded skies.

On the penultimate floor of the airbase control tower, General Ramzi Bader looked around at the carnage his sister had wrought. It had been twelve seconds of butchery, delivered without a flicker of emotion.

All five flight controllers lay dead, each one shot through the head. There were splatters of blood across the digital consoles, across the windows and the floor.

'What are you doing?' Bader asked, horrified.

'What is necessary,' she said. 'Because only destruction can bring renewal.'

She busied herself with the controls. He gestured at the bloody bodies around them.

'What if there is nothing left? Nothing to rule over?'

Latifah turned fully to face him, a thin smile of triumph on her narrow face. 'I knew you never really believed.'

'I do believe,' he insisted. 'But I thought we would rule together, that this country could be ours. Think of it,' he said. 'All we could achieve.'

'It is not enough.'

'How is it not enough?' he asked, bewildered.

But her answer was just a set phrase from the terrifying and familiar liturgy. 'Everything must burn.'

Behind his back, General Bader released the safety on his weapon.

'Surely, sister, this is madness.'

Before he could aim and fire, Latifah raised her own gun and shot him squarely between the eyes.

With the pad of his right thumb on the biometric release panel, Sabie opened a steel cupboard on the wall of his office and took out a small, snub-nosed automatic pistol, the only projectile weapon in the whole of DGIS headquarters. From the desk, he picked up his transmitter-detonator.

On the screens, all seemed quiet in the so-called new republic of Cyrenia. No matter. Soon the place would be an international pariah, its puerile fantasies of tolerance and harmony exposed as lies. When the rebuilding finally came, it would be reabsorbed into greater Libya, the nation it should never have left.

He glanced at another monitor, showing Sébastien slamming the fire extinguisher into the disintegrating door to Fayard's private quarters.

Nothing mattered any more. Death and life were immaterial.

Still, just because he could, he thought he might go up to the sixth floor and put a bullet between the big man's shoulder blades.

He tapped a screen to reactivate the lifts and disable the locks on his own armoured door.

As soon as Mariam heard the sound of the locks on the armoured door releasing, she readied herself. When Sabie stepped out into the corridor, her sonic immobiliser caught him full in the chest. He fell twitching to the floor, dropping a snub-nosed automatic on the polished concrete. She stepped in and he reached out a hand towards her, an expression of pained rage on his lean grey features. At point-blank range, she shot him again and a small radio transmitter dropped from his spasming fingers.

Mariam picked up the transmitter and made sure the safety guard was closed over the button. She popped the magazine from Sabie's weapon, then dragged him inside the office, ripped a length of electrical cable from a paper shredder and used it to tie his hands behind his back. He was barely moving. For a second, she wondered if he might be dead, then she heard his rasping breaths.

She turned her attention to the monitors.

The first screen showed her a dim image of Sébastien, slamming his fire extinguisher into the ruined timbers of the concealed door into Fayard's private quarters. She saw the top panel collapse under the onslaught, leaving a fragment of the top rail still fixed in place by the mag-lock. In a few moments, she hoped, Fayard would be out.

Then she saw a notification pop up, telling Sabie that someone was trying to call her.

She glanced at her comm-watch – nothing.

She took the anonymous audio-call via Sabie's system.

'Who is this?' she asked.

'Mariam? It's me, Amaury. Alex told me to call. Are you at—'

'DGIS headquarters, yes. Come as quickly as you can.'

'Where's Alex?'

Good question, she thought, scanning Sabie's monitors.

'Be careful, Amaury. You're under surveillance.'

'Don't worry about me,' said Amaury. 'I'm on my way.'

Amaury ran up the stone staircase to the road, looking for an autodrive. He carried his prosthetic in his left hand, the bleeding stump of his right arm held firmly in his sling.

Alex had only one weapon left to deploy. The Falcon itself.

He banked the jet in a tight arc. Through the cockpit windows, he could see aircrew on the ground, scrambling to get the fighters in the air.

It was now or never.

As the nose of the Falcon came round, he disabled the automatic assistance from the onboard computers and aimed the jet at the launch pad. He hoped to impact the rocket a few metres above the ground, but any kind of direct hit would do.

When Mariam located the launch countdown on Sabie's middle monitor, only ninety seconds remained. The rocket was on the launch pad, surrounded by a cloud of smoke from burning propellant. A graphic in the corner of the screen displayed an intercept path with an object in orbit – an object labelled with the French flag and the cryptic title *Tonnerre de Dieu*.

'*Merde,*' she breathed.

She didn't know what 'God's Thunder' meant, but it couldn't be good news.

She turned back to the screen where she had taken Amaury's audio-call. It showed all the personal communications that Sabie had been intercepting. Alex was on the list.

She hesitated. She feared she knew what Alex would do – that he would sacrifice himself for the greater good.

Would it be wrong of her to distract him?

No, she thought. To hell with that. At least let us say goodbye.

She touched a fingertip to the feed from Alex's devices, activating an audio icon, hoping he would be in range of the comms towers on the airbase, that she could speak to him one last time.

Alex had no intention of sacrificing himself, of saying goodbye. He felt his comm-watch vibrate but he had no time. He could see the initial thruster ignition on the rocket on the launch pad. In under thirty seconds, it would be too late.

He pulled open a small safety guard to reveal a chunky red lever.

'Okay,' he said aloud, 'let's do this.'

On the centre screen in Sabie's office, Mariam saw the Falcon appear, nose down, heading straight for the camera, straight for the launch pad. Her heart contracted. She felt a surge of grief, of loss. She wished she had told Alex more about her life – where she went each Sunday, the tragedy of her sisters' births.

That she thought she loved him.

Now it was too late.

Then something was different. She leaned in, trying to see what had changed. Was it the Falcon?

For a moment, she couldn't figure it out. Then she realised. The cockpit had flipped open. A moment later, the ejector seat was shooting out into the night sky.

'Thank you,' she breathed, not knowing who it was she thanked.

Twelve seconds later the jet hit the rocket and gantry. The plane exploded in a bright fireball and the rocket itself came skidding across the tarmac, directly towards the camera, filling the frame.

Then the feed failed and there was only darkness.

Alex was falling. He caught a glimpse of his seat, plummeting away beneath him, then a sudden violent tug upwards as the circular parachute unfurled and caught the air. Already he could feel the bruising where the ejector-thrust had slammed his shoulders against the straps of his harness.

All that remained was to hope that the chute would decelerate his fall sufficiently for him to hit the ground without significant injury

Mariam dragged Sabie into the lift and took him straight to the sixth floor. With Sébastien's help, she caried hm to the carpeted area near the windows and untied his wrists. His grey complexion had turned blue. She put an ear close to his lips and listened for his breath.

'That's enough, my dear,' said Professor Fayard.

Mariam kneeled over him and started CPR, pumping his chest to a rapid violent rhythm.

'I had no choice. I know we should have questioned him, but he was about to flip open the safety-guard on his transmitter and…'

And what? She didn't know.

'Let him go,' said Fayard. 'It's better that way.'

Mariam couldn't stop. 'It's my fault. I should have found out where the explosives are and—'

'I will order a search of the building,' interrupted Fayard. 'I have no doubt we were his target. You did the right thing.'

'It was the second son-imm hit,' Mariam gasped, beginning to lose her rhythm. 'It must have damaged his heart.'

He touched her shoulder. 'That's enough.'

Mariam stopped. The room became quiet, apart from her quick breathing. She contemplated the innocuous but congested face of the traitor who had moved so easily among them.

'He's gone,' said Fayard.

It was true. Sabie was dead.

Amaury appeared in the doorway. 'What's happening? Where's Alex?'

'Come in, Monsieur Barra,' said Fayard. 'We will explain everything.'

Mariam stood up. Sébastien fetched a rug from Fayard's private rooms to cover Sabie's body.

'Yes, what about Alex?' Mariam asked.

'He's well,' said Fayard. 'I was able to use Sébastien's comm-watch to contact Madame Poiret. She took the precaution of sending fighter support after him. He survived, thanks to the ejector seat. One of the fighters has landed and is bringing him home.' He frowned at Amaury. 'Monsieur Barra, you appear to be bleeding?'

'It's nothing.'

Amaury gave Fayard a concise account of what he had seen and done. 'I left the bodies on the embankment, below the Tour d'Argent.'

'Sébastien will organise for them to be collected and disposed of,' said the old man, wearily. 'This all has to go away.'

The big man spoke into his comm-watch.

'Secrecy is a mistake,' Mariam argued. 'There should be a trial.'

'No,' said Fayard, glancing at the rug covering Sabie's corpse. 'We are compelled, as always, to work in the shadows. People must never know how close we came.' Fayard slumped down onto one of the uncomfortable swivel chairs, his shoulders hunched. 'How was I so blind?'

'You are unwell,' replied Mariam. 'Your judgement is clouded.'

'Perhaps.'

'All the same, you knew. That's why you wanted Alex to join the family.' Then she added: 'Sabie meant to die, didn't he, with the rest of us, from his bomb, wherever it is?'

'He has his wish,' said Fayard, coldly. He sat up a little straighter. 'Sébastien, take the traitor's remains to the incinerator where they disposed of the Portuguese boy. And the bodies from the embankment. That would be justice.'

'At once, Professor,' The big man picked up the empty corpse of the man who used to be Administrator Sabie and carried it away to the lifts.

There was a moment's silence.

'I want to go to the airport,' said Mariam.

'So do I,' said Amaury.

'Of course,' Fayard agreed. 'But our aircraft has only just left Cyrenian airspace. There will be time enough.'

EPILOGUE

The rocket that should have destroyed the satellites and brought down God's Thunder skidded across the Al-Jaghar tarmac, propelled by ignition and the impact of the Falcon, careering into the control tower. It did not detonate. The next day, crushed by the rubble, Latifah Bader's body was found, along with that of her brother, General Ramzi Bader, shot through the head at close range. The two corpses were stripped and left out on the desert sands to be disposed of by jackals and vultures.

After impacting the control tower, the rocket broke up and some pieces came to rest a couple of kilometres away. Although the vast shrapnel bombs didn't explode, the object itself caused considerable damage to one wing of the massive solar array, the area at the southern tip, looked after by an Egyptian refugee worker.

From fragments of testimony from members of the scientific and engineering staff – and from a report respectfully submitted by the Egyptian frontier authorities – the outline of Zeina Yaseen's story was assembled. Steps were immediately taken to find out what had happened to her. Prime Minister Mourad was determined she should be located and rewarded for her part in preventing a global disaster.

Mourad and Sanchez landed safely, far enough away from the airbase to witness the final climactic moments of Alex's apparently suicidal flight. When Mourad saw the cockpit flip open and Alex descending to earth on his parachute, the prime minister was elated but angry that no one had told her that Alex would be able to save himself.

'You might have informed me sooner,' she complained.

'*Je m'excuse,*' said Sanchez.

Back in Paris, Claudine Poiret managed to get in touch with the magistrate in Calais, using an old-fashioned fixed telephone line, shortly before the midnight deadline. The magistrate proved surprisingly decisive and competent, mobilising the city police to intercept the mortuary attendant just as he was preparing to introduce the pathogen into the regional water supply – a pathogen that might have spread from the Atlantic to the Urals within just a few months.

Poiret also used her international network of diplomatic contacts to try to prevent the attacks on the undersea cables. The authorities in the US and the South Pacific acted swiftly, but the dredger lying off the Cypriot coast had already moved into position and done considerable damage before it was boarded. The impact was very minor compared to the devastation the obliteration of the satellites would have brought about.

Director Philippou killed herself with poison when she found out the worldwide disruption had failed.

Director Genmis at GFU in Norway ordered the synthesis of an effective antiviral compound to treat Gloria Lamarque and Professor Fayard. Their extended treatment would last six months, but both were expected to make a full recovery. The same treatment was being rolled out in Cyrenia with immediate success.

As for God's Thunder, the office of the French president ordered the platforms' entire fuel loads to be employed in boosting all three of the devices out of orbit to roam directionless through deep space where, eventually, a gravitational field would draw them into a star where their destructive payload would be dwarfed by natural processes.

Or they would disappear into the singularity of a black hole.

As it turned out, both Gloria Lamarque and Professor Fayard recovered more quickly than expected. Two weeks later, they were both well enough to attend a small private presentation of twin honours from the Cyrenian and French governments, a ceremony conducted in secret in a small room at the Ministry for Foreign Affairs. Prime Minister Mourad was present, fresh from her reinstatement.

Captain Alexandre Lamarque of the Directorate-General for Internal Security received both countries' highest honour. In the case of Cyrenia, it was the first time such an award had ever been made. Other medals were presented to Mariam Jordane, Amaury Barra, and several others for their contributions to undoing Sabie's plot.

As soon as it was polite to do so, Alex and Mariam slipped away. They made their way along several splendid corridors to the privacy of Poiret's office, overlooking the esplanade of Les Invalides. They went inside and shut the door.

They kissed. For a time, nothing else mattered.

After a while, Mariam opened the window and Alex stood behind her, looking out.

'You realise this makes you a hero,' Mariam said.

He laughed. 'What does that even mean?'

'It means they will have plans for you – Claudine Poiret, Professor Fayard.'

'I suppose so.' He put his arms round her waist. 'Nothing is safe. There are still people out there who believe in Sabie's cult of destruction.'

'I know,' she told him.

It was dusk. They heard the evening song of a blackbird in a lime tree, pure and sweet above the noises of the city. Alex remembered the day when he had walked into this same office to resign. It seemed like a lifetime ago.

'Now Gloria is better, Poiret has no hold over you,' said Mariam. 'Will you walk away?'

Alex thought about how close the world had come to disaster. Was it his responsibility to fight for light, to ward off the darkness?

Perhaps it was.

'Whatever I decide, will you stand by me?' he asked.

'I will,' she promised.

'Then we have already won.'

ACKNOWLEDGEMENTS

First, Martha Mosse, Felix Mosse, Benjamin Graham and Rosie Turner - attentive and intelligent 'family' readers. You helped at the crucial in-between time of: 'It seems good, but is it?' Thank you.

Second, three generous early professional readers, in alphabetical order - Lee Child, Anthony Horowitz and Lesley Thomson - whose support was invaluable in conversations with BKS Agency - Jason Bartholomew and Joanna Kaliszewska - and perhaps helped persuade Moonflower Books - Christi Daugherty and Jack Jewers - to take this chance. Between you, supported by Emma Waring and Jasmine Aurora, you made it happen. I will always be grateful.

Third and last, the person from whom I learnt to write books - the best and only Kate Mosse.

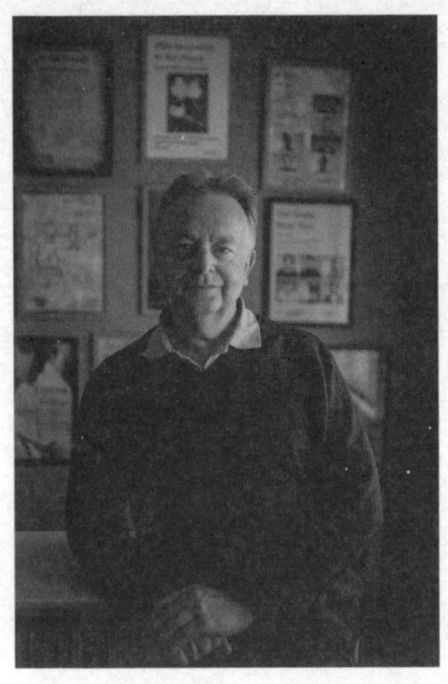

ABOUT GREG MOSSE

Greg Mosse's first career was in theatre as an actor, director and writer. He has lived and worked in Paris, New York, Los Angeles and Madrid, mostly as a translator and interpreter for a variety of international organisations. In 2015, he returned to theatre, writing and producing 25 plays and musicals as well as four short films. He took advantage of 2020's lockdown to fulfil a long-term ambition to sit quietly and write a thriller. *The Coming Darkness* is the result.

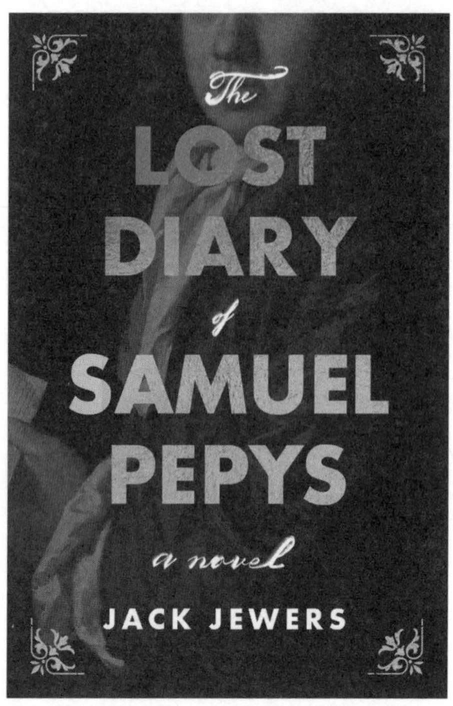

Best Historical Fiction 2022
Sunday Times

Book of the Month
The Independent

'Debuts don't come better than this…
a page-turning crime thriller.'
The Sunday Independent

'Swashbuckling action-packed drama.'
Woman and Home

Book of the Month
The Independent & The FT

'Brilliant.'
Heat Magazine

'If there's one teen novel this year that readers will never forget, it's this one…'
Books for Keeps

'Gripping.'
The Guardian

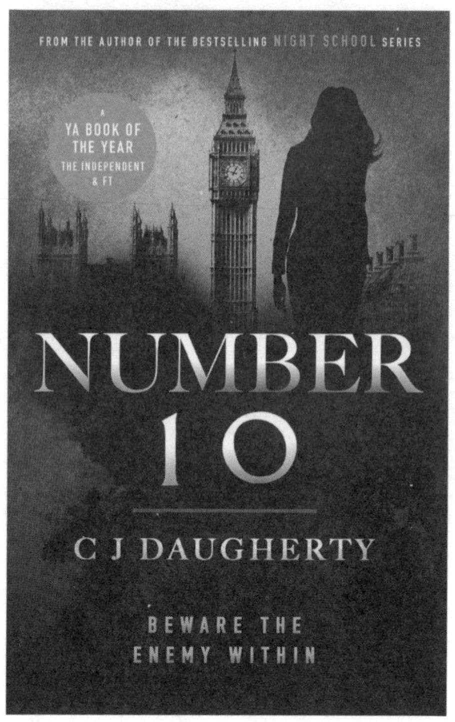

'YA Book of the Year…
CJ Daugherty is a YA big hitter.'
The Independent

'Exciting and unique… action
packed and thrilling.'
The Guardian

'The most exciting teen book
series to hit our shelves in ages.'
Now Magazine

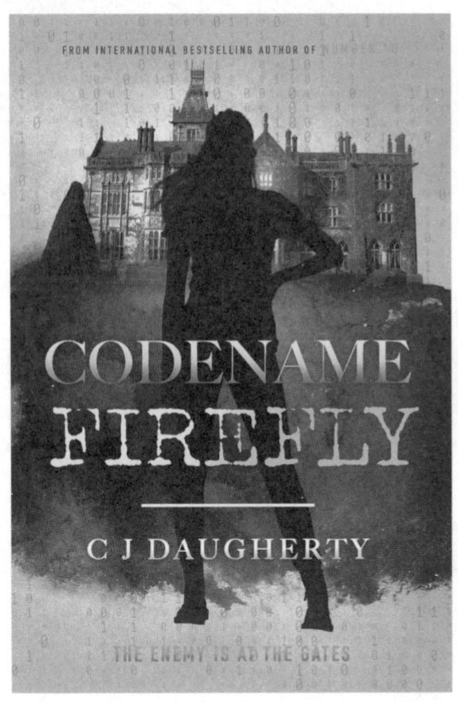

YA Book of the Year
Woman and Home

'YA Book of the Month… Daugherty expertly mixes thriller, mystery, action, and romance.'
The FT

'Exciting and tense… A captivating adventure.'
The Reading Cafe

FOLLOW US

www.moonflowerbooks.co.uk

@moonflowerbooks

@moonflower_books

/moonflowerbooks